Hidden Rainbow

MOODY PRESS
CHICAGO

Hidden Rainbow

Christmas Carol Kauffman

Illustrated by Allan Eitzen

Copyright © 1957 by Mennonite Publishing House, Scottdale, Pa.

Library of Congress Catalogue Card Number: 57-13005

Moody Press edition 1963

ISBN 0-8024-3807-5

24 25 26 27 Printing/GB/Year 88 87 86 85

Printed in the United States of America

To
John's and Anna's
children
who greatly helped in
furnishing material
for this story

Preface

This is not a story dug out of the long ago, nor is it one of my own creation. Should anyone doubt the reality of any part of it, he may make inquiry of John Olesh (Papa), who lives with his daughter Anna and husband Nick Ninkovich, at Bethel, Pa.

Clustered around John Olesh in beautiful Berks County valley below the Blue Mountains you may locate his devoted children, each of whom contributed material for this story. John, now in his climbing seventies, is active in personal witnessing for Christ, particularly to prison inmates in nearby cities. He can converse in five languages.

The invitation came to me from the official board of the Meckville congregation near Myerstown, Pa., to come to Bethel and meet personally the Olesh family and hear this remarkable story. For a number of days I lived in the home with John, Nick, and Anna. As long as I live, God will receive my thanks for this privilege.

Born in Yugoslavia to Catholic parents, John and Anna were led to truth, light, and true happiness through the ministry of a Protestant missionary. Their courage, faith, and suffering for the sake of soul peace will put many of us to shame for ever thinking our way was difficult. Mother Anna, whose life story on earth has just closed, was considered by all who knew her nothing less than a miracle. Many drove fifteen miles just to hear her offer a prayer, not eloquent, not wordy, but one that described her Christian life of quiet, unwavering courage, serenity, and a passionate love for those still in darkness. Her afterglow is an enduring chal-

7

lenge and inspiration to her church, her children, and her many friends.

My one desire and prayer, like that of the Olesh family and the official church board, is that many, both young and old, who read this story will come to find their own rainbow arching from bended knees heavenward.

C. Carol Kauffman

Chapter 1

Anna paused at the step of the straw-roofed house, handed the sickle and hoe to her husband and, with a solemn pensiveness, looked out through the broad, open street of the ancient Yugoslavian village of Miletinac. She drew a long, deep breath as she gazed silently at the sun-burnished Blue Mountains horizoned against a low-flamed sky.

There was a shadow on Anna's young, olive-skinned face —an expression of wonder and concern mingled with fresh anxiety. She tucked a loose strand of black hair up under her white headkerchief and scanned the baked-clay houses built in a straight row on the west side of the street. The houses were all alike, twenty-two on the west side of the street, twenty-three on her side. Anna Olesh could name each family in each house in the village.

"My John," she whispered almost inaudibly, her one hand now on the knob. Anna bit her lip, turned the knob, but did not open the brown-stained glassless door. Instead, her searching glance followed John, her husband, cleaning the garden tools with a hunk of hard earth. She watched him with big questioning eyes, full of devotion. "Would he?"

Ann had worked hard all that afternoon along with John in his father's sugar-beet field. The penetrating heat of the sun and the summer dust had made her coarse cotton blouse stick to her damp body. She had walked the hot earth barefooted, slipping into her hand-knitted scuffs when they neared the village.

But Anna had been happy all day in the field — happy because she was strong and could help John; happy because they could work and plan and be together; happy because they could come home together to their little rented earthen house nestled securely with the other forty-four in Miletinac.

Anna had not complained about the warmness of the day, nor the stickiness of her body. Neither had John heard her once complain about the unusual lack of rain the past weeks which made hoeing more tiresome. Nor had she complained about the scarcity of fuel, the stunted pumpkin crop which meant there would be a shortage of lamp oil, nor yet the meagerness of their home furnishings. And Anna had never complained because of inadequate transportation or their scarcity of money which meant walking twenty-eight miles to Daruvar if they had to see a medical doctor or a dentist, twelve miles to the nearest Catholic church in Djulovac, or five miles to Vilieki Bastaji to buy matches, yard material, or a tool. Anna was as well fixed and as well fed as the majority of village wives and loved by her husband a bit more, she was confident.

John was strong, lithe, and sun-tanned. His hands, sturdy and quick, were made for work. Below his high forehead, clear gray eyes seemed to temper everything he did, even the laughter that rolled not often, but with depth and muffled fervor, from his robust body. John was of a serious nature and sensible, particularly for one entering his twentieth year. He carried himself with a natural, unstinted poise— the thing that had first, but secretly, attracted Anna. And when John spoke, his words were strangely convincing.

It was in the month of March that John Olesh had asked Anna's parents for their daughter. He had been successful in convincing both that at nineteen he was mature, level-headed, and capable of supporting a wife.

John's parents had made it known that in order for Anna to be well accepted in the Olesh family they must be married by Father Jardell in the Catholic church in Djulovac. To this Anna had agreed. So the union had been an acceptable and happy one, and the couple were living in a two-room rented house and in peace and harmony with John's family as well

10

as with everyone in the village. They had been married five months. Anna was not yet eighteen.

"You don't know how much I love you, John," whispered Anna. "I love you at this moment as never before." She stood at the door watching him work, like always, with diligence. Her lips moved as she continued to whisper her young, quickening, vigorous love for her husband.

Anna was confident John had not proposed what he had — the big, the startling, the unexpected adventure — a few minutes earlier while on their way in from the field, without first having turned it over carefully in his own mind.

John had stopped to wipe perspiration from his forehead with the homemade handkerchief she had given him that very morning and ran it back over his tawny hair. Something about John held her with a new fascination. She scarcely moved.

John's proposition definitely startled Anna. She looked up sharply, stunned, mute. Her strong young arms which had never known anything but honest hard work felt suddenly weak and limp. John noticed and caught the rake lest she drop it.

"Anna," he said quietly, "it would be the hardest thing I've ever tried to do in my life, but I'd do it all for your sake."

Anna stood, hardly breathing. Her face turned pallid.

"I've been thinking about this for weeks already," he added with warmth in his voice.

"But, John," Anna ventured at length, after a prolonged silence. "But, John," she repeated, searching his warm face, "would you — would you really think of going to America now?"

"It would be harder later on, Anna," answered John with tenderness. She was watching his face so intently that she tripped on an earth clod and might have fallen, but John stepped close to steady her.

"You mean how much later on?"

11

"After the little one is here. If I could leave soon, I could get an earlier start. You could go back to your folks for a while, couldn't you?"

"An earlier start?"

"Yes. There's no chance here of getting ahead. You know how poor we all are. Father Jardell in Djulovac is almost the only person who prospers, it seems. I don't begrudge giving him his portion. But it's not that, Anna. Aunt Tena tells me Uncle Jose is making good in America. He sent her a money order last week and she cashed it in Daruvar. She said she's going to buy one of those iron stoves with an oven built in it."

Anna was following John's story with widening eyes. She had not often heard John say so much in so short a time.

"When did your Aunt Tena tell you all this?"

"We met at the mill last week."

"You never mentioned it to me," Anna remarked in disappointment.

"But I've been turning it over and over in my mind aplenty," admitted John. "We need to get ahead more than Father Jardell or Uncle Jose does. I don't see how I can provide for a family on a rented two acres — I mean the way I feel a father ought to."

"A father," whispered Anna. She looked away for a moment. Her lips quivered. "I'm glad you want to get ahead, John," she faltered. "But I've not been complaining, have I?" Quickly she brushed a tear before he would see it. "You'll make a wonderful father, John," she whispered.

"It's time to be thinking about these things," commented John in kind seriousness. "No, you haven't complained, Anna. I am the one who is complaining. If America is all that I imagine it to be, it would pay for me to go for several months at least, and give myself a try. If I would find work, I'd send home to you all I could above my expenses."

Anna thought a long minute. "Suppose, suppose you didn't find work?"

"I judge from what Aunt Tena said that in America there are plenty of places where I could find work. I can't get this out of my head. I want to earn enough to buy a farm of our own as soon as possible. A place we could call our own, Anna."

"But how could you go, John?"

"On a boat."

"Of course," agreed Anna. "I mean, where would you get the money to go on? Doesn't it cost a great sum to ride one of those big boats to America?"

"I suppose it would, Anna."

"But you don't have it," Anna stated with excited emphasis.

"I know," agreed John. "Henry Schmidt might tell me of someone in Daruvar who would loan me money. He seems to know a lot of men over there. It's one of my ideas, Anna. It might even be a foolish one. But this one thing I do know, I'll have to borrow money from someone."

"Borrow —" Anna's voice was apprehensive. "Then you would be in debt to begin with," she sighed, "and have to pay that back first before you could start getting ahead."

"I figured all that, Anna, before I decided to mention this to you. Just trust me, Anna. Don't be frightened. Uncle Jose borrowed money to get his passport. Aunt Tena said he got a job almost right away in a stone pit breaking up rock, and made as much in one day as we were able to save all last month."

"Truly? Oh, but —" reflected Anna, "that's not very much, John. Is it?"

"No," agreed John. "Not if you look at it from that angle."

"John, already, even before I know you are actually going, I feel sort of sad. You understand, don't you, John?"

"But you're a brave girl, Anna." John looked down at her. His tone was not even a trifle chiding, but affectionate. "That was one thing about you that I noticed when you worked in the depot at Vilieki Bastaji. You were brave and

13

strong and industrious. You didn't know I watched you in particular twice when I stopped by, did you? You were busy serving meals both times."

Anna shook her head. "You never told me before," she whispered.

"Of all the girls in Vilieki Bastaji and Miletinac and Daruvar — of all the girls I've ever seen in all Yugoslavia — not one looked as good to me as you, Anna."

"You've not seen many girls," — color crept into her cheeks — "now have you, John?" she demanded softly.

"Enough," came the answer. "And I think you are the kind that would be brave and — and stay here and let me try at least to make good where other men have done it. I'm young and I'd like to try before I get as old as Uncle Jose. Miletinac is just like it was when our grandfathers were boys. But Aunt Tena says in America things are changing, growing, and people are more free to do as they please. Even the women, she said, choose different patterns for their dresses."

"How strange!" exclaimed Anna, as though she doubted that.

"Everything over there must be different," continued John. "I mean better. I want to go and find out for myself. I know," he added, "many a wife would object, but you won't, will you? It's for *your* sake I want to provide a better home and better living if I possibly can."

As the two were nearing their house, other villagers, both young and old, men and women, were coming in from their respective fields, each laden with a sickle, rake, or hoe, some pulling hand-drawn carts or carrying gunny sacks of corn, wheat, or sugar beets. Some were gaily chatting back and forth to each other as they came.

The rolling farm land around Miletinac, one of the more backward villages east of the gorgeous Dinaric Alps, was only moderately fertile; nevertheless it was a beautiful and quiet place to live. Rainfall was usually quite plentiful,

14

winters mild, and summers not oppressively hot. The Blue Mountains to the south, the heavy forests to the west, the profusion of flowers on the plateaus blessed the country with a rare scenic grandeur that gave the native people an inborn love for their restful country, even though they had to work hard for what they raised.

"I love it here," said Anna wistfully. "I do hope, with you, that we can own our own farm someday. How could we be happy living any place else, John? Could you be happy living in America even for a few months?"

"That I don't know yet," he answered. "I love it here in Miletinac, but my head is full of dreams. Dreams for you, Anna, for us, for our family. Do you understand?"

The people of the Balkans were taught to control their emotions, particularly husbands to wives and vice versa, especially in the open. But all at once Anna wanted to throw her arms around John and tell him he shouldn't let his dreams go any further. She wanted him to make good, yes, a thousand times yes, but she wanted to keep him close to herself, especially now. She saw herself being torn from him, separated by the endless Atlantic which might never bring him back, that Atlantic which had swallowed whole ship-loads of people. She tried to visualize herself living contentedly back in her former home, a young mother-in-waiting, working to keep busy while waiting for the arrival of both infant and father. Even worse, she saw her true love threatened by those fashionable American women each of whom dresses in her own costume. Anna visualized, but for a rash moment, a number of other suspicions to put her happy young heart in terror.

Then one more long glance at John quelled those fears. The sweet confiding things he had just told her gave her that quiet assurance she had known since the day of their marriage. John look at another woman? Never, though a million miles of land and sea separate them. John had not once given her the slightest reason to fear anything like this.

"But the priest," suggested Anna, suddenly and with solemnity.

"What about the priest?" asked John.

"Well, if you sent me money from America, wouldn't he expect additional offerings for my safekeeping and the child's — wouldn't he, John?"

"Maybe. I wouldn't know. There he comes now," observed John. "What can this mean? Someone in the village must be very ill, for it is not the season for him to be sprinkling the holy water on our homes."

"Oh, John," sighed Anna. "Just suppose tonight would be the last time he would be coming to bless us and our house before you leave!" Anna's voice almost had tears in it. John had never seen his wife so stirred. "Just suppose, John!"

Chapter 2

John was very thoughtful before he spoke.

"That sounds as though you think my dreams will come true," he breathed. "You really do make me happy." There was pride in his tone. "You will be brave and tell me to go ahead and make plans then? I was almost sure you would, Anna. It's for *your* sake that I want to try this. Look! The Father is going into Franz Milosh's house. He must be worse."

Anna Olesh had learned in five months of married life that her sensible, serious-minded husband possessed a rare convincing manner. Her look of anxiety vanished as she ran the palm of her hand across her forehead. She opened the door.

The house was as she had left it, tidy though scantily furnished, the hard earth floors swept immaculate. Quickly she started a fire in the crude corner clay cookstove and put on a kettle of water to make cornmeal mush. She counted the potatoes in the basket by the stove, and selecting two, put them in her only, and highly prized, brown enamel pan, a wedding gift from her grandmother. Before she had the potatoes peeled, John came in with a nest of fresh eggs in his hat.

"The sun is going down behind a bloody sky," he said, "and I noticed only a thin streak of clouds far away. There'll be no rain tonight. Another reason why I believe I should try America. Unless it rains soon, we'll see some hard times this winter, I fear."

"Well, John," began Anna, a faint smile like delicate needlework brightening her plain but striking young face,

17

"rain or shine, let's be thankful for what we have. We're happy even if we don't have much." She looked in the hat. "Six eggs!" she exclaimed softly. "Good. Put them in that dish on the table. We'll each have one for supper. Tomorrow I'm going to make a raised coffee cake for our Sunday breakfast."

"And I know this," beamed John. "Not a woman in America could make one like it or half as good."

In the dresser drawer Anna kept a homespun cloth which she put on the table only on special occasions. Almost tenderly she got it out, unfolded it, and looked at it thoughtfully before she spread it on the table. The black-handled knives and forks and plain heavy tan plates seemed to take on new value as she placed them on the cloth with lingering care.

The houses in Miletinac, though made of native red clay, were as firm and sturdy as concrete, and as rain-resistant. Scarcely a house in the village had more than two windows, and very few families owned more than one lamp, a homemade affair, usually a tin can large enough to hold about a cup of pumpkin-seed oil. A five- or six-inch pipe cut out of tin and rolled tightly together through which was fed a cloth wick was placed upright in the center of the can. The lamp produced more smoke than light, but no one in the village had anything better, and each was content with what he had.

The children of Miletinac attended a public school, fair for the day. They were taught to read, write, and cipher, but the teachers were extremely rigid, often cruel, and punished the pupils severely regardless of age. Seldom did a child have more than one slice of butterless, jamless coarse bread and an apple wrapped in a cloth for his noon lunch. If a hunk of sausage could be spared from the smoke rack above the kitchen ceiling, then the apple must be kept for another day.

The usual evening meal was bean soup, mush, kraut, potatoes or turnips with meat, for those who were fortunate

18

enough to have pigs. Very few families could sit down to a table blessed with more than two dishes and bread. Clothing was frequently handed down from one generation to the next.

Anna put the supper on the table and from the kitchen window she and John could see several neighbor children who had already finished their meal, running and laughing in the street.

"You are not eating much tonight," John said tenderly at length. "You are only watching the children. Come, Anna, eat your egg before it gets cold."

Anna knit her brow as though trying to gather together her spirits. "The children?" she asked. "Oh, I wasn't even seeing the children, John. I was only thinking —" She pressed her fingers against her warm cheeks.

"About what, Anna?"

"Well," she said, "I was wondering how I can really be as brave as — as you seem to think I am, John."

Anna had never seemed more beautiful to John than now in the gathering darkness. He looked at her a long time before he spoke. Reaching across the table he caught her one hand in his.

"I cannot imagine you being any other way," he said with tender confidence. "While you clear the table, I might walk over and inquire about Franz Milosh. He must be very ill."

The following week John made the trip to Daruvar, had his picture taken, and applied for a passport. He left home long before dawn, repeating his morning prayers twice on the way.

Covering ground afoot was almost an art with John Olesh, and as he strode with ease and grace in the cool of the morning before the hungry sun had a chance to wilt the green fields, he drank in the fragrant dewy odors of the cabbages, fruit-laden vineyards, and savory pasture grasses. John felt energetic, hopeful, and happy because Anna had agreed to his going. He hummed snatches of Slovenian folk songs, jagged gay little tunes that gave expression to his feelings.

Anna, rising very early, had prepared him a delicious breakfast of sliced cold corn mush fried in some of the greenish pumpkin-seed oil, a scrambled egg, roast barley coffee, and a slice of raised coffee cake which she hid away and saved purposely for this very morning.

"After the chickens are fed and you have your work all done," John suggested, "you might go over to your folks and let them in on this. Find out how they feel about your coming back home for a while. Explain carefully and exactly why I —why *we* feel it is important." She followed him to the door, stood there silhouetted by the meager smoking, sputtering light of the pumpkin-seed oil lamp, and listened until she could not hear his steps, which were filtered at first between her own heartbeats. Then when she could hear only her own heart, she firmly closed the door, made the sign of the cross, brushed a spoon across the flannel lamp wick to put out the flame, then stretched herself across the end of the bed to rest and wait for dawn. One moment she hoped John could get a passport, and then the next she hoped he could not. With one breath she hoped some kindhearted and generous person would loan him money for a passport, and with the next she caught herself praying Holy Mary to let no such person be found. Anna's trust in John was nevertheless implicit. His motives, she knew in her own mind, were untarnished. But the risk, the separation — life within her quivered.

Anna lay thinking until through the curtainless windows she saw, up among the pale stars, the cool sky turning white and she knew dawn was near. "Brave," she said, aloud. "John says I'm brave. I dare not disappoint him. He said it's for *me,* for *my* sake."

Anna got up, washed her face, recombed her silken black hair, tied on the kind of kercheif worn by all the married women of the village, and went out to hoe the turnips before the morning got warm.

John saw her in the dusk, waiting for him at the edge of the village. He all but ran to meet her, and Anna knew before he had time to tell her that his mission had not been futile.

"I can go third class for fifty dollars!" he exclaimed.

"Fifty?" Anna's eyes widened.

"Yes," cried John. "I can hardly believe it. That's in United States money, of course. From Le Havre, France, to New York. And a boat sails from Le Havre on the seventeenth of September. I'm almost positive I'll get my passport. There were several other men in the office making arrangements too. One was a German from Travnik, one a Croat from Knin. And I can borrow what I need from — why, what's wrong, Anna? Aren't you pleased?"

"Pleased?" she asked. "Why — why, yes, John," she said softly. "Of course, I'm always pleased when you've been successful. I didn't mean to look displeased. I was only following you. It's all so unbelievable. You can borrow what you need from whom?"

"From a Jewish man in Daruvar who knows my father. Anna, I know it's almost too good to be true. And did you talk this over with your parents today?"

"Yes. Yes, I did, John."

"And they are agreed? You may come home for a while?"

"What else do you suppose they would say, John? My mother said I'm her daughter until I'm dead, and even though the house is small, they'll manage to make a place for me. But you know that little sister of mine listened in when I was talking to Mother, and she ran down the street like a weasel, told the Kasha children, and they told the Pauts, and so already it's all over Miletinac that John Olesh is going to America to get rich."

"Rich?" John laughed one of those deep muffled laughs Anna always enjoyed.

"She seems to think it's something perfectly wonderful," continued Anna, "that her brother-in-law is going to undertake such a thing. And she got the idea from someone that

21

you'll soon be back laden with money and all sorts of wonderful things from America."

"I fear little Elizabeth has allowed her imagination to run too high and wild this time," laughed John. "I doubt if it's quite that easy a matter."

The evening was perfect. Beyond the grassy, unfenced borders, fields were yellow with ripe corn, wheat, and pumpkins, golden daisies and multicolored dahlias waving in the gentle breeze. The vineyards were almost black with ripened fruit that scented the cooling air. Acorns were falling on the leaf-carpeted ground. Happy, healthy children were playing the day's last games of toss-and-catch in the one wide avenue of the village. Summer, almost over, was turning into the splendors of autumn, and nowhere in the Balkans was the evening more serenely beautiful, peaceful, and inspiring than it was that night in Miletinac when John and Anna Olesh walked home together.

There was peace in the vast open heavens, peace in the golden sunset, peace on the purple Blue Mountains, peace on the shocked wheat fields, peace on the rye-thatched roofs, peace in the slowly fading twilight, peace in the clay path on which they were walking, peace throughout the village and across the land as far as eye could see.

"It's so beautiful tonight," whispered Anna. "It almost hurts."

"Hurts? What do you mean by that?"

"Well," answered Anna, "it just does. Sort of a happy hurt. I can't explain it, but when you're gone I'll be seeing all this —" she hesitated, "without you." She slipped her hand into his. "Nothing in America could be as beautiful as Miletinac, do you think? Watch, John, how the sun is reflected on the mountains over there. Now they are red, now blue. Look now over there, orange-purple and black. I just *know* America can't be more beautiful."

"No," agreed John. "Nothing in America will ever be more beautiful or more peaceful. Of that I am very certain.

And no girl or woman in America will be half as beautiful as you, Anna. I know that too."

Anna blushed. "It makes me happy to hear you say that, John," she cried softly. "Then I know you'll hurry back to me. There comes Father Jardell again. What can this mean? Is Franz dying?"

"Good evening, Father," the two addressed the long black-robed figure whose full red face shone in the dusk.

"Good evening," answered the priest, touching his black hat. "I just heard the news from one of the villagers that you may be leaving us to go to the States in America. Is that correct?"

"I'm planning that way, Father," answered John.

"And if you go," said the priest, "I want to urge you to keep up your daily prayers and attend church regularly in America. You won't have to walk twelve miles there, I'm very sure."

"I hope not. I mean — yes, Father," answered John. "I'll try to."

"You will be doubly duty-bound leaving your wife here; this you know, John," said the father in his characteristic priestly tone.

"Yes, Father," agreed John. "I know."

"But I fear," added Father Jardell, squinting and rubbing his double chin, "that you'll not find everyone in America good and honest. And moreover," he added, "not all Americans will give you a hearty welcome. You may be glad to come back to good old Miletinac in a hurry. There's no place in the world like our own country. And besides," he continued, "there are devils in America."

"Devils?" inquired John, raising both eyebrows. "Have you ever been there to see any, Father Jardell?"

"No," answered the father, stroking his double chin again, "and I doubt if I'll ever make such an attempt. This is good

23

enough for me right here." And he swept his skirts across his black shoes and glided on southward.

"John!" exclaimed Anna, half horrified. "You still feel like going?"

Chapter 3

John wrinkled his sun-tanned forehead and made a prompt reply. "If I meet an American devil, Anna," he said, "I'll politely go my way and let him go his. I won't even speak to him."

"Yes, I'm thinking," stressed Anna, "that you won't be able to talk to either angels or devils when you do get there. How will you know one from the other if you won't know what they are saying? You've never seen either."

John pondered. "People's actions speak louder than their words anyhow, don't they, the world over?" he asked. "Don't worry about that now, my brave girl. Maybe Father Jardell is a little jealous. Oh —" John caught himself. "What am I saying? I must not think such thoughts of the father."

"Just the same I wish you could speak a little English. That troubles me, just that alone, when I think of it."

"If Uncle Jose made out, I guess I can," answered John. "But you know we forgot to ask the father what brought him to our village again."

"We'll likely find out soon," answered Anna.

September was the big harvest month of the year and all over the farm-strips and hills of Miletinac, families were busy working together. Potatoes, the staple food of the Yugoslavians, were stacked in piles on straw beside the houses, the stacks then carefully covered with a layer of earth. Cabbages were cut fine and stamped into kraut barrels by many clean little bare feet.

Wheat was hauled by ox-drawn wagons to the nearest mill, where it was ground into one or several grades of meal and flour. Prunes were cooked into delicious prune butter, in copper kettles over open fires in the yard. Pumpkins were hauled in from the fields in large numbers, split open with axes, the pumpkins fed to the hogs or choice ones baked for supper, the seed dried during the night in large trays on top of the stove after the fire had died. Apples were sliced and dried, corn ground, beans hulled, turnips checked for later pulling, and then when all of that was done, there were nuts to be gathered.

The end of the first week in September John received his passport. The house had been spoken for, the garden harvested and sold (that is, what Anna didn't give to her parents toward her board and keep), and the loan from Mr. Hauenstein, the Jewish friend, had been obtained. John had his woven-grass valise partly packed. The chickens would be sold shortly and then their few pieces of furniture would be stored in a neighbor's empty shed, for the day of John's departure was drawing near.

Men, women, and children gathered each evening around the front of the Olesh house, asking John and Anna every conceivable question about John's contemplated trip abroad, oh-ing and ah-ing and aye-ing, giving suggestions, offering warnings, then discussing the adventure glibly one with another. Some of the younger men envied John. The older men shook their heads fearfully. The young girls pitied Anna. The older women put their motherly arms around her, promising to stand by her and at the same time assuring her that God and Holy Mother Mary were especially near to such as she.

Anna's mother prophesied that John would soon realize he had formed an erroneous conception of a glorified America, and would be back with Anna before her day. Her brother, Jose Dorge, was the only man of their village, she added, who had as yet gone off to America, and there always had been something vain or exclusive about Jose, as if he were in a class apart from the rest of the people in Miletinac.

26

Strange how Tena Dorge seemed so perfectly content to live month after month with Jose in a foreign country, saying always he'd be returning one of these days. It wouldn't be so with John and Anna, she figured, for they were too devoted to each other.

The children of the village also gathered around with the parents, listening with wide-eyed amazement, believing that surely now if one of their number, one like John Olesh, strong and brave, crossed the ocean and returned, their country would be ever after one of the most important spots on the earth, and would be discussed in school for generations to come.

Those nightly neighborhood gatherings made Anna feel as though John belonged to the village almost as much as he did to her. But after the "good evenings" had been said and their own door closed for the night, she knew better. They talked over everything. There was nothing left to say but "good-by."

In due time Anna was safely placed in the shelter of her parental home, and the last long "good-by" had been said. Anna watched John until he was out of sight, suppressing her feelings, for many eyes were watching her.

John walked to Daruvar, carrying his quaint straw valise, and from there rode a train to Zagreb, on to Basel, Switzerland, to Paris, then to Le Havre where on the seventeenth of September the *Santonita* left harbor on schedule.

The nine-day voyage was pleasant and quite uneventful except that John put himself laboriously to the task of learning a little German from several of the shipmates, for he was told it would be greatly to his advantage in more ways than one.

And young John Olesh soon did learn that a man who couldn't speak English and only a very little German could not expect to earn above twelve cents an hour, for he'd had no experience running "no machine, un no nozings, but mid han' or wagel un ox."

Anna held her breath while she tore the letter open. It was postmarked Steelton, Pennsylvania, October 10, 1901.

DEAR ANNA,

My thoughts have been with you always since the day we parted. The trip to Le Havre was both pleasant and exciting. I wished often you could have been at my side, knowing you enjoy beautiful scenery and flowers. I surely did not imagine Zagreb was so large and wonderful a city. Not one thing at all like Miletinac. Such houses and buildings you never dreamed of, nor the vegetable markets. In the depot there were people of many languages: Germans, Turks, Hungarians, and Austrians, not to mention our own Slavs, Serbs, and Croats.

The cathedral was very beautiful. It looked like many brown suns behind clouds. I said the rosary there. There were many images, even on the front and top.

Switzerland was yet more beautiful, but Paris I did not like. It was night when the train got there. We were nine days on the water, which gave me a great appetite. I loved the ocean. The meals were well enough prepared, but I never knew there were so many different things to eat. Twice we had roast sparrows and many kinds of soups and cheeses. I did not refuse to try anything, nor did I once get seasick as some others did.

I tried to learn some German from two friendly men who had once been to America and were returning. They had great sport helping me, but were very kind. Already I can say, but not well, a few words in English, but I am sure it is one of the most difficult of all languages and I fear I could never master it.

Those men on the boat advised me to go to Steelton, Pennsylvania, where many foreigners have found work. They helped me in New York to get on the right train. You could never dream how New York is so stacked, one house on top of another and close together, and streets full of carts and wagons. I actually did see a horseless carriage driven with a wheel. Very strange indeed. I have work in a stone quarry loading stone into a huge basket that runs out on a cable. You shall not worry about me although it is somewhat dangerous. I get $7.20 a week and it costs me $4.50 a week for room and meals. I stay in a three-story house where two other quarrymen stay. The lady makes my dinner in a tin pail. Write to me soon and send it to the post office general delivery, for I may not stay here longer if I find better paying work. Write me many things and how you are.

With fond love,

JOHN

It was exactly fifty-one days later when John received his first letter.

DEAR JOHN,

I was made joyful to get your long letter. I read it many times to myself and to some of our people in the village. Everyone asks about you. I am very well and keep myself ever so busy so I will not miss you too greatly. But that I do just the same. Yesterday Grandfather came and helped us butcher. We stuffed four links of sausage and hung them in the attic. Already we can smell them in the smoke.

Elizabeth says the teacher talks about you in school and will try to get a map to show them where you are. Right now Elizabeth is busy stringing an acorn necklace for herself. We have been having good rains which make all in the village glad again.

I have been helping Mother gather English walnuts and apples. They are especially fine this fall. Tomorrow or the next day when we finish chopping all the meat we will make soap. I will then knit myself some new scuffs and some very small shirts.

A very sad thing happened last week. Franz Milosh lay like dead for two days before he died. The witch doctor came and spit on ashes and put an egg on the window sill besides doing other things, but it did no good, and Milosh's wife borrowed quite a sum to pay her. It will take Milosh's wife many years to pay her bill to the father. I know you always liked Franz very much, and I have been going over to see wife Milosh every day since he died and she says it helps her to forget her sadness.

Last week I went along with the Kasova girls to take their pumpkin seeds to the mill. On our way home we met a strange man who was selling little black books called Testaments. He said they contained a very important message we should all know about. Of course, we had no money. The girls said Father Jardell would be very, very angry if he knew the man was in our village, and if he knew we talked with him he would make us kiss both his hands and the cross on his neck for sure. I can't help wondering what's so important in that book. Do you go to church as he told you to, John?

Be good, John, and I hope you soon find a kind of work that is not dangerous. Remember, I miss you. It looks like a storm coming. The chickens are already in the trees. I wonder, do the women in America wear each a different pattern? I am glad we went to school and learned to write even though mine is not as perfect as yours. Do read my farewell affection in these lines.

ANNA

Joe Twig was a six-foot, powerfully built Negro that gave one a first impression that he could push over a store counter if he leaned hard against it. But the most extraordinary thing about Twig wasn't his height, nor stature, but the way he talked. His voice had the depth of a bass viol, the silkiness of satin, and the soft warmth of a feather bed. He had a heart that befitted his voice — warm and tender.

Joe lived with his Mrs. Amelia and five little Twigs up the alley and at right angles to the drab gun-metal-gray rooming house on East Malone Street, where John boarded. Joe and John met one evening in the corner variety store where one hoped to find almost anything from a shoestring to an iron skillet. Joe was immediately captivated by the painful helplessness in which he found this new young lad of a stranger, for John was desperately trying to tell the storekeeper what he wanted. John was at the point of giving up in despair. Oh, for the right word in English! John fumbled. No, it wasn't a pocketknife, no, not a putty knife, not ointment, not a cabbage slicer, almost, but not a whetstone. He scanned the shelves and shook his head for the tenth or twentieth time when Joe Twig stepped up and placed a sinewy black hand on John's shoulder.

"Frien'," he said, "maybe I kin hep you. What is it yo-all want? Say it with you han'. Try it on me, Mister," and Joe showed two rows of fine pearly teeth while he demonstrated with his big pink-lined hands. "God made dese 'fore He made yo talk, anyhow. Show me now — with your hands."

John had determined that since his face seemed to tell everyone he was a foreigner even before he spoke, he would try to keep it as well groomed as possible, though he worked in a stone quarry for only twelve cents an hour. By appearances some of the other quarrymen rarely used a razor.

John had a fairly good straightedged razor which he applied every other day except to his upper lip. A trim mustache he felt would give him a certain dignity and the touch of maturity he needed.

John caught Joe's idea and proceeded to do a pantomime, shaving his face with his forefinger and rubbing it carefully across the palm of his hand.

"Bet I know," grinned big Joe, black eyes twinkling; "bet it's a hone he's awantin'. Got one, Duncan?"

Storekeeper Duncan fished one out of a drawer behind the counter, held it out, and John nodded.

"Wall, bless mah soul!" laughed Joe. "Couldn't yo hab guessed dat? Good thing I mosied in right now. How much fer sich a hone, Duncan?"

"Thirty cents," answered reddening Duncan, adjusting his tarnished-rimmed glasses. "Know the man, Joe?"

"Neber met till now," answered Joe, "but I'll be his frien' if he'll let me be." Turning to John, "Thirty," he repeated as though John hadn't heard, and to make sure he understood he dug a handful of change out of his own pocket and selected a quarter and a nickel.

"Like-a dat, Mistah."

John understood. His young gray eyes gave big Joe a warm "thank you," and nodding, he found his own thirty cents.

Chapter 4

Joe Twig and John Olesh carried on a dramatic conversation right there on the street in front of Duncan's variety store. And although John failed to understand much of what Joe was telling him, their efforts at communication were not altogether lost.

First of all, the two discovered they were neighbors. They discovered next, without actually realizing it in so many words, that each possessed a deep emotional personality, and they took an impressionable liking each to the other. In the third place, each felt a sense of brotherhood and a spontaneous desire to live as good neighbors should, regardless of color or nationality.

Although Joe Twig could speak neither German nor Slavish, to John's utter astonishment big Joe seemed to comprehend most of what he was trying to explain, where he was working, how much he was making, where he had a wife, and all of that. John soon learned how to talk with his hands. Then to John's still greater amazement, Joe Twig put a big arm across his shoulders and ushered him to his own back yard. He showed him graciously to a dilapidated wooden bench, disappeared into the house, and returned with two slices of juicy watermelon, one for John and one for himself.

The two men understood each other better as the evening slipped on. Sometimes they grunted to each other with only bits of sentences, then finished with laughter, sometimes a nod, sometimes a shake of the head.

"Mah boy," said Joe, as if assuming he was John's senior, "wanna work for me? Huh? Wanna drive a horse an' wagon up an' down de streets, gathering up leaves an' sich?"

John didn't quite get it at first, but Joe wasn't ready to give up. He repeated, "Wanna drive a horse an' wagon for me?"

Joe took John to the barn at the rear of the lot and showed him Doll and Dick and his two iron-wheeled wagons. "I could use you," Joe told John. "Could gib you a nickel more a day an' work not so hard. Lots of people in de better parts of town want der leaves an' trash gathered up dis time o' year. De ole man I had hepin' me is no good. Sick. Lazy. You tak dis here wagon wes' ob town an' I tak de other on de eas'. One dollar an' twenty-five a day. You mus' mak more if ya kin, my boy. You'll neber get ahead till ya do."

That evening John looked at himself in the dresser mirror in his room. A new, compelling something shone in his eyes. "John," he said, eying himself seriously, "you've got to make good, not only for Anna's sake, not only for our own children's sake, but for the sake of men like Joe Twig." John walked across the room several times, his hands in his pockets. "God," he said, "Mother, Holy Mother Mary, I want something. I don't know what it is, but something —"

John started working the following week "mid wagel un horse" hauling leaves and trash for his big black boss, Joe Twig. The horse, Dick, seemed to understand John perfectly, but alas, the people!

'What did you say?" demanded a thin, pointed-faced woman on his fourth day. Her voice was irritable, impatient, stern. "Speak English," she snapped, "so I can understand what you want."

A moment of sickening failure possessed John. He remembered how Anna had said it disturbed her that he wasn't able to speak English. This naked truth had been his one nightmare from the day he set foot on American soil. It had been broken at times by short intervals of hope that tomorrow would go better. Others had lived through this stage, he consoled himself, so why couldn't he?

The frown on the woman's face was definitely not the medium by which John's nightmare would be broken by hope. Rather, by stage fright. Would she hiss at him next, or spit on him? But, all John could think of saying as he tipped his hat was, "Gudday, Ma'am. I so goot spak English as I kin. Pardon. Pardon." So he left, but even in the midst of his fright, he was surprised he had done this well.

The clear noonday December sky was almost cruelly bright. A crisp wind set tumbleweeds chasing each other across the street with a whisk-broom rustle on the hard-trodden ground. Anna, on her return from the village mail depot, clutched the letter, pressing it against her thumping heart. Her feet could not get her home fast enough. She lowered her head against the wind and the blinding brightness of the sun, and the playful breeze seemed to move the earth and send her along with it. She filled her lungs and laughed aloud. She grew light with anticipation, lighter than she had felt for weeks. Her mother held the door open as she bounded into the kitchen.

DEAR ANNA,

May this letter find you in good health and content. You asked about the American women wearing different dresses. I have all your letters before me and will try to answer all your questions. Yes, it is true, Anna. Many patterns and many colors, but that does not make them lovely. In fact, some are most unlovely, at least to a foreigner.

No, I have not gone to a church as yet, for before I go I must first buy better clothes and I am trying to save all I can. Do not be impatient with me if I cannot send you any money for a while yet. I will soon.

Joe Twig, a kindhearted colored man, has hired me to drive a horse and wagon over town, gathering at first leaves and rubbish, now ashes and rubbish. I do get fifty cents a week more than at the quarry. I still hope each day to make more. If only I could speak English, I could find a better job. It is a great trial to me, or I must say with the people who do not understand me, nor I them. But I keep trying. I stay at the same place. Tell all the village I am well. Today I ate my first banana. It is a long white fruit inside a yellow shell. I may learn to like such a thing. Nearly every man carries a little clock in his pocket. Someday I would like to have one.

It is very different here when someone dies. They keep them perfect for several days by some means, and after the funeral they are carried away in fine carriages with glass windows.

Your mother is ever so kind, but had better kill the goose when it is ready, for I cannot know when I will be able to come back.

Many loves,

JOHN

Slowly Anna folded the letter. A tear dropped on her blue blouse.

"Doesn't sound like he'll get the loan paid off very soon, does it?" remarked her mother, trying for Anna's sake not to sound morose. Anna made no answer. The lump in her throat grew.

In the middle of the night Anna's mother woke with a start.

"Yes?"

"Light the lamp," whispered Anna, "and bring it into my room."

She named the baby Mary, a dainty, fine-featured, perfectly formed child with blue eyes and dark hair.

"John will be so pleased when he hears about this," beamed the proud grandmother, holding the baby close to Anna's face.

"I wish he could see her now," sighed Anna. "And, Mother, was — was I brave?"

"Yes, dear," nodded her mother. "I'd say you've been brave all along. Just rest now and try not to worry about a thing. We'll help take care of little Mary, and when the day comes we'll have her baptized and everything will be all right."

Women throughout the village came to see the sweet new baby whose father, so far away in America, wouldn't know about her for nearly a month. Every woman seemed to feel almost duty-bound to help in the proper raising of the little fatherless one who wasn't actually fatherless, of course.

Little Mary did not suffer from receiving too little attention either, for Elizabeth was thrilled beyond words to have a little niece. She would have neglected studying her spelling and arithmetic to hold her new niece every evening after school, but one mention of the teacher's stick put lessons before pleasure.

DEAR JOHN,

You are a father now. Mary came the tenth of December before daybreak. She seems healthy and strong. I only wish you could see her, John, with her blue eyes; she is very sweet. I cannot tell you now whom she looks like—more like you than like me, I believe. I tried to be brave.

By this time are you not getting more money? Is it not as easy as you thought? Your Aunt Tena said that Uncle Jose likes it in America very much. He has been gone now close to two years. I surely hope it will not be so with you.

Someday we'll have our own farm, won't we, John? And we'll be living together. I dream about it nearly every night. Bv the time you get this letter little Mary will be baptized. Mother and Father are taking the little one to Father Jardell at Djulovac on the eighth day. Everyone has been kind to me. Will you not be here for Christmas? I wish the day was already past. The goose will not taste as good as it would if you were here to help eat it. Mother is outside now just pulling the bread out of the oven. Aunt Tena's new stove is beautiful. I would rather have my husband than many new stoves, but I will try to be ever so patient.

Father said if he could afford it, he would have Mary's

37

picture taken in Daruvar sometime so I could send it to you. But no picture would be like seeing her and touching her. I will try to be brave always.

Many affectionate loves,

ANNA

All winter long John hauled ashes. The people on his route through west Steelton soon recognized him as an honest, reliable man, and gave him trade without the exchange of many words.

The three boys behind the big maple tree tittered at each other.

"He didn't see us, did he?" giggled one. They huddled, tramping on each other's feet. "Wait until he's closer, then shoot. Won't he be mad?"

"Anything I like," chuckled the second, "is to see a guy get poppin' mad an' can't sass back."

"Ready," signaled the third. "There he is, kids."

Three stones whizzed through the air. Three more. One struck John on the left shoulder, one on his left ear, cutting a small gash. Two hit Dick, who jumped, nearly throwing John from the wagon.

John pulled the reins, jumped from the wagon, and ran for the tree.

Boys scrambled in three directions, but John overtook the clumsiest and caught him by the coat. The boy wriggled, clawing the air and screaming with rage.

"I no hurt you," said John, grabbing the boy by the shoulders in a firm grip. "I —" he shook him, but not severely. "Boy no goot." John shook his head, looking straight into the lad's dirty face. The boy sniffled, puffing between sniffles. He tried to kick John, but John held him at arm's length.

"You crazy baboon of a foreigner," hissed the lad between chattering teeth. "You let me go or I'll have my dad beat your measly brains out and it wouldn't take him long, either, 'cause they're mighty few."

John held the boy. He spoke not a word. " 'Twasn't my stone that hit you, nohow," he bawled. "Hey, you guys." He saw the other two runaways creeping back. "Hey you," he shouted, "pelt him till he lets me go."

The two gathered stones, but at that moment a slender little aging woman appeared at her front door and called out in no uncertain terms.

"Drop those stones, boys." They turned in surprise. "Hear me?" she demanded, coming toward them. "I've been watching you boys," she shook her finger, "and if you throw another stone I'll have to report you. Sorry, but I will."

The boys slunk away.

"Shame on you," she continued. "This is the third time I've seen you torment that man. I saw you from my front window and I've not seen him do a thing against you. That's very unkind of you."

"Ah, well," ventured one boy. "Come on, you guys." And as the three tore into a run, one called back over his shoulder, "Hunkey trash! Hunkey trash!"

John tipped his hat to the slender graying little woman.

"Those are bad boys," she said.

"Bad," agreed John, nodding.

Then she said, "Those little devils need to go to Sunday school."

John shook his head.

"Oh, yes they do," insisted the woman. "The Sunday school has done a lot to make fine young men out of boys just like those."

John stared. "Pardon," he said. "I go on mid wagel un horse."

That night John lingered at the barn after he had Dick unharnessed and fed.

"Joe," he asked, running his hands into his pockets, "vat iss Sunday school?"

39

Chapter 5

The early March sun, beginning its slow downward cycle, sent soft rays through the budding tree branches outside the open barn doors, making latticework on Joe Twig's chocolate face. He gave John a long scrutinizing glance.

"Sunday school?" he asked, still eying him. "Whar yo pick up dat word?"

"Bad boy devil go. I know nozings vot iss."

Joe leaned backward and laughed, a low rumbling laugh. He scooped a can of oats from the feed bin and poured it out for Doll. Then the same measure for Dick.

"You fed Dick?" he inquired.

"Ya," answered John.

Joe threw the oats back. He unbuttoned his patched blue denim jacket and folded his hands behind him.

"You say bad boy debil go ta Sunday school? What yo talkin' 'bout?"

John shook his head. He held up three fingers. "Boy mid rock" — he showed Joe the size by forming a circle with his forefinger and thumb, "to my" — he pointed to his damaged ear.

"Say," observed Joe, stepping close, "yo did get a whack. What boys did it, John? Now tell me."

"Un," John pointed to his shoulder, "un Dick — Dick jump. So I vonce run, mid han' get boy. Un voman im house run un say," he shook his finger, "bad boy, stop. Go vay. Go so — so," John scratched his head. "Bad devil un Sunday school."

Joe's face grew almost as serious as John's, yet a twinkle like a kitten getting ready to chase a ball of yarn lurked around the corners of his black eyes, wanting to break loose any second into a dashing smile.

"I jes done like to hear all dis," began Joe Twig, tenderly examining John's gashed blood-stained ear. "Who were de boys who threw stones? Can't yo tell me dat?"

"No vot name. No vot nozings un I — I no vork mid horse un wagel. No more. No more," repeated John.

"Yo — yo mean," stammered Joe, stepping back. "Yo mean you'll quit over dis!"

John floundered like a horse in the mire. If only he could explain in his native tongue. John nodded.

"Yo can't quit me, John," Joe plunged bluntly to the bottom. "I'll fix dem rascals. Take me to whar it happened. I'll fix 'em if you can't. Yo say yo ketched holder one?"

"Yeh."

"Den why under God's heaben didn't yo flounce him good?" Joe demonstrated, beating the air.

John shook his head. "I no mak mad. I no kin make English. Fader Jardell say votch Merican devil. I votch un stay vay. I no vork mid Dick un wagel more. I vork mid han' un mid stone un no people ven I no more goot English speak."

"Well," said Joe. "Well," he repeated with deep feeling. "So you've made up your mind already an' I can't talk yo out of it? And who's Fader Jardell?"

"Mine priest fader."

"So," inquired Joe in surprise, "yer a Catholic?"

"Yeh."

"Neber knew," answered Joe.

"You no Catlic?" asked John.

"Nope," answered Joe. "I keep all my 'ligion in my heart and it's a pretty good place ter hab it, too. Nope, I'm no Catholic."

"I know nozings Sunday school is."

"Shur," readily answered Joe. "Catholics hab mass an' no Sunday school. Go early an' pray on beads, den gad round

41

all day on de Sabbath. Not for me. My ole mammy kep de Lord's day holy all day. An' my Amelia, she teach de young-uns to be hones' an' tell de truf, and mine der own business, and neber sass back. She larns 'em good. Ders a Sunday school right down dis street four blocks whar mine go. Not regular, but 'nuf I know don't hurt 'em none 'long wid der mammy's teachin'."

John didn't comment. His thoughts seemed far away, many furlongs, perhaps miles, or even seas.

"Dey won't be liable ter torment yo agin," ventured big Joe in a fatherly tone. "Come now. Aren't yo a brave man, John?"

John straightened. He looked into big Joe's kind face as if to ask what all he had been telling him. His clear gray eyes revealed, however, careful consideration of Joe's last question. Brave?

"I no make mad," John said at length. He worked the toe of his shoe in the dirt of the barn floor.

"Explain yourself," said Joe. "What yo mean, John? Yo 'fraid yo'll make dem rascals mad? Huh? Dat it, John?"

"I," said John, slapping his hand on his chest. "*I* no make *my* mad. No goot. No," John made a fist and beat the air, all the while shaking his head.

"Yo mean yo done wanna get yourself mad an' fight?" asked Joe. "Won't hit? Beat a boy? A bad boy? Why not?"

"I no hit," said John firmly. "No," he repeated. "I no work mid horse un wagel." And John's voice was decisive, final.

"Den," answered Joe with disappointment, "dat means I pay you now. Sorry. Sorry, John."

She read aloud:

DEAR ANNA,

You will notice I am sending you twenty dollars with this letter. Use it as you decide for the best. It is now six months today that I left you in good old Miletinac. I long to be with you and dear little Mary tonight. My evenings are long and lonesome, for I will not go out to the saloons or gamble even though the men here in the house urge me. I stay in my room or sit sometimes in the park close by when it is not too cool, and try to fasten more English words into my head. I try to listen to children at play and reason out what they are meaning by their speech. I wonder if you could learn it with more ease. How sorrowful if I would have to write you letters in English. I would, by all means, have to ask someone to do it for me; so I would not do it often.

No, I have not as yet gone to church here. I am sending you the money instead of buying myself better clothes. I could send you more, but I must keep enough for trolley fare to and from work. I am working in a different stone quarry now where I get a dollar more a week than I did hauling leaves and ashes. It is not much gain since I need to pay for trolley rides, but each little bit helps. At least, Anna, it is my everyday hope to work steadily upward. Some joyous day I expect to surprise you with glad words that I can prove to these American chiefs that I am worth by my hands and my head more than my mouth can tell them. You need not let Father Jardell know I send you this much money. Ask Aunt Tena where Uncle Jose is over here. I would like to locate him. He could be of help to me perhaps.

You will soon be spring planting. How I wish we could be planting our own fields together! But let no one suppose I am sorry I came to America, for I am not. This is a great experience and I will have countless things to tell you that I cannot put in letters for space and time and cost of postage.

The winter with snow is very cold. I doubt if you and little Mary would enjoy it, but the houses have beautiful stoves that send out warmth even to all corners of the room.

I cannot understand why there are so many religions here and every one having their own church and preacher, as they call their priest-leaders. They certainly cannot all be right, and sometimes I think they might all be wrong unless there are many gods. There are many Americans, I believe, who have not tested any one of the religions; so I think they must not be much good. The women wear hats, not kerchiefs like you do; they go even into churches with chicken and bird feathers and flower gardens on them. That is not to my liking. Shall I tell you "good-by" so soon? I could write on and on, but press little Mary to yourself for me, for I am very lonely tonight, and although she is not old enough to understand, whisper to her that her father in America longs to see her.

My many loves,
JOHN

Anna stood thinking. "I know what I'll do," she cried. "Every bit of this money will go toward paying off what John borrowed from the Jewish man."

"He didn't say you should use it for that," said her father thoughtfully.

"But the sooner we pay that, the sooner he can save up enough to come home on. Here. Please take it to Daruvar and give it to the man."

"It's yours, Anna," objected her father. "Keep it a while and think it over. Anyhow, I'm quite certain you'll need to cash it yourself."

"Even so," answered Anna. "I'll go along with you the next time you go and you'll take the money to him, please, for I don't know him. Will you say 'yes'?"

"Think it over, Anna. It may be the thing that John would like you to do, but wanted you to decide."

It was the day of fundamental importance — Easter Sunday. There was an early rustle in the rustic village of Miletinac. Anna was getting ready to go with a group of conscientious worshipers to the annual celebration in the Catholic church in Djulovac.

Anna had selected her best, her daintily hand-hemstitched blue blouse which she wore in Miletinac fashion, loose over

44

her matching gathered skirt. Her cheeks had been washed and rubbed until they glowed. Tiptoeing carefully to the crib she made certain Mary was sound asleep before she joined the group gathering in the wide village street.

"Elizabeth," whispered Anna, "it's sweet of you to stay here with Mary today. Good-by now."

The sun was still hiding behind the pine-covered hills when the group started on their twelve-mile walk. From nearly every house stepped someone, or two or three, all freshly dressed in their best. Only the very old or very young of the village would miss this important event of the year.

The church in Djulovac could not hold the crowd that came; so the priest stood on a platform just inside the door and the people gathered in silence and with heads bowed in conscious dignity outside the church while he chanted and spoke in strange words. Then, as he held out his hand over them, the crowd answered, "Christ the Lord is risen today. Glory, Hallelujah."

One by one the people went forward, placed their offering of flowers on the red-clothed altar, then kissed the priest's extended left hand and the gold cross which hung from his neck by a long chain. Each gave him an offering of money.

Repeatedly he picked up a small glass of wine and drank its contents while a white-robed lad refilled the glass from time to time from a silver-lidded pot.

Silently and with strange awe the people stood again in a mass in front of the church. Even here there seemed to be a great fixed gap between the priest and his people. When the last person had given his flower offering, Father Jardell held out his hand again and the people answered his words in one accord, "Christ the Lord is risen today."

"And do you suppose," whispered Anna to her mother on their way home, "that John has remembered to go to church in America today?"

"Surely," came her mother's answer. "Surely John would not forget that."

Chapter 6

It was the first of June when Anna received the answer. This time she tore it open close by the mail depot. And to add to her unhappiness over it, Father Jardell came sweeping along as she was reading the letter.

"Aye," said the priest, tapping her gently on one shoulder. Anna jumped, for she neither saw nor heard him coming.

"A letter from John?" he asked.

"Oh!" gasped Anna, pressing it to her. "Yes, Father."

"And he's behaving himself as a good father and as a good member of the church should, I presume," added Father Jardell, arching his eyebrows in question.

Anna's face got hot. She folded the letter around the money order and tucked it quickly into the envelope.

"Why, Father —" she stammered weakly. "Why, Father, I — I trust John. He wouldn't be anything but a good father, I'm certain, and I am also certain he's behaving himself very well, for he wrote once that some men tried to get him to go out with them evenings to gamble and drink and he wouldn't go."

"And when will he be returning?"

"Father, he doesn't know yet," answered Anna.

"Is he working?"

"Yes, Father."

"And is he sending money home to you?"

"He has sent me some three times, Father." Anna's hands trembled a little. She picked at the corner of the envelope.

"Very fine," blinked the priest. "Very fine. I haven't seen you for several weeks."

"Yes, Father," agreed Anna. "I only wish we had a church here in Miletinac."

"We may have someday," said the priest, and he started to glide away, then stopped short. "I meant to ask if your husband is going to church over there in America."

Anna's face felt crimson. "Well, it's like this," she began. "He hasn't good enough clothes yet to go to such fine churches as they have in America, Father. But I know John says his prayers at home. Oh, I just know he does, Father."

"Then he's not doing penance, you mean?"

"Well, Father," answered Anna with a sigh, "perhaps by this time he is. I'm sure it—it isn't because he wouldn't want to or doesn't feel he needs to. John isn't that careless. But he's trying hard to save up enough to come home on."

"You write and tell him," Father Jardell said, "he's to do penance while in America or he'll have much to care for when he gets back."

Anna walked home with slow steps, staring hard at nothing in particular. She decided not to relate the conversation to anyone, not even her mother.

August came. There was uneasiness and painful embarrassment in John's silent distress. Morning after morning when he walked between the green rows of maple trees on his way to the trolley line, he muttered inward self-scoldings for not having been able to obtain a better paying job.

Noon after noon when he opened his tin dinner pail and sat munching, staring into the naked, colorless, sun-baked quarry walls, his thoughts traveled with uncontrolled habit to the cool, full green pastures back in Miletinac: happy, strong fathers with their kerchiefed mates working by their sides in the potato and cabbage fields; little children prancing along in innocent gaiety; sweet fragrant country air, grape-scented and invigorating; the distant pine-wooded hills, and warm sun shining kindly on the rye-strawed roofs.

Night after night inexpressible longings and searchings tossed and tormented him from the time he caught the trolley until long past midnight. The "why" about life now and about a hereafter troubled him more than the "why" he hadn't been more successful in advancement financially. The day he saw the foreman in his crew fatally wounded had made its lasting impression. It wasn't the accident, the snapping of the cable, the crash, the terrified shouts of the men, but the look on Bargelley's face and his pathetic cries before he died that haunted him. That very morning Bargelley had called his crew together and had given them another one of his safety-first lectures. "And remember, fellows," he had said in conclusion, "let's all be careful today to save our own lives and the lives of our buddies on this job. None of us are ready to die yet," he added laughing. "I know I'm not, and I'll bet none of you are either."

There was a dreadful wordlessness when the frightened men crowded close around their dying boss. They all knew when they saw his ashen lips and when they heard the deep gurgling sound come from his chest that, though he had said he wasn't ready, death had its claim. John heard with paralyzing horror Bargelley's cries to God for mercy before his collapse into unconsciousness. The rest of the day the men moved about in the quarry talking only when necessary and in muffled tones. John wondered what they were wondering in their unusual quietness. That night he said his prayers twice and then paced the floor in restless longing.

From his bedroom window in the drab and cheerless rooming house on East Malone, everything John looked at in the street below made him more lonely and more perplexed at his own uneasiness and incongruity: couples sitting and chatting on public park benches; a store window gaily trimmed with green and white paper and filled with strange new wares; an American flag waving in the breeze on a nearby schoolhouse; tight-waisted women mincing by on shoes with amazingly high heels, some pushing baby carriages; a young man pedaling past on a bicycle.

John sat down and picked up his pencil. He shook his head. Anna should never know his questions and unpleasant

48

experiences. His grief and mental struggles were partly, at least, self-imposed, the result of his own romanticism. He could blame no one; so he would tell no one. No, not even Anna should know the extent of his loneliness nor how perfectly and how personally he was learning that his ignorance of this foreign tongue had forced him to the bottom. His expectations had already been dashed. His daydreams had been blackened by cyclonic winds that blew and twisted to near shreds his fond hopes. Why relive to relate?

Always in the center of each new struggle, Anna's young tender face, full and expectant, lustrous brown eyes, mature in devotion yet sweet and childlike in faith, stood out with compelling vividness—lovely, patient, and above all, brave. But for Anna and his little one John would have tried to shrug his shoulders at his unhappy complexity. He could have shoved embarrassment, fear, and incongruity down the back steps of America and gone home. Or he could live on alone indefinitely on his limited wage, searching silently for the answers about life. He wasn't hungry, bedless, nor entirely friendless.

John decided to go for a long walk when he met Joe Twig at the door.

"Jes on my way ober," warmly grinned Joe. "Haben't seen yo lately. Still workin' whar yo was?"

"Ya," answered John.

"Goin' someplace?" asked Joe.

John shook his head.

"Den come along ter a ball game."

"I?"

"Shur. Come along. Promised ter play wif de gang tonight. Bet you'd make a good one at it, John. Dat's one time ya kin work yerself up 'thout speakin' 'so goot English,' as ya put it."

John hesitated. Joe had his big hand on John's arm.

"Bet ya kin run like a deer. Let's go."

On the way to the field Joe said, "Heard dey's wantin'

four men at de foundry. I'm a-goin' ober der and ask fer me a job fust thing real early in de mornin', so I am."

John looked up sharply.

"Wanna go along?" asked Joe.

"Ya!" exclaimed John, "I go mid yo."

The following week John wrote:

DEAR ANNA,

At last I'm making better wages; so I'm sending you another money order. Save what you can toward our little home. I'm working at a wheel foundry. It's a very warm job since I help to feed a huge firebox called a furnace where scrap iron is melted. I would not like to do this all my life. A very rough group of men work here who make constant fun of God and Hell, and Catholic priests and Protestant preachers alike. Two men from Rumania work near me and also have a difficult time with English. The foreman can speak German and that helps somewhat.

I learn a new English word nearly every day, but one reason why English is so difficult is because many words have several meanings. This seems very odd to me. I am told to dump a load fast, which means to do it quickly; then I'm told to hold fast to the brake, which means to hold it tightly so it will not move quickly.

I've played ball several times with men and boys of this neighborhood. I like it and it is a fine time to learn words. But sometimes I do not know whether I'm to come or go or stand still. You will laugh at this, I'm sure.

Little Mary will likely be walking and talking when I come home. I know it's too far to take her to Daruvar and too expensive to have her picture taken; so I'll just keep on making my own picture of her in my mind. You are both in my thoughts always, Anna.

How is the garden this summer? The pumpkins especially. I hope someday we can own a glass lamp such as I have in my room. It makes a wonderful, bright light that shines through a glass chimney and smokes very little. I have many other things I hope to get you some glad day.

Yesterday who should come to see me but Uncle Jose. He said you told Aunt Tena where I was and she wrote and told him to find me. He has been working in a coal mine not over seventy-five miles from here. He's going farther west to hunt for another job. I think he likes to see more new country. But, Anna, I feel much better since he told me how it went with him the first year he was in America. It just takes time and patience since we are foreigners and without a trade or money to start up a business of our own. He is not a bit downhearted. Of course, he has been making more than I do as yet, but I will always be looking for a better job.

Dear Anna, do not fret, please, because I have not gone to church yet. I must get better accustomed to these American ways and feel my way around. I cannot seem to make you understand.

Uncle Jose said he never bothered to go to church here and since he's a good Catholic, Father Jardell should be satisfied if Uncle Jose is. Isn't that good enough? I walked past a Protestant church one evening and heard music coming from the open windows. It was the people themselves singing and I never before heard anything like it. I felt like slipping in, but to be sure, I did not.

I must close before this gets too long. Uncle Jose said I could go west with him if I wanted to, but I'd rather hold my present work and perhaps go later if he is first successful. He will let me know. My good friend, Joe Twig, also works at the foundry.

My many loves,
JOHN

"What is it?" asked Elizabeth. "What makes you look so sad, Anna?"

Anna handed the letter to her mother.

"You read it," she said. Then she took her baby out of Elizabeth's arms and pressing its soft little head into her neck, she hurried into the bedroom.

"What's wrong?" asked Elizabeth, following her.

"Please go on," begged Anna, covering her face with the baby's dress. "Go," she sobbed softly, "and let me be alone."

51

Nor did Anna come out of the room until she had her emotions well under control.

Anna went out into the garden and dug a square hole in the ground in the center of the cabbage patch, lined it with a clean gunny sack, then went back into the house to get Mary. Carefully she placed her little one in the ground bed, then built a canopy with baskets to shield her tender eyes from the sunlight.

"Mary," Anna whispered, kneeling to caress her baby, "your father says he may not see you until you are big enough to walk. Think of it, you dear little baby girl." She kissed her on the forehead. "You can watch Mother work now from here. I won't go far away. No, you won't cry. We've got to be brave, both of us, when Father is so far away. But he will come back someday." She caught her baby's uplifted hands and pressed them against her lips.

"I must run along now and help hoe the cabbages. Someday my little girl will be running along beside me to the cabbage patch."

Anna got to her feet and picked up her hoe. "And someday," she added, "you'll be walking straight into your father's arms. Won't he be happy to see such a pretty little girl!"

Chapter 7

In March Anna received the short but welcome letter saying John would be sailing on the tenth of April. "Our John is coming home at last," rejoiced his father, "but I fear there's more than one young man in Miletinac who has one foot already on American soil and once John returns with a favorable report will want to go off too."

When John did arrive two weeks later nearly half of Miletinac followed Anna to the edge of the village to meet him. It was the same as before. John seemed to belong to the village as much as to his wife.

"And there he comes," shouted a husky lad who had run ahead and climbed up a tree.

Anna could not help cringing a little under the fact that there was no hope of her meeting her husband but under the gaze of what seemed to her just then almost a myriad of eyes. She squeezed Mary's little hand and held her breath. Where was John? She couldn't see him. People began to move toward a figure in the distance, men removing their hats, getting ready to wave them in the air.

"Papa?" Mary questioned impatiently.

"He's almost here," comforted Elizabeth, brushing the little girl's hair and pushing through the crowd at the same time.

"Yes, dear," said her mother. But Anna couldn't hide the tone of suspense in her voice. "Why!" she exclaimed. "There! There he is, Mary! Your papa! Look! It's John."

The boy in the tree had leaped to the ground, dashed ahead of everyone, and grabbed John's bulging valise out of his hand. The excited crowd moved forward, his parents, his brothers, his sisters, his home folks. Half a dozen boys raced

53

to see who could touch John first. Then followed shouting, jumping, and laughing. Every boy wanted to carry John's valise. The older people held their eagerness with a little more restraint, however, and one man shouted out with a tone of consideration that Anna inwardly thanked him for, "Why don't you let him have at least a glimpse of his little Mary and the wife first?"

But Anna's feet were suddenly glued to the ground. Her heart missed a beat. She wanted to hurry toward him, but couldn't. But she didn't need to. John pushed through the crowd toward her.

"Anna!" cried John. His eyes were as moist as hers. He clasped her outstretched hand in both of his and pressed it against his heart. Her head for a moment rested on his shoulder. Mary clung to her mother's skirt, too bashful now to look up. John reached down and tenderly gathered her in his strong arms.

"Can it be?" he exclaimed, ignoring the group of onlookers for a moment.

"Oh, Anna," he whispered in her ear. "She's wonderful. I can hardly believe this is our Mary."

"Does she look like you thought she would?" asked Anna.

"Better, Anna. Better than my poor imagination," he laughed.

"Do you know I'm your papa, Mary?" He kissed her. Mary smiled, showing her perfect row of teeth. "Or can't you talk yet? I'm your papa. Yes, I am, Mary."

Mary kept on smiling, then touched her father's warm cheek with her fingertips.

"She'll talk after a while, John," whispered Anna. "She's too excited now."

Then John turned to the group. "Hello, Mother and Father. Everybody! It's good to see you all. Hurrah for good old Miletinac and all you good neighbors!"

The crowd could wait no longer. All around John they pressed in. Yes, it was their good friend and neighbor, the

54

John Olesh they had grown up with, the same John, but mysteriously different somehow.

Everyone talked at once. Everybody wanted to touch him.

"Look at that American haircut."

"And his shoes. Leather, aren't they?"

"Don't they hurt his feet?"

"See his pants, and his store coat."

"Think he'd let us try them on sometime?"

"Did they cost a great deal, John?"

"What did it cost to come home?"

"You say only forty-five American dollars?"

John carried Mary while Anna walked as close to his side as possible, but they could scarcely move for the crowd which was growing now. Anna knew it was useless to begin on any of the thousand and one questions she wanted to ask him until they were once alone in the privacy of their own room. And where was that room? And where that privacy?

At the door of the house, Anna's father clapped John on the shoulder. "Well," he said, "now that you've finally come, we'll have to kill the hen the girls have been trying to fatten for the occasion. How does that sound to you? Here, take a chair. You've got your arms full with a mighty sweet little girl, haven't you, John?"

"Indeed I have," answered John, "and the hen sounds mighty good to me, too. There's only one thing that would sound better, and that's news of a place I could buy."

"There is a two-room house for sale down the street here," said Anna's father. "The Sam Pirggio place. Did you know she died last week?"

"No. How much does he want for the place?"

"I don't know, but we'll inquire."

"But what's Sam going to do?"

"He'll go and live with one of his sons in Daruvar as soon as he can sell, so I've heard. If you'd rather build, I think we could find several men to help you put up a house. You might be able to buy a piece of ground from Schmidt."

55

"I'll price both," answered John, "and see what's the best buy. One thing sure, I want to make my hard-earned American money go as far as possible."

"So you really think it was to your gain to go to America?" inquired Anna's father.

"There's no doubt about it," answered John. "But you see, I didn't stay long enough."

"Long enough?" Anna's eyes widened. "But you were gone nineteen months, John."

"Long months for me, too," answered John. "But it's like this. It takes a person so long to get accustomed to American ways of living and working. Just about the time I would have been able to get a better job, I felt I had to come home to see you and my baby. I couldn't stand it away any longer. I felt it was my duty to come home and buy you a place and get you settled in it."

"Me a place?" inquired Anna with surprise. "You mean us, *our home,* don't you, John?"

"Certainly. Certainly," answered John. "But as I was saying, it's not exactly an easy matter to get started in America. Most foreigners, I think, find that out when they get there. The first year or two is the hardest. You feel so stupid and lost when you can't talk to anybody. You feel at first like giving up, but well, you see it takes time, Anna, and lots of patience. You just have to keep trying and trying, and I'm certain that if I'd go back again I could start in where I left off."

"Go back again?" gasped Anna. "You—you mean—"

John caught Anna's hand and pressed it. "I came home to make you happy, Anna," he said, "and as comfortable as possible. I came home to buy a house, or build one, to work beside you in the garden and field, to father little Mary, and eat your homemade bread and coffee cake. I got very hungry for it, Anna. Don't fret about my going back. I promise you I'll never do it unless we both feel certain it would be for the benefit of the family."

Anna drew a long, deep breath. She stared at John.

Little Mary, on her father's knee, was watching him in wide-eyed silence. He gave her a hug. "Now," he said, "I want to open my bag; so you stand here beside me and watch. Want to?"

John handed Elizabeth something wrapped in red tissue paper. "This is what I brought you. I know you've been good to help Anna with the baby and I really appreciate it. It's not much, Elizabeth, but a gift from America."

"A ball?"

"That's an orange, Elizabeth. It's good to eat."

Elizabeth squealed with delight and held it to her nose. "It smells good."

"And will taste even better," added John.

"I'm going to take it along to school to show everybody."

"A nice idea," said her mother, "but you may not have any of it left for yourself if you do that, Elizabeth."

"And this is for you, Anna." With great pride John presented his wife a small glass oil lamp wrapped inside four yards of brown and yellow flowered print.

"John! How wonderful!" cried Anna with delight. "I'll have the nicest dress of anybody in the village now. Oh, John, it's too pretty to wear. And the lamp! Will pumpkin seed oil work in it?"

"I wouldn't know why not. We'll try it. In America they burn a clear coal oil. And here, Mary. Something for you too."

"Shoes!" cried Elizabeth. "Look, Mary. Little shoes from America with buttons on them. Let's see if they fit. They're too big, aren't they, Anna?"

"Stand up," said Anna. "Now walk, Mary. They won't be too big very long the way she's growing."

Mary could hardly stop walking to go to bed that night. All the next day she played with her shoes, pulling them on and off dozens of times.

"Now," announced Elizabeth when she came in after

57

school, "I'm taking you and your shoes and my orange to see every grandma in Miletinac."

John and Anna decided on the Pirggio property, the two-room house with the three acres and several pieces of home-made furniture. A week from the day of purchase, they had the house set in order and part of the garden planted.

"And now," beamed Anna when the three sat down to their first meal in the house, "at last—at last, John, I have you to myself and we can talk and talk and talk."

John stroked Mary's soft dark hair. "Us three and no more. Just what we've been working toward for a long time. And now—"

At the open door stood a tall, thin man, hat in one hand and a small leather case in the other.

"Pardon me," he said. "I'm a long way from home and I wonder if I could get a bite to eat?"

John looked at Anna. "Do we have a little extra?" he asked.

"Well, John," replied Anna, "I—I guess we should never turn a hungry person from our door, should we? We'd better invite him in, don't you think?"

"Yes, of course. Come in, sir," said John. "We haven't a feast prepared, but I believe we can share what we have. My good wife will cut an extra slice or two of bread."

"Thank you kindly," said the stranger.

"Here, sir, is water with which you may wash." John filled the basin.

Anna looked again. She cut the bread, but while she was doing so she looked the third time. The man's face seemed strangely familiar. Her hands trembled a little when she put the bread on the plate.

"Take this chair," John said. "How far from home are you, sir?"

"I came from Daruvar today," replied the man in a pleasant voice. "That's where I have my family right now. I'm really from Budapest. This is very kind of you to take me in.

I do appreciate it."

The man bowed his head and closed his eyes. "Thank you, dear Father," he prayed, "for Thy love and watchful care over us. And just now for these table comforts to sustain our bodies. May we use our strength to do those things which will count through all eternity. Amen."

A prolonged hush followed. John and Anna exchanged glances.

"A mighty sweet little lady you have here," said the visitor, smiling down at Mary. "I have a little girl about your size. Her name is Miriam. What is your name, little girl?"

"Mary."

"One of the sweetest names in all the world, too." Turning to John, "Your name, sir?"

"Olesh, and yours?"

"Lutz."

"Help yourself to the potatoes, please, and here's cabbage, Mr. Lutz."

"Thank you. Thank you."

Anna sat fixed before she took her first bite. She tried to catch John's eye.

"I want to pay you friends for this fine meal. It is very kind of you to take a stranger in like this and so unexpected."

"Pay? No, indeed," objected John. "But I'm inquisitive to know what brought you 'way over here from Daruvar. Do you have relatives or business here in our village?"

"No relatives in the flesh," answered Lutz, "but I hope someday to have some in the Lord."

Anna looked at John, but John's gaze was fixed on the stranger.

"You see, I'm in business for the King."

"The king?" inquired John. "The king?" he repeated.

"Yes," answered Lutz. "I'm an ambassador for the King of kings. The King of Heaven and earth. I've been saved to serve and with great joy I will work for my King until I die. I'm out offering the Bread of Life, the Living Water, the cure

59

for all ills, the best and most important thing in all the world."

Anna caught her breath and held it. She stared at John and he read alarm in her widening eyes.

"Do you folks have a Bible or a New Testament in your home?"

"A Bible?" asked John. "No. No," he repeated, "never even touched one."

"Then here," said the man, pulling a small black book from his coat pocket. "I'll give you one of these New Testaments as pay for this good dinner."

Chapter 8

Anna dropped her fork. She sat up very straight. The man held the Testament out to John, but John did not take it.

"We're not expecting any pay for this dinner," said John, shaking his head. "Please keep your book and sell it or give it to someone who really wants it."

"You mean," remarked Lutz in a kindly manner, pressing the Testament between both hands, "you mean you wouldn't accept this precious Book as a gift, a gift of love from me to you?"

John put both hands on the table edge. He gave Anna a quick glance. "Sir," he replied, "I don't know that I would. Not—not today. This is a strong Catholic village, as you can't help knowing."

"But my dear Mr. and Mrs. Olesh." The man's gray eyes reflected tender compassion and when he spoke, his voice was warm and human. He seemed lost for a moment in deep meditation. "Blessed be the Lord forever, my dear friends," he said. "Yes, I am fully aware of this, but that should not bar you from having the Bible in your own home. Why should it? This is God's Word for everyone—Catholic, Protestant, Jew, Gentile, black, red, yellow, or white. It's a 'whosoever' Book."

"But the father—" broke in John. "He would be greatly displeased if he'd find out I took it, even as a gift. I don't know what he'd require of me and he certainly would find it out sooner or later. There are no secrets in a village this size, Mr. Lutz," and John knit his brow as he faced the man across the table. "I don't mean to seem rude. Thanks for your generosity, but right now I don't think I'd better accept your offer. I repeat, we don't want any pay for this meal."

When Lutz spoke again his voice was clear like fresh, sparkling spring water flowing gently over smooth rocks. "This is God's Holy Word of eternal life, my friends. Regardless of your profession or your lifelong teaching—and I say this in all respect, for I am sure I understand your situation— God tells us in this Book that we should call no man Father, for we have but one Father and that is our Father in Heaven. The one Father, God, so loved us that He gave His only Son, Jesus Christ, to die on the cross, to shed His own blood that whosoever believes on Him should not perish, but have everlasting life. This Book contains that precious story of the life of the Father's Son, Jesus Christ. It tells of this great love for all of us and what we are with Him and what we are without Him. It tells us how we are completely transformed by His Spirit and how He gives us joy unspeakable, rest, peace of soul, and assurance that passes all human understanding. It tells us, too, that no one can buy or work his way to Heaven. Salvation is a gift that we accept by faith. This Book of God tells us that in Christ is life and that life is the light of men. My friends, how happy I'd be if I could leave this little gift of life with its message of love and good cheer with you, so you could read it for yourselves."

John looked across the table at Anna. "What do you say?" he asked in a near-whisper.

Anna drew a long, deep breath. "You're the head of this house, John," came her answer. "I don't want to say."

"Well, tell me this," reflected John, addressing Lutz. "You've been in our village before?"

"Yes, over a year ago."

"And," John's voice was a bit husky, "has anyone in this village bought or accepted one of those books from you?"

Lutz shook his head. "Not yet."

John bent forward and looked Lutz straight in the face. "And yet you come back?"

"Of course," came the man's ready answer. "The love of God in my heart won't let me stay away. Something tells me there are hungry, troubled, and lost souls here in Miletinac. I cannot give up. God pleaded with me over and over before I yielded to His call. It's my duty to offer my fellow men everywhere this true way, this only way to eternal life. This is the glorious Gospel story, Mr. Olesh. Of course I came back, but I might never again."

"But," insisted John, "have you actually talked to very many as you have to me—I mean here in this village?"

"I've tried to."

"And what did the others say?"

"Just what you've said, Olesh," replied Lutz. " 'The father would object; Father Jardell would require penance.' "

"And he would," declared John. "He'd call it a terrible sin if I took that book." John put the palms of his hands down on the table top. His mind seemed to be struggling with thoughts unexpressed.

"But, my friend," continued Lutz, "you see, it's not Father Jardell any of you need to answer to, but the Father in Heaven. Christ is our only mediator, our only way, our only hope. He is all we need. He is the only one who hears and answers prayers and forgives. Not an earthly man or woman or priest. Let me read to you what the Holy Scriptures tell us. Now there was a—"

A loud rap on the door! There stood John's father panting, his face wet with perspiration.

"John," he called, "come out here and help me, will you? My cart is tipped over in the ditch yonder. I need a lift."

"I'll be right out."

"I'll gladly help, too," said Lutz, and he followed John out of the house.

Without any difficulty the three men soon had the cart set upright.

"Thanks, men," panted John's father, wiping his damp face with his homemade handkerchief.

"You're welcome," answered Lutz. "Glad to help you."

John's father grabbed John by the arm and spoke in a

serious, excited tone as he held him. "Stay here, son," he said. "I want to talk to you a minute."

"I'll go on back to the house and get my case and hat," said Lutz as he walked away.

"Now," began his father, his face close to John's, "that man had better stay out of our village if he knows what's good for him."

"And what do you know about him?"

"I don't know very much, only that he's a nuisance and we don't need or want what he's got to offer. We've gotten along all these years without that Bible book; so why do we need it now? You know as well as I do that Father Jardell would be furious if he knew you let him inside your house. Why did you let him in, John? And why was he in there so long?"

"How did you know he was in our house?"

"Because I was watching since I first saw him in the village. John, why did you invite him in, or did you?"

"I didn't know who he was, Father," answered John. "He asked for something to eat and I wouldn't refuse to feed a hungry man, would I?"

"Something to eat? Indeed! But you certainly didn't buy one of his books."

"No, Father. I didn't even accept one in payment for his dinner."

"So that's—"

"I must go," broke in John. "Don't be so excited. I'm not a boy. I've got a mind of my own, haven't I? And after all—well, I *must* go. The man went back to the house."

"To be sure, you must go, John. But being in America for a while—well, I just didn't know how you stood. I was determined to call you out of the house for something, if I had to purposely tip over my cart."

"Why, father!" exclaimed John. "You didn't!" and John hurried back home.

"I still would like to pay for my dinner with this New

Testament, Mr. Olesh," smiled Lutz, "and your wife said it's for you to decide since you're the head of the house, which is the right attitude for any good wife to take."

"And when she said that," answered John, "she was quite certain I'd say exactly what she would expect me to say, that we don't want any pay of any kind for the meager dinner we gave you. It wasn't much, but the best we had and not worth the price of your book, I'm sure. We don't need the book."

"So you wouldn't even take it, then, as an outright gift, forgetting the payment for the dinner?"

"Not today," answered John.

Lutz bowed politely and stepped to the door.

"It's been very nice to meet you folks," answered Lutz. "And I've enjoyed having this little chat with you. God bless you, and you, Mrs. Olesh, and your little Mary. God bless your house and all you do, and give you a real hunger and thirst for the truth. Good-by now." At the door he hesitated. "In case you ever get over to Daruvar, look us up," he said. "We live in the two-story cement-block house right across from the depot. It's not hard to locate and in the front window is a sign 'Gospel Center.' My good wife would be glad to serve you a meal without charge."

Anna and John stood at the door and watched the man until he was out of sight. The long, wordless silence was broken when John rubbed the palms of his hands together in a slow uncertain manner.

"John," whispered Anna, "I do wonder and I can't help it."

John looked down at his wife as though he were trying to pull the thread of her thoughts through the needle's eye of his own.

"Wonder what?" he asked at length.

"Well, just what all is in that New Testament book. Look, John, Mary has fallen asleep at the table. I'll lay her in on our bed. Bless her little heart."

"Let me do it, Anna."

She followed John and pulled back the top covers.

"Let's begin all over again," whispered Anna. "Come, let's sit down at the table and forget the work for a little."

"What do you mean, begin all over?"

"I mean, I said we were going to talk and talk, and then that man came," sighed Anna. "John, you know how it's been since the day you came home. I've been wanting to ask you so many things, ever and ever so many about America, and I—well, I had a thousand things to ask you today and now since that Mr. Lutz came, I can think of nothing else. Close the door, John. He was different, wasn't he?"

John closed the door. He nodded.

"Very different, wasn't he? Something unusual about him and—and likeable. What did you think when he began all at once to pray the way he did at the table?"

John shook his head.

"Is he right that we shouldn't call Father Jardell 'father'?"

John shook his head.

"He said we don't need to answer to Father Jardell for what we do or don't do. Is he right or wrong?"

John shook his head.

"Well, John!" exclaimed Anna a little impatiently. "I said we would talk together and you do nothing now but shake your head."

"I don't know what else to do right now," laughed John. "I'm thinking."

"I'm thinking, too, but let's think out loud to each other. I can't, or at least I won't, discuss this with anyone but you, John, ever."

"Why not?"

"Would you, with anyone but me?"

"No."

"Why not?"

"I wouldn't feel like it."

"But why wouldn't you?"

"Why wouldn't you?"

Anna bent forward and looked John full in the face intently. "Let's be honest with each other, John," she said. "It's because we'd be afraid to. I guess that's why, isn't it?"

"Afraid of what?"

"You know as well as I, John. We're both afraid, aren't we?"

"Afraid of what?" John scratched his head.

"That's it. What is it we're afraid of? I ask myself. You called me brave, didn't you?"

John nodded.

"But there must be different kinds of bravery then, John," said Anna thoughtfully, "for we're both afraid of what people will say. We're afraid of Father Jardell. Afraid the neighbors saw that man come into our house. Would you discuss this with your own father or mother?"

John laughed. "Not today."

"Why not?"

"Anna, I fear we're going around in a circle, aren't we? This will get us nowhere fast. But I'll tell you one thing, if you promise you won't tell it to a single soul. Not even your own mother."

"I promise. What is it, John?"

John tilted back in his chair and rubbed both hands slowly over his thick dark hair before he spoke. "Well, it's this, Anna. That man, Lutz, has something that Father Jardell hasn't got."

"And it's something that—that rather attracts me," added Anna. "I hope someday we'll meet again. Father Jardell won't come twelve miles without being well paid for it and he knows the people here can't afford it, yet this man came twenty-eight because—well, you heard what he said."

"Yes, I heard, and he said he feels there are some in this village who are lost and troubled."

"Wonder who and what he meant by that? I can't understand it, can you?"

John shook his head.

"I almost wished for a moment—oh, dear, I'll have to

confess to the father, I guess, if I say it out loud."

"Anna," John stood to his feet, "you mean if I'd accepted the book you wouldn't have objected? You mean you almost wish I would have?"

"You are older and wiser than I am, John," answered Anna. "You are the head of this house and although I was frightened at first—well, if you would have accepted it, I—I guess I would have read it."

"But I didn't. And he's gone. We've got to get to work and get our cabbages planted, Anna. Let's forget Lutz—at least not talk about him in front of Mary."

Chapter 9

The latch on the door of the Olesh home clicked frequently the day after the man named Lutz had been in Miletinac. And Anna felt increasingly glad that John had refused to take the Testament and that she could honestly add to her inquiring neighbors that he had turned down Mr. Lutz' repeated offer of payment for the dinner. Furthermore, she was glad she could insist that John had no idea what the stranger's mission was when he invited him into the house. She was getting weary, however, and bored and almost resentful, repeating her explanation so often. But in a village the size of Miletinac any bit of news was carried, handled, sifted, fanned, graded, and stamped before it was finally put on the shelf to dry.

"He'll surely never come back to this village again," laughed one plump neighbor to three other women as they stood in front of Anna's house the next evening, sharing freely their impressions and conclusions about that Bible seller. "My husband," she repeated for the third time, "told him off in a hurry."

"And," added another, "Father Jardell would have no reason to get stirred up over this. He ought to be proud of the people here, the way we all gave him the cold shoulder."

Anna, who had unavoidably been in the group, excused herself by saying, "I must run along and get a pail of water. John will be coming in to supper soon."

The more Anna heard of the village discussions, the heavier her heart, even in spite of her increasing gladness. This strange paradoxical feeling bewildered her. The man's conduct and his strange new words were still fresh in her memory and she had lived over and over the entire incident, repeating snatches of his sentences which she could neither

69

comprehend nor forget. To be sure, she had not related any of this to her neighbors.

Perplexed, her olive cheeks burning and her forehead damp, Anna walked with heaviness to the well. She wanted to hold the love and the respect her neighbors all seemed to have for her, but an inexplicable, tiny gap seemed to be forming between herself and them. Lutz had done no harm in the village that she could see and something within her rose silently to his defense. Since the hour he had walked out of their house a jumbled confusion of yeses and noes, rights and wrongs, pluses and minuses had thrown her into a continuing mental debate about him and the father. She sometimes wished she could forget the man entirely.

Slowly she filled her water pail and waited until the women had finished their discussion before returning to the house. For several minutes she looked out toward the distant blue mountains, but the trees took on strange, unhappy shapes and the hills, gloomy, meaningless colors, as she gazed distractedly.

"Mother," cried Mary, running toward her with arms outstretched and clasping tightly something green in one hand. "Look, Mother," she cried.

"You've been in the garden, haven't you, Mary?" asked Anna. "Did Mother tell you to pull the onion?"

"Papa. Papa," cried Mary. "For Papa." Mary's blue eyes sparkled and danced as she clasped her treasure.

"They're hardly big enough to pull yet, dear," remarked her mother, "but you may put that one beside Papa's plate for supper. In a week or so you may pull some for all of us. But no more tonight, dear."

Mary was unusually happy and talkative at the supper table that night. She laughed and jabbered with her father as she hadn't since the day of his arrival.

John smiled with pleasure and glanced at Anna across the table. "Sounds like we're really getting acquainted, doesn't it? Was this your idea about the onion for me?"

"It was her own. She went to the garden and pulled it herself when I didn't know it."

"Well, Mary," said her father, "how did you know I like onions?" He patted her head gently.

Mary dimpled.

He asked, "You just guessed it, didn't you, Mary? And do you know what I'm thinking of right now?"

Mary took a bite of bread and shook her head. John put a gentle hand on her shoulder. "I'm thinking that it won't be long until you'll be big enough to help Mother hoe the onions and set the table and knit stockings and do lots of things," he said proudly. "I believe you've grown just since I came home. Remember that evening you and Mother met me down by the hemlock tree? You were too bashful that evening to speak to me, remember?"

Mary dimpled again, showing two rows of beautiful white teeth.

"What a wonderful evening!" exclaimed John. "I feel like taking a walk. Why don't we walk down to the hemlock tree before dark, Anna?"

Mary clapped her hands in glee.

"I'd rather do that than—" Anna pinched her lips.

"Than what?" asked John.

Anna shook her head. "Yes, let's take a walk," she said. "I'd like to get beyond my doorstep tonight."

The air had been summerlike all day, balmy but not hot. The valley was radiant in the soft green springtime of year and the shooting, full, promising gardens were bordered with feathery sprays of delicate white alyssums and pink and lavender tulips. The lowering sun was playing magic colors on the silvery clouded sky when the three started out for their stroll.

Mary, laughing with joy, skipped and ran on ahead of her parents, and the earth seemed to spring under her feet.

"She's a happy little thing, isn't she, Anna?" remarked John. "And how I love her! She's so bright and pretty and

71

sweet. I hope to give her a better chance in life than—Mary!"

Before John had finished his sentence, the child tripped and fell. John made one dash and picked her up quickly.

"You're not hurt very badly, are you, Mary? There, there. You'll soon be all right. You were running too fast. Don't cry, dear."

But Mary cried convulsively, leaning on her father's shoulder as he knelt beside her.

Anna carefully examined Mary's face, her arms, her legs. "There's nothing but a little scratch on this one knee. Why do you cry so, Mary? She'll soon be as happy as ever, John. I think it knocked the breath out of her. It scared her. She's been just too happy and gay and frisky all evening. Now don't cry any more, Mary. You'll soon be all right. Can't you stand up? This leg? Try it, dear."

Anna rubbed her hand up and down on the child's leg. "It's not hurt much, Mary. Let Papa carry you for a little way, then you'll soon be walking again. Too bad this had to happen to our happy little girl."

But Mary continued to cry as though in pain, pointing to her right knee.

"Maybe we'd better give up our walk and take her home," suggested Anna sadly.

Mary cried all the way home. She cried herself to sleep in spite of all the caresses she got. The next morning Mary still cried and flinched when her mother tried to straighten her right leg.

"But I know it's not broken," insisted John. "She couldn't move it at all if it were. Mary, you be a good girl, dear, and let Mother rub some warm oil on it and that will make it feel a lot better. Now Papa must go and work. When I come in for dinner you'll be better." John kissed Mary.

But three weeks later Mary was limping. She cried whenever her parents tried to straighten her leg. Anna shuddered. She had tried everything that anyone in the village had suggested—everything except the witch doctor. An unhappy re-

72

sentment she could not exactly explain kept her from submitting to that, though her parents tried to persuade her to send for the woman.

"It might help," said her mother, "and it wouldn't do any harm, Anna."

"But who has she ever helped? And it costs terribly."

In front of others Anna tried desperately to conceal her longing to cry out and weep, but in her own room she shed tears frequently, asking the questions over and over, "Why was our joy so suddenly turned into suspense and melancholy?" "Why does little innocent Mary have to go through such an experience?"

"Oh, John," she cried one evening, "tomorrow it will be a month since Mary fell. Look, it seems her knee is getting stiffer every day. I'm afraid she'll never be able to straighten it. What more can we do? I wish we could take her to Daruvar to the doctor."

"I think that's what we'd better do," agreed John, "but where would we get the money, unless I'd borrow it?"

"Wouldn't your father help us out? I believe mine would. I'm sure he would if he had it, John, for he dearly loves Mary and he feels so sorry for her."

"Almost looks as though we've got to do something and we'd better not put it off much longer."

Anna sank on the edge of the bed and, with her face in her hands, looked at the bare earth floor, her lips drawn and her tired eyelids drooping from anxiety and sorrow.

"Do you know what I've been thinking about, John?" she asked.

"What? The priest?"

Anna shook her head. "That man from Daruvar," she whispered.

"Lutz?"

Anna nodded. "He said that book was the answer to all our needs."

"But he couldn't have meant this kind of need, Anna. We

couldn't open the book and find money in it to take a child to a doctor."

"You're not making fun of me, are you, John?" asked Anna in a hurt voice. "Anyone would know he could not have meant that. But he meant something that I don't understand and I wish I did. John," her voice was almost inaudible.

"Yes?"

"If—if we take Mary to Daruvar and—and his house is right across from the depot, do you—suppose—?"

John did not smile. He did not frown but looked at his wife with long, silent penetration. His lips parted, but he did not speak.

"Oh, John," whispered Anna, "don't be so shocked and displeased with me. Don't make me feel so—so wicked, John. I'm sorry. I shouldn't have mentioned it. I'm tired, I guess, and—and sad and worried. John, I was thinking."

John stepped close and put one hand on Anna's shoulder. "I'm not displeased with you, Anna," he said softly. "And I don't know why you say I make you feel wicked. Don't fret, please. I think perhaps it frightens Mary to see you so distressed. We'll do all we can for her. This hurts me as much as it does you, Anna. But you've been a brave woman and you'll be brave about this, won't you? Her knee may get all right in time. She's young."

"But why did you look at me so, John, as though I said the wrong thing?"

"I was just thinking," he answered. "It seems that ever since that day Lutz was here you've not been yourself, even before Mary fell. You don't suppose he cast some kind of spell over our house, do you?"

"Oh! Oh, John!" exclaimed Anna. "I surely hope not. I never thought of anything like that. But—but, John, how could that be—how could it—when he seemed so kind and sincere? Has anyone suggested such a thing?"

"I hate to tell you who," answered John. "Don't ask me."

It was not until the end of the next week that arrangements were finally made to take little Mary to Daruvar. Nearly every mother in the village had stopped in to see the child and examine the poor little knee. Each rehearsed fragments from her own family history of various tumbles, bruises, and injuries and what had cured this and that, and what had failed. Anna's own mother wasn't a bit satisfied that they hadn't tried the witch doctor. Nor the priest.

"If the doctor in Daruvar can't help her, we might try the witch doctor," consented Anna. "If it would make you feel better."

Since John's father said he had business he wanted to attend to in Daruvar, it was agreed that he and John could very well take turns carrying Mary as far as Vilieki Bastaji where they could catch the train. It wouldn't be necessary for Anna to go along and since John's father was going to help John borrow some money, he wanted to be there and hear what the doctor would have to say.

That was a long day for Anna with one constant struggle to keep back tears. Her mind ranged over her problem like a wild animal seeking to escape the bars of his cage. Her lips twitched at the bitter thought that the kind-faced bookseller might have cast an evil spell over their house because they refused to accept the Testament; then again they relaxed when she repeated his tender words: "God's Holy Word of eternal life . . . and that life is the light of men . . . joy unspeakable, . . . rest and peace of soul."

She did not accept her mother's invitation to spend the day with her. Anna wanted to be alone.

Part of the day Anna busied herself in the garden, but more than once she caught herself chopping off a beanstalk instead of a weed. She made a raised coffee cake and forgot to add the salt.

When John returned that evening after dark he looked

75

worn and troubled. Gently he laid Mary on the bed and faced Anna.

"Well," said John, taking her one hand in both of his, "we saw the doctor."

"Yes?"

"And he said there's nothing to do but operate. And if he does, the knee will be stiff anyhow. He can bring her leg out straight, but then it would always be straight and be very unhandy whenever she sits down. I'm sorry, Anna, but there's nothing we can do about it now. He said the kneecap is split and has damaged the joint under the cap. He said this same thing has happened to others and they lived on. He said she'll learn to walk and hop around before long and we should help her forget about it and make her happy in spite of her handicap."

Anna reached up and put her left hand on John's shoulder. The light from the beautiful glass lamp John brought from America made a distinct glow on her sad face. Her eyes filled with sudden tears.

"Then," she said, "that's what we'll do. Bless her heart, she's sleeping, isn't she?"

"You don't know how I dreaded to come home and tell you this."

"John," said Anna, "all day I had a feeling you might. I thought I just couldn't take it, but—" she faltered. "Well, when it comes right down to it," she brushed away a tear, "you can take more than you thought you could. Like when you left me to go to America."

John pressed her hand. "This is our first real disappointment, isn't it, Anna? And I—I hope you'll always be able to take it this way when other hard things come."

"You—you didn't see him?"

"Who?"

"That man in Daruvar?"

"No."

"The house?"

76

John nodded. "But I never let on because of Father. I tried all day long to avoid mentioning the man to him. Anna, let's forget him. Let's forget he exists. It's best. We've just got to."

"Oh." Slowly Anna stepped over to her sleeping child and gently removed her shoes and stockings. "Mother will be after me now to call the witch doctor, or Father Jardell, or both."

"But we can't afford it, Anna. We can't. I have something better in mind."

"What? Oh, John, tell me."

"We'll wait a while first."

"Tell me, please."

"I'm very tired, Anna. Cut me a slice of bread, then let's go to bed. I must sleep over it."

"It's not about—not about the man—the book, John?"

"Anna," whispered John, "I said just a minute ago we're going to have to forget that man Lutz, and his book, and his ideas, and everything he said. If the doctor in Daruvar can't help Mary, what more help could he give?"

"I don't know," came Anna's sad answer, "unless he could help me."

"Help you?"

"I—I just feel like I need something. I don't know what, but something to help me to be an extra-good mother to her now." Anna buried her face in her apron.

Chapter 10

John and Anna did not neglect their daily prayers. Although they could see no evident change in Mary's knee, their prayers had a somewhat soothing effect on their own spirits.

Mary ate well, slept well, and complained less and less about her knee as the days passed. It was Anna's mother who manifested the greatest grief and anxiety over the child. One morning she faced her husband suddenly and with tears, cried in distress.

"No matter what they say, let's ask the witch doctor to come. They should have called for her when Mary first fell and it wouldn't have cost them what it did to take her to Daruvar. Anna says she doubts if she ever helped anyone, but she has. She stopped Ab Kelboe's nosebleed and she got rid of Henry Bisais' fever. Remember?" Her voice was raised with a firm determination and an unresigned grief.

"Mary's such a dear, beautiful child, I can't bear the awful thought that she'll be crippled all her life unless they have tried everything, and they haven't. I can't understand Anna," she continued. "You can see the hurt, sad look on her face even though she tries to smile and seldom says anything about it any more."

"You really think we should send for the doctor without their knowing it?"

"Yes. Couldn't you just tell her to come over to Miletinac? It could appear, you know, as though she happened along. I'm getting almost desperate," she cried. "Maybe John might have to borrow the money to pay her, but if it would give little Mary lifelong relief, what's that? Since you're going to Vilieki Bastaji anyhow, why not try to slip off without their

78

knowing it and look her up? If I only had a goose or two, I'd offer them to pay her."

The bland, almost listless little breeze, that scarcely stirred the air that afternoon, made working in the garden a tiresome job. Quivering with fatigue, Anna leaned on her hoe to rest a little.

"I hope it rains tonight," she remarked to John, who was hoeing several rows across from her, in the cabbage patch.

"Any more water in that jug?" he asked.

"Yes."

John laid down his hoe and started toward the jug. He stopped abruptly. "Look," he said, "someone is talking to Mary at the doorstep. I thought she was inside sleeping."

Anna turned. "It's—why, John!" she exclaimed, "it's the witch doctor, I do believe."

Together the two hurried to the house. At the same time Anna saw her mother coming, half running.

Bending over the child on the doorstep, the witch doctor ran her long pointed fingers over the crippled leg.

Mary drew back, frightened. Her big blue eyes filled with sudden tears. Terrified, she called for her parents.

The witch doctor raised a bony hand, as John and Anna ran up. "I can fix it," she said, smacking her thin lips. "How long has it been so?"

Perplexed, John and Anna stood speechless. Impatient and perhaps a little annoyed at their silence, Anna's mother answered for them.

"Too long," she offered, "but you can help it, can't you? That's my grandchild. Isn't she sweet?"

"Sure, I can fix it," answered the old woman, dropping suddenly on both knees beside Mary. She peered closely at the knee, and smelled it. "There's an evil spirit in the joint," she said, "and it will be harder to get out than one in an open wound. But it can be done. We should go inside and lay the babe on the bed."

"But wait," said John, taking Mary up in his arms. "I did not send for you to come here." He held the frightened child close to his breast.

"Someone did," muttered the old woman, shifting her weight from one foot to the other. Her bony ankles cracked.

"But it wasn't I," answered John, pressing his child still closer to himself. "This is my child, my house, my responsibility. You will charge me how much?"

"I must get paid for my trip over here," said the witch doctor, frowning. She rested a brown hand on each hip bone. "You wouldn't expect me to walk 'way over here on a warm day like this for nothing, would you?" Her earrings rattled when she shook her head.

"But I didn't ask you to come."

"But a man did. And," she wailed, "I must be paid whether I treat your child or not." Her black eyes snapped. Her gaze was unwavering.

"Who was the man?" asked John.

"I didn't ask his name. I never saw him before. An older man than you."

"What did he tell you?"

"He told me I should come over to Miletinac, that there was a little girl here who had fallen and hurt her knee. I stopped at the edge of the village," she pointed, "and inquired where the child lived. I guess this is the child, or is there another?"

John and Anna exchanged glances.

"I do hope you'll let her treat Mary, since she's here now," said Anna's mother with insistence. "It just has to help somehow."

The witch doctor seemed to have some uncanny power. She laughed a weird, hideous laugh, then stepping close to John, took hold of his arm above the elbow, and said as she squeezed it tightly, "She's too pretty a child to neglect. I won't charge you much. Take her inside and get me an egg. She's such a pretty babe, pretty babe."

80

Almost dazed, John obeyed. Anna and her mother followed. Anna handed the woman an egg.

"Don't be afraid," whispered John to Mary. "She won't hurt you. I'll stay right beside you."

From her satchel the witch doctor brought out an oily red rag and in this she wrapped the egg and moved it over and over the child's knee, all the while saying strange, incoherent phrases in undertones. Carefully she placed the rag with the egg on the window sill. Then she took a few ashes from the stove, spit on them, and sprinkled them on the child's knee. Next she took a small transparent quill from her satchel, licked it with her tongue, tapped the windowpane with it many times, then took it outside and buried it in the ground at the edge of the garden.

"And now," she announced triumphantly, when she re-entered the house, "when the egg has disappeared from the cloth on the window sill, the evil spirit in the joint will be torn loose. And when the quill in the ground has gone back to the bird from which it was taken, the spirit will be carried away and your child's knee will be loosened and she will be able to walk like new."

John and Anna stared in mute wide-eyed astonishment. Anna's mother smiled with new hope. She nodded.

"And now my pay." The old woman held out her bony hand to John.

"Where shall I get it?" John looked at Anna, but found no answer in her despondent look.

"Can't I pay you later? I do not have it now. I didn't know you were coming. I'm not prepared."

"Later?" frowned the witch. "And so you would have the miracle of the spirit to start working later, too?"

John and Anna stood paralyzed. Anna tried to swallow, but couldn't. Suddenly John picked up the glass lamp on the table and held it out to the witch. Anna gasped.

"How about this?" John asked. "This beautiful lamp from America, worth much more than you ask."

The witch doctor waved her hand in disgust and mockery. "What would I want with such a thing? I need no light. There's money in the village and you can get it. It's money I want and I've only charged you a mere trifle."

For a moment everything in the world took on fantastic, unreasonable proportions for John and Anna. Everything they possessed turned to dust. Everything but Mary. There she lay on the bed. Anna could hear John breathing faster and heavier each passing second, and John saw Anna's face turn ashen.

"I know," suggested Anna's mother suddenly, as though she had seen a vision. "Aunt Tena got a money order the other day from Uncle Jose. She may loan you enough, John."

Without a word, John hurried out of the house and the witch doctor gathered up her satchel and followed, walking. She stood waiting outside the house into which she had seen him disappear. Soon John came out and handed her the money. There was no exchange of words.

With a grunt, the woman tied the money in a small cloth, which hung on a red cord around her dirty neck. Then she went her way. Anna's mother also left. But before she walked out of the house, she said in words that were quiet and even, "I'm glad you let her do it."

Her face burned feverishly, but Anna tried to prepare supper, for which neither she nor John was hungry. All she wanted to do was close the door and hold Mary on her lap. Her heart throbbed with a dull ache. She bathed her face in cool water, tied on a clean apron, and put herself resolutely to the task of peeling a few small potatoes.

Undoubtedly, many eyes in the village had seen the witch doctor as she left the house. That meant many would be calling to find out what she had done, and to see if Mary's knee was loosening any. As with John, Mary belonged to the village, it seemed. Anna sighed.

"I wish we could fly away tonight," she whispered to

She took it outside and buried it at
the edge of the garden.

John when he returned. "I wish we three could fly all the way
to America."

John grabbed Anna by the arm and looked into her sad,
troubled eyes. "Anna," he whispered. "Anna," he repeated,
"are you awake or talking in your sleep?"

"In my sleep?" she asked wearily with a dry, crippled
laugh. "Sleeping right after this? I'm stunned. I'm troubled.
I doubt if I'll sleep all night."

"Maybe I won't either," answered John.

"Oh," shivered Anna, "why do witch doctors have to be so ugly and hideous? I don't like to think of repeating it all evening. But folks will be coming any minute now. Wish we could lock the door. If this doesn't help Mary, I'll never be able to forgive the man who sent her over here, I'm afraid. And I hope I never learn who it was. If the people of the village would only let us make our own decisions. She frightened Mary. And you said the doctor in Daruvar said we should try to make her happy and forget her knee. How can she now? Poor child."

"Sh!" John glanced at his child on the bed.

"I know," whispered Anna, looking at Mary through tear-blurred eyes, "but she heard her say there's an evil spirit in her knee, and ever since she's gone she's been trying to ask me something. My head hurts. My legs hurt. I hurt all over. After—after—" Anna brushed away a tear. "Oh, I know you said we shouldn't mention it again, but just this once, John. After that Mr. Lutz left, I didn't feel like this."

Her eyes beseeched John's. "He didn't frighten Mary. I know there's no comparison, John, but—but, I do wish—" she stepped close to him. "I know it sounds silly, and it is, I guess, but I wish we could pick up and fly to America tonight and nobody would ever find out where we went."

"Why, Anna Olesh!" exclaimed John. "You said you'd never want to leave Miletinac. You said you loved it here."

A tear fell on her blue blouse. She brushed it away quickly. She tried to laugh. "Doesn't sound like I'm very brave right now, does it, John?" she said remorsefully. "I never felt like this until now, but something is wrong. Terribly wrong. And if this doesn't help Mary, I'll know it for sure."

John slipped one arm across Anna's shoulder. "But if it does," he said, "we'll always be glad, won't we?"

"John," Anna picked up the third potato and started peeling it.

"Yes."

"You've slept over it a good many nights and you haven't told me yet. Your other idea."

"No, but if this doesn't help, I will."

"That's a promise, John?"

"It's a promise."

"How soon can we expect the egg to disappear? Tonight? In a day, a week, a month?" Anna's voice sounded like a dull echo in a big empty cave.

"She didn't say," answered John, peering at the window sill with a frown.

"Papa," cried Mary, "hold me, hold me tight." She held her arms outstretched until he took her.

Most of the people who dropped in that evening expressed confidence that Mary's lame knee would now be healed. Everyone seemed glad that the witch doctor had come.

"You must be patient," said one neighborly old gentleman. "It may take quite a while because it's been in there so long. Those spirits are terrible things to get rid of, you know."

Mary clung to her father and hid her face constantly on his shoulder.

"I know what you must do," solemnly added the man. "John, you've got to go more often to church again."

John looked a little smitten. "You think so?"

"I do." He answered with conviction.

"But it's like this," explained John, "it's too far to carry Mary. One of us has to stay here with her. And since Anna and I were separated for so long, we like to be together on Sundays."

"You mean you haven't seen the priest since you came home?"

John admitted it.

"It might help," suggested the old man kindly. "It might help."

Heretofore, Anna had always found a sort of satisfaction and consolation in walking twelve miles to Djulovac, to attend church. She had taken for granted that John did, too. But she had been somewhat dismayed to discover his indifference since his return from America. He manifested little interest in even meeting Father Jardell. Anna had mentioned the fact to John twice, and both times his answer was slow but deliberate. "We've been baptized and we've been faithful in the past, and we still faithfully say our prayers; Uncle Jose says that's enough. I've learned that a person can take this religion too seriously."

"This religion?" asked Anna.

"Any religion," answered John. "Does it actually trouble you that I haven't seen the father since I'm back?"

"I don't know," answered Anna almost feebly. "I can't explain exactly how I do feel. One day it troubles me a great deal. The next it doesn't. But," she added, "if the neighbors are thinking about it, you'd better plan to go, John."

The following day was Sunday. John walked the twelve miles to Djulovac.

"And what did Father Jardell have to say to you, John?" asked Anna when he returned.

"Nothing."

"Nothing?"

"I don't believe he even noticed that I was there."

"John! Weren't you disappointed?"

John shrugged his shoulders. "I was there," he said, "and I'm sure God knew it. I prayed. I said an extra prayer for Mary."

Anna blinked. She rubbed both hands back and forth across her arms. "I thought surely he would see you," she said slowly, "and talk to you, and ask about us. He doesn't know yet that Mary got hurt, does he?"

"But we haven't got the money; so what good would it have done? Money," muttered John. "Money," he repeated bluntly and with meaningful lack of emotion.

Anna and John worked hard all summer. Their diligent and united efforts and the plentiful rains yielded them a bountiful harvest. Potatoes were stacked beside the house, "enough," said John, "that we can sell some and buy a few more chickens." Anna dried beans, made kraut, and traded extra cabbages for prunes with which she made butter.

October came, but the egg in the shell was still on the window sill securely wrapped in the oily red rag. No one had touched it. Eagerly, anxiously, daily, Anna's mother called to glance at the window sill and to examine Mary's knee. At the end of six weeks her eagerness had grown to deep disturbance, and at the end of four months to anguish and dejection. Mary's knee, though free from pain, was stiffer than ever.

Chapter 11

Elizabeth spent many an evening after school entertaining Mary, teaching her simple games and gay little songs. The child learned readily. In spite of her handicap, she developed a cheerful, winsome personality, and continued to be the much-loved child in the village.

"Anna," said Elizabeth one evening, "is the egg still inside that cloth on the window sill?"

Anna looked up with a forlorn expression on her face. "Must be," she replied in a sadly muffled voice.

"But how do you know," insisted Elizabeth, "unless you look?"

Anna frowned, and a long tired sigh escaped her slightly parted lips. "I don't," she murmured. "But," she hesitated and cast a sad glance at Mary's knee, "it hasn't loosened any, as you and Mother and all in the village can see." Anna walked over to the open door and looked out toward the Blue Mountains.

"May I peek?" asked Elizabeth, skipping over and tapping Anna on the back.

"Better not." Anna did not turn around, for she did not want Elizabeth to see the struggle she felt creeping from her inmost soul to her face. "Grandma Jerobe said that would break the charm," Anna said drearily, still gazing toward the mountains. She pressed her fingers hard against her hot cheeks.

"Well, then I won't," agreed Elizabeth.

But while Elizabeth was busy playing with Mary on the bed, she accidentally bumped the red object of mystery with the back of her head. Something popped, and immediately a terrible odor filled the room. Elizabeth screamed, waving her hands frantically above her head.

"Horrors," cried Anna. "Quick, Elizabeth. Pick it up. Throw it out this door."

A sickening feeling swept over Anna. "It's there, isn't it?" she cried. "The egg? Take a stick and poke it open, Elizabeth."

Elizabeth obeyed. "Here it is, Anna, but rotten! Rotten as can be!" Elizabeth dropped the stick and ran home as fast as her feet would take her.

"And now," choked Anna, "what will Mother and all the people have to say? And the quill is still in the garden too, I dare say. Broken charm indeed."

Wretchedly she looked at the stenchy mess on the ground outside her door. Gathering her frightened child up in her arms, she kissed her twice. "My dear little Mary," she cried softly, "you can't understand all this, can you?" She kissed her again. "And we'll never try it again, no matter who in Miletinac tells us to."

The dying day cast an ashen light on Anna's sad face, as she stood in the open door.

"What's happened?" asked John. He came running. "I heard someone screaming. And what stinks?"

"Looks as though the fates are against us," answered Anna. "Look out there on the ground." She pointed. "You can go tell that old witch doctor that her treatment didn't work, and the egg burst as soon as Elizabeth touched it. I never did believe in it."

"Elizabeth? Who told her she could touch it? And where is she?" demanded John.

"Don't be angry with her, John. It was an accident. She was frightened terribly, and ran home. What will Mother and the people have to say now? Perhaps we peeved the witch doctor, or didn't pay her enough, or waited too long, or something. Something." Her voice was almost bitter. "We won't try this again, will we, John?"

"You're right," John answered emphatically, "we will not

try the witch doctor again, and if anybody sends her over here, close the door. Don't let her in."

Anna stepped close to John. "I'm ready now for you to tell me your other idea." Her hand was on his arm.

"You're sure you're ready? Right now?"

Anna nodded. "I can't wait another minute, John."

"You haven't tried to guess?"

"I've tried, but I can't. Please tell me now."

"Well, all right then. It's America."

Anna's eyes widened. She stepped back. The color in her warm cheeks vanished. "America! What can you mean, John?"

"I mean, I want to go back and see if I can't find a doctor there who can do it."

"But," Anna grabbed John's arm, "but if you did find a doctor who thought he could, he wouldn't really know without seeing her knee. Would he, John?"

"But I could inquire. I could find out how much it might cost, and if such an operation has been successful on others. That's my idea, Anna. Now I've told you. But remember," he caught her hand in his, "I promised you I'd never go back without your consent, and unless you felt it would be for the benefit of the family. If you'll agree, I'm ready to go and .try"—he drew a deep breath—"try the hardest thing a father ever tried."

Anna was still holding Mary. She walked over and sat down on the edge of the bed and was very thoughtful before she spoke. "But I never supposed," she said slowly, holding the child's head against her cheek, "that such a thing as this would have to happen to make me willing." She tried to swallow the lump in her throat. "It wouldn't be easy for me to tell you to go. Not a bit easy, John."

"And do you suppose it would be easy for me to leave you two? I'd take you along, but, Anna, I know we couldn't afford it now. You have the home here, the garden, the chickens, and plenty laid up to eat." He sat down beside her on the bed. "Do you think—?" He rubbed his hands together. "It's hard to say this, Anna, but—" He stopped. He swallowed. "Do you suppose you and Mary could get along for a few months without me?"

"A few months? You wouldn't stay a year?"

"I wouldn't plan to. I wouldn't want to."

"Oh, John," cried Anna, pressing Mary still closer, "I—I feel I could do almost anything for Mary's sake." She hid her face in Mary's dress a moment. "Do you really think there might be a doctor in America who could do it?" Her big brown eyes searched John's face.

"We must not build our hopes too high, Anna," he replied. "You're a mighty, mighty brave little woman, when it comes right down to it. You surprise me every time." He took Mary out of Anna's arms and held her on his knee. Anna reached over and took hold of John's one arm with both her hands.

"I think you're the one who is brave," she said softly. "I have my parents, Mary and Elizabeth, and all the people in the village. But you'd have to go back among those strangers you can't talk to, and who don't understand you, and who don't even care."

"I know, but as long as I know you care, and I hear you're both all right, I think I could stand it. Don't say anything to anyone about this yet. It may be a month or two, or maybe longer before I can get enough money together, and I don't want to borrow this time."

"John," whispered Anna, "if you really feel that's what you should do, yes, it would be best for you to go first." She sat thinking. "But now, John, please, go out and bury that mess before we eat supper. Rag, shell, and all."

"No, no," differed John. "Let's leave it there for a while, so all the people in the village can see it for themselves."

To Anna's surprise her mother did not come rushing over. In fact, it was the next afternoon before she made her appearance. Anna had never seen her look so haggard, sad, and dejected. There were dark rings under her tired eyes,

91

and a sort of stifled wail in her voice. With unmasked misery her gaze followed Mary, limping but smiling, as she played happily with another little girl beside the house.

"I'll never be able to understand why it didn't work," was her gloomy remark as she stood watching from the open door.

"And you really expected it to?" asked Anna.

"I believed with all my heart. I would like to talk to the witch doctor."

"Oh, please, Mother, please," cried Anna, "let John do it if anyone does. This is our problem."

Before Christmas, everyone in the village knew that John would be going back to America in less than a month. A few seemed excited; some shook their heads.

John's father and Anna's father discussed the situation at length, when they met on the road the day before Christmas.

"It's like this," said John's father. "I know for a fact that John hasn't been as faithful as he should have been in attending church. He's missed confession entirely too often. Seems strangely indifferent. I told him once, maybe God let Mary fall because he didn't go to church when he was in America. Now if he goes back and doesn't do better, I fear something worse will happen."

"Have you ever tried to talk to him about this?"

"Not much. Just can't get started. I'm tempted to think it might be as much Anna as John."

"No."

"John's a good boy in many respects," reflected his father. "Never caused me any trouble to speak of. But he never did seem to really appreciate Father Jardell as I thought he should. Can't understand John. He always was— what shall I say?—bolder, more independent or something, than the rest of the family. Works his brain too much. It bothers me a good deal that I can't draw him out about this. Father Jardell hasn't been in the village for six months or more. Guess you heard he wasn't a bit well."

"Heard that, yes. And when a man his age develops a heart ailment, he's got to take it easy. I hope he'll be able to come over for the house blessing ceremony next month. If he comes, since John's not leaving until the fifteenth, he may see him then."

"That's right. Hope he does."

"They're coming to our house for dinner tomorrow, and if I have an opportunity, well, I might try again to draw John out. Nothing like trying."

"Do. Perhaps a father-in-law can do more than a father, in such a matter."

Anna stood at the window and watched Elizabeth and Mary playing outside. "John," she began, still looking out the window, "I know after you're gone I'll wonder lots of times why this has all happened. I seem not to be able to forget it when you are here with me. After you're gone it will be harder, I'm afraid."

John made no answer. He was getting ready to shave. Slowly he ran his razor back and forth across the hone.

Anna continued, "My folks still seem to have faith in that old witch doctor. It frets me when they think there's a reason why it didn't work. Wonder what reason the witch would give if you told her."

John started to shave. Anna stepped close to him and touched him lightly on the shoulder.

"Wonder what your folks think."

"Well, I know this," answered John, holding the razor in mid-air, "they think I'm pretty bad."

"Bad? What do you mean?"

"They think I've stayed away from church too much. Maybe I have. I know they're very displeased about it. My father told me it worries him that I didn't go to church in America. I just can't seem to make him listen to reason." John made two strokes down across his cheek.

"If—if that's why—" He made two more strokes. "Anna," he said, "let's not discuss this at your home today. I have

93

come to the conclusion that *no one* knows anything about 'why this,' and 'why that.' People guess and jump to conclusions, but nobody really knows anything. Mary fell. We know that. She hurt her knee. We know that. It's stiff and we know that. But if we try to figure out why, we'll both go crazy. If it's my fault, I hope someday God will give me the full punishment I deserve."

"Oh, John!" cried Anna. "You never talked quite like this before. Don't you think maybe we'd better leave Mary with Mother and go to church next Sunday, and try to talk to the father if it would make everyone feel so much better?"

"It's *you* I'm concerned about," answered John thoughtfully. "Would it help *you?* We can't live to please everyone else. I'm sorry so many think we're wicked, but how could we afford to give any money now? If the father is able to come to sprinkle our houses, that will cost us something, too."

Anna watched John until he had finished shaving. "And have you forgotten that the man in Daruvar exists?" she asked, her hand again on his shoulder.

John glanced down into Anna's inquiring face. "I sup-

94

pose," he answered, after a prolonged pause, "just about like you have."

"Well, John," and Anna stepped over to the hook on the wall beside the bed and took down her jacket, "I don't know how you feel 'way down deep inside, but I feel sometimes as though I'm passing between two rows of fire, dodging this way and that, trying not to get burned. When you get to America, why don't you go to some priest over there?"

"What for?"

"Well, you know."

"How could I, until I learn to speak English better?"

"Oh, that's right. Then how can you talk to a doctor about Mary's knee?"

"I'll make him understand somehow," answered John.

The chicken, well done and juicy, had been baked to a beautiful golden brown, in the outdoor oven. Around it in the savory fowl sauce lay mealy, whole potatoes and dried green beans. With pride Anna's mother placed the filled platter in the center of the table. Elizabeth set on dishes of hot mashed turnips, plum butter, and stewed apples, while Anna poured the steaming roasted barley coffee and cut a plateful of delicious-looking nut bread and coffee cake. But Mary and Elizabeth did most of the talking at the table. No one else seemed to think of anything worth saying.

"You two aren't eating much," fretted Anna's mother at length. "Anna, take more chicken. John, I made this coffee cake especially for you. Take more."

"Thank you, Mother," answered John, "your dinner is wonderful, but I've had plenty."

"I know. You dread leaving, don't you, John?"

"In a way, yes. Yes, I do, Mother."

"We wish too you were already back."

"I wish I could take Anna and Mary with me."

"Oh, no! Never!" cried Elizabeth. "Not 'way over there to America."

"By the way, John," slowly ventured Anna's father, bending forward a trifle, "don't you really think you ought to go see the father before you leave?"

"What about?"

"Well," he rubbed the back of his neck with his left hand, "about what any of us want to see the father about, I guess. Don't you think it would make you feel easier about leaving your family behind?"

"It might," answered John at length, "and again it might not."

"Might not? Might not, did you say? Why, John, what do you mean?"

John drew a long breath and glanced at Anna before he spoke. "I'd better not try to attempt an explanation," he said carefully. He cleared his throat. "We did talk about going to church on Sunday, if we can leave Mary here."

"Of course," smiled Anna's mother, "we'd be glad to keep her. Ever so glad."

Chapter 12

Before midnight Saturday, it began to rain, and rained steadily all night. By five, it was pouring and the rain was accompanied by a strong wind, and a weird whistling sound. When John looked out the door at daybreak, the street was a sheet of water, and rain was still falling.

"This is our answer," he said as he closed the door. "We can't go to church this morning and I'm sure no one else will either. We'll say our prayers at home today, Anna."

Five days later the father did come to the village. It was the most important day of the year in Miletinac. School was closed for the day, so every boy and girl could be at home to witness his or her own house being sprinkled. By ten o'clock, excitement was high. A face or two, or even three, could be seen peering anxiously from a window in every house in the village, for in breathless eagerness, everyone was watching for the arrival of the black-robed father, who had not been in the village for many months. And when he was finally spotted at the far end of the village, slowly but surely working his way from house to house, parents as well as children began to speak to one another in undertones. The aging father, with his pewter water jar, was a holy personage and most highly revered. Some even feared him.

"And now—now," whispered starry-eyed children, clinging excitedly to one another, "see, he's coming to ours next." And when the father finished the task of sprinkling the water on the door and frame, one of the children might even be given permission to dart out and place the family offering in his outstretched hand. "And why did he sprinkle our house?" those same children would ask year after year. And the parents, year after year, would answer, "It's to keep the evil spirits away from our house, and to give us health and happiness all year."

Anna and John were likewise standing at their window, silently waiting, watching. John had Mary in his arms.

"Who is it, Papa?" she asked, repeatedly patting his cheek.

"It's the priest who has come a long way," answered John. "See, he's blessing our house now with holy water. Anna, do you want to go out and hand him the money, or shall I?"

"I'll take Mary. You go, John."

"Ah," remarked the father, raising his heavy eyebrows. "So this is where you live? And when did you come home?"

"I came in April." John placed the money in the father's outstretched hand.

"April!" exclaimed the father. "You mean you've been home for nine months and I haven't seen you all this while?"

"I've been tied down," answered John.

"And what has tied you?" inquired the father. "You surely have not been farming on Sundays, have you?"

"No, no indeed, Father." John cleared his throat.

"Sickness?"

"Our little Mary fell and hurt her knee."

"Her knee? But your legs," observed the father, frowning a little. "Aren't they strong and nimble? I haven't seen you in church since—well, a long time. Since before you went away, if I recollect."

"I was over once, Father, recently."

"Once! Only once in nine months! What a record! It doesn't sound good."

John shifted. "I was there, but you did not notice me."

"Well, well," answered Father Jardell. "Neither did you come to me for confession. I recall no confessions from you in many months. Are you that good, John?"

John made no answer. He felt the father's eyes piercing him through.

"I hope while in America," added the father, "you did

98

not learn that doctrine of devils, that you can get by without it."

"Oh, no," answered John quickly. "I heard nothing of such a doctrine while in America. Anna and I both fully intended to come last Sunday, then that big rain spoiled our plans."

Father Jardell slipped his hand into the deep pocket in the fold of his long black robe, and fumbled with his money. "You know," he said, "this house blessing helps, but it's not enough, John. You've been sadly neglecting not only your own soul, but the souls of your family. You're far behind in your holy offerings, too. I suppose you made good money in America, did you not?"

"Money's not as easily earned over there as some think," answered John, "nor as I had expected. I soon discovered that a foreigner like me has a long hard hill to climb."

"But you'll find it harder and longer than you ever did before," answered the father, rubbing his double chin, "unless you do penance and do it mighty quick. You are tempting God. Are you prepared now to take care of those sins?"

"Sins? You—you mean with money?"

The father's expression grew a bit stern; his voice a little impatient.

"I mean," he said, "since the rain prevented your coming last Sunday and I'm here to ease your load of guilt, how about settling for part of it now?"

"I—I just can't," faltered John. "No, I'm not prepared today."

"You can give me what you were going to bring last Sunday."

John looked troubled. "But I gave you all I can spare right now," explained John. "I'm going back to America on the fifteenth, and that'll take all I've been able to scrape together."

"What!" exclaimed Father Jardell. "You mean you have

99

money to ride the ocean and no money for your father! What has come over you, John Olesh? I'm alarmed, and I observe that you have sometimes failed to address me properly today."

John put both hands in his trouser pockets, and looking past the father, saw his wife and child watching from the window. He detected a look of strange, new alarm on Anna's face. "You'll be getting chilled, I fear," John said with strained concern. "You've not been well and you have many more houses to bless."

"And how right," agreed the father. "I must be moving on. But I hope you get as uneasy about your soul's condition as I am, John." The father fumbled with the cross on the chain. He held it up before John. "I hear there's a man from Budapest living in Daruvar, who calls himself a Protestant missionary. I've never seen the man, but I'm told he's got one of the most deceptive doctrines any man ever devised. And one of the first things he tells people is that he's got a Bible that will open their eyes and give them a new sort of revelation on divine truth, and it makes them very wise, and so on, so they don't need to confess to the father. He tells people many more very absurd and foolish and even wicked things. Surely you have not been over to Daruvar to listen to such a man, have you?"

"No, no," answered John.

"Nor talked with one like him in America?"

"No, no, Father." John started toward the house.

After John went into the house, he sat for a long time, his gaze fixed to the bare earth floor. Anna could hear him breathing.

"It looked as though the father was displeased about something," Anna remarked at length. There was uneasiness in her voice.

"He was."

"What have we done, John?"

"It's what we haven't done."

100

"Yes," she sighed, "I am not surprised he thinks that. But what shall we do about it?"

John shook his head. "Better not say more until a little girl with big, blue eyes is fast asleep," he said wearily. "Come, Mary. Let Papa hold you while Mother puts a little dinner on the table."

Mary climbed up on her father's lap. He cleared his throat. "You know," he said, "I think you ought to sing me one or two of those nice little songs Elizabeth taught you. How about it?"

The child needed no coaxing. In sweet, innocent, tender simplicity, she sang not two, but four without a mistake. "Are they pretty songs, Papa? Did I make you happy again?"

Anna saw John brush away a tear. She saw him plant a tender kiss on Mary's forehead. She saw him hold her close and whisper something in her ear. Slowly she cut some bread, and set out a dish of cottage cheese.

John and Anna talked well into the night.

"It's much harder for me to see you leave this time," said Anna. "I wish that man hadn't stopped here. I'm so tangled up in my thoughts, and now I feel worse than ever since the father came by. Is there really a God, John?"

John tapped his shoe toe on the earth floor. "We've been taught there is. Why, Anna, of course there's a God."

"Does He see us?"

"I hope so."

"Does He really care about us?"

"I hope so. Sometimes I wonder."

"Do you really think the evil spirits will stay away from our house while you're gone, if you don't give the father more money before you leave?"

John shook his head. "Wish I knew," he answered. "The father tried to make me feel very wicked. I don't know whether to ignore him or feel bad about it all. Right this minute I'm half tempted to give up the trip, and settle with him. Maybe we'd both feel a lot better."

"But John!" cried Anna. "You can't do that now. You have your passport. I'll go to church whenever I can while you're gone, I promise. And, John, I'll say prayers three times a day. That ought to help. Oh, John, I'll try to be as good as I know how."

"If the father knew that Budapest missionary once sat at our table," John's voice was husky, "I doubt if the house and the three acres would bring enough to cleanse us."

"But, John," exclaimed Anna, "he didn't have any influence on us. Did he?"

"Of course not. Nor did he convince us of anything— except, well, except that he had something new and different, and that he was a pleasant man and happy about something he believed in."

"I wish I knew," sighed Anna sadly. "Oh, I wish I knew what he did to us that day."

"Mr. Lutz?"

"Yes."

"Why, Anna," reproved John, "didn't we just get done saying he didn't? Don't ever let me hear you suggest that he did. We didn't let him."

"All right, then," agreed Anna. "I'm sorry. He didn't— only, I mean, I never had this funny, funny ache here in my heart until he came. I mean, that's the part I can't understand."

On Sunday it rained again. John and Anna prayed at home and in earnestness, for the next day John would be leaving after early breakfast.

The depot in Daruvar was filled with people waiting for the eight o'clock train to Zagreb. Since John would have over an hour's time to wait, he decided to walk to the nearest store, where he could purchase two things he still needed, a comb and a cake of shaving soap. Near the entrance of a drugstore, about three blocks from the depot, he

102

came upon two poorly clad little girls, each carrying something in a paper sack.

"Here," said the taller one, "let's trade. Maybe mine isn't as heavy as yours." In the exchange, the smaller child dropped her sack. "Oh, Mary," she sobbed, "look! What will we do? It's coming out!"

John stepped up and put one hand on the child's shoulder. "Don't cry," he said, "everyone has accidents. Maybe I can help you."

"But we can't get it home now," she sobbed. "The sack's burst open and—"

"Wait," offered John. "I'll step inside and ask the storekeeper for a new sack."

"But we didn't get it in there."

"Where did you get it?"

"A man gave it to us. We needed it," she sobbed.

"But you wait," repeated John. "I'll go in and ask."

John soon returned. Carefully he lifted the broken sack and dumped the contents into the new sack. "See," he said, "not much is lost after all. How's that?"

"Thanks, mister," said the older girl. "Thanks very much."

"How far must you carry your sacks?"

"Down the street a little way and around the next corner, mister."

"That's not far. Here," said John, "give me both. I'll have time to carry them for you."

The little girls led the way to a dingy, poorly furnished basement apartment. On a broken chair near the stove sat a thin, pale-faced woman, holding a tiny baby on her lap. She looked up in surprise when John entered.

"Mamma," said the one little girl, "Mr. Lutz gave us a sack of cornmeal and a sack of sugar. And he said we won't need to pay for it. But he wants us to come to his Sunday school on Sunday, and I told him we would if we could. We can, can't we, Mamma?"

John put the sacks on the table.

"I think so," answered the mother. "But who's the gentleman, Mary?"

The woman stood up. She held her baby closer to her when she spoke, and pulled the blanket up around its tiny face.

"Millie dropped her sack, right there in front of the drugstore, because it was heavy for her, Mamma, and this man came along just then and got a new sack, and then he carried them both home for us. Wasn't that nice of him?"

"Well, I guess it was! Thank you, sir. That was most kind of you."

"You're welcome," answered John. He put his hand on the doorknob.

"Do you live close by, sir?"

"No, I'm from Miletinac. I just walked down the street from the depot, and met the girls in their predicament. I'm on my way to America."

"You are? Thanks again, sir," smiled the woman. "We need the meal, God knows, and after Mr. Lutz was kind enough to give it to us, I'd sure hate to lose it on the street."

"Of course," John agreed. "And—" he hesitated, "who's the Mr. Lutz, if I may ask?"

"He's a man of God, sir," answered the woman. "That's the best I can tell you. I never knew anyone like him. I was left a poor widow two months ago, and that good man and his wife have done more to keep and comfort me these two months than—well, sir—you say you're from Miletinac and I'm told that's a strong Catholic village, and I don't want to cast any reflection on any father, for I have a brother who is a priest in France, and I dearly love him. But when a young mother gets down low and out of everything like I've been, and you have two little girls crying for something to eat and your own stomach is empty, and then a man like Mr. Lutz comes to your rescue, it leaves an impression, no matter if you've been in the church all your life. I think one night I might have committed suicide if it hadn't been for those good people, I was so depressed. He said Christ didn't come to get all He could out of people, but to give to others in need, and that's the way he wants to live. He does it, too. I've even seen him go along the streets, shaking hands with poor ragged boys and girls, and giving them little books to read. Once I saw him stop and talk kindly to a drunk man. Tell me, sir, what would make any man do such a thing, but the love of God in his heart? That's why I say he's a man of God. Mary dear, put a kettle of water on and I'll make some mush. I know you girls are hungry."

John stopped at the drugstore, made his purchase, and hurried back to the depot. Until the train pulled in, he stood outside facing the cement-block house across the tracks, but all he could see was the soft glow of a light from the front window.

January 30, 1904

DEAR ANNA,

Send my letters to General Delivery, Barberton, Ohio. I found a job at once in a foundry starting at ten dollars a week, and the promise of a raise in three weeks, if my work proves satisfactory. I stay in the cheapest room I could find. It's not very good, but I can get along. As soon as I can, I'll send you a money order. This is close to Akron, and since that's a large city, I will likely go there to look up a doctor. Write and tell me everything. I pray always for you and Mary. Holy Mother Mary will surely hear our prayers, won't she?

All my love,
JOHN

May 1

DEAR JOHN,

We miss you even more than we supposed. But everyone is so very kind to us, especially to Mary. She never frets nor complains about her knee, and is happier each new day. Elizabeth has taught her more games and songs,

105

and all day she and the children around us have great times. In the evening, however, she talks constantly about you coming home. I hope you'll be back by September. You said I should tell you everything. The most important thing I have to tell you may be a surprise. There will be another little one in September. I have most of the garden planted. Mother and Father helped me, and so did several of our good neighbors. Don't worry about us, John; we're getting along. Just pray for us every day. I do for you.

In love,

ANNA

Chapter 13

Anna's next letter smote him to the heart. The second page read,

John, I can't forget what you wrote about your experience with the children and their widowed mother in Daruvar. I hid the letter. Mother has asked me a dozen times if I heard from you again. I told her everything you wrote but that. But I'm *so* glad you helped those dear little girls. I thought all night about what you told me, and couldn't sleep a wink. I wish I could call on that woman and have a long talk with her.

The letter in John's hand trembled.

But I don't suppose I'll be going to Daruvar, and if I did I would hardly dare do such a thing, would I? I'm terribly confused. Will we ever really know who and what is right? Can't you try somehow to find out in America? Listen, John. The father is seriously ill and the villagers are afraid he'll never be able to come again. I cried a long time last night. I felt so empty and lonely. If I could only have you here to help me forget these things that trouble me.

John folded the letter and, rolling it nervously in both hands, looked out into the narrow alley through the dirty rain-splashed windowpane in his room. He groaned. "Why did I write it? Oh, shame on me. After all I've said." He twisted the letter and drew his breath through his tightly set teeth.

With sharp and painful vividness, John relived each confusion, each disappointment, each doubt and fear he and Anna had experienced since that day Mr. Lutz had made his appearance at their door. For thirty minutes or more he stood staring into the alley. No one passed but an old man carrying a bundle of sticks on his back.

John also relived the evening he talked to himself in the mirror in his room in Steelton. "You've got to make good." His own words mocked him now, tormenting him. "Make good," he repeated. "And I'm not. And what's more, now I've failed Anna. Why did I tell her?"

John did not step over to the stained mirror and face himself again. Instead, he sank on the edge of his sagging bed, and dropped his tired, aching head in both hands. The twisted letter fell to the floor. The room, with its faded, dingy wallpaper, smelled stale and musty. The floor was rough and dirty. The bed was full of bumps and dips. John wanted to get up, pack, and rush home to comfort Anna, and beg her to forgive him for writing about things that upset and confused her. But how could he comfort her when he himself was so uncomforted and miserable? And why was he? Hadn't he gone his limit to try to be a good father, a good husband? John rubbed his aching head. He shook himself. Finally he picked up the letter, stuck it in his pocket, and went out. He started walking. He did not return to his room for over an hour.

Anna leaned hard against the end of the bed and read the letter the second time.

MY DEAR ANNA, *July 5*

At last I had an interview with a doctor in Akron. I feel certain I made him understand about Mary's knee. He was kind to me, frank, and I believe honest. We waited too long. He could operate, but he wouldn't promise more than the doctor in Daruvar. Not at any price. He said we should be glad it wasn't her elbow. I had hoped you could come to Daruvar to meet me when I come, but I doubt now if you'll be able. Yes, I am planning to come home in September. I pray Holy Mother Mary to watch over you, my dear Anna. I went to a big Catholic church in Akron Sunday.

Many loves,

JOHN

The expression on Anna's face did not change, nor did the color leave her flushed cheeks.

"Is Papa all right?" asked Mary.

"Yes, dear," answered Anna, "and your papa is coming home in two months."

The last sixty days before sailing seemed like a year to John. He worked hard every day, then tossed restlessly at night. His thoughts tormented him as they twisted over and over in his mind. He did not forget that Anna asked him to search for the answer to her troubled and confused mind. But where? And how?

The meeting he walked into on the street corner one night only added to his own distress and bewilderment. A small group of people, with radiantly happy faces, were singing. John stopped to listen. He caught a few of the words. "Jesus, only Jesus." He stepped a little closer. A large man with a clear, convincing voice talked fast and with great earnestness. Something about Christ. He held a black book in one hand. John stepped still closer, but hard as he tried, he understood only a little of what the man was saying. "One of those deceptive doctrines, I suppose," thought John. Still he lingered.

A middle-aged man, in a ragged shirt and dirty trousers, staggered up and shook hands with the man who was speaking. John stood on tiptoe. The speaker drew from his inside coat pocket a small red paper-covered book and handed it to the man. John watched. Then he heard his own name mentioned. Strange. He bent forward. He heard unmistakably a second, and a third time, his own name. What could it mean? Something about John and the book. John who? The man who had taken the book looked at it a moment as he held it in his unsteady hand, then handed it back to the speaker, shook his head, muttered something, and staggered away. John was completely baffled. What was the little red book? And why did the man hand it back? John walked on down the street. Tomorrow he would sail.

It was daybreak when John reached Miletinac. He ran most of the last two miles, and was panting when he knocked gently on the door. He walked in.

"John!" cried Anna, sitting straight up in bed.

110

"Anna! How are you, my dear?" John dropped his valise, threw his hat on the table, and rushed to her.

"All right."

"Are you really?" he asked.

Anna laughed. "Of course I am, John. We have another little girl." She pointed to the crib. "I waited until you came to help choose a name.

John tiptoed to the crib, then back to Anna. "I came as soon as I could. Believe me."

"I know you did, John."

"Where's Mary?"

"Over home."

"When did the baby come?"

"Day before yesterday. Why, John, you're all out of breath. And you look worn and thin. What's wrong?"

"Nothing."

"Nothing at all?"

"Nothing new. I've been terribly anxious about you and Mary. Lost some sleep wondering how you took it all."

"Took what?"

"Everything."

"Like what?"

"The baby. And then my letter about what the doctor had to say."

"Well, John, of course I was disappointed about that, but you said we shouldn't build our hopes too high. Remember?"

"I know. But I hope you don't hold it against me now for leaving you when I've failed in everything."

"Hold it against you? John! Don't talk like that. I worried about how you took it. Don't look so troubled. Listen, John."

"Yes, I'm listening."

"Mary's a happy child. She's always singing and laughing and learning. You should hear her. She doesn't fret about her knee. Let's not let her find out how we've worried about

111

it. If there was an evil spirit—well, it certainly hasn't spoiled her disposition. Even Mother admits that."

"You mean it?"

"Really, John. Mother is amazed. I know she is. So is everyone in the village. Mary has been the joy and sunshine of my life while you were gone. I don't know what I would have done without her. We played, we sang, we worked, we prayed together, and even got ready for the baby together. She's so thrilled over her new sister. Mother brought her over for a while today." Anna rubbed John's hand. "John?"

"Yes."

"What shall we name her?"

John studied. "I always liked the name Kathrine."

"Then Kathrine it is," agreed Anna. "I'll get up now and make you breakfast. You look so weary, John."

"I'll be all right now that I know you are," answered John. "Let's just talk a little before we eat. My, it's good to be here. I got homesick. These last two months were almost torture. Even though I made a little money, I came home feeling like a failure. By the way, how's Father Jardell?"

"He's gone."

"Gone?"

"He was buried last Saturday. You will not need to confess to him now, John."

John breathed deeply. He sat in silence, looking at Anna.

"Don't feel blue, John. You did more than most fathers would have even tried to do. Don't say again you've failed."

The worn, tired lines on John's face melted into a gentle smile.

"And please don't talk to anyone else like that. Since Mary is so happy, why can't we be too? Cheer up, John. Now we have Kathrine as well to live for and love."

John took Anna's one hand and held it to his lips. He said not a word.

"And, John," added Anna, "the evil spirits were kept away from our house while you were gone. I worked hard

112

and the garden turned out very well. And you're here now to help harvest it. Don't feel sad."

"Anna," exclaimed John, his eyes brightening, "you sound like your brave, happy, sweet self, like you were when we were first married. And before we had these troubles and disappointments and confusions. What has happened? Tell me quickly, so I can be happy with you."

Anna did not answer immediately. She brushed one hand slowly over John's dark hair.

"And you're not troubled?" he whispered. "You're not confused any more? You know, your letter."

Anna laughed softly. "I'm happy over your coming home. Can't you see how I need you? Why shouldn't I be happy? I know now that it was Holy Mother Mary who heard my prayers and brought you home safely. And she heard your prayers for me, didn't she? I'm all right. And so is little Kathrine. I kept my promise and went to church a number of times, when the weather was nice. I must admit, it made me feel a lot better, John. Really it did. I went with several other girls, and we had good times on the way. And you wrote that you went to a big church in Akron once. I feel sure God was pleased. It made me happy, too. You see," she continued slowly, her expression growing serious, "after you left I kept rolling things over and over in my mind, even though I told myself not to. I simply could not keep from it. Then you wrote about that widow in Daruvar, and what she said about Mr. Lutz. I felt worse than ever. Everything he had told us that day came back, and troubled me greatly. I was wretched."

"Forgive me, Anna," cried John. "I shouldn't have written that to you. I knew it after I mailed the letter. I've hated myself ever since."

"Oh, no, John. Don't feel that way. You must always tell me everything. Please. I cried that night a long time. Yes, I did, John, but it was the turning point."

"What do you mean?"

"Well, I asked myself, *Why am I crying? What's wrong?* And I didn't know. I had to admit I didn't. I decided right then I was plain silly for crying over something and not knowing why. It was worse than silly. I knew I'd have to take myself in hand, for this confusion and unrest was ruining my life, and Mary's and yours. Finally, after lying awake nearly all night, I began to pray hard to Mother Mary. Then I prayed to all the saints I could think of. I begged them all to help me dismiss this whole silly mess. Everything. I promised Mother Mary I'd be as faithful as possible in going to church. I told her I realized Father Jardell had reasons to be displeased with us. Don't you really think so, too, now that he's gone?"

John hesitated. "Go on," he said.

"And now that you're home safe and sound, I'm *not* going to allow myself to ever get confused like that again. I know Mother Mary will help me. Why, John, I didn't even care to talk to my own mother for several days, and I know she and Elizabeth both thought I'd heard sad news from you. I could hardly do my work. And, John, that's not pleasing to God to be like that. I determined I would be happy when you came."

"And you've been like this ever since that night?" inquired John. "Happy like you are right now?"

Anna slipped her one hand inside one of John's. "I only wish," she said softly, "that I could tell you honestly that I have been. Hard as I tried, hard as I prayed, there were a few times when I wasn't. I'm really ashamed."

"Ashamed?"

"Yes."

"Explain."

"I—I can't. I wish I could. Surely no one else in all the world has had such experiences. It just simply can't be the way to live. What has been wrong with me? One day I was sitting right over there on that chair, busy knitting while Mary was sleeping. All at once everything came back to me.

114

It seemed I could even hear Mr. Lutz saying, 'I hope God will make you hungry and thirsty for the truth.' I began to ask questions. The truth. What is it anyhow? Who knows? Does anyone know? I felt awful. All those foolish questions no one can answer. You know, I thought about Lutz, then the father, then him, then the father. I soon was more confused than ever. Don't you think I've been silly, John? The whole thing is absurd, isn't it, and ridiculous?"

John sat on the edge of the bed thinking. He made no reply.

"Didn't you find anything in America to set us straight?"

John shook his head. "There seem to be many religions in America, many churches, many ideas, many books. That alone was very confusing to me. No, I wouldn't have had any idea where to go to try to find out. But, Anna—"

"Yes?"

"You got over it. You said—"

She nodded. "I prayed harder than ever, and begged all the saints again to let me be happy and forget, forget, forget. It helped. All the next day I prayed to forget. And now that you're here to pray with me, John, it's going to be so much easier to stay settled. Just think how busy we're going to be with two little girls."

John pressed Anna's hand. "I still think we've both taken our religion much, much too seriously," he said. "But since you've found the way to be happy, hold to it, Anna. Please, whatever you do, keep on forgetting. Let's not talk about it. Stay happy, and satisfied, like you are right now." He looked into her thoughtful brown eyes. "And then you'll make me the happiest man in Miletinac." He stood up. "Oh," he stretched his arms above his head, "it's good to be home again. And it's good to know you've taken this disappointment so bravely. You're wonderful, Anna. I can't stand it to ever see you distressed again."

"I'll try," whispered Anna smiling. "I'll try as hard as you did when you went off to America."

115

And Anna did try. The Olesh family of four settled down to happy, healthy, busy living. John put himself completely and conscientiously to the task of being the hardest working, thriftiest three-acre landowner in Miletinac. As the busy weeks and months passed, Anna continued to be unusually happy, and in unruffled calmness performed her many duties. She put wholehearted enthusiasm into everything she did, from knitting socks to making a bowl of potato soup. John Olesh was proud of his wife. If he couldn't make good, it wouldn't be her fault, he often told himself. The tiny gap Anna once feared was coming between herself and her neighbors, had completely disappeared. If either she or John experienced days, or even moments, of confusion or unrest of soul, neither discovered it in the other. They worked, they planned, they skimped, they saved together. They were at peace with all the neighbors. They repeated their daily prayers, and even took occasional turns attending church. The parents smiled approvingly.

The new priest, Father Markum, was younger than Father Jardell—tall, thin, and serious-faced.

John was poor, as poor as the other men in Miletinac, but he gave the father what he could. And their disappointments and secret confusions of former days were buried deep beneath the peace and contentment under their own rye-thatched roof. As the girls grew physically and in appetite, the wherewithal to meet their needs was scarcely sufficient. Nevertheless, with cheerfulness Anna did her part in helping to make ends meet, and her expressive brown eyes, deep and trusting, gave John daily inspiration and courage.

Mary grew stronger, brighter, and rosier every day. Baby Kathrine developed into a normal, healthy, and beautiful child, and made Anna comparatively little extra work.

When the pumpkin-seed oil ran out, Anna did not fret nor complain. John exchanged cabbages with a neighbor for oil. When there were no more potatoes, he worked for potatoes.

116

Anna's pretty print dress from America was faded, worn, and patched. The little buttoned shoes were put away for Kathrine to grow into, and Mary was wearing homemade, knitted scuffs with cardboard soles. But she was happy. They all were well and happy, and Anna told herself repeatedly that was worth more than anything money could buy. The two little girls entertained each other, which made it possible for Anna to work outside with John a good deal of the time. That she enjoyed very much.

Two years later Joseph came. John was thrilled. On the eighth day he took him to Djulovac to be baptized by Father Markum.

But before Joseph was a year old, Anna noticed a troubled expression growing on John's face. He talked less, laughed seldom, frequently woke up during the night, and tossed and turned when he did sleep.

Chapter 14

For weeks Anna tried outwardly to ignore John's troubled look. She put forth added efforts to be cheerful, helpful, and happy. Often she helped Mary sing the gay little songs Elizabeth had taught her, and did so when John was within hearing.

True enough, she also was having a real struggle. It took careful planning to properly feed and clothe her three dear children. But others in Miletinac were having the same struggle. Smiling through her problem, Anna thinned the soup each evening, and scrubbed the potatoes instead of peeling them. She altered and patched and pieced so the children would have enough clothes.

John must be worried about their poverty. Surely the man from Daruvar had not been back in Miletinac to upset John again. If John had seen him, he hadn't mentioned the fact to her. He prayed, she observed with inward gratitude, as much as ever. About once a month he walked the twelve miles to church.

One cool evening in late November, John was unusually quiet at the table. He ate only one slice of dry bread.

Anna could ignore his troubled look no longer. "Aren't you feeling well?" Carefully she pinched the words through her unsmiling lips.

John nodded. "I'm well." He forced a feeble smile.

"But you took no soup," she commented feebly.

"That's all right. You eat. You and the children."

"But, John, yesterday you ate but little too."

For a moment John seemed lost in solemn thought. When he looked up, his gray, serious eyes had a tender warmth in

118

them. "Just so you and the children have enough," he replied softly. "Don't be anxious about me."

"Oh, but I am," declared Anna. "You—you can't go on this way. Here," she pleaded, "you take half of mine. We do everything else together." She held her bowl out to him.

John smiled and shook his head.

Reluctantly she set it down. "Have I complained, John?" Pent-up tears filled her eyes. Twice she tried to say more, but her tongue felt warped and thick.

"Never," came John's tender answer, "not even now when I noticed the flour box will soon be empty. You've done remarkably well, Anna."

"Then please take part of my soup." She held it out to him again. "It would make me happy, John."

"Not this time." John adjusted himself on his chair. He picked up his spoon and put it down again, trying hard to seem calm. "We ought to have a cow and a team of oxen and more ground."

"We should," agreed Anna. This was not a new idea. She had agreed to this before.

"With Joseph growing like a weed"—he glanced lovingly at his small black-haired son tied securely in the high chair, his plump, rosy cheeks plastered with bread crumbs and soup —"we're just not going to be able to make it on this patch of ground."

Anna agreed to this with a long deep breath and a look of mutual understanding.

A pause followed, interrupted only by the clicking of three spoons scraping the bottoms of three bowls. Thoughts raced madly through Anna's mind. She knew John said the truth. She knew, even better than he, how many things they were in need of.

"Then that's what's been troubling you? That and nothing else?"

The heaviness in John's heart seemed to drop loose. His shoulders slumped. Then she had noticed. As though he

119

could try to hide anything from Anna. "A father must provide better than this," John said with a sigh. "Maybe others can be satisfied, but I can't. Yes, it troubles me." His tawny, strong hands covered his face for a moment, as he rested his elbows on the table. "I dread to think of it again," he muttered sadly. He cleared his throat. He reached over and put one hand on Mary's shoulder as he often did at the table. "If I could figure out any other way, but I can't." He hesitated. His eyes met hers across the table. Each read the anxiety, and the same genuine parent love, in the other's. "Can you?" he asked.

Anna knew what John meant. And he was certain that she did. He moistened his lips as he glanced again at his three children around the table. "If I could go—long enough to tide us over until winter is past." His sentence was hardly above a whisper.

Anna showed no surprise, even though she swallowed the lump that formed in her throat. "Are you asking me?" Her voice, too, was scarcely audible.

"We've got to decide together." John's voice was a little unsteady now. "I've told you before I'd never go unless you agreed. We've got to do something soon. Real soon, Anna."

"I know."

"And I don't want to borrow to buy more land, if there's another way out."

"No."

"You wouldn't blame me then if I can't figure out something better?"

"Blame you? Why, John. You know me better than to say that." There was nothing but implicit trust and devotion on Anna's face and in her voice. "Here," she said, "please finish this soup. Please, Papa John. I've had all I care for."

John took the soup.

In January John Olesh made his third trip to America. It was in the year 1907. He found immediate employment in a steel mill at Harrisburg, Pennsylvania, with wages above his expectations. Before two months had passed, he had saved, by careful skimping, one hundred dollars.

Anna was dumbfounded when she unfolded the letter and looked at the money order. She stared at the figure with rapt attention, then sank on the wooden bench beside the table.

"What's wrong, Mother?" exclaimed Mary, hurrying across the room and throwing her arms around her mother's neck. "You look like you're going to cry. Don't, Mother."

"I might." She laughed softly, her eyes shimmering with glad uncontrolled tears. "It's money from your dear papa. Now I can buy corn meal, sugar, matches, and yarn, to make you children new shoes. It's almost too good to be true. I wonder if I am reading the figures right."

Trembling with excitement, Anna read the letter—the last paragraph out loud. "After you get what you need, save the rest toward a down payment on a farm. I'll send another hundred as soon as I can."

"Don't cry, Mother," pleaded Mary, pressing her lips against her mother's forehead. "Isn't Papa all right?"

"Yes, dear, but I fear he's doing without the things he needs himself, to send this much home already. Mary, will you do something for Mother now?"

"What?"

"You're my good little stand-by, aren't you? You watch Kathrine and Joseph while I run over to Grandmother's house."

"What for?"

"I want to see if she can't come and stay with you children while I go to Vilieki Bastaji today. I'll hurry."

But before Anna opened the door, her hand still on the knob, she reconsidered that decision. "The storekeeper in Vilieki Bastaji won't be able to cash this. What am I thinking of? I'll have to go to Daruvar to the bank. But I'll hurry over and ask Grandmother if she won't come and stay with

121

with you children tomorrow. It will take me most of the day to make the trip. You little ones be good for Mary now," and Anna all but ran across and up the village street.

The air was cool and crisp when she started for Daruvar the next morning before daybreak. She pulled her jacket collar together at her throat, and held it as she walked as fast as she could. Again and again she repeated the items she needed most, wondering how much she would have left for their nest egg toward a farm. She prayed, face tilted upward, eyes looking heavenward, making the sign of the cross not once, but three times.

Before she had gone five miles, the gray sky parted at the horizon and through the jagged tree edges, the oncoming day shone crimson. In spite of her anxieties and problems, there was a healthy glow on her cheeks, and a new gleam in her eyes.

The store in Vilieki Bastaji wasn't open yet. Anna knocked on the door at the rear of the store. The storekeeper came to the door.

"I wondered if you would let me borrow enough for train fare until I come back this evening. I have an American money order from my husband and I'm going in to Daruvar to cash it. I'll give it back this evening. Can you help me out, please?"

He nodded, disappeared for a moment, then returned, opened the door, and handed Anna two coins.

There were only a few passengers in the coach. Tired, Anna sank into the first seat she came to. She leaned back, resting her head on the high leather-upholstered seat back, and tried to relax. She closed her eyes, drawing one deep breath after another as the train lurched on its way. There was a strange tugging at her heart, but it had to do with going into Daruvar. She opened her eyes and sat up straight, gazing out the window. The next minute she felt a gentle tap on her shoulder. Anna lifted her head and looked into the face of the man standing in the aisle beside her.

"Aren't you Mrs. Olesh?" he asked.

Anna's mouth opened with speechless astonishment.

"Aren't you from Miletinac?"

Anna's hand went over her thumping heart. "Yes."

"I didn't mean to scare you. Aren't you Mrs. Olesh, the mother of little Mary?"

Anna was almost too excited to speak. "Yes," she whispered softly.

"And didn't you let me eat a meal in your home one noonday, let me see, about three years ago?"

"Yes," answered Anna, "or four."

"Then you remember me?"

Anna nodded. "I remember."

"I suppose you're going into Daruvar?"

"Yes."

"So am I. May I sit here beside you and chat a little?"

Anna's cheeks grew warm. She could feel the color creeping into them, but her hands turned cold, her arms weak. She moved over closer to the window. He sat beside her.

"You know, I've never forgotten your kindness to me that day, Mrs. Olesh."

Anna clasped her trembling hands.

"I've tried time and again to get back to Miletinac, but each time my plans were changed at the last minute. How's little Mary?"

"She's not so little anymore. She'll soon be old enough to go to school, but—but she can't."

"You say she can't go?"

"Mary fell and injured her knee."

"Oh! Lately?"

"No. Soon after you were there. She's crippled—for life. We waited until it was too late to help her." Anna went on and told the whole story.

"I'm really grieved to hear this, Mrs. Olesh," said Mr. Lutz. "You know, for some reason I've never forgotten you people, you and little Mary and Mr. Olesh."

123

Anna could hear her heart pounding violently.

"But God is grieved much more deeply when people He has loved and suffered and died for, wait until it's too late to do something about His salvation. That is far more important than a knee. You know, Mrs. Olesh, these bodies will go back to dust someday, and we'll have new, perfect bodies in Heaven. These frail bodies of ours weren't made to last throughout all eternity. But our souls were. I'm so glad we have a great physician we can go to. His remedy for the sin-sick soul is free. Isn't that wonderful?"

Anna sat rigid, her gaze fixed on the back of the seat in front of her. She did not answer, nor move her head. She did not even take notice of the beautiful fast-moving landscape.

The man continued in a soft-toned voice: "I've just been back to my old home in Budapest, to see my mother before she made her departure into the next world. It was an experience I'll never forget. My mother had a badly twisted, worn-out, and pain-racked body, but my, what a beautiful soul! What a triumphant passing! How is it with you, Mrs. Olesh? Have you tried the Great Physician?"

Still Anna did not answer. Her cheeks burned. Her legs shook.

"How's Mr. Olesh?"

Anna drew a deep breath. "He's in America again. Left in January."

"To hunt up another doctor?"

Anna shook her head. "We're very poor, Mr. Lutz." She did not look up. "We have three children now. John's working in a steel mill. Yesterday I got a money order from him."

"And so you're going into Daruvar to spend it?"

"I want to save what I can toward buying a farm. But there are things we must have. John's a hard worker, Mr. Lutz. John's a good man. A good father. A good provider."

"And the Bible says that if we seek first the kingdom of

124

God and His righteousness, all these other things we need will be added unto us."

Anna looked perplexed. She pressed her fingertips deep into her cheeks. "It says that?"

"That's right, Mrs. Olesh. It's God's true word in His holy Book. I remember how I tried to give you a New Testament that day."

"You remember?" asked Anna.

"As if it were yesterday. Have you forgotten?"

Slowly Anna shook her head. "I tried to. I wanted to. John said we—we had to." Anna cleared her throat nervously. She folded and unfolded her hands in her lap. She pinched her fingers. "I almost did." Her voice was scarcely above a whisper.

"Almost," repeated Mr. Lutz. "And no one has offered you a Bible since?"

"No, sir."

"I can't help feeling that the Spirit of God planned that we meet like this, so unexpectedly today. It's just like Him to do this very sort of thing. I've often prayed that you'd have a hunger for the truth, you and your husband."

Anna looked up sharply as though something pricked her to the heart.

"Have you never felt any desire to know the truth?" he asked.

Anna moved closer to the window. "Yes," she faltered, "many times—but I think no one can know. John said in America there are many churches, many religions. Oh, it's all so confusing. I — I —"

"But the Word of God is truth, Mrs. Olesh. It sets us free from all this confusion. There are many false religions, yes, in America, and everywhere in the world."

Anna sat up very straight. "Oh, Mr. Lutz!" she cried. "Stop! Please." She clenched her fists in her tightly folded arms. "If there is a God who knows all things and cares,

125

then why— Oh, please, Mr. Lutz, the things you told us in our home that day confused and tormented us until we wished we'd never met you. Please, Mr. Lutz," begged Anna. "I can't think of going through that struggle again with my husband so far away. He wants me to be happy. I prayed to Mother Mary and to all the saints to help me forget the things you told us that day. I can't think of—" Anna's cheeks lost their color.

"My friend," said Mr. Lutz, "Mother Mary doesn't hear prayers, nor do the saints. No one but God hears and answers prayer. He is the only Mediator."

"How do you know?"

"Because the Bible, the Word of God, tells us so. I'm sorry I gave my last Testament away yesterday, or I'd read it to you. I have more at home in Daruvar. When we get there, I'll run over and get you one. It will take only a few minutes. You—you won't refuse to take a Testament as a gift this time, will you?"

Anna's breathing became more labored. Her lips moved, but Mr. Lutz could not understand a single word. He waited, but she did not repeat her sentence.

"You say you will accept it?" he asked.

"I'm—I'm afraid I—I might," she whispered, "but—"

"But what, Mrs. Olesh?"

"John!" she cried. "What will John say? Oh, I shouldn't do it, Mr. Lutz, with John in America. I told him the other time he went, to try to find the truth about these things over there and he didn't know how to or where to go. If your Bible is the truth, why then don't more people—why doesn't everybody take one?"

"It's not my Bible, Mrs. Olesh. It's God's message to all of us. But see. Here we are at Daruvar already. I will run over to the house and get you a New Testament. You'll take it and read it if I get it for you, won't you? Don't wait until

126

it's too late, my friend."

The train stopped.

"Daruvar," called the conductor.

"Will you wait outside here?"

He saw her lips tremble. "I'm afraid I might. Hurry, Mr. Lutz."

Chapter 15

As Mr. Lutz followed Anna Olesh out of the train, he noticed her faded, mended dress below her worn and patched jacket. Her black hand-knitted, leather-soled scuffs, tied on with heavy twine, were worn nearly threadbare at the toes and heels.

"We live right over there in that cement-block building. See?" Then he waved. "That's my good wife standing there in the doorway. I suppose she's been watching for me every time a train came in for the past several days." He waved to her again. "Wouldn't you like to go along over with me and meet her?"

"Oh." Anna scarcely looked up as she shook her head a little. "No, Mr. Lutz. I'll—I'll wait here."

"And I'll be right back. It will take me only a few minutes."

As in a dream, Anna stood on the cobblestone walk and watched the man dash across the tracks and kiss the woman who was waiting for him at the open door. For a moment she swayed, for she felt a little dizzy and sick at her stomach. What was she allowing this Mr. Lutz to do to her? The very thing both she and John had declared never should—never would—happen? She shook from head to foot. She pressed her tongue between her teeth and bit it.

Must she wait? She hadn't exactly promised to, had she? Anna's thinking was confused. She twisted one hand in the other. She could hurry on to the bank and save herself a lot of trouble. For a moment she thought she would, yet she didn't. There was something so profoundly different about the man. He seemed so confident in what he believed. His unmistakable sureness that the Bible was the truth kept her waiting.

Anna wanted to know the truth. She knew she did, even though she had tried desperately to avoid thinking on the matter for months—years. She stood waiting in sickening anxiety, trembling, eager, yet fearful.

Daruvar. Since that day the man Lutz left their house in Miletinac the name had always sent a strange unexplainable feeling over her. And now she, Anna Olesh, was actually in the city, facing the house in which he and his family lived. She bit the inside of her cheek. Was he coming? A few minutes? It seemed like many since he had disappeared into the doorway yonder.

"Mr. Lutz." Anna repeated his name over and over half audibly to herself. The man? No. Not the man, but what he had said, what he was, what he professed, held her there.

The house. This was it? There was nothing attractive about the cement structure, gray, dull, severely plain. She had often wondered what it looked like. And now this was it? Anna frowned. She noticed the sign in the window to the right of the entrance, "Gospel Center," in bold black letters.

The door was opened. Mrs. Lutz stood watching as her husband hurried back across the tracks, springing light-footed, almost buoyantly.

"And here you are, Mrs. Olesh," he announced smiling. He handed Anna a small book bound in inexpensive black, imitation leather. "And God bless you as you read its pages," he added a little out of breath. "Undoubtedly you'll read portions which you will not understand. Don't be alarmed. Don't give up reading or be discouraged. Perhaps it would be best to start with the Book of John."

"John?"

"Yes. I marked it with the blue ribbon for you."

"Oh," Anna stared at the book in her hand.

"And whenever you get over here to Daruvar, please feel

"And here you are, Mrs. Olesh,"
he announced smiling.

free to drop in and visit us. Tell us how you're getting along. If I should happen not to be here, my good wife will entertain you. She's very friendly, Mrs. Olesh, and eager to help you or anyone. She can explain the Scriptures to you if you can't understand some things."

"Oh." Anna was still staring at the closed book in her hand.

"And she told me to invite you to come for dinner."

"Dinner?" Anna looked up sharply. Her eyes widened. Her lips parted.

"Yes."

"To—today?" she gasped.

"Yes, yes, Mrs. Olesh, she meant today. It's only ten o'clock now. Can you be through with your purchasing by noon, and come over and eat with us?"

"Mr. Lutz!"

"Why are you surprised? I've always wanted a chance to return your kindness, Mrs. Olesh."

"But, but this," she held out the Testament.

"That's not payment for the dinner you gave me 'way back there. You'll come then?"

Anna hesitated. "Oh, thank you, Mr. Lutz," she answered. "And Mrs. Lutz. But no," she took a step, "not this time."

Mr. Lutz took a step too. "Remember," he said, "you won't be able to get a train back before two. You'll be hungry before you get home. We'd be glad to have you, but we won't insist."

Anna thought.

"You're welcome," he said gently.

"I can't," came her answer. "No, not this time."

She wanted to laugh and cry at the same time. She wanted to run, run until she found John somewhere in that strange big city in America, explain to him how all this came about, and ask him what to do. She could see his anxious, disappointed, startled eyes on her. She was completely overwhelmed with both fear and gratitude. She could not comprehend this personal interest, this unusual kindness from the man, Mr. Lutz. Never before in her life had anyone given her similar attention.

131

Right then, Anna wasn't at all certain she'd be hungry by noon. Her stomach quivered at the thought of eating.

Suddenly tears almost blinded her. She felt bruised and crippled, torn by indecision. Should she give the Testament back to Mr. Lutz, apologize for waiting, and make a bee-line to town before she could hear another word from his lips? She saw before her, in a pitiful heap, every resolution broken. She knew it would mean misery, old and new, in unbearable days ahead.

She took another step to go.

"Mr. Lutz," she cried in distress. "The Mother!" She choked. "The Holy Mother Mary," she clutched the Testament in both her trembling hands, "she'll be greatly displeased with me now. And John—John—" Without another word she bit her lip, slipped the Testament deep into her jacket pocket, and hurried away.

Anna took a quick backward glance before leaving the cobblestone walk. Mr. Lutz was still quietly watching her.

It took Anna quite a while to calm herself. She was still nervous and excited when she took the hundred dollars the cashier in the bank handed her through the iron-barred window. After counting it twice, she tied it securely in her handkerchief and tucked it into her inside jacket pocket. Her knees felt weak and uncertain; so she leaned hard against the building when she got outside the bank, and tried to decide where to go from there. Not often had she been in Daruvar, and now everything seemed unfamiliar. Down the street she noticed a mill sign. She'd go there first and price corn meal, and unless it was cheaper than in Vilieki Bastaji, she wouldn't buy any.

During the next hour as Anna walked from store to store, her arms full of sacks and bundles, she pressed her right elbow against the little book in her right-hand pocket. It was still there.

Noon came. Anna could not convince herself that she

132

should accept the dinner invitation, though she had a definite desire to meet Mrs. Lutz. But she was getting hungrier every minute. The hands on the clock in the dry-goods store where she purchased yarn pointed to noon. "But why should I go there?" she asked herself. She made the sign of the cross, moved her lips in prayer, gathered up her bundles, and walked out.

In a bakery shop window, freshly baked loaves of bread in several sizes were stacked on wire racks. Anna stopped. It looked good. She stepped inside. It smelled delicious. She placed her bundles on the counter, took out her money, and counted the change. It would take so much to ride the train back to Vilieki Bastaji and so much to pay back the storekeeper.

"Yes, ma'am," greeted the plump, red-faced baker, wiping his hands on the corner of his soiled apron.

"Do you have any stale, or damaged, or—or little loaves, sir?" Anna inquired. "I mean that you'd sell for half price?"

The baker nodded wordlessly and reached under the counter.

"Here you are, ma'am," he said, pushing a small crippled loaf across the counter.

"How much?"

"Got a copper?"

Anna fingered her change.

"If you haven't, ma'am, it'll be all right this time."

"I have. Thank you, sir."

Slowly Anna made her way back to the train depot. Once she glanced shyly over toward the cement-block building, just long enough to read the sign in the window. She chose an empty bench in the farthest corner of the waiting room, placed her bundles on it, then seated herself in the midst of them. For at least thirty minutes she sat motionless, one hand pressed tightly around the book in her pocket. A few people came into the depot, bought tickets, and sat down on one of the benches in front of her. No one seemed to notice her and she was glad.

"Well, William," remarked Mrs. Lutz, placing a bowl of steaming mush on the table, "it looks as though your lady from Miletinac isn't coming."

"She's filled with fear, Agnes. I don't remember when I met a person the Spirit was dealing with more gently."

"Gently?"

"Yes. She's having a real battle on right now, I dare say. In her fear and superstition, she wasn't sure she was going to take the Testament, yet the Spirit so gently had her take it, and slip it into her pocket. While the children are washing their hands, let's just bow our heads in a word of prayer for her."

"Of course, William. Apart from the aid of the Spirit the Testament will mean nothing to her, and your efforts will be useless."

The five Lutz children, ranging in age from six to fourteen, understood well why they were living in Daruvar. They shared reverently in the concerns, disappointments, and victories of their parents. They had often heard them mention Mr. and Mrs. Olesh in prayer, along with a long list of other unsaved souls. Lillie, the oldest, had frequently prayed, too, for this couple in Miletinac who had showed kindness to her dear father, but who were bound in spiritual darkness.

They listened intently as their father told of his experience with the precious young mother, Mrs. Olesh, who boarded the train at Vilieki Bastaji.

"David," said Mr. Lutz to his eight-year-old, "I'm going to ask you to do something. You'll have time before you go back to school."

"To do what?"

"Mrs. Olesh is a young woman with a pretty face and big brown eyes. She's wearing a black kerchief on her head, a dark blue dress and jacket. Listen, you go over and see if there's anyone in the depot who looks like that, will you?"

"Why, Papa?"

"We invited her to come here for dinner, but she's too timid. It'll be night before she gets home. Think how hungry she'll be."

"And what shall I tell her?"

"Don't say anything to her. Just walk all through and around the depot and come back."

David was soon back. "She's in there; I saw her."

"All right. Thank you, David. Now you children run off to school. I'll have Mother take her something to eat."

"But she was eatin'," said David.

"Eating what?"

"Bread."

"Are you sure?"

"I saw her. I walked right past her. She was sitting back in the corner."

"Did she see you, David?"

"She never looked up."

"You're sure she was eating?"

"Sure she was. She had some bread in one hand. And she was reading the Testament you gave her."

"Really, David?" exclaimed Mr. and Mrs. Lutz in unison.

"Go, see for yourself," answered the boy. "She was reading so hard she never noticed me walking past her."

"Praise God!" exclaimed the boy's father. "No, indeed, I won't go over to find out. Mother," he said softly, "we'll kneel this time to pray. Run along now, David, and the rest of you children, or you'll all be late for school."

It was a tired, troubled Anna who lay awake that night until long past midnight. She awoke early the next morning with a strange heaviness around her puckered eyes, and a painful weight deep in her chest, the kind of weight that often follows nightmarish and fitful sleep. The children were evenly, peacefully breathing in sound sleep. Anna clasped her hands under the back of her head and tried to patch together fragments of the dream that trailed across her conscious mind.

She sighed. She tossed. She stared searchingly at the monotonous brown ceiling. The dream. It was coming back bit by bit. Yes. John, stranded in quicksand, somewhere between Vilieki Bastaji and Daruvar. She had heard him calling to her from some faraway place for help. Frantically she ran, stumbled, ran again, through brush, over rocks, and wet, slippery, sometimes steep places, until she found him. He was sinking slowly until he was past waist deep in the treacherous, horrible sand that would soon take him forever from her sight. With arms outstretched he was pleading for her to help him. She had screamed and cried in her dream until she woke with a start, trembling, her heart pounding violently.

Anna scolded herself. "Just a bad dream," she said. She got up and dressed. She tiptoed across the room and made sure each child was sound asleep.

From under the mattress she drew out the Testament and held it in both hands for several minutes, then without opening it, tucked it back where it had been all night.

"Dear John," she wrote, "I hardly know how to begin this letter." Her hand shook. Her head dropped on her arm.

Chapter 16

One at a time John added other words to his English vocabulary. Alone in his dingy, poorly heated room, above a barber shop in one of the low-rent districts of Harrisburg, he repeated over and over and aloud, words, phrases, and sentences he wanted to master. It helped to pass the long, lonely evenings. John never went out at night except on walks.

At times there loomed up in him terrible feelings of insecurity, sometimes with rude and shocking suddenness—not only financial insecurity, but emotional and spiritual, with deep inexpressible yearnings. It troubled him, for he had determined that this time he would not be the victim of despondency while away from home. These times were distinctly disappointing and in an effort to pull himself out of them, he'd write to Anna. As his heart grew more lonely, he tried desperately to hide the fact from her by making each letter sound happier than the one before.

Had he ever worked harder? No. Had he ever skimped more to save toward that dream farm in Miletinac?

DEAR ANNA,

Another week has rolled around already; so winter is a little shorter for you and the dear children, and spring a little closer. Before long I plan to send you another hundred. Keep your eyes open for a place. I can hardly wait. My hands itch to plant and tend and reap, to feed my beloved family. Tell me things about each of the children. To raise a family in a big city like this is no good thing. That I am more convinced of every day. I am glad you are where you are.

No, Anna, I have not attended a church here yet. I would be at a loss to know which one to go to. I am only as a visitor in America. If you were here with me and we lived here, it would be quite a different thing. To be sure, I pray every day even though most of the men at the works say we might as well jabber to the wind. I am depending on you to pray, not only for yourself, but for the children and for me. I will leave it up to you from now on, to decide how much to give the father. I would not think of going to church here without an offering, and I'd rather it would go to our own priest back home.

Please write and tell me all is well, and that you have enough to eat. Save what you can, but don't ever go hungry. Never worry about me, for I'm getting along fine.

With love,

JOHN

But John had a strange gnawing pain with unusual heaviness around his heart when he walked back from the mailbox that evening. Something inside cried out in silent anguish. Doubts about God and religion, and a sense of the futility of life, ate at his very soul. He tried to ignore it, evade it, shake it off. He walked several blocks north, then east, and tried to read the signs in every shop window. That brought no relief.

As he continued walking, he began to search for one happy face, but found not one that impressed him as being really happy. Had no one found a real joy in life? Was everyone as lonely and dissatisfied as he? Slowly he went back to his room.

The next evening the letter came, the letter Anna had started the third time before she finally finished it. He hurried home, tossed his hat on the bed, and tore it open with eagerness.

DEAR JOHN,

The next day after I received your letter with the money order, I went to Daruvar. Mother stayed with the children. It was for me a very exciting day, the train ride, cashing the money order, and getting what we so much needed.

138

In Daruvar I bought yarn to make the children and myself new scuffs, also bought thread, ten pounds of cornmeal, five pounds of sugar, five of beans, salt, and matches. That was all I could carry home; so the next day I went back to Vilieki and bought flour, turnips, and oil.

I am still tired from the two trips, but how thankful we are for what you've done to make all this possible. I have a little more than ninety-two left, and it's safe under the mattress. I won't spend any more of it unless I absolutely have to.

Joseph was very sick yesterday, and during the night. I don't know yet what was wrong with him. For a while I was almost afraid I'd have to send Father to Daruvar for medicine, but before noon today his fever broke, and he's a lot better. I am much relieved, as you can know.

John, please, do not be angry with me, but I've got to tell you something. I'm almost afraid to, for I know it will be hard for you to understand how it all came about. I fear that after all that has taken place in the past years, and after what we've both pledged each other, you'll lose all confidence in me.

John's heart beat rapidly. He stepped close to the window, clutching the letter.

It all happened so unexpectedly. Even now as I try to relate it to you, it seems almost like a fairy tale, yet it's not. Oh, John! Please don't be very angry with me. It's this. The man from Daruvar. Yes, that Mr. Lutz was on the train when I got on at Vilieki Bastaji. I didn't notice him but he saw me, and remembered me. He remembered everything we talked about that day, and little Mary. He asked about her.

I was greatly surprised when he asked to sit down beside me, and made himself friendly. He talked to me until we reached Daruvar. He told me that neither Holy Mother Mary nor the saints hear or answer our prayers. He says he knows, and can prove it by the Bible. He offered me a New Testament.

John's arms sagged. He almost let the letter slip from his hands.

I must not let you think that he forced it upon me, John, for he didn't.

After we got off the train, he asked me if I would wait until he hurried over to his house to get it for me. I waited. John, that's the part I fear you won't be able to understand. I'm not at all sure I can explain it either. I didn't want to wait, yet I did. I felt terrible to stay, yet I would have felt worse not to. John, did you ever go through such an experience about something, about anything? There seemed to be two of me, two voices inside, two somethings tearing me both ways. If ever I wished for you, I did then. You may be horrified, or even angry with me, John, although I have never seen you so. I am almost afraid to tell you all this, yet I am more afraid not to. I don't want to keep anything from you. In fact, I can't do it, John, and feel right in my heart.

Will you be upset very much over this, John? I hope not. Will you be upset when I tell you I have the Testament under the mattress, and that I've been reading in it every morning before the children wake up? No, they do not know it's in the house and no one else either. I must admit I'm a little interested in what I've been reading in this section called John. It seems so real. I can't explain it. But I wish you had one like it, and could read on pages 135 and 136. Better yet, I wish you were here and we could read together. You are older and wiser than I am.

Now if you think I have been very wicked, tell me, John. For some reason the pages I've read make me love you more than ever before. Truly, John, I want to do what's right by you, and by God and the father and our family. Don't think that now I'm about ready to lay down the religion we've been raised up in. I'm not. I'm only interested in knowing what's so important in this book, and in knowing why Mr. Lutz believes what he does, and what it is that makes him so kind and friendly, and different. If he is wrong at all in his belief, then he is terribly wrong. And I want to know it before we should ever happen to meet again. I could write much more, but the letter would get too long. If the weather is nice on Sunday, I will ask Mother to stay with the children and go to church.

Mary sends "Papa dear" much love, and Kathrine is repeating the same words right now. Joseph can say several new words. I wish you could hear him try to help when Kathrine and Mary sing together.

As always,
Many loves,
ANNA

John read the letter again, then sat by the window, gazing down into the busy street until long past dark, past his usual suppertime, but with no thought of eating. Finally he got up, lit the gas light, and read the letter once more before he tucked it in the top dresser drawer.

He did not answer it that night, nor the next, nor the next.

Anxiously, Anna waited. It was a week past the usual time to receive a letter, when it came. Her father brought it to her, smiling triumphantly, and sat down to enjoy its contents with her.

"Come to Grandpa, Joe," he said. "Sit here on my knee while Mother reads the letter to us."

The little fellow obeyed. But Anna had to try hard to hide her nervous anxiety. Carefully she opened the letter with her paring knife. She felt weak and her hands trembled. Slowly she pulled the folded pages from the envelope.

"Let me read it—to myself first—Father," she said feebly. "Please, if you don't mind."

Her father tapped the floor with his heels. "Hurry then," he remarked, "for I'm in a rush. I'm on my way to Vilieki Bastaji. We're out of flour and matches."

"In that case," suggested Anna, clasping the letter against her breast, "why don't you stop in on your way back? You'll have to be going, Father, if—if you want Mother to have fresh bread for supper."

"Well," he said, "all right then."

Anna thought that her father acted a little hurt, as well as a little disappointed, when he set baby Joe down and stepped out of the house. "Do come back," she touched his arm. She stood quietly at the door for several minutes before unfolding the letter.

"Will this one make you cry because you're so glad for the money?" asked Mary, eyes widening.

"Papa didn't send any money in this one, dear," she answered softly. "Don't you want to get Joe a drink so he'll be quiet while I read what Papa has to say?"

"Of course."

DEAR ANNA,

At first I was stunned at what you wrote in your last letter. But I was not angry with you. I am not angry now, even though I cannot quite understand why you accepted the Testament after you promised so faithfully never to allow yourself to become unsettled again with anything that Mr. Lutz had to say. I hate to think of you living now with the distressing and disturbing thoughts you once experienced. I remember all the things you told me the morning I came home the last time, when Kathrine was a baby. Are you happy now? Or do you lie awake and fret and worry and cry at night? If you do, you'd better burn that Testament at once. You say it makes you love me more? Good. But I can't understand why or how. However, if that is true, then read it some more, for I can't have too much love.

I do get lonely for you and the children. But my time here is half spent now. I plan to come home in September. Although I am really quite alarmed over your taking the Testament, Anna, I will not say I have lost all confidence in you. If you had kept all this from me and I would find it out later, that would both hurt and disappoint me greatly. I trust you, and I believe you want to do what's right. If you can keep this secret and read in it without getting all unstrung and upset, I won't object too much. If you want to read the book purely for information, it may be all

142

right. This is my answer after thinking it over for several days. More than anything else, I want you to be happy now, to stay happy all the time while I'm gone, and above all, to be happy when I come home. I haven't any idea what's in the book, but I must admit you have me wondering now. Be very careful and don't let Mary and Kathrine know you have it, or they might tell someone. You know what could happen then and we don't want to ever experience anything like that, if we can possibly avoid it. We must respect our parents and the father. I do hope God and Holy Mother Mary both understand how it all happened. Please don't take to heart everything Mr. Lutz told you, Anna. Do be careful if you go to Daruvar again. I'm not angry, but I am very, very anxious about you. I'm also anxious to come home and see for myself what's so important in that book. I can't warn you enough to take care, and let no one learn that you have it in the house.

Yours,
JOHN

"Mother," exclaimed Mary, searching her mother's face as she came over and stood squarely in front of her, "why do you look so sober?"

"Oh. Do I really?" Anna tried to smile. She stroked Mary's head gently.

"Isn't Papa all right?"

"Well, yes. Yes, of course he is. I'm sure he is, dear."

"Didn't he tell you in the letter?"

"I haven't quite finished reading it; just wait a second." Anna scanned the last few sentences, and folded the letter. "Your papa is coming home in September," she said with tenderness.

"September? When will that be?"

"Four and a half more months."

"Is that very long?"

"Plenty long," she answered with a sigh and a faraway

143

look, "long for us, but longer for him."

"Why?"

"Because we have each other, dear. But Papa is all alone in America."

"Poor Papa," exclaimed Mary.

"You know what would make Papa happy when he comes home?"

"What?"

"If you could teach Joseph to sing, like you did Kathrine."

"I will," agreed Mary. "Come here, Joseph. We'll begin right now. Come, you and Kathrine, sit on the little bench beside me."

Anna was determined to win the battle. She dared not let what happened nor anything in the book make her unhappy. John's letter had been beyond her expectations. Parts of it gave her definite relief from anxiety. Life from that day on was never quite the same. She rose before dawn almost every morning, tiptoed across the room, bathed her face in cold water, then drew from under the mattress the hidden book.

One morning verse fourteen in John four held her attention. Over and over she read it. "But whosoever drinketh of the water that I shall give him shall never thirst; but the water that I shall give him shall be in him a well of water springing up into everlasting life."

Anna closed her eyes for a moment while her one hand smoothed the pages of the open book. "Beautiful," she whispered under her breath, "but who can understand it?"

Chapter 17

Her feet clad in the new black yarn scuffs, Anna stepped from the train at the Daruvar station, and with quick purpose hurried straight for the bank to cash her second hundred-dollar money order. This time she did not so much as glance toward the building across the tracks.

For the past two weeks the questions she wanted to ask Mr. Lutz had rapidly multiplied. She had even marked with her pencil a dozen or more verses in the Book of John that she wondered about most. But John had warned her to be very careful, and she intended to carry out his request. If there was any asking for explanations on what she had read thus far (she told herself), it could be postponed until John came home. Perhaps he, too, would like to have satisfying answers to the same, and they could inquire together (should they ever have an occasion to go to Daruvar together), or John alone could do the inquiring. So Anna made her purchases and returned home without seeing a sign of Mr. Lutz.

In her new life of early morning reading, there was one thing that gave her a feeling of encouragement, comfort, and hope. John had not been angry with her, and more than that, he had written that he was anxious to come home and read in the book, too. She kept that letter in the Testament, and occasionally reread it.

True enough, however, she read passages that were not only perplexing, but disturbing, that gave her a sense of undoneness. She couldn't exactly interpret how she felt, but it was there. An inner restlessness, a longing, a looking forward to something really satisfying, at some future time. Either that, she told herself, or forget the whole silly business again. She must be happy when John came home. She must be.

One morning, when she was reading in the first chapter of Acts, Anna closed the Testament, drew a deep breath, shook her head, and chucked it back under the mattress. "No use," she sighed wearily. "Beyond me to understand it. I dare say only a few people in the world do and I'm not smart enough to be one of those few." A deep disappointment gripped her sensitive spirit. For three consecutive mornings after that, Anna woke at the usual time, but instead of getting up to read, she lay thinking until the children wakened.

On the fourth morning, however, for some reason, she got out the Testament again, and standing close to the window, read slowly, carefully, some of the verses she had previously marked. "He that believeth on the Son hath everlasting life: and he that believeth not the Son shall not see life; but the wrath of God abideth on him." "Wrath of God," she repeated seriously, "what is the wrath of God?" "I am the good shepherd, and know my sheep, and am known of mine." She read it again. "Heaven and earth shall pass away: but my words shall not pass away." She read that twice. "Ask, and ye shall receive, that your joy may be full." "My joy?" whispered Anna, looking out through the wide, quiet street of Miletinac; "how would that make my joy full? How can I receive? What shall I ask?" She turned several pages. "Without me ye can do nothing." "Do nothing?" she whispered, knitting her brow. She shook her head. "Blessed are they that have not seen, and yet have believed." She paged again. Her eyes caught these words: "All things, whatsoever ye shall ask in prayer, believing, ye shall receive." Anna pressed the closed book against her throbbing heart, while her bowed head touched the window casing. "O God," she prayed silently, as she drew in a long deep breath, "I suppose maybe you know what it is I need. I don't. But someday I hope I will."

Anna did a remarkable job of appearing happy before her children, her neighbors and parents. In fact, no one would have guessed she was even holding any problem conferences within herself. Nearly all of May was spent.

The Sunday after she cashed the second money order she, with two other young women, walked the twelve miles to church in Djulovac.

Anna had a feeling that she ought to go, not so much for her own sake as for the sake of the villagers.

The day was perfect. Beyond the lush green fields, starred with yellow buttercups, stood the majestic dark pines. The air was fresh, yet balmy, and the countryside all the way was enlivened with an incense-like fragrance from thousands of wild roses, nestled in the grass on either side of the road.

Anna enjoyed the earthy smell of the prelude to summer: the fruit trees in blossom, the freshly planted vegetable gardens, the beautiful wooded hills in the distance. She enjoyed also the friendly chat with her two companions, the one a childless young wife, the other a mother of two small toddlers. They talked about everything from seeds in the hand to bread in the mouth, from husbands to Heaven, everything of common interest to young women in beautiful Yugoslavia.

As she passed him at the door of the church, Anna placed three coins in Father Markum's hand. Nodding, the priest tapped her gently on the arm with his finger tips. "Faithful daughter," he said in a kind, muffled voice, and smiling, looked straight down into her eyes. His were almost luminous. Anna was surprised, quite taken back. She did not know whether he was that well pleased with her offering, amused, or trying to be extra friendly. He said nothing to the other two women. Quickly she walked to her pew, dropped on her knees, and bowed her head. A train of thoughts, not prayer; a storm of thoughts, not prayer.

On the way home, Anna had very little to say. She enjoyed the out-of-doors, the beautiful scenery, the walk with her friends, but was she glad she had gone to church? Was it worth the effort? Was she any better for going? Any nearer to God? When she went to bed that night the questions in her mind were still unanswered. She rolled. She tossed. She begged for sleep.

Three weeks passed.

DEAR JOHN,   *June 20, 1907*

Miletinac was never more beautiful than now. I hope you'll be pleased when I tell you that today I made a payment of one hundred and fifty dollars on a twelve-acre farm, the Wakgri place south. You know. They are moving to Vilieki in three or four weeks. The house is in fairly good condition. We will be living in it when you come home, and I'll have a late garden started. I'm so happy about it, John, and Mary is really excited. I have been sending up special prayers for such a place and I'm sure you have been too. Ever since you left, I've been watching and inquiring around as you told me to, and when this opened up I felt sure it was the farm for us. Now we can raise more pumpkins, potatoes, beans, and turnips.

Oh, John, I can hardly wait for you to come home and help me. I hope now you will never again need to leave us. We'll try as never before to make ends meet. The children are well and surely have good appetites. The Testament, yes, it's still securely hidden under the mattress and I'll take extra care of it when we move. Don't worry. The more I read it, the more I love you and the children, but it's true as truth, the less I think of myself. This morning I read this, "Draw nigh to God, and he will draw nigh to you." I hope it's true, but I don't know how to draw nigh to God. Would you? I think it will take me years to understand just a little of this strange, strange book. I am not surprised now that many people are not interested in taking or buying one. Neither can I explain why I have such an urge to open it again and again and read these strange sayings. Can it be that I want to know more about God than all these my good neighbors do? Well, I'll admit, John, that I do. Every time the children look up into my face with their bright questioning eyes I have a terrible desire to be able to answer their many honest questions and to lead them into the truth. No one ever really did that for us. We just grew up.

Now that I've written you about the farm I can hardly wait till you get this. Bring just a little something for each of the children if you can. Never mind about me. All I want is you, dear John, and your fatherly help to raise these lovable, sweet children of ours.

Your faithful one,
ANNA

The letter was sobering to John Olesh. It made him gravely conscious as never before that whatever the future held of good or bad for his family was keenly his responsibility. Anna would do more than her share, to be sure. But John felt a sudden lonely sort of freedom, a freedom to do but one thing and do it to perfection if it cost him his life. He wanted to prove not only to his wife and children but to all the world that America had no attraction, no growing interest, apart from the opportunity it gave him to help them to a higher, happier plane of existence. Every thought, every ounce of energy would be spent in the light of their happiness and security.

All the way home John was planning. As he sat or strolled or stood on deck during the days of his ocean voyage, his gaze fixed on the glass-clear endless Atlantic, he saw but one thing, his own ocean of opportunity with responsibility as deep as the sea and as high as the open heavens above him. He was going home to the most beautiful spot on earth, he mused; not so because of the scenic mountain formations, nor the fruitfulness of the lush valleys, nor the awe-inspiring sunsets, but because it was where he'd find the trusting, responsive eyes of his beloved kerchiefed Yugoslavian queen.

"Lonely?"

John jumped. The eyes in the long peaked face of the six-footer beside him looked down into his as though he had been assigned some very important prophecy to be delivered from the oracles of the high priest. "The truest hearts sometimes waste away in the pangs of separation and privation, you know." The man had a forefinger hanging limp in both vest pockets.

Mouth open, John nodded, not knowing to what, even though the gentleman had spoken in his own native tongue. "Ah — sir," stammered John. He was conscious of his awkwardness at the moment.

"Now cheer up, mate," continued the six-footer, placing one unsteady hand on John's shoulder. He produced a sickish smile. "Fate and love are not always tyrants. No indeed. We must learn how to master ourselves in the throes of whatever becomes ours to face. Even a death. That's hard to say, I know, but we dare not allow ourselves to appeal to the sympathy or pity of others." The gentleman knit his heavy eyebrows and looked out over the blank green waters. "For pity ofttimes is cruel, yes, cruel," he repeated. "Envious, hostile, stinging our souls like nettles. Certainly. That's it. I say it over and over to myself daily, hourly." Here the man drew a laborious breath. "Though I face what the fates would call open defeat, I must and I will keep alive a pulse of joy in my breast." Lightly the man patted himself below the chin. "Which assures me right now, yes, even right now, that in the midst of seeming failure with all its disappointments and blasted dreams there is delight and satisfaction in having once tried. I may soon die and someone else more fortunate will kiss my dreams when I am stiff and cold and forgotten, forgotten. You must do the same, sir."

John stepped back speechless. He ran both hands deep

into his pockets. He fumbled with a few coins. The man's hand on his shoulder became increasingly heavy.

"You're from Yugoslavia," John ventured, trying to compose himself. He cleared his husky throat.

"From Bitola. And you?"

"Miletinac."

"Never heard of the place."

"It's not far from Daruvar."

"Bitola's 'way down in the southeastern corner of Yugoslavia. Going home, sir?"

"Yes. Home." John was not conscious that when he spoke his eyes became vivid with life.

"To stay?" The man drew back, arms dropping limp.

"I hope."

"Hope?" His whisper sounded like a breeze playing through the pine-coned forest.

"Why not? My wife is there." John's pupils dilated. "And three children waiting to welcome me. I'm going home!" shouted John.

"Ah," sighed the man with a sad groan. "To mix your cards and mine I see now it is very unhealthful." He turned, but took only one step. "At least for me. And for you too. Your loneliness will soon be over, but not my own."

"Explain," cried John with sudden impetuousness. "You're a perfect stranger. I don't seem to be getting the drift of what you're telling me."

"As I supposed." The gentleman faced John, stroking his face. He had an expression of being frightened at himself.

"Explain," repeated John. "You thought I was lonely and at the same time you —"

"Ah, that's it," interrupted the man. "I seem to have no concept of the difficulties I still must master." There was a thin clarity in his words. "I must practice, I see, extraordinary critical expressions for sufficient self-control to safeguard the purity of the class I belonged to. Even though the noose is

151

around my very neck, so to speak, I must repeat, repeat, repeat this ideal — this philosophy in order to quell the evil hideous spirit that looms up within me. Broken in health and, they tell me, in mind also. Sent home to die and be forgotten. I cannot believe it. Yet I must."

"Who?" insisted John. "Who, sir? Explain."

Distress, depression, and consternation froze the man's face. He looked almost ghastly. "Started out to be a priest," he whispered at long length.

John waited with furrowed brow.

"For life." The man's hands grew moist with nervous sweat. "And now the noose. Got an incurable disease, they told me — in here." He pointed a bony finger to his heart. "And in here." To his head.

The ashen face came maddeningly close to John's. He drew back. The man turned abruptly and, with feet dragging, disappeared. John did not follow. Frantic impulses leaped into his thoughts and, with hands clasped behind him, he stood in the same spot until the supper gong was heard. Slowly, reluctantly, he followed the line of passengers to the third-class dining room.

Chapter 18

On into the night John walked around on deck, aimlessly and in complete silence, trying to forget the incident. The night was practically windless and an almost hidden moon tipped the clouds. He stood at last without moving, one hand gripping tightly the other wrist behind him. He very emphatically did not want the strange creature to run into him again, yet irresistibly he found himself focusing his attention on the face of every tall man, long enough to be convinced it was not he.

He stood at last as if not exactly sure where he was, so frantically was he struggling with things the man had said and with the man himself. He tried to understand why any man who started out to be a priest would arrive at such a state. He surely was being most cruelly treated or was cruelly disillusioned. Should he report this to Father Markum for just and proper investigation? Or dismiss the entire incident? Or—and John's eyes brightened at the sudden idea. The man may have been jesting, acting the clown for the sport of watching John's reaction. He recalled now that the man's eyes had snapped with suddenness from gloom to self-defense; from despair to a sort of trickery. Yes, he remembered. And yet he had such a deeply rooted look of fear.

John shrugged. Why bother or wonder or stew about a quirk from 'way down south? A stranger who had disappeared as suddenly as he had appeared? They would soon be lost from each other forever.

Then like a smoldering ember in the underbrush, memory fanned his thoughts into a blaze. Clearing his throat he dropped both arms and stood stiff, erect as a marble pillar, his eyes fixed intently on the silent shifting cloud-waves playing around the moon in the sea-heavens.

"Lutz," he said to himself. "The man from Daruvar could help the man in despair if anyone could. I do believe it."

But before John walked off the gangplank the next morning he had crammed the stranger, Lutz, and the little Testament all into the back of his mind in a carefully prepared forget-it-all pigeonhole. He wouldn't relate the incident to Anna. And the Testament—well, he'd let her bring up the matter and if it really was very important she would.

A dozen pulses throbbed within him as he hurried, head erect, eyes direct and clear, steps brisk, toward the train depot in Le Havre. A tinge of frost in the morning air painted his eager face a healthy deep red. He was going home! Home to make a new start on a new place. Truly God, and the Holy Mother Mary of the Christ child, had helped him these past almost ten months to find employment. He whistled half under his breath.

And Anna. John's steps quickened. He tingled with anticipation. His compressed lips stretched into a delicate smile. To have his feet on earth again made him surprisingly refreshed. He wanted to feel its moist softness, and seed it with his bare hands, and watch his children eat of the fruits it bore.

It was a joyous reunion. Joseph turned somersaults to give vent to his happiness. To this John laughed outright repeatedly.

"Josie, you little mischief," exclaimed John. "Are you actually that glad I've come home?"

In the weeks following John's third home-coming he and Anna were drawn together with the immensity of their love. It was not a demonstrative, irrational sort of affection that diminished with the passing weeks, but a continuous, growing understanding and appreciation for each other, with a mutual desire to please, satisfy, gratify.

154

With their three alert, fast-growing, and affectionate children they both had ample opportunity to have their parental love tested, strengthened, demonstrated.

Anna, as John had expected, had made a good choice of property. The fall lettuce, onions, and turnips were flourishing in sturdy top greenness. Cress, the milk cow, was content on a plot of thick pasture grass. The house was common but cozy and the roof did not leak. Each of the children had developed physically and mentally far beyond his expectations. But best of all, Anna was more energetic than ever, even though she was deluged with work. Her large brown eyes glowingly searched John's face with kind, intimate smiles as she nodded approvingly at his daily accomplished tasks. What could give a husband and wife more true satisfaction than the pleasure of working, planning, planting, reaping together? Of all the hard-working wives in Miletinac, John was sure Anna was the most efficient, and more than that, the most beautiful.

It came up one afternoon when John and Anna were busy in the turnip patch. She was cutting off and stacking the tops in one basket, the turnips in another, as fast as John pulled them. Side by side they had been busy at this since the noon lunch, moving back and forth steadily across the patch, talking little, but in the mutual quietness of love and adoration. "Never saw nicer turnips, Anna," John had said at the outset. To this Anna agreed.

"Must have had just the right amount of rain," he mentioned minutes later. "Wonderful turnips." To this Anna agreed smiling.

They worked on in silence, enjoying a communication beyond the handling of turnips. Anna was certain John was buried in the interests of his little family and perhaps thinking intently about the opportunities the twelve acres could produce for their welfare. He had expressed repeatedly to her his vital concern about the children's growth and problems, especially Mary's with her one stiff knee. But so far she had been doing remarkably well under Elizabeth's thrice-weekly calls for private tutoring. She could sing, print, read, and memorize better than the average child her age.

Anna wasn't going to be the one to bring up the subject. She had vowed that within herself before John came home, and had stamped the vow with another when she saw him coming toward her, half running, half shouting, half crying for joy.

"Anna!" he had cried, his whole face bursting into a glad smile.

"John!"

"Mother!" He turned long enough to take in Mary, Kathrine, and handsome little Joseph all in one loving glance. "Mother of my children," he whispered in Anna's ear. He had said the last three words softly, increasing their tenderness. Anna's heart hammered with happiness.

John seemed overjoyed to be home again. Why bring up anything to hamper their happiness? She wouldn't. Not this time. Perhaps John had found it. In America. He said he'd try. But she would not quiz him. He was the head of the home and must take the lead now, about things on the farm and in the major decisions of life. Regrettably she had too often been the instigator and promoter of unrest and spiritual bewilderment.

The New Testament was in its usual hiding place under the mattress. Anna could think of no better, safer place to put it. It would stay there until John asked for it or took it out of his own accord. She had written and told him where she kept it. If he wanted to see it, he could help himself, but she would not shove it under his nose. He must take the initiative.

Weeks passed. No mention was made of the book under the mattress. Anna wondered tormentedly. Yet she outsmiled and outsang those wonderings. She missed her before-breakfast readings greatly at first, but as the days ran into a month she got accustomed to it. It was like dieting. The craving lessened.

John went to the Djulovac church once. That was largely, Anna was certain, because his father insisted so vigorously. On John's return he made but one significant comment and that was in reply to Anna's pointed question.

"How did Father Markum impress you this time, John?" she asked, trying to appear calm.

He looked at her for a moment, then tore his gaze from her wide-open eyes and looked out the kitchen window. "Well," he said at length with a note of gloomy dissatisfaction, "I don't want to judge any man, let alone a man of God as Father Markum surely is but," he stroked his hand across his lips, "he seems sort of worldly-wise—smooth. It seems as though he enjoys looking down on us." John took a step closer to Anna and gripped her shoulders with both his hands until it almost hurt. "But, Anna," he said as he looked her straight in both eyes, "remember you are not to quote me. You are not to be persuaded nor to draw any conclusions from me. I've become too critical since seeing more of the world." He shook her slightly in his firm grasp. "Anna."

"Yes."

"Remember."

"Yes."

"Go on thinking what you always have of the father."

"Yes."

"Let's not discuss it again."

"Why?"

"Because."

"Because why?"

"Enough, Anna. We're happier not to. Let's remain so." He smiled down into her uplifted face and catching it in the cup of his two hands planted an affectionate kiss on her forehead.

After that Anna was more determined than ever that she would not be the one to start a discussion about Father Markum or any other spiritual leader. The New Testament remained untouched where she had tucked it in a folded scrap of woolen cloth under the mattress.

John handed Anna another crisp, juicy turnip. "You know," he said, "time surely flies. Almost before we realize it we'll be sowing more turnip seed in this ground."

"And I was just thinking about ground and seeds this very minute," chuckled Anna softly. Yet her expression was serious.

"How?" John handed her another turnip.

"Oh, nothing."

"Well, go on. What is it? Wasn't I right?"

"Ever so right, John. Yes, we'll be sowing seeds again

158

soon. Seeds are such wonderful little things, aren't they? Or is it the ground they fall on?"

"Takes both."

"I know. They're both made by God, aren't they?"

"Suppose so."

"Suppose? We know that much, don't we?"

"Why, yes." John looked up sharply. "And what were you about to say?"

It was a subject Anna could postpone no longer. Her eyes, modestly downcast for only a split second, met his inquiring ones.

"I read about seeds and different kinds of ground in the— in the," Anna's legs trembled, but her voice remained calm and sweet, "little book Mr. Lutz gave me, John."

He dropped the turnip in his hand. He stood waiting for the next sentence which Anna suddenly determined not to say. She had failed. She had broken her vow. But the ripeness of the opportunity had been irresistible. Out of the abundance of her inmost heart the words had slipped, for all that afternoon in her mind she had seen seeds from the hand of a sower falling on good, rich, ready, newly tilled ground that bore a hundredfold.

John's earth-soiled hands closed. "The book?"

"Yes."

"You still have it?"

"Why, yes. Of course, John."

"Under the mattress?"

"Yes."

"Who knows?"

"No one. No one but you, John."

"You're sure?"

"Absolutely sure, John. Are you afraid because it's there?"

John smiled faintly. Hunger for something shone in his eyes. "I won't admit that," he answered. "Maybe I should be, but," and he clasped one soiled hand firmly over the other to grip his words to his own determination, "I'm not." He laughed and a look of fresh courage edged itself across his ruddy face.

Anna could scarcely speak for the lump that came suddenly in her throat. A sort of guilty delight mingled with optimism made her tingle.

"And so?"

"Well," he said a little hesitatingly, "if I'm not afraid, guess it wouldn't hurt if I'd get it out and take a peek in it when no one's looking."

"I've—I've been waiting for you to say something first, John."

"Me?"

"Yes. I've waited, not wanting to spoil your happiness. I seldom missed reading in it a while each morning before the children woke up, but since you came—"

"Why have you changed?"

Anna fumbled for an answer. "I—I really haven't, John."

"You haven't?"

"No."

"But when—where then have you been reading?"

"I haven't been."

"Then you have changed since I came home, at least on that point."

She admitted it. Insistent thoughts started working. "Well, John, you see, I thought you should ask. The book is there. It's yours as much as it is mine."

"You modest little wife. You wrote and told me the book made you love me more."

"I did. It did."

"Then didn't I write and tell you I couldn't have too much love?"

"Yes."

John picked up the turnip he had dropped.

"What about ground and seeds in the book?"

"We'll read it together after the children are asleep. I think I can find the place. It's about a man who went out to sow seed, and some fell on the wayside and the fowls of the air ate it up at once. Some fell on rocks but died shortly. Some fell among thorns and was choked out. But what fell on good ground grew and increased a hundredfold."

"Anyone could write a story such as that," remarked John.

"But it means something, John."

"Means what? That is only nature."

"But the seed is like the Word of God, it says."

"I don't understand."

"That's what I've been telling you, John. Even though I don't understand most of it, it draws me back."

John shook his head and handed Anna another turnip. "Must be a powerful book. Let me see what I think of it."

Chapter 19

Neither John nor Anna was ever idle. Whenever John was caught up with his own work, he hired himself out for pumpkin-seed oil, potatoes, meat, or even clothing for the children. Sometimes he'd help a neighbor mend a leaky roof or rehang a broken-down door for milk, the amount depending on the generosity of the neighbor rather than the hours consumed. The children needed sweet milk to drink to fill out their diet, and Anna could make good use of it in a dozen other ways. Cottage cheese was always a prized dish at any meal.

Then came the butchering season when the late November nights were crisp enough to thoroughly chill the pork slabs and strings of stuffed sausages.

The children's eyes widened with delight and their eager lips smacked as they clustered around Grandfather Olesh's meat-chopping board. How quickly, how exactly, how fine he minced the pink chunks of meat. And what know-how Mother had for preparing the entrails for the stuffing.

It was in the midst of the busy Friday morning butchering merriment that Grandfather spoke to John when he entered the house with the pork hocks.

"I've got something on my mind, John," he announced.

"You have?" John chuckled. "So have I."

"What's on yours?" Grandfather's steel-gray eyes squinted and his long, thick, graying eyebrows twitched.

John handed the hocks to his mother for the singeing, scraping, and washing process.

"Step back a little, Josie," John said good-naturedly. "I don't like to see you so close to Grandfather's knife. It's awful sharp. Well, it's this," he remarked. "I've been trying to figure out how I can get another sow. With the children growing we'll need more meat. Joe, there, will soon be eating like a man." John glanced over at Anna and smiled faintly.

"I can hardly wait till dinner," Mary exclaimed, twisting the end of one of her light caramel-colored pigtail braids round and round her finger. "You'll fry some, won't you, Mother?"

"Very shortly, dear."

At this all three young Oleshes jumped up and down in glee.

Grandfather rapped the handle of his knife nervously on the cutting board on his lap. "I want to ask you something, John." With this he bent forward intrusively. "This is important and I've had it on the end of my tongue several times." He moved the knife slowly up and down, pointing it first at John and then at Anna, but his eyes were fixed on John when the question was asked.

"How does that Budapest Protestant missionary, as he calls himself, in Daruvar, know you so well?"

John winced a bit. Anna's heart missed a beat. She stopped cleaning entrails.

"I didn't know he did," promptly came John's answer.

Silence. Then: "Well, why don't you ask me why?"

John's forced laugh sounded a little sensitive. "Yes, why?"

"You're really curious?"

"Of course I am. The only time I ever met the man was the day he called at our house over there. That was at least five years ago. Wasn't it, Anna?"

"Mary was still very small, I remember."

John was afraid to look again at his wife. He kept his glance unmoving on his father's bold-featured, well-groomed face. The irregular lines of his mouth were moving as though counting—years, days, or perhaps beads.

Anna's strength ran out of her arms and limbs like water, leaving her weak. She felt herself shaking inside and her hunger for the fresh sausage suddenly disappeared.

All the month's happiness which had enveloped her and John with warmth and radiance flashed through her mind. Since the first night they had read together from that carefully hidden little book, the mysteries of love, life, and death had encompassed them, shut them in together in a strange place from all the rest of the world. They had pledged to discover these mysteries together. Quite skeptically at first John read baffling verses such as Romans 5:1, "Therefore being justified by faith, we have peace with God through our Lord Jesus Christ." Or, "If any man be in Christ, he is a new creature: old things are passed away; behold, all things are become new" (II Corinthians 5:17).

"I don't get it, Anna."

"Neither do I, John, but isn't there something beautiful about it? Let's not give up altogether and stop trying to understand. At least we can understand these simple words, 'We love him because he first loved us.' And I guess that means God, doesn't it? Couldn't mean anything else."

"Couldn't mean Mother Mary," added John pensively. "It says 'him.' "

And so by the aid of the crudely made low-flamed pumpkin-seed oil lamp John and Anna had read to each other in whispered tones short portions nightly since the opening of the subject in the turnip patch. They had taken every precaution against peeking eyes or fits of sudden wakefulness. Each was positive no one knew of their possession.

Only the Sunday past John had remained with the children and agreed that Anna should take that long-postponed twelve-mile hike to Djulovac. It would likely be the last such trip for many months, for winter was just around the corner and another little one was due by early summer. Anna had enjoyed the trip to the full. In the first place she knew John would be happy entertaining and caring for the children. In fact, the whole next day each related to her some antic, some story, some treat they had enjoyed from dear Papa.

The day had been a relaxing one for Anna. On the way she filled her lungs with the tingling freshness of the morning, and chatted with the overgrown teen-aged Leskovik girl who accompanied her. It was the toast-brown rustic time of year Anna loved when the distant sun-burnished Blue Mountains had a bluish-gray cast under a powdery-white sky.

It was on the return trip that Anna realized anew, with a mixture of vague understanding, shame, and anguish, that

"Couldn't mean Mother Mary," added John pensively.

she had not been honest. She knew she had not gone to church out of desire. Fear of being suspected, besides a dutiful feeling to family custom, had instead propelled her to the church. All the way home reality began to press in again—reality of her own unsolved undoneness, reality of differences of opinion and inevitable opposition. Her prayers, she was certain, never went beyond the ceiling, yet she persisted to the last bead. Anna's heart filled with heaviness and pain.

Twice Anna had caught the searching eyes of Father Markum riveted on her. It troubled her somewhat. Did he know something she thought no one knew? Smooth, clever, confident. Was that how John had put it? As she listened, head bowed, his voice was almost toneless to her, except at one point when he broke abruptly from the memorized Latin phrasing. There was a thin clarity in his words that threw a warning out to her she dared not ignore. "He that insists on playing with fire is very likely to get burned. And to remove burn scars is very, very painful."

The heaviness in Anna's chest, however, had soon worn off after sharing her feelings with John.

"Fear can do funny things to people," he had told her. "Come, come. You imagined he was staring at you. I could have thought the same the last time I went to church. Don't worry. This is a free country. Let's not allow ourselves to feel guilty."

She had given in gracefully. Surely John had changed in his attitude during the last months. Three happy days had followed, busy days, crammed full of work. Yet they had read a small portion each evening.

John's father continued: "I met the man Monday morning when I was in Daruvar. Rather, we ran into each other on the street corner outside the mill. Hadn't seen him for many months and I wasn't anxious to either. He's a pest. That's what I'd call him. Trying to undermine our unity of faith and start a new church." His face took on a contemptuous expression. "I hate any man who is a sneak."

John kept silent. He looked at his father until he was sure he could paint his portrait after he got home.

"Tried to hand me a 'tract,' as he named it." The knife point hit the cutting board. "I told him, 'Keep your trash.' Wait till I tell Father Markum how I shoved him off. Then he tried his sweet stuff on me. Asked me my name. The minute I said Olesh his eyes opened as if I were some long-lost friend. 'You're from Miletinac,' he said, 'and I know your son and family.' Asked how Mary's leg was. Now how does he know that?"

Anna swallowed hard to keep from coughing.

John scratched his head as if hunting for stray pieces of the puzzle. "Well, perhaps someone from the village told him. I'm sure I didn't. The only time I've seen the man was that day 'way back."

"But you'd know him if you'd see him?"

John stretched his neck. "Well, let me see. He was—" John hesitated, trying to recall the face he could not possibly forget—"tall, and not too heavy, if I remember."

"He's got an unforgettable face," interrupted Mr. Olesh, peeling off his emotions. "It almost startles a person. It's so—what shall I say—significant of—well, of the trade, the thing he represents." His eyes snapped. What was Grandfather Olesh saying?

Deep within her Anna felt a constriction around her heart. How truly, how rightly he had described that face. Tiny beads of perspiration dampened her forehead. She wanted to laugh. She wanted to cry. Instead, she unconcernedly swished the cleaned entrails back and forth in the pan of water.

"Pa," suggested Grandmother Olesh, "you'd better quit arguing about that fellow and get to work or we won't get our sausage stuffed before dark. You're only workin' yourself into a lather over nothing."

Agreeing with a quick blink of the eye John walked out o the house and soon returned with a pail of water and another slab of freshly carved pork.

The insight only increased John's and Anna's loyalty to each other. Not once when they were alone did John reproach his wife with an accusing word for taking the Testament from Mr. Lutz. The occasion, though a little nerve-racking to Anna in particular, only proved to be the threshold to a larger world of investigation for truth.

It started the moment John's father bristled. Anna could sense John was going to fully protect and stand by her regardless of the outcome. The remainder of the day was sprinkled with pleasantries, laughter, and satisfaction in seeing the job finished. No further mention was made of the man in Daruvar.

"A big day it's been but a happy one," beamed Anna, reviewing the links of sausages hanging high on the wires above the kitchen stove. "And we certainly do thank you both for coming over and helping. Don't forget your pan of meat."

"As though we might," laughed Grandfather putting on his hat. "We'll be looking for you to come and help us next week."

"We'll be right there," answered John good-naturedly.

"Papa," Mary stood close to her father's knee. One little arm found its way across his shoulder. When he turned his head, he felt her gentle breath on his cheek.

"Yes, my dear."

Supper was over and John had pushed his chair away from the table.

"Who was that bad man Grandfather was talking about today?"

"Oh," John's bootless foot dropped to the ground floor. "I—I wouldn't call him a bad man, Mary."

"But Grandfather said he was. Didn't he?"

168

John stalled a moment. "Grandfather evidently thinks he is, but—but really, Mary, Grandfather doesn't know."

"Who is he?"

"A man. A missionary Grandfather doesn't like. Mary, listen"—he roped one of her long braids around his hand—"don't bother your poor little head with such things. It was a mistake to bring this up before you children. The man lives far, far away from here, Mary."

"I know. In Daruvar where Mother went to get her money an' things."

John drew her closer in the half circle of his arm. "Yes."

"But how does he know me?"

Anna stood stock still listening.

"He was in our home once when you were a tiny little girl. Come, sit on my lap and sing me a pretty song. That one Elizabeth taught you last."

She perched herself. But she was persistent.

"Will he ever come back again, Papa?" Fear filled her eyes.

"I wouldn't know, Mary. I—I doubt it." He pressed her closer.

"You wouldn't let him in if he came, would you, Papa?"

"How does that song start now? It was about a north wind blowing, wasn't it? A gay little tune I like."

"I remember." And Mary did sing it in a voice as clear as a delicate bell. She sat thinking.

"What is a track, Papa?"

"A track? A train runs on tracks. Or we make tracks in the mud with our feet."

The child looked up into her father's face bewildered.

"How could he? The naughty man Grandfather thinks is bad tried to give him a track. I don't understand how."

John stroked her head. "There are lots and lots of things I don't understand, Mary dear, old as I am. It was a tract, a piece of paper with something printed on it. Grandfather didn't want to bother to read it. He doesn't like to read very well."

"Do you?"

"Very much. When I have time."

"But how can you? We have no books."

John pressed Mary's head against his shoulder. "We are not rich enough. Rich people can have many books. They cost money."

"I wish we had just one—just one. Don't you, Papa?"

"Which one?"

"I don't know. Just any one with good stories in it."

John looked up at Anna, his face aglow above the dim light of the oil lamp. "Perhaps someday," he said softly. "Now it's time to go to bed, Mary."

Chapter 20

The funeral had been a simple one. A prayer in the widow's meagerly furnished basement kitchen and then a few fitting remarks along with the reading from the fourteenth chapter of John's Gospel, out by the newly dug hillside grave.

Mr. Lutz and his wife Agnes walked ahead carrying the small pine coffin which Mrs. Lutz had neatly lined with part of a much-used but freshly washed blanket. The resigned mother and her two little girls, Millie and Mary, followed. The non-Catholic potter's field was about six furlongs beyond the northern edge of Daruvar in an overgrown Godforsaken-looking place.

Huge purplish-gray clouds floated across the cold sky sending their shadows across the little group as the boychild's wasted corpse was placed gently into the grave. Mr. Lutz, with hatless head uplifted, offered a prayer of thanksgiving to almighty, all-merciful, all-knowing God who gives, who takes, and does all things well—the One who comforts, who heals, who cares.

There were no convulsive sobs, no piercing wails, no ill feelings, but deep, heartfelt emotions which wet the faces of all five. While Mr. Lutz covered the grave, Agnes placed her arm lovingly around the young widow's slender waist. There was nothing more, nothing new to say. It had all been said in the early hours of the day while she was keeping vigilance at little Nordy's bedside.

For weeks Agnes and her husband had been preparing the young mother for the transition Nordy was destined to make. He had never been healthy. His body refused to respond to any medication. Nothing but mother-love had sustained him for his few short years on earth.

"Without you two dear people I couldn't have stood it," the widow said as they turned to walk away.

"We have been placed here to help dear ones like you, Ella," said Mrs. Lutz.

"You've proved to me that you actually believe that too. I can't understand all your many kindnesses to me."

"Neither can we understand God's love for us, Ella."

"You've taught me so much, Mr. Lutz. Oh, so many things I'd never have found out if it hadn't been for you. Thank you." The woman's sad eyes shone radiantly through a film of tears. "Thank you, Mr. Lutz."

"Don't thank me. Thank God. I am only His messenger boy, His love slave. We'll be back in a few days to see how you all are." He patted Mary and Millie on the shoulder.

An hour after they got home Mr. Lutz closed his Bible and got to his feet.

"Agnes," he faced his wife from the opposite side of the library table. He rested his hands, palm down, on the poorly varnished top. "You know, I can't get that Olesh family out of my mind somehow."

"Again?"

"Wonder if they're in trouble."

"You seem to be good at sensing such."

"Have a notion to go over to Miletinac, but—"

"Too far, isn't it?"

"Not that."

"Too cold?"

"You know me better."

"Afraid?"

"Me? Afraid of who, what?"

"Any one of a number of things, William."

"For instance?"

"Well, losing a whole day's time and accomplishing nothing. Or getting run out of the village. Perhaps mobbed.

172

Or getting told off by the lady's husband if he'd be at home, or—"

"You're teasing, Agnes," he broke in.

She blushed in reply.

"Come. Come. Where's my faithful wife?" he protested reprimandingly, but at the same time wrinkles formed around his eyes as they always did when he smiled..

"Really, Will, to be honest now, I wish you could find out somehow if the woman has been reading the Testament you gave her. You know, I've been concerned from the first."

"I have an uneasy feeling about them."

"Any reason for it?"

"Well, the woman has never come to see us."

"Is there anything strange about that, Will?"

"No. But it seems to be related to the attitude the senior Mr. Olesh manifested toward me when I tried to hand him a tract on the street Monday."

"I haven't heard about that yet. Why, William Lutz! You surely didn't expose that sensitive little soul, did you?"

"To be sure, I did no such thing. He remembered me and my helping hand when he had a tip-over with his cart in the ditch. I sensed that day by the way he eyed his son that he didn't appreciate my presence in the village. I'm only speculating, but I say I have a wary feeling that if he found out his daughter-in-law accepted a Testament from me, there's serious opposition on hand. Should I satisfy myself by taking a trip over there?"

"You've never seen her in town again?"

"Not once."

"Well, what did the senior Mr. Olesh do or say?"

"It wasn't what he said but the way he glared, then scowled, and drew back as though I might bite him." Mr. Lutz chuckled. "Almost amuses me. But, anyhow, I let him know I haven't forgotten and I inquired about the little girl who's crippled. Let's make it a matter of prayer. Let's put out the fleece."

"What shall it be?"

"Well," William Lutz sat down and placed both hands over his Bible. "What shall it be? I couldn't go this week any more. I'll plan for Monday. You write at least ten Scripture verses on slips of paper. Only one verse will have the word 'go' in it. If I choose the one with 'go,' it means I'll go."

"Regardless of the weather?"

"If God wants me to go, He'll take care of the weather." Agnes nodded.

"Let's pray."

"If we don't soon go to bed, John," whispered Anna, closing the Testament in her hands, "the night will be much too short. It must be past midnight."

The two had been talking since the last pair of eyes had closed in sleep. Those were Mary's.

They had gone back and rehearsed everything from the beginning, wading together through past fears, doubtings, blunders, heartaches, and misunderstandings, but with no personal pinchings. They plunged into the "now." They could choose one of three possibilities. John outlined them.

"You see what we're facing?"

Anna nodded. Of course she knew. He was reminding her of nothing she hadn't reviewed a thousand times.

"We can get rid of that book, or go on reading it on the sly and try to live a double life, or we can out with it and take the consequences."

Anna pressed the little black book against her throbbing heart. "You say, John," she whispered, "which we should do."

"To deliberately go against our parents would be something terrible, Anna. It's never been heard of in Miletinac. Someday we might sit and imagine how we could have spared ourselves a lot of grief."

She breathed heavily.

"Let's try the second."

"Keep the book?"

She nodded.

"Run the risk?"

She nodded.

"Live double?"

Silence. "If that's what you want to call it, John. But let's not call it that. We're only undecided. Something may happen to completely convince us our parents have the only way."

"Let's sleep over it once more. But wait. What was that you read the other night about being confounded?"

Anna paged through the book. "I don't know where to find it now. But it was something about not getting confounded if you believe on Him. But I don't know who that means. It's so hard to understand, John."

"Well, let's start at the beginning and read through the book one page at a time. Maybe then we will discover what it means."

Mr. Lutz' Sunday evening drawing turned up no "go." "If it's not God's time, I'd only cause confusion. So that's my answer for now. But, Agnes, we must make those folks a special matter of our daily prayers. Something tells me they are passing through unusual struggles."

The season came for the annual house blessing. John almost dreaded it, but nevertheless got his offering ready to give to the father. He purposely stayed close to the house that day so Anna would not be alone. But before Father Markum had finished sprinkling the third house in the village the wind began to send clouds of dirt through the air and great raindrops came splattering on the windows. Naked tree limbs scraped and cracked and then came a downpour.

The father took refuge in the Jectavo home. Two hours later, holding his long robe high above his ankles, he hurried up one side of the village and down the other performing his sacred duty. There was no extra time. He lingered in front of the Olesh home only long enough to accept the coins John placed in his outstretched hand.

"That is over with," said John with a sigh of relief. "Now I'll get to work."

The baby was a dainty, well-formed little girl with silky, creamy skin, soft brown hair, and blue eyes. John would consent to no other name for her but Anna.

"This one has to be named after you, Mother," he insisted.

"Under one condition, John. If the next one is a boy, it will be John."

"So?"

The days were never long enough after Anna came. Not that the baby wasn't a welcome addition, for physically, mentally, and even spirtually Anna was more fit to receive this one than any of the previous three.

Though still searching in and debating with the Word, she felt a something invisible and indescribable hovering around her day and night. She was surrounded by a warm something, sometimes like a voice that wasn't. She tried to describe it to John.

"Don't you feel it too? I think you must, John, for you and I are so close."

"When you are able, let's plan to go into Daruvar together. We'll have your mother stay with the children, for you should go to the dentist."

Anna looked up in surprise. "Oh, John! And take the Testament along?"

To this he made no reply.

But there were the huge garden, the potato patch, the washings, the meals, the bread baking, the knitting, the mending, the combings, and again and again the weeding of the garden. Anna spent more time there than in the house. She knitted after supper while John softly read a portion, usually one chapter.

"Verily I say unto you, Except ye be converted, and become as little children, ye shall not enter into the kingdom of heaven."

"John," Anna dropped her knitting. "Read that again."

He did.

"Be converted. I wish I knew what that means."

The points of the knitting needles in Anna's hands touched each other as she tried to bring together the dangling, ragged ends of her thinking. "As little children. John, are we making ourselves ridiculous? Wasting our time? I don't think we understand much more than we did when we began over ten months ago."

"I've found out there are about as many words I can't pronounce or understand as what I can. Shall we quit?"

"Shall we?"

"Might save ourselves a heap of trouble."

"Father Markum said those who play with fire are likely to get burned. He meant something."

"Come." He took his wife by the arm. "Put the socks away for tonight. If this little book is the fire the father had reference to, and he'd find out we had one, I'll bet he'd be the one to see to the burning." John pinched out the light.

It was her custom of the season (late June) for Anna's mother to spend a day, or more if need be, helping Anna prepare her green bean harvest for drying.

"Nice morning to work," said her mother, snapping beans with skilled fingers. "Why such a face, Anna?"

"I've got a tooth that has to ache every now and then."

"You may have to go to Daruvar and get it pulled."

"I'd rather get it filled if we could afford it."

"Try pumpkin-seed oil with a little cinnamon in it."

"We're out of cinnamon. It's about at the place where nothing helps much. John said as soon as the plums are ripe he'll try to sell enough to pay for a filling. It kept me awake half the night."

"How's little Anna behaving?"

177

"Never had a better baby. She cries only when she's hungry or needs attention. Hear Mary in there singing to her? She's the best little nurse."

"Let me know if you decide to go get that tooth taken care of. I'll come over if you give me notice ahead."

"I'll ask John when it would suit him."

"Suit him?"

"He may want to go along."

"Go along? To stand there and watch you suffer?"

"Not that. Go along to—to sell the plums maybe."

"Maybe Pa could get away easier than John. He might sell your plums for you while you're at the dentist and sell some of ours too. I'll ask him."

Anna ran into the house to take a look at the children, try a bit of oil, and ease the sudden tinge of disappointment.

Chapter 21

Anna was sharply aware both of his nearness and of his eyes riveted on her the moment she stepped off the train. For an instant she stood fixed. Her scuff-clad feet were as if glued to the ground, stubbornly refusing to go on. Her father, heavily boxed with plums, moved slowly ahead of her.

It was a tense moment. Anna felt suddenly transported into a foreign country with no sense of direction and loss of communication.

All the way to Daruvar she had wondered if she might by chance get a glimpse of him. Most of the way she had argued and debated with herself what she would do.

She had discussed the possibility of seeing Lutz in Daruvar with John the evening before, imploring his advice. But he was optimistic.

"There is only a slight chance that it will happen," he said assuringly. "And if it should, just act as though it is of no concern to you. Just ignore him. With Father along he surely wouldn't try to stop you and talk to you."

She raised her eyebrows. "Hardly. The other time I was alone." Anna shook her head and made a sigh. "After all our planning how we could manage to go together just once, now it had to be this way."

"Well, it can't be changed now. I wouldn't have dared to insist." John shrugged his shoulders. "Maybe it's best. If I'd go along, we might even run into fire. You know."

"Maybe so. I hope he doesn't show up on some street corner and try to hand Father one of his tracts. He is as dead set against it as your father."

"Worse, if I know anything. I heard him telling Clem

179

Verbeki this morning when we were working together over Clem's sick cow that if either of his children ever took a tract or one of those New Testaments from that rascal Lutz, he'd disown her."

"Why, John Olesh!" Anna dug the tips of her fingers deep into her cheeks. "Did my father actually say that?"

"I heard him."

"Why did he? What brought the subject up?"

"I didn't get the beginning. I didn't ask them to repeat it either. I let on I didn't catch it."

"But you did. What else?"

"I told you what I heard. Clem said something about someone being in Daruvar and that that crazy fanatic tried to shove a piece of religion onto him. I didn't get who it was or when it happened. I had just gone to the well when Clem started on it."

"John," Anna bit her lip. "Do you suppose my father said what he did for a reason? For a special purpose?"

"Your guess is as good as mine. I wouldn't know why. He doesn't know we have the book."

Anna stepped close to John and pressed her hand against his chest. "Would he do a thing like that? Disown me if he knew? He might. He loves me, I know, but he loves his church more."

Her arm dropped limp. She fumbled with the folds of her faded print skirt. "I really wonder," she stood debating with her own thoughts, "if it's worth the risk."

"To go to Daruvar?"

"No, I mean to have that Testament there under the mattress and Mother here alone with the children all day."

"She certainly won't go to turning beds upside down."

"No." Anna laughed. "I wouldn't think so."

"You're entirely too much on edge, Anna. I shouldn't have told you what your father said."

"Yes, you should have. It's all in the picture now, and dear, oh, dear, what will it turn out to be?"

"Go on, dear. Go get your tooth filled and see to it that nothing else happens to hurt you. You are smart enough to handle a situation. Your train will get into Daruvar before that city man is hardly out of bed, I dare say. Go straight to the dentist. Mind your own business and nothing will happen."

"You're right, John. You're wonderful. But send up a prayer for me just the same."

"Of course." Then he kissed her. "Your mother and the children will have a great time tomorrow. She enjoys them and they'll love you all the more when you get back."

A smile brightened her spirits as well as her face.

"And let's not take time to read tonight," John concluded. "You're tired and need all the sleep you can squeeze into this short night. Anyway, since your father sounded the way he did this morning, we'd better lay pretty low on this whole thing for a while. Maybe a good long while."

Anna's head dropped. She picked at her fingernails. "All right, John," she whispered. "You're the head of this house."

In spite of a thumping toothache, Anna felt emotionally set and sure of herself when she and her father left Miletinac before daybreak. It was after they were seated on the train that she began her imagining. She remembered the seat where she sat before.

She was unmistakably certain. Anna knew Mr. Lutz knew her. There was something so fresh, so clean, so bright about his smoothly shaved face. Then a sudden gleam came in his eyes as they looked at her inquiringly. He tipped his hat.

A deeply buried desire made her answer with a slight nod of her head. But her face turned pale.

"Mrs. Olesh," he extended his hand. Someone behind wanted to pass and gave her a gentle push.

Anna shot an anxious sidewise glance toward her father and at that moment he turned around.

"Aren't you coming, Anna?" he asked.

Then Mr. Lutz understood why the hand he offered to shake wasn't uplifted. He watched her hurry toward the man with the boxes of plums. "Just a minute," he called, dashing up beside the two. "Are those for sale, mister?"

"Yes. You wanting plums?"

"Look nice enough to eat, sir," exclaimed Lutz. "How much for a box like that?"

Anna stood trembling, astonished.

"What would you give me?" Anna's father put the boxes on the ground and watched the man pick one up and feel its full juicy perfection. His toe tapped the earth. "Break it open. Taste it. Best plums——" As though lightning struck him, Anna's father realized who he was talking to. An embarrassed, awkward, almost boyish expression swept across his angular face. Then he smiled ruefully and shifted uneasily. He actually seemed frightened, not at Mr. Lutz, but at himself. His firm body sagged. He knew it did.

Anna stood baffled, her eyes downcast.

"Mighty good," said Mr. Lutz. "My children are wild about plums. So is Mrs. Lutz. She can make the best pudding and jam a human ever ate. I'll give you what they're worth."

Anna's heart jumped. She noticed the Adam's apple on her father's thin neck go up and down helplessly. He took an inventory of his fruit, bit his lip, and said huskily, "Well, the one box is hers," motioning to Anna. "She has to have enough out of it to get a tooth filled."

"Of course. Of course." Mr. Lutz ran his hand into his pants pocket. He counted his money and handed Anna four coins. "Here, Mrs. Olesh. This ought to pay for two fillings and take you back home too."

"Oh, Mr. Lutz," exclaimed Anna, fumbling the coins. "We intended to walk home. The plums were too heavy for

Father to carry in, you know." Anna's own voice shocked her. It was clear and firm. Not a bit unsteady. Mr. Lutz seemed to have a way of taking the disagreeableness out of the situation. "No one else would have given me this much, I'm sure." She moved her position. The warm July sun beat down on the trio and when she looked up she had to squint against the dazzling brightness that glistened in her eyes.

"Let it be that way, Mrs. Olesh. It could be that no one else is as deserving. These," he gathered up the box, "are exceptionally nice plums and the wife will be highly pleased. Here," he set down the box, reached quickly in his shirt pocket, and pulled out a folded pink paper and held it toward her father.

To Anna's amazement her father reached out and took the item offered. But she was immediately horrified, for he tore the paper into bits without unfolding it and threw them to the ground.

Not a word did Mr. Lutz say. He didn't even appear to be surprised. Instead, he smiled at Anna and walked away whistling.

The reaction of Anna's father was rather sarcastic.

"Mrs. Olesh," he began, and Anna knew he was tight full of frazzled, unhappy thoughts.

"We'd better hurry on, Father." She meant to ignore his mimicking remark. "I hope the dentist can take care of me at once."

"So he even remembered your name?"

"It's an easy name to remember, I guess." She tried to laugh.

"Why was he so overly friendly to you?" He covered her with a jealous glare.

"I wonder myself."

"You shouldn't be so talkative to strangers, Anna."

"Oh. Was I?"

"Yes. John wouldn't approve of it. I'm sure of that."

"Then I shouldn't have taken this money either?"

"How does he know how deserving you are?"

Anna remained silent.

"I'm certainly glad I am with you today."

"So am I, Father."

"He's a slick one. I'm glad enough I got rid of the one box of plums that soon, but I can't stand the man, even if he is a little good-looking."

"Do you know many bad things about him?" asked Anna, somewhat hesitatingly.

"I don't know one good thing about what he's trying to do. What a man spends his time at tells what he is, doesn't it?"

"I believe you're right, Father."

"I know I am," he said, relieved. "Now, Anna, right over there is the dentist's office in the front room of his house. See. When you get done, you go back to the depot and wait there for me. You can go inside and sit in the shade."

"I will. I hope you have luck selling your plums for a nice price."

Anna was the dentist's first patient. He examined the tooth. Yes, he'd fill it for half the amount she had received for her plums. But he couldn't guarantee it would hold forever. It would take possibly thirty to forty minutes.

Before the dentist was finished, a pleasant-faced woman entered and asked how long the lady would be in the chair.

"I'll be finished soon," said the dentist. "Be seated. I can take care of you next. You're the preacher's wife, aren't you?"

"Yes. I came to see her, sir."

"Please be seated, ma'am."

Anna lifted her head for only a second. It dropped heavily back on the headrest. Her first impulse was to get up and run straight to the depot. But that certainly would be most ridiculous. The dentist was ready to press in the filling. She wished she could make the woman understand without saying it straight out that it didn't suit at all to see

184

her today of all days. Of all things. Her nervous fingers picked at the arms of the chair. No one but Mr. Lutz sent her over. Maybe John's father was right when he called him a pest. Nevertheless there was but one person who gave the clue to her whereabouts, her own jealous-hearted, thoughtless, tactless father. Her own dear father. There was no getting away. If she was destined to be caught talking with the preacher's wife, she would just have to take the consequences. God help her.

"Mrs. Olesh." The woman's voice was sweet, subdued. Gently she led Anna by the arm to the door. "I'll take only a minute's time to speak to you. Do you still have the little Testament my husband gave you?"

"Yes."

"Have you read any of it?"

"Yes. Yes. A good bit."

"Wonderful. My husband wants to know how you're getting along."

"What do you mean?"

"Your husband. Does he still oppose you?"

"No."

"Good. More wonderful."

"It's our parents."

"As we supposed."

"Very much would they oppose if they knew."

"We understand. But you. Do you understand what you read, dear?"

"Much of it we don't. It's very difficult."

"Can you come over?"

"Now?"

"You couldn't, I guess."

"No, indeed. My father's in town."

"Yes, I know."

"I must not stay longer here. I must meet him at the depot. Soon."

"I see. I'll go on. But don't be discouraged. Keep on read-

185

ing. The Spirit surely will unfold little by little. And remember, we always pray for you."

"Always?"

"Always. You've been much on our hearts. I'll run along now. Can't you come to Daruvar sometime and drop in for a chat?"

"I don't know."

"Try."

"We will. If I come, John must come too, if possible. What we do we'll do together."

"That's the spirit, Mrs. Olesh. Good-by."

"Good-by," whispered Anna. "We've never forgotten your husband."

"He's been talking of coming over to Miletinac to—"

The frightened expression which gripped Anna when her fingers went to her lips checked Mrs. Lutz from completing her sentence. "Please," Anna begged, "wait."

"All right then. I'll tell Will to wait."

"For a long time."

Nearing the station Anna relaxed. As she entered and sat down to wait, there was an eased and reassuring feeling that the unexpected she had met up with wasn't going to put a gap between her and her father after all. He met her in the depot with a broad smile and seemed in extra good spirits. She had been waiting almost an hour.

"Well, so you beat me. Got your tooth filled?"

"Yes."

"Hurt you?"

"Of course. Did you think it wouldn't?"

"Here," he said, handing her a baker's roll. "Let's eat before we start back."

"Thanks, Father, but the dentist told me not to eat before evening. I see you sold your plums."

"Sure. The banker bought them."

"What did he give you?"

"Well, not what your buyer did." Then her father sat

down beside her, took a bite of his roll, and leaned over until his arm touched hers. "Guess we needn't get so excited about that Mr. Lutz, after all."

Anna's eyes asked the question.

"Just had a lengthy chat with a couple of townsmen who know his scheme from A to Z. He's working at it like a fired-up steam engine, only he's got mighty few people in his train. Not getting any followers to speak of. Perhaps a few who never did help out the church very much. They think he'll soon wear himself out and skip the country. Has six children to feed and clothe and where he gets his spending money no one knows. He doesn't get it out of the people of Daruvar. Must have kin over in Budapest who help him out. So cheer up, Anna. He'll likely be shipped back to Hungary one of these days. Sorry I talked to you like I did."

Anna picked at the folds of her skirt. "That's all right, Father," she said softly.

Anna relaxed about her father, but she wondered whether the men who had informed her father about Mr. Lutz had told the truth. If they did, John might as well take the Testament and bury it deep in the garden some night after dark, bury it so deep that no one in this generation or the next would ever unearth it.

Chapter 22

It wasn't the first time Aunt Tena had called to proudly display some handsome never-before-seen-or-heard-of article, a gift from her husband in America. Once it had been a pair of fine-ribbed machine-made black hose that were almost too elegant for her to wear with her homemade yarn scuffs. Again it had been a high-pedestaled oil lamp with a wick strung through a turn-key contraption into a half-pint-sized glass container. The lamp had a transparent glass chimney. She never would have had the courage to light it at home alone had John not done it for her the first time. To her amazement the same amount of oil burned longer in the American-made lamp than in her home-made tin one and produced ten times more light and without smoke. Next she brought over a unique cabbage slicer that with its five sharp blades sliced a whole head of cabbage in seconds. With it Jose sent a dainty, soft, white muslin handkerchief with a bright pink border that really seemed too flimsy to use.

While her own beamed and twinkled, Aunt Tena smiled down into the three pairs of eager eyes clustered close around her. To prolong the children's and Anna's eagerness to see her latest gift, she talked first about the weather, the chickens, the gardens, the neighbors, the old, the young, the middle-aged, things local but nothing new while she held the treasured boxed object on her lap. At last she removed the lid.

"Oh!" How Aunt Tena loved to hear the children make that sound as their eyes widened!

"What is it?" asked Anna.

"Here," she said. "Hold it. Feel it. Smell it. Make a guess."

"Smells like roses and coffee cake and something else I can't think of right now."

"Let me smell it," cried Kathrine and Mary in unison.

"And me," added Joseph.

"Just what do you call it?" asked Anna. "It feels like it might be soap."

"That's what it is!" exclaimed Tena. "Toilet soap. Doesn't Jose send me nice things? 'Perfumed toilet soap,' he wrote or I might have tried to taste it."

"Will it make you smell good like that if you wash yourself with it?" inquired Mary.

"That's what I'm aching to find out," answered Aunt Tena. "Only I hate to use it for fear all the pretty smell will wash out. And look here." She unfolded a twenty-four-inch lacy, scalloped square made of silky gray yarn and held it up. "It's called a 'fascinator.' I guess I said it right."

"A what?" asked Anna.

"Mother, let me hold the soap," interrupted Kathrine.

"It's a fancy name for a fancy head scarf. Jose said the ladies over there wear them pinned under their chins or hung across their shoulders. Like this I suppose." She demonstrated.

"It's beautiful, Aunt Tena." Anna ran her hands over the softness of it. "But listen."

"Yes, Anna. You're going to ask me when I am going to wear it. Well, dear," she folded it and placed it tenderly in the box on her lap, "I haven't decided yet. Really it's most too elegant for me to wear and anyhow I don't like to be dressed finer than the other women of the village. Now if you had one like it, we could wear them together sometime. But then when would that be? I seldom feel spry enough any more to tramp those twelve miles to church and there's no other occasion to dress up. If I were as young and nimble as you, Anna, we might go a few places together. John

189

never saw any of these when he was over there?"

"I don't know. He may have, but he saved every cent he could to buy this farm. Yes, Aunt Tena, John's told me about a good many fine things the women in America have that we don't. What I was going to ask you is this: Isn't Uncle Jose coming back?"

"He hasn't said anything about it yet."

"But doesn't he get lonely for you?"

"He never says much about it."

"And you?"

"Get lonely for Jose?"

"Yes. I'm just remembering how it was when John was gone."

"But you had the little ones. I think that makes a difference. I never suggested that Jose go and I wouldn't like to suggest that he come back. If he's better satisfied over there and sends me money and things, I'm not of any notion to complain."

"Do you ever have a—well, a longing to go to America to—to live?"

"To live? Me leave Miletinac? I'd have to feel a lot different than I do now. No, I haven't the slightest desire to cross the ocean, Anna. Would you?"

"I don't know what I'd do in your case, Aunt Tena. John and I enjoy working together. Those seemed like mighty long months to me while he was gone. But I had something to look forward to. I knew he was coming home at about such a time. It kept me planning and working toward a happier day. Isn't it that way with you?" Aunt Tena tapped the box ends with her hard-worked fingertips. "Oh, well, I suppose," she mused. "I suppose someday Jose will surprise me and come walking in. Would be just like him, wouldn't it?" she laughed.

"Where is he now?"

"In America."

"I mean where in America?"

190

"It's a little hard to keep track of that man. You know he moves from place to place if he can get a job making more money. My letter this morning says he's in Lancaster, Pennsylvania, working in a smelting plant."

"Wonder if John would know where that is."

"I'm sure I don't. Jose sent me a little map of the United States long ago and I got it out and tried to find the places, but the letters are too tiny. Could be I need eyeglasses. But that doesn't really matter. I mean, the exact spot where he is. The main thing I'm concerned about is that he's around decent people and goes to confession when he ought to."

"You think he does?" Anna bit the inside of her cheek as soon as she had asked the question. But she realized her mistake too late.

"Why, Anna! Why would I think he doesn't? Didn't John when he was in America?"

Anna's vigor drooped. She forced a faint smile which was all too sickly. She groped for an answer she could not catch hold of; so she caught hold of Kathrine first, then little Joe. "Say," she suggested, "why don't you children slip on your jackets and play outside while the sunshine is nice and warm? It would do you good. Mary, you need a little fresh air in your lungs too."

But Aunt Tena was insistent. Nor did she delay her insistence until the children were shoved kindly out of the house. Mary looked back over her shoulder at her mother's strange expression. It was a little perplexing for the six-year-old to understand why she wasn't welcome to stay and listen in on the conversation if she wanted to. No visitor had ever called who was quite so fascinating as Aunt Tena with her twinkling dark eyes and easy-flowing words.

"You mean he didn't?"

Anna ushered Joe, the last one, over the threshold, then slowly closed the door. Her thoughts raced until she was almost panting for breath. "Well, I'll tell you, Aunt Tena," she ventured facing her squarely. "I'm not going to lie to

191

you about it. I don't believe in that. He went to Mass once, but I have my doubts if John went once to confess to a priest when he was in America."

"You mean the first time?"

"I mean either time."

"Why, Anna Olesh!"

"He couldn't have talked English well enough to make one understand if he had tried."

"But that's no real excuse, Anna. I think those fathers can understand what anyone says no matter what language they speak. They have a way. They're smart. If a man from any country would go to any father anywhere on earth with something to confess, there's not a father who wouldn't understand what it's all about. Even if the man couldn't do more than grunt. The father could pray to God and explain. He'd understand. Anna, that's a poor excuse. Well, well. I certainly hope Jose doesn't excuse himself that way. I'm going to ask him the next time I write. No wonder your mother said she hopes John will never get it into his head to go back to America."

"Mother? Did she tell you that?"

"Yes, she certainly did."

"When?"

"Yesterday. I was over. We got to talking as we always do about everything. She says John's a lot different since he went across."

"Different? How? If I know anything, he's— But tell me first what Mother said."

"Well, now maybe it wasn't anything real serious. I hope not. And I don't want to be called a talebearer. Jose always did remind me I talk too much when I get started. I suppose your mother has discussed this with you, hasn't she?"

Anna sat down on the edge of the bed. "I don't know until you tell me, Aunt Tena."

"Now, it isn't that John's not as ambitious as he was before. Sakes no. She's highly pleased with the way he works and gets things done. And he's extra good to you and the children. She told me so more than once. Everyone in the village can see that. And everyone likes John as a neighbor. And I think most of the younger men envy his experiences over there, but none of them had wives as brave as you. Or the men themselves lacked the courage. I tell you, Anna, your parents think you were mighty plucky having a baby twice with him over there. I wonder sometimes if I'd have done as well. You have four sweet, pretty little ones, Anna. Smart too."

"But you still haven't told me."

"Yes, I know. I'm coming to it, Anna. You see your mother—and father too for that matter—feels John's too careless about going to Sunday Mass and confession. Surely you can't help knowing how they feel about it. Don't you, dear?"

"In a measure. Yes. But they can't say he never goes. Mother frets too easily."

"You're right, Anna. She always was natured that way even before you were old enough to remember. She worried terribly when Jose left. Of course he, being her only brother, made it worse."

"But just why does Mother worry so about John? He's old enough now—"

"But it's you and the children she thinks of."

"Explain," begged Anna as though it were some dark secret they were keeping from her.

"You know, dear, it's the sacred duty of every father to keep his life clean and up-to-date with the church father so nothing will happen to his family."

"So Mother's expecting something bad to happen to us?"

"She fears it worse than anything I could mention. After what happened to Mary— Oh, Anna dear, I didn't mean to make you cry. I shouldn't have—"

Anna brushed two tears away quickly. She looked away for a moment. "I'm not going to cry. And you're not telling me anything new, Aunt Tena. We know the folks imagine some evil spirit took over Mary's knee and it might not have happened if John had—Oh, dear, I just don't want to go into all that again. They've been so good to us. But nothing bad has happened to you."

Aunt Tena sat in meditation. "I'm going to ask Jose," she concluded at length. "He'll tell me. I can't believe he's not doing all right."

"Whether you know it or not, the folks always blamed that German for influencing Uncle Jose to leave. And ever since, they don't like to see a foreigner show his face in Miletinac."

"We talked about that too yesterday. They're even afraid of that Hungarian missionary over there in Daruvar because he's been in the village a few times."

"It makes a person miserable to live with such fears," remarked Anna with thoughtfulness.

"By the way," her aunt said, "Drew Datlore told your father that some man who lives in Daruvar said he saw you once talking with him."

"With whom?"

"That Hungarian missionary, that Protestant from Budapest. You know."

Anna felt prickly, then queer in her stomach. "Yes." She swallowed. "That's true. But Father was with me. He sold him my plums. We were hardly off the train. He was there watching for someone who didn't get off. There was nothing alarming about that, that I can see."

"But it was some other time. I don't know when. But I told your mother it was foolish for her to let her mind run wild. I know if it had been you, you would have told her about it. Now don't feel bad, Anna. Come on. Smile about it. My, my, as sound and grounded in the faith as the Dorges have always been and the Oleshes too, let the man try to sell his little Bibles. I'm not going to lose any sleep over what Jose wrote."

"What's that?"

"He said America is full of not one but many kinds of Protestants. He can't understand it. And around Lancaster there's still another. I forget now what he called them, but he said they're very good farmers and take such wonderful things to a great market place—fruits, vegetables, meats, cheeses, and even baked things of all kinds. He said one day when the machinery broke down they couldn't work; so he walked out through the market and one man was there selling Bibles."

Anna's lips parted. Her eyes widened. "Did—did he buy one?"

Aunt Tena laughed. "Goodness no. How could he read one of those things when he never finished the fourth grade in school? He said some people in America own one as a sort of charm against evil."

"You mean?"

"Well, they just have one in the house someplace. I guess they don't have to read it or believe it. Just let the evil spirits know it's there. And God too, I guess. I don't know. Sounds funny doesn't it?"

"Well, I don't know whether it does or not, Aunt Tena. It seems that everyone fears something. You'd be afraid if you'd learn Uncle Jose doesn't go to confession. If there could only be someone who could tell us of a better way to live. I mean without fear. John says he doesn't think people should go to church out of fear and pay dues to the father just because they have to. I think I agree with him."

Tena Dorge got abruptly to her feet. "So John's been doing some free thinking since he's been in that free America."

"Don't blame America, Aunt Tena. John thought about that before he ever went over there."

"Yes? Well, John always was a boy to think and dream. Here he comes now, stepping it up as if he has some new thought on his mind."

Chapter 23

There was something to what Aunt Tena surmised. John did have something on his mind.

The three children followed him into the house.

"Good afternoon, busy farmer," greeted Aunt Tena. "Just had a pleasant chat with Anna."

"You needn't rush off because I came."

"It's time for me to get home and feed my chickens. Know anything new?"

"Well," John Olesh bent low to unbutton his small son's jacket. He also removed Joe's cap and straightened the straggly hair. "I know we just finished a new roof on the Megotina place."

"Who else helped?"

"Henry Prolop, Drew Datlore, and Anna's father helped for a while. Looks very nice, too," added John. "I hurried home for a pail and a pan, Anna. They're going to pay me with walnuts and sausages. And a few garments Mrs. Megotina thinks you can work over for the children."

"Oh, goody," cried Mary and Kathrine, clapping their hands. "Walnuts and sausage."

"I guess that's the newest thing in the village," concluded John as he turned to face Tena Dorge. "Do you know anything newer?"

"Not newer," laughed Aunt Tena. "I told Anna my bits of news. I must run on now or darkness will overtake me."

"Come back," called Anna from the open door.

"I will, dear. But you hardly ever come to my house any more."

"You understand how it is, Aunt Tena. You have no little ones to tie you down."

John gave Anna a prolonged glance, then hurried off with the water pail and her one and only enameled pan.

Elizabeth came home from school crying.

"Child alive. Coming home late again," remarked her mother who was in the act of drawing a pan of freshly baked bread from her outdoor oven. "And what's the matter now?"

Elizabeth nodded. "I can't help it," she sobbed. "I hate school! And I hate that old teacher. He's getting meaner every day. And I hate Mat and Hank."

"Elizabeth, do tell! Open the door quickly. Come. This bread is hot. Now," she said once the bread was on the table, "take off your coat and scarf and try to calm yourself. Last night you said the teacher whipped you, and made you stay after school because you missed two spelling words. Monday he punished you because you were tardy. But I know you started plenty early this morning and you knew every one of your spelling words before you left. You didn't forget, did you?"

Elizabeth shook her head. "It wasn't that this time. I remembered every single word." She pulled off her scarf and coat and dropped heavily on a chair beside the table. "I'm just thankful little Mary can't go to school."

"Why, Elizabeth. How can you say such a thing? You—"

"Because I am. Mr. Polti would be mean to her too."

"What makes you say that? Who could be mean to a dear, sweet little child like Mary? And in her condition?"

"I don't know how anybody could, but I'll bet he would be. He's mean and cross to everyone, but to me especially now just because I'm Anna Olesh's sister." She rubbed her wet handkerchief across her swollen eyes.

"What? I don't understand, Elizabeth."

"Father Markum came to school today."

"He did. But he usually visits your school once a year. My, I hope you were very polite to him, Elizabeth."

"I was, Mother. All the children were. We said, 'Yes, Father,' every time he spoke, and kissed his hand."

"Then I don't understand this."

"After catechism he talked mostly about that wicked Mr. Lutz in Daruvar and the awful things he is trying to do to people, even to good Catholics."

"And of course you agreed, didn't you, Elizabeth?"

"I didn't do anything, Mother. I just sat perfectly still and listened. You could have heard a pin drop all the while he was there."

"And what did he say about you being Anna's sister? Hurry."

"He said he heard."

"Oh, no, Elizabeth! Not what Aunt Tena told me yesterday."

"He said he heard Mr. Lutz was in our village several times and he wanted to know if he talked to any of us children."

"Well, had he?"

"Everybody shook their heads. Then he asked if any of us had ever seen him."

"Did you, Elizabeth?"

"Not that I know of."

"Of course you didn't. Go on."

"Then he asked if any of us knew of any house in the village where he had been inside."

"Oh, Elizabeth." The mother caught the bottom of her apron and twisted it around her hands.

Ready tears filled the child's eyes. "I felt sick, Mother. I didn't want to tell. Oh, I didn't want to tell on my own sister when it wasn't her fault. But Hank and Mat rolled their eyes around and looked at me, then the father asked me straight out, 'Do you know?' I never wanted to tell a lie so bad in my life, but I knew if I did they would tell. Then I'd be all the more wicked." Elizabeth shook with sobs.

"Then what?" whispered her mother with a shudder.

198

"The teacher told me to stay after school."

"Only you?"

"All the others were allowed to go home. They all promised never to talk and never to speak to Lutz if they ever saw him anywhere."

"And didn't you too?" Her voice was almost hysterical now.

"Of course I did, but I had to stay after school anyhow."

"Why?"

"So the father could talk to me alone."

"What about?"

"About how awful it was John let him into the house. And their house should have a special sprinkling and it's a wonder something awful hasn't happened to them long ago. And he told me how John and Anna haven't ever confessed this to him and he's thought for a long time something was hanging over them. He made me say John and Anna were naughty and had done very wrong. I didn't want to say it. But I did. I was scared not to. But I don't think they're bad, Mother. They're as nice to me as ever. I wanted to go over tonight and teach Mary some more new words. Now I won't with my eyes all red. I feel awful and I hate school. That old teacher made me stay after Father Markum left and write one hundred times, 'I will never disobey the father.'" Elizabeth buried her face in her arms on the table.

A long, painful pause followed before the mother spoke. Her voice was husky, fearful, and strained. "He probably asked you to do it for your own good, Elizabeth. Don't cry any more. The father is very jealous. He is concerned because he has to be. It's his religious duty, Elizabeth. Mr. Polti is too severe. I'll agree to that. But maybe he asked you to write that so often to impress you and all the children how important it is to obey the father at all times. You didn't get another whipping, did you?"

"No."

"And you were polite to the father?"

199

"As polite as I knew how to be, Mother. I kissed his hand again when he got done talking to me and thanked him." Elizabeth jumped up, grabbed her coat, and flung it across the room. It landed dangling on the end of the bed. "But I'm not ashamed Anna Olesh is my sister, and I think she's about the nicest, kindest woman in all Miletinac. I don't think people have any right to talk about her the way they do."

The door had opened and the father's tall muscular frame filled the doorway. He stood with his right hand on the doorknob. "I hope you're right, Elizabeth," he remarked in a grave mood as though debating with his own thoughts. "The whole village, I suppose, is passing comments tonight, but John and Anna can blame no one but themselves." He closed the door and hung his cap on the nail beside it. "And it's entirely up to them now to pull themselves out of it into the clear and stay in the clear."

"So you've heard already what happened in school today?" demanded the mother almost crying.

"In school?" Then he noticed Elizabeth's sad, tear-traced face in the dusky shadow of the kitchen. "In school?" he repeated in a low, hollow-sounding voice. "I hope what I heard hasn't been dragged on to school. And whatever you do, Elizabeth, don't go over there and repeat everything you've heard or will hear. Part of it, I know, is not so."

What a supper the young Oleshes had!

The sausage was delicious, not too fatty, and seasoned to perfection. Beside it on the table Anna placed a bowl of chopped potatoes in thickened white sauce and a pan of stewed apples.

"Tomorrow," she announced, "I'll make a raised coffee cake with a few of the walnuts in it. But we'll save the rest of them for nut bread for Christmas."

"So Aunt Tena had bits of news," remarked John. He didn't look at Anna when he spoke. He was busy spreading plum butter on Joe's bread. "There you are, son. Don't take such huge bites or you'll choke."

"Oh, Papa," exclaimed Mary. "She had the prettiest-smelling soap you ever smelled that her Uncle Jose sent her in a box."

"Uncle Jose is her husband, Mary," corrected John. "He's my uncle."

"Is he? Well, he's the one in America who sends her things."

"Yes. I know. Do you wish I was in America so I could send you soap and things?"

"No, no!" cried Mary. "We'd rather have you here with us, wouldn't we, Mother?"

"Indeed we would. Tena Dorge can have all the sweet-perfumed toilet soap, fancy head scarves, fine-ribbed stockings, and potato slicers in the world if she wants them. I'd rather have my husband on this side of the ocean so we can work together, eat together, live together, and figure things out together."

"Like what, Mother?" Mary asked.

"There are ever and ever so many things for fathers and mothers to figure out for the good of a family like ours. Like," Anna looked at John and winked, "this one. Here's one small piece of sausage left." She picked it up with her fork. "Who needs it most?"

"Papa," answered Mary. "He worked the hardest today."

"I'm not sure about that," answered John. "Mother worked as hard as I did."

"No, John. I only worked with my mind while Aunt Tena was here. You were up and down a ladder all day. I had enough."

"Cut it in two," suggested Mary. "Then you will be alike."

"I know," stated John. "Give me the sausage. I'll cut it into three pieces and each of our children shall have one more bite. Is that all right, Mother?"

Anna smiled. "It's all right, Papa," she said. "You did the

201

figuring and I agreed. You're the head of the house."

Both laughed with the children.

"Anna," began John after the four were asleep, "the Testament is still under the mattress, isn't it?"

"Unless you took it out."

"I didn't. But I want it now."

"You're sure? To read? I thought we were not going to bother about it for a long time."

"That's right, Anna. Go get it, please."

She did. "What are you going to do with it?"

"Don't ask," answered John. "Don't ever ask me what I did with it. I've figured this out today and—well, like at the supper table, you're going to agree as a good wife should." John tucked the Testament inside his shirt and held it snug under his left arm. "It's all for your good, Anna," he added. "For mine too. This thing dare not be in our house. Not another day. Someone is trying their level best to prove something on us and they're not going to succeed if I can help it. Understand?"

John noted the look of fresh alarm on Anna's face. He put one hand on her shoulder. "I'll never blame you for taking it. Never, as long as I live. I'm not sure I wouldn't have done the same that day. But since you did, no one will ever find out by me that you took it or that it's been under our roof this long. Not because I'm ashamed or sorry, but for your protection, Anna. So now," he buttoned his coat and reached for his cap, "I'm going out. Do not follow. Go on to bed."

"But, John," whispered Anna. "Are you going to tear it up?"

He shook his head.

"Burn it?"

He shook his head.

"Well, if you're going to bury it," she whispered sadly, "bury it so deep that no one will ever find it. And—and, John." Anna pressed her tightly folded hands against her thumping heart. "I hate to think of dirt getting on it. Let's wrap it carefully in a cloth first so—"

"But I didn't say I was going to bury it." He inched toward the door.

"You didn't say you weren't either. What else could you do with it?"

"I have it all figured out, Anna."

"But, John," she followed him to the door and held him by the arm. He heard her breathing rapidly.

"Pinch out the light before I open the door," he said softly.

She did. "Please destroy it as gently as possible, John," she begged. "It's been something so mysterious and precious to me somehow."

"But I didn't say I was going to destroy it."

"Oh!"

"I'm not."

"Oh!"

"In one year from today I will either destroy it or bring it back into the house."

"A year from today?" repeated Anna in a whisper.

"That's right. If anything is going to happen, it will happen within a year, I figure."

"Happen?"

"I mean to Mr. Lutz. If he's a fake and is run out of Daruvar and all his efforts go to nothing within the next year, I'll destroy this Testament. But if he's still at his job in spite of all this opposition and gossip—well, I'm not sure what I'll think about him, Anna, but I'll bring this book back to you. How does it sound?"

In the darkness Anna bit her lip, thinking fast. "John," she answered, "you're wonderful. It's fair. You're right and I agree. Aunt Tena said when she saw you coming toward the house you were walking as though you had some new idea."

"Oh, that Aunt Tena and her bits of news." John adjusted

his cap. "Remember," he said, his hand on the doorknob, "if anyone ever comes here and asks you if we have one of Mr. Lutz's tracts or holy books in our house, tell them to come in and turn it upside down and hunt if they want to."

"You don't think anyone will, do you, John?"

"You never can tell. Now go on to bed."

"I'll not sleep one wink. I'll not even close my eyes until you come in, unless—unless it's to pray."

Chapter 24

John was not gone long. Carefully he opened and closed the door, took off his shoes, and slipped into the adjoining room. He stumbled against her kneeling beside the bed.

"Anna," he whispered, grabbing her by one arm and helping her up. "You didn't fall?"

"No; I—I couldn't go to bed until I tried to explain to God about all this. If the book is part of God, it seems to me He deserves to know how I feel."

"I see. Come. You'll get chilled."

"You're sure it'll be all right? I mean where you hid it?"

"I think so."

"No one will ever discover it?"

"Hardly, unless there would be something like an earthquake. Now you're not to worry about it. I did the best I knew."

"I'm sure you did, John." She patted his arm. "Many things came to my mind since you took it out. Snatches of things in the book. 'Let not your heart be troubled,' and 'We ought to obey God rather than men.' 'My words shall not pass away' even though earth and Heaven will, and believe all things that they will 'work together for good,' 'I will never leave thee, nor forsake thee.'"

"You remember all that?"

"I didn't know I did really, until it was taken away. It made me feel sort of weak. But there was a verse about strength made perfect in weakness or something like that."

"Well, time will tell how much truth there is to the whole thing and whether or not it's worth remembering."

John held his voice clear, steady, and remarkably indifferent whenever approached on the subject of the Budapest missionary who had wedged his way into Daruvar, as his father put it, and was worse than a pest. He had carefully instructed Anna to do the same.

"After all," he reminded her, "there is nothing to be nervous about. The less we say or act excited, the better off we'll be. The only thing that bothers me now is that Mary and Kathrine had to get in on this. They are both much too young to be frightened or confused over religion or to know anyone else is. We must continue to treat our folks and neighbors like always. Let's not show any resentment or alarm or anxiety if we can help it. And we're not going to try to find out what everyone is saying or thinking. We'll try to be extra kind to Elizabeth. She's been doing wonders for Mary." To all this Anna readily agreed.

But no one rushed over with reports or accusations. No one put any point-blank questions to either of them. Not even John's own father. Opinions, comments, threats, and fears were freely given, men among men, women among women, in John's and Anna's hearing.

Anna fully expected her mother or father or both to pay them a special visit. She struggled and labored endlessly shuffling answers she might draw out to meet their questions. Finally, after the third day had passed, their absence not only perplexed her but Mary as well.

"I wonder what's wrong, Mother?"

"Wrong about what?"

"Elizabeth hasn't come for a long time. Do you suppose she's sick or something?"

"Guess I ought to run over and find out. If she doesn't come tonight, I will."

"And Grandma hasn't been here for a long time either."

"Seems like a long time, doesn't it? It's been four days."

"But she used to come every day."

"Just about."

"Is she cross at us?"

"I wouldn't know what about, dear. I know we're not cross at her about anything."

"Well, Mother, what was it that Aunt Tena was talking to you about that day?"

"Well, let me see. She talked about a lot of things. Uncle Jose, and the things he sent her. I can't remember everything, Mary dear. Look. There comes Elizabeth now."

"Oh, goody." And Mary flung open the door.

"John," related Anna that evening, "Elizabeth called me outside when she finished Mary's lesson tonight. She's terribly upset."

"What now?"

"Over remarks she hears the children make going to and from school."

"More of that?"

Anna nodded.

"About the naughty John and Anna Olesh? About the poor unfortunate Olesh children, and the Olesh house and farm all being condemned, I suppose. Well," John laughed dryly without humor.

"That's about what it all amounts to."

"And what did you tell her?"

"I told her not to pay any attention to it; to act as though she doesn't hear any of it and never enter in on it or talk up."

"A good answer."

"I told her it wasn't troubling us any."

"Right again. That's the way to talk to her."

"Then it hasn't been troubling you one bit?"

John tilted his head to one side and looked into Anna's face meditatively. "What's more," he remarked in a low tone, "I'm not rushing over to Djulovac to satisfy the worried neighbors and give Father Markum a gift I haven't got."

Anna was silent.

"That's so. I haven't got it."

"I know. But Mother sent word by Elizabeth that she'd gladly stay with the children Sunday so we could both go."

"Both of us?" John scratched his head. "Now wouldn't that please everyone and the father? But truthfully, Anna," he added, his expression changing to one of seriousness, "your mother means well. She is sincere. I'll always respect her and my parents for that. And what's more, I believe every person in Miletinac talks only because they're anxious about our welfare. No one has been unkind or rude to me yet. They talk the way they do to warn us. They've always been like that. Don't you remember how everyone in the whole village grieved and carried on and talked when Franz Milosh lay sick so long before he died, and when Uncle Jose left for America? When the Pogiea place burned, and when Mary hurt her knee? It will always be like that here. We're one of the village family. We belong to everyone. I believe either your parents or mine would be willing to give their right hands to save us from doing the wrong thing. And I believe your mother spends most of her time figuring out something more she can do for our happiness."

Anna nodded.

"Of course the question is," John went on, "what is for our real happiness? I stopped in over there today. Your mother asked me a dozen or more questions."

"She did?"

"I mean about you and each of the children. And did we have enough of this and that? You know how she is."

208

"Never mentioned?"

"Not one word. Of course I could easily see she had something on her mind. I wasn't there long."

"Was Father there?"

"No."

"Why haven't they been over?"

"I told her we'd been missing them. I think she's been grieving. I didn't ask. When I passed Grandma Prungle's place, she called me in to help her move her bed to the other side of the room. She's a dear old soul too. Grabbed me by both hands to thank me and said with big tears in her eyes, 'John, my boy, I've got lots of good things to say for you. You're going to come out on top, I know.'"

"What did she mean?"

John shrugged his shoulders. "I didn't ask. I just said I hope so. You see we're part of the village family, Anna. Underneath all the talk these folks all really care about us and want us to be sure to remain one of them. Don't you see?"

Anna studied John's ruddy face, his sturdy legs, his straight shoulders firm and uplifted, his hard-worked hands crossed to grip his upper arms. She drew a long deep breath. "It's good to feel wanted, isn't it? Everyone has been very kind to us. We're so—so at peace here and yet so fearful and anxious. Doesn't seem right. Everyone is anxious over something or someone else all the time. It's been us ever since the day they found out you were going to America, then worse since the day we fed Mr. Lutz, then Mary fell and, oh, dear, it's been us too long now. And if they really knew." Anna shook herself.

John sat down and kicked off his shoes. "Our village is too small. Everyone lives too close to everyone else. Work alike, dress alike, eat alike; so we must believe alike too." He tapped one stockinged foot on the hard earth floor. "Advantages, yes, but too many disadvantages. I'll tell you what I'm going to do. I'm going to make your dear-hearted mother and old Grandma Prungle and all the rest of our relatives and concerned village folks happy one of these days and go to church like a good man should. And," he concluded as he rested his face in both hands, "maybe I'll think of something to confess to the father too."

For a moment it was deathly quiet in the house. The four children were asleep.

"You mean—" Anna stepped close to John and pulled his hands away from his face. "You mean you'd have to think for long?"

John hesitated. He cleared his throat. "I'm not perfect. Not by a long way. I've no notion of confessing that Mr. Lutz defiled our house or children or you or me. No. I refuse to believe that sort of thing. It's hard to know what to do to make these good people happy."

One day before John made that trip to church he spoke out with sudden and shocking boldness so that every man in the group would hear him. Young John Olesh's indifference on the current topic came to an abrupt and functional end. He stood erect facing Rufus, the last who voiced his sentiments. Each of the four villagers' hoe handles came to a standstill and four mouths gaped.

"Listen, men," he said, "do you actually think that that man Lutz is worthy of all the attention he's been getting from all of us of late? I think we could talk of something more worthwhile. He's not going to come back over here in our village and do any damage to any of us unless we let him. And if he's going to have to skip the country—well, God haste that day."

John's short and carefully worded speech accomplished what he sincerely hoped it would. His own father looked astonished, pleased, tickled, then slowly wet his lips and smacked them with gratitude and relief. Anna's father reacted in a similar manner. Then each of the four exchanged glances, nodded, and proceeded to mix mud plaster with renewed vigor.

"Sounds as though everything ought to come along all right for John and his family," whispered one man to the next.

"Always did think he'd sooner or later come to it. Well, let's shut up about it now."

"Got good news for you," announced Anna's father upon opening the door when he arrived home.

"Finished with that barn already?"

"Better than that. I just about concluded today that we've been worrying and fretting unnecessarily over John."

"You mean it? How's that?"

"He expressed himself today. Openly. Of his own free will."

"Who did?"

"John. Either he's been misjudged, misunderstood, falsely accused, or he's just had his eyes opened and is taking his stand with the rest of us. And it's just as his father pointed out to me confidentially after John went on home; he has a good head on him, and when we sift this whole thing down, what have we got to prove anything but that they did invite in and feed that Lutz and they—I mean especially John— have been plenty careless about going to confession?"

"And isn't that enough?"

"It is if other things develop. But wait till I tell you what John said. You'll scarcely believe me."

"Then hurry with it."

The good news was passed from mouth to mouth, from house to house in the ancient village, from house to school, and even reached the ears of the father before John made his appearance at church.

It was remarkable how soon the talk throughout the village took on a new slant. Anna's emotions raced all the way from surprise to near tranquility, from secret alarm to inner balm, from amusement to suspense. Could it be that John's little speech which did not voice his convictions at all brought about such a change? Would it last? What would happen should the people discover why he made that speech and how he actually felt? Anna pondered.

It was not her imagination that very soon the women of the village spoke to her with a decided new warmth and with more natural smiles. Nor could she help noticing how Elizabeth's countenance brightened from day to day. Her own dear mother came often to the house and beamed on her and the children—baby Anna in particular.

"John," exclaimed Anna one night a week later, "I can't tell you how glad I am for Elizabeth's sake. She's her happy self again. The little girls even notice the change. And what's more, she reports the teacher is a bit more kind to her too."

"Well, fine. But did he tell her he's sorry he made her stay in and write that sentence one hundred times?"

"I didn't say that. I'm not joking."

"Neither am I. It was unjust, and if he hasn't, he ought to."

Anna threw the yarn over her needle point several times. "I'm wondering," she said slowly, "if the day may come when you and I will have to say we're sorry too."

"What for? I thought we were being nice to her."

The oil lamp sputtered and a tail of smoke curled high above the kitchen table before the light flickered out. Anna continued knitting in the dark.

"I didn't mean her."

"What then? Because we let Lutz in?"

"No, John." Her hands dropped in her lap. She looked out through the kitchen window to the cold, gray moon-tipped clouds hanging above the distant mountains. "I was just remembering some more of those strange sayings in the little Testament." Anna dug the point of one of her knitting needles into her cheek. "And if there's any truth to them, well—"

John did not insist she finish her sentence. He glanced from her face to the same slowly shifting clouds she was gazing at. "And tomorrow," he said, "remember I go to see the father."

Chapter 25

John decided to strike out earlier than usual to avoid company. He was naturally a faster walker than most of the men or boys of the village and he disliked lagging. Too, he wanted to be alone with his thoughts.

Anna prepared a tasty breakfast: two eggs fried in pork grease; two thickly cut slices of bread spread generously with plum butter; coffee; and a piece of her famous raised coffee cake. She sat opposite him at the table.

"I hope the children sleep on for a while," she whispered. "Then I'll dip back in bed and rest a while."

"What a breakfast!" exclaimed John. "Could you spare two eggs for me?"

"It's going to be a long, chilly walk," she remarked. "You'll need all that."

But Anna did not add that she would go without an egg herself so the children would each have one.

"You'll tell me all about it, won't you?" she whispered.

"Have I ever kept anything from you?"

"One thing."

"What's that?"

"Where you put the Testament."

"But you know why. I didn't take it out of the house without letting you know."

It was not exactly the kind of ordeal John had tried to prepare himself for. Father Markum was standing just inside the door adjusting his stiff celluloid collar when John entered.

"John Olesh." By his tone John wasn't sure whether the father was surprised or impressed. Perhaps both. "You're early," he added still adjusting his collar.

"Well, it's been some time since I've gotten over," began John. "I wanted to come early."

"Yes," remarked the father. "You've stayed away much too long for your good. I'm sure you realize that now. And I'm glad to learn you realize too the importance of every Catholic performing his sacred duty in voicing his convictions against these terrible heresies." The collar finally fixed, the father held out his right hand. John hesitated a second, then bent forward and touched it with his lips.

"You came early for confession," stated the father without emotion.

"Yes," admitted John, and he followed the father to the curtained-off confession room.

"No doubt you have much on your mind," remarked the father almost kindly. "Your parents and your wife's parents and all the good people in Miletinac have been concerned about you ever since that brazen heretic from Daruvar entered your house."

"But was it a sin, Father Markum, when I did not know who he was until after I had fed him? I thought it was my Christian duty to be kind to a stranger."

"Then you absolutely did not realize who he was?"

"I had never seen the man before."

"And is the report true that he offered you one of those books he carries around?"

"That he did as pay for his dinner. But I did not take it."

"Nor did your wife?"

"She knew as well I that to do such a thing would greatly displease you, Father Markum, and besides would require penance. My wife is as sincere about this as I am. Neither of us would want to do anything wrong in the eyes of God."

"I'm delighted to hear this free confession from your own lips, John. However, it was a great sin. One can commit unintentional sins, you know. And, of course, you know too that whatever displeases me displeases God also. We work together. And we will continue to do so. His Church will go on and prosper to the end of time regardless of the number of false men or groups or religions that try to work against it. They cannot ruin the true Church."

John must have displayed a look of astonishment, for the father pressed his fingertips against John's chest and continued: "That's right. Since Christ gave Peter authority and power to build His Church, it has grown to cover the entire earth in unity of faith, in unity of worship, and in unity of obedience under the oversight of faithful men, as Father Jardell was for years. Of course the pope is over us." He paused. "Now you must hurry, for others will be coming; what is it you need to confess?"

John looked down a moment, pinching his lower lip. "To be honest, Father Markum," he faltered, "right now I—I can't seem to put my thoughts into words."

"How strange! Oh, come now," he said impatiently. "What's the biggest sin that bothers you?"

"They all bother me," answered John frankly. "I don't know that one is bigger than the other in God's sight."

"Well, one thing ought to bother you exceedingly if it doesn't."

"What's that?" John looked up sharply.

"You've never asked me to come over to purge your defiled house. And until you do, you'll never get ahead."

"You mean?"

"I mean nothing you do will prosper. What's more, you'll never find peace of mind until you have that done."

"And how much would you charge?"

"Charge?" gasped the father. "Your own conscience should set the price. I would have to intercede long, hard, and often to have that stain completely removed. The greatest sin anyone can commit is procrastination."

"Is what?"

"Repeatedly putting off what you know is the right thing to do. Every day, every week, every month your obligation gets larger."

John knit his brow and shook his head. "Then," he said, "it is already more, I fear, than I can ever meet."

"Ever?"

"I'm a poor man. Here," he said, handing the father one small coin. "It's all I had to bring today."

Father Markum dropped the money, without looking at it, into the large pocket in the folds of his long black robe. "Self-sacrifice for a worthy cause is greatly rewarded," he remarked in what seemed to John a tone of disappointment.

"I know it," agreed John. "And we will have to go without lamp oil for at least a week now."

"Isn't it worth it?" came the father's terse words. "Wouldn't you rather sit in the dark in your own home for a week than to run the risk of being cast into the darkness of purgatory forever?"

John's strength shriveled for a moment. Then he took one lingering look at the father and asked as gracefully as possible: "May I go home and think all this over again? I mean more prayerfully than ever before?"

"You may. It's the only thing to do, John. Holy Mother Mary, the saints, and God will alike tell you what your sacred duty is. You owe not only a debt to God and the church but to your family. God bless you. I'll look for you next Sunday."

John stayed for Mass. He felt embarrassed, then sick at his stomach, then indifferent.

"The only good I can see that has come out of this trip," he told Anna, "is that it pleased our people."

Eleven months later when John Olesh looked back to that Sunday morning interview with the father, he realized that it was one of those small but significant pieces that fit into the puzzle pattern of their lives. It was the day his namesake was a week old that he came to this realization.

The year up to the end of the eleventh month had continued without startling events. There had been the everyday round of honest hard work, planning, skimping, and stretching to make ends meet with never more than enough of anything except the appetites of the growing children. Those, to be sure, neither parent would want to pinch. Anna managed somehow to mend, patch, darn, add to, reline, or reinforce so that John had decent enough clothes to wear to town, or to church (if and when he felt moved to go, which he did about once every five or six weeks).

"I'm going to be fair with myself," he told Anna. "Fair with our parents, our good neighbors, and with God. I'm willing and anxious to learn and if we keep on begging God, or the saints, or Holy Mother Mary, or all of them, or whoever it is that does really hear prayers, I think some time, somehow we'll know who and what is right. Or perhaps discover every one is wrong. I can't say it makes me happy, but I'll go anyway."

Without arguing Anna agreed, remembering John's promise about the hidden Testament.

If they were still the objects of criticism and anxiety, John and Anna were not aware of it. The uppermost concern and talk among the Miletinacans had turned to the Parot family who lived in line to the south on the west side of the wide village street. The subject of concern was the fourteen-year-old and oldest of Mat Parot's four husky boys who had fallen from a ladder and injured his back. The father had twice paid the old witch doctor to come from Vilieki Bastaji and work her charms over him. But after six weeks he still lay in great pain and was hardly able to turn himself over in bed. Anna's mother shook her head in sad dismay but all the while insisted she believed as strongly as ever in the witch doctor's methods and ability to cast out evil spirits and the "matter" must lie with the boy's parents. Or it was another of those obstinate deep-seated covered-over evils which required more time to be torn loose. The egg in the oily red rag on the window sill must not be disturbed as it had been in little Mary's case.

Anna refused to discuss the witch doctor or the boy's

illness with anyone including her own mother. The neighbor women sensed the reason for Anna's silence and discussed that among themselves. "She hasn't gotten over her own disappointment yet," they concluded. "And she knows there's a reason why the old woman's charms did not work on Mary and so she has practically forbidden anyone to mention the name 'witch doctor' in Mary's presence."

What really disturbed the villagers about the Parot boy's misfortune was the fact that the fates would let the evil spirit capture the smartest, the most obedient, the best loved of the four, the one his parents depended on to help with the heavy farm work, and the one that went twice as often to confession as the other three. Folks seemed to think he'd go into the priesthood before many more birthdays. Why now was he the one to fall off that ladder while working so diligently for his father? The boy had begged for Father Markum that he might confess again every sin he had ever committed and kiss both his hands. Mat had unstrawed and carried all the way into Vilieki Bastaji potatoes from his fast-dwindling supply and sold them that he might be able to pay the father for coming. And while the father was in the house two dozen or more villagers stood reverently outside waiting to bow and salute him as he came out. A few who had not been able to go to church for some time quickly confessed their shortcomings and sins along with explanations for their absence, but assured the father of their constant prayer life, and handed him a coin or two and kissed his hand.

Baby John had a bad start with the colic. Unlike the other four, he cried a good deal at night.

"Here," suggested John after six consecutive nights of interrupted sleep, "let me try my luck with him."

But his floor walking and patting and talking had little effect. "All right," he declared, handing him to Anna, "tomorrow I'm going into Daruvar to the drugstore and get some of that Ideal colic relief. You look at me as though you

218

wonder how I'll do it. You know that new pair of socks you just finished for me? I'll sell them."

"But you need them yourself."

"Not as badly as the baby needs the medicine."

Daylight came when John was half way to Daruvar. The nippy wind had gone down and the light fog lifted, revealing an occasional milch cow licking crisp, frosty grass-blades. John walked with sure-footed swiftness, head erect. His lungs tingled with the fresh morning air.

The manager of the drugstore did not need the socks, else he gladly would trade them for the colic remedy. They were lovely, but his good wife had just finished knitting him two new pairs. John might try the banker or the baker or the ticket agent in the depot. He was a widower and undoubtedly bought all his socks.

Neither the bakery nor the bank was open yet. Before John reached the depot he looked across the tracks. There it still was in the big front window. "Gospel Center." And freshly painted. John looked every direction first, then crossed over.

He rapped twice before anyone came to the door. He bit the inside of his cheek.

"Good morning, Mr. Olesh! Good morning!" Mr. Lutz grasped John's hand in both of his and held it in a firm grip. "Come in."

"Thank you."

Lutz closed the door and ushered John through the hall into the large simply furnished living room. "Here, take a seat. You rapped twice, I know, but we were just finishing our morning worship in the kitchen."

"Oh! I'm sorry, Mr. Lutz."

"Never mind. That's quite all right. This is an answer to prayer, Mr. Olesh. I just finished mentioning your name to God again. We've often asked Him to send you and your wife here to us. I thought you'd come together sometime. She said you do everything together."

John laughed nervously, softly. "We do, Mr. Lutz. As far

219

as possible. But—well, you see we have five little ones at home."

"Five? Reason enough."

"The baby is less than a week old. I came to town to get some colic medicine. All our home remedies have failed."

"I see."

"I—I came to get straight on something." John cleared his throat. His strong hands trembled. He felt suddenly helplessly weak, timid, afraid. What if he had made a terrible mistake now? One he'd be sorry for forever?

Mr. Lutz sat down beside John. "By God's help I'll do my best to set you straight, my friend. What's on your mind?"

"Well," ventured John, "how soon are you going to leave?"

"Leave for where?"

"For anywhere."

"I don't quite understand, Mr. Olesh. Did you hear I was going somewhere?"

"I heard you might have to."

"Have to?" Mr. Lutz's face broke into a pleasant smile. His warm eyes, direct and clear and kind, swept John from head to toe. "I'm quite aware of the fact that some people in Daruvar would like to help me move on, but God hasn't told me yet to start packing. There's no law that I know of that will force me out. We're happy here. God brought us here and He is blessing our efforts."

"He is?"

"Of course He is. Our Sunday school and church attendance is growing. I mean a little, and we've won three souls to Christ during the past year." Mr. Lutz got to his feet and faced John.

"Three?"

"Three. Yes. Think of it. We're simply thrilled. Of course I wish I could say one hundred and three. But, Mr. Olesh, I'm glad I can say three souls were won for Christ. The joy it gave us to help those two women and that one man come through from darkness to light can't be expressed in words.

220

To hear their testimonies now and to see them live daily in victory over sin, superstition, and haunting fears and bondage is the greatest joy we've ever experienced. Leave Daruvar? When I have these three precious babes in Christ to feed and take care of? And when there are others almost persuaded? Did you get the report from good authority that we might have to leave?"

John fumbled a moment for the answer. Warm circles raced round and round his heart.

"Never mind," said Mr. Lutz good-naturedly. "I'd really rather not know. It's been reported to me that I was going to be stabbed and hung and shot full of holes and all of that, but we've actually had our meeting disturbed no more than a half-dozen times. But tell me, friend, you have a special reason for asking your question."

"Yes. But this is all I need to know." John rose to go.

"But you make me inquisitive, Mr. Olesh."

John moved toward the door. "Someday I may explain. I must hurry on."

"But you're not going to leave so soon. Come to the kitchen for breakfast. Agnes," he called, "set another plate."

Chapter 26

This now was more than John had expected. He felt miserable, even a little shaky inside. No. He couldn't think of accepting. Why hadn't he thought about it that city folks seldom eat breakfast as early as they did in Miletinac?

Now that he had found out firsthand what he wanted to know, he ought to leave immediately—before anyone who might recognize him might chance along at that critical moment. John twisted one hand in the other. What a fool he'd made of himself!

"I must be going, Mr. Lutz," he said with his hand on the knob. "I shouldn't have disturbed you at such an hour. I'm sorry."

"Please," insisted Lutz in a sincere tone. "It was no disturbance at all. Believe me. We like pleasant surprises like this. Don't we, Agnes?"

"Of course," came the cheery answer from the kitchen. Then freshly aproned Mrs. Lutz made her appearance. "Good morning, Mr. Olesh," she greeted him. "It's no trouble at all to have you stay and eat with us. We'll be ready to sit down in a few minutes."

John felt helpless. There was no getting away now without appearing obstinate, ungrateful, or even rude. Furthermore, he could not deny that he was hungry. As the tantalizing odor of freshly brewing coffee and frying cornmeal mush wafted in from the kitchen, the temptation to stay nearly overcame his determination not to do so.

"I understand, John," ventured Mr. Lutz confidingly. He took hold of John's one arm. "It's plain old fear again, isn't it now?"

John looked up sharply. "Then you—you do understand? I don't mean to be unkind." He tried to laugh but couldn't.

"Perfectly. Perfectly, John," Lutz said. "This country seems to be possessed with fear. We meet up with it every day. It's the main reason why our little church here hasn't grown faster. We see folks coming near, hesitating, looking in, then hurrying on by as though someone might bite them. We understand. We've even had a few slip in at our back door after dark and ask questions about the tracts I've handed out, about our purpose for coming here, about our Bible, and what not. Then they slipped out, scared stiff they might be found out by others. I know how you feel. I'll help you leave safely."

John stood thinking, half-disappointed that he could not find another fitting excuse. He drew a long heavy breath as if trying to convince both himself and Mr. Lutz that in spite of those kind words he had made a terrible mistake. He looked around. If he could only fade out of sight!

"Don't scold yourself," Lutz said. "Everything will be all right. Please come to the kitchen. Agnes says she's ready. I want our children to meet you. They've often helped to pray for Mr. and Mrs. John Olesh."

Reluctantly John obeyed. But uncertainty clung to him like milkweed seeds to a woolen coat.

Lutz offered a short thank-you prayer for the steaming food. Immediately he launched an interesting conversation without being preachy. He didn't even ask if they had been reading the New Testament. Instead, he asked about John's family, his farm, his crops, his trips to America. Occasionally he laughed heartily at the amusing incidents John related and permitted David and Lillian to enter into the conversation and ask questions.

John's tension gradually melted away until he was surprisingly relaxed as well as refreshed. The mush and coffee were more delicious than they smelled.

"And what is it you're going to get for your baby?" asked Mrs. Lutz.

"Ideal Colic Remedy. As soon as the stores open I want to get it and start back."

"Wait a minute. I thought that's what you said. We've got almost a full bottle of that here in our cupboard. Left over from our last baby. We'll never need it, I'm sure. There's nothing better."

Lutz noticed a look of relief pass over John's face. He saw him close his eyes tightly for a moment, swallow hard, then take a sharp breath.

Lutz would have given a good deal to know at that moment all that was going on in young Olesh's mind. He had endeavored to train himself to understand these people of the Balkans, deeply rooted in their traditional religion. But there was something unusual about John Olesh, or was it that he had a great deal more to learn? For a minute Lutz sat in deep thought.

"Well, John," he exclaimed with a sudden, exuberant tone, "God bless you anyhow for stopping in. And we sincerely hope it won't be the last time. It's been a very happy occasion, one we'll look back on and remember. I am sure it was God Himself who led you here."

"You think so?"

"Of course I do."

"Well, I—I hope so," John heard himself saying. His heart pounded. He thanked Mrs. Lutz for the medicine and moved again toward the door.

A sort of guilty delight possessed him. He must go. Of course he must. Yet he felt strangely at ease, comfortable, even reluctant to leave. Was this Lutz a real human minister of God? Or was he allowing himself to be cruelly disillusioned by the man? Could a Gospel missionary actually be that common, that on-the-level, that understanding with a poor commoner like himself? Tangled incongruous thoughts raced through his mind like mad. Had he deliberately walked into a honey-baited trap? In any case, for the moment at least, he felt a wave of unfamiliar happiness he had not before experienced. It was as though something touched a chord in his soul he never knew was there.

"Thanks for the breakfast," he heard himself saying.

"The way is clear as far as I can see," declared Lutz, looking out in every direction. "Go now in safety and God bless you all the way home. Blessings on your wife and little ones, including the new baby. And remember, John, our doors are always open to you any hour of the day or night. We'll be looking for you."

"I'm surprised you didn't say more to the man about his spiritual condition, William," remarked Mrs. Lutz after the two watched John cross the tracks.

"I wanted to badly enough. But today wasn't the time. I didn't want to spoil a good start and send him back into the world of fear for good. God's been working. Our prayers haven't been for nothing. But Mr. and Mrs. Olesh aren't the kind that will be rushed."

Agnes Lutz looked at her husband with trust and confidence as she nodded assent.

Anna stood speechless. She looked at the Testament John had placed in her hand, then at him. She glanced into the next room to see if the children were all asleep.

"The year is nearly up," he said simply. Then he blew out the light.

"I know," she agreed softly. "I've been counting the days. Wondering, too, if you were and remembering your promise."

"Of course I was remembering. And Lutz is not leaving Daruvar."

"He's not?"

"Neither has his work gone to nought. It's even growing."

"You mean you actually found out today?"

"Straight from his own lips."

226

"John! You mean you talked to him on the street in Daruvar?"

"Sh! One better. But maybe when I tell you, you'll say I made the biggest mistake in my life. Maybe I did. I don't know. But on the way over today I determined about daybreak that if I kept my promise it was time to be finding out somehow. After I got there I didn't know whom to trust to ask. The stores weren't open yet and all at once I looked over there to the place. And I got a sudden crazy impulse to go ask him myself."

"John!" Anna grabbed his arm. "I—I can't believe it."

"I hardly can myself. But I did just that. What's more, I sat at their table and ate breakfast with them."

"No! What's going to happen?"

"I've been trying ever since to decide whether or not I feel defiled."

"Do you?"

"I don't know exactly how I feel."

The baby had responded almost immediately to the colic medicine. The two sat in the dark and talked undisturbed for over an hour. Anna sat rapt, almost breathless at times, as John related every detailed happening of the day.

"Now won't you tell me where you hid it?"

"I discovered just the very nook up under the eaves of the house out there at the southwest corner."

"Up there?"

"I told you I wasn't going to burn or bury it and I couldn't find a safer, drier place to keep it."

"You're wonderful, John. It's not ruined. Oh, I'm so glad. Just think, all this time it was so near and I never knew."

"And we never had to lie about it either," reminded John.

"No. But several times I was sure someone was going to ask me if I ever touched one. What a relief!" Anna pressed the Testament between her two hands. "I'm glad to have it back." Her voice trembled a little. "And especially since you've told me how kind they were to you today."

227

"It may cause us a lot of trouble now. And we've got to be more careful than ever."

"John, why is there such a difference between Mr. Lutz and the father? The father always makes us afraid of him. Mr. and Mrs. Lutz try to make us feel just the opposite, don't they?"

"I haven't figured it all out yet."

"I wish we could read a little before we go to bed."

"We'd better not light the lamp again. It might waken the children."

"More than that, John, the oil is about gone again. So are the matches."

"Put it back where it was under the mattress. Listen! Didn't someone knock? Hurry, Anna. Stick it under quick, then jump in bed and cover up."

Before John reached the door someone knocked again and opened. "Anna."

"Oh, yes. Yes. Is that you, Father?"

"Are you in bed, Anna?"

"Well, not exactly, Father. I mean, I was just ready to crawl in. What's wrong?"

"I didn't want to frighten you, but Elizabeth's awful sick."

"Since when? She was here this evening and seemed all right."

"Just came on her since supper. She wants you to come over. Is it so you can leave the baby for a while?"

"Yes. Yes, of course. John's here. And the baby's been sleeping ever since I gave him some of that medicine John went after."

"So he got it? Well, good. Bring it along. A dose or two might help Elizabeth."

"But it's colic remedy, Father. It's for babies."

"Bring it anyhow. Could be she's got something like colic. I don't know what's gone wrong with the child. And I don't know why she's calling for you this time of night."

"Go ahead," John insisted. "I'll get along all right. You surely won't stay all night."

After Anna left, John went into another long rehearsal of his interviews with Father Jardell and Father Markum, the one with Father Markum eleven months prior in particular. He relived every dread, every rebellion of heart, every shame and fear of that morning. His face got warm and the cords of his neck twitched. Forever in the darkness of purgatory unless the house is cleansed? "Don't scold yourself. Everything will be all right. I understand. Perfectly. Perfectly." John walked stocking-footed back and forth across the kitchen, then stood at the door looking out into the dark street. "Both can't be right," he declared to himself. "The one seems always to take; the other gives and gives."

Elizabeth was sitting on the edge of her bed moaning, holding both hands on her stomach. Anna set the bottle of medicine on the table beside the smoking pumpkin-seed oil lamp and dropped on one knee beside her sister.

"What can I do for you, dear?"

"I don't know," cried Elizabeth. "I just wanted you near. I'm so sick."

"Your head is warm. She may have a little fever, Mother. What have you done for her?"

"Everything I could think of. Warm salt water, clabber and burnt bread crumbs, cinnamon tea, and what not."

"I can't take any more of that stuff," fretted Elizabeth, "and I don't want that old witch doctor to come either."

"Who said the witch doctor was coming?" asked Anna.

"Well, I'm afraid if I don't get better, Mother will have someone go after her. Oh, please, Anna, do something for me quick."

"You'll soon be all right, Elizabeth. You probably ate something that didn't agree with you. Surely," said Anna comfortingly, stroking Elizabeth's forehead, "we wouldn't think of calling in the witch doctor yet. You're scared and all worked up. Let me see. What could we do?"

"Here, try some of this," suggested Anna's father picking up the bottle and holding it out.

"Did John sell the socks?" inquired the mother, taking the bottle and looking at it closely. "Who bought them, Anna?"

Anna made no answer.

"The drugstore man?" she asked.

Anna held her breath. She stared blankly at the bottle in her mother's hand.

"And my goodness!" exclaimed the excited mother. "You don't mean to tell me that already this evening you've given that baby this much." She held the bottle closer to the dim light. "Why, it's about a fourth gone. Horrors, Anna! Look, it says here to give an infant only five drops. He's liable to die for you."

"Don't be alarmed, Mother," begged Anna. "I read the directions before I gave it to him. The bottle wasn't full when John brought it home." She cleared her throat. "Well, Mother—," she stammered.

"Never mind about the trade," interrupted Father. "If you're going to give her some, go ahead and give it. None of us will get any sleep tonight."

"Shall we try it, Elizabeth?" asked Anna. "Say about one spoonful? I really don't think—but if Father insists, I guess it won't hurt you."

"Come here, Anna," whispered Elizabeth. "Sit beside me."

Anna sat close and put one arm around her sister.

"I want to tell you something," she whispered out of the corner of her mouth. "I don't want anyone else to hear."

"Tell me quickly," she whispered. "While Mother's getting a spoon."

Elizabeth put her face against Anna's ear. "Some of the children told me today if you don't hurry up and get your house blessed, the father won't baptize your new baby and then," sobbed Elizabeth, "he'll—"

"You haven't told them?"

Elizabeth shook her head. "What are you going to do?" Tears rolled down her cheeks. "He's too sweet to go to that awful bad place, Anna. I can't think of it!"

Anna pressed Elizabeth's trembling hand. "Don't believe it," she whispered quickly. "Sh! Don't fret."

"Here it is now. Open your mouth, Elizabeth." Her mother stood over her, spoon in hand. "And I hope it helps."

Elizabeth looked at Anna wistfully. "Shall I?"

"Try it. It'll make Mother and Father both feel better."

"Will you stay here with me for a while?"

"I'll stay until you tell me to leave. What did she eat for supper, Mother?"

"It couldn't be over what she ate, for she never ate more than a bite. She was feeling bad when she came home from school and had to throw up. I can't remember when she's had a spell like this. It reminds me of the way she cried when Father Markum talked to her after school. He wasn't there today, was he, Elizabeth?"

She shook her head.

"Did the teacher punish you for something?"

"No."

"Now try to lie down and relax," suggested Anna. "There now. Don't you feel just a little better already?"

"A little, I guess."

"You two go on to bed," said Anna, drawing a chair close to Elizabeth. "I'll stay here with her until she's asleep. Please, Mother. You and Father are both tired."

"How about you?" asked Father.

"I'll be all right. She wants me to stay and I promised I would. I hardly believe there's anything seriously wrong. See, she's not moaning the way she was when I came in."

The two took Anna's advice.

It had been a long time since she and her sister, who was not little any more, were together alone to talk at length. It had been years. Before Mary was born. John was in America. To be sure, they had seen each other and talked nearly every day since, but always around other people. Anna rubbed Elizabeth's back and legs until she was certain her parents were asleep.

"Anna," whispered Elizabeth. "Won't you pray hard to Mother Mary that he'll baptize little John?"

"I pray as best I know for all my children. Every day."

"Father said once that if only he had the money he would pay to have your house blessed. I would too if I had it."

"You are kind, Elizabeth."

"Well, I don't want anything bad to happen to any of you."

"For some reason it doesn't bother me, Elizabeth. I wish it wouldn't you. I can't tell you why because I don't know how to explain it, but something tells me our house doesn't need to be cleansed. And if Father Markum doesn't want to baptize my baby, he can save his holy water for someone else's baby."

"Oh, Anna! I hope all the people in the village don't begin to talk and say things again."

"If they do, dear, please don't let yourself get upset like this. John is a good father. He will do the best he can for his family. Believe me, that he will."

"Yes, but I want everyone to think my sister is the best in the village. I want my nieces and nephews to be the nicest and best, don't you see?"

"What the people say doesn't make us good or bad, Elizabeth. It's what we really are that matters, I think."

"Maybe so, but just the same—"

Anna planted a kiss on Elizabeth's forehead. "You're going to rest now, aren't you?"

" I feel better. I guess you can go now."

"Then good night, dear. Sleep well."

Chapter 27

To Anna's surprise John met her at the door when she returned. "John. You mean you're still up? Has the baby been crying?"

"Only once. I don't think I need the rest as much as you do. What's wrong with Elizabeth?"

In the darkness of the kitchen Anna could not see John's facial expression, but she was confident it registered neither alarm nor anger when she reported what Elizabeth had said. He simply took her by the arm and led her across the room. But the warm pressure of his hand told her that on his face was written determination and courage to face a new and difficult situation. It told her they would head right into it hand in hand.

"So that's it," he remarked. "Well, if it is, we'll be ready for it. And in a different way than anyone will be expecting."

"What do you mean?"

"I mean, we'll plan right now not to have him baptized."

"You mean—?"

"Yes, I mean we will plan not to before Father Markum refuses us. He'll not get the chance to turn down our baby. Come," he added in a solemn tone, "you're tired. And if you don't get your rest, you'll be sick. Tomorrow night after the children are all asleep we might as well read a little again in the missionary's little book."

"Why not in the morning?"

"Depends on how early you'll feel like getting up."

Anna wasn't able to relax as easily as John was. She repeated over and over his words before she finally fell into a troubled sleep. They were the first in her mind when she woke with a start. "We'll plan not to." Something broke in on her suddenly strange dream. Where was she? Oh, yes. Now she remembered. Week-old John was crying lustily to be fed.

"John," she whispered. "Why don't you get up now and read a page before the children get awake? I'll have the baby asleep in a minute or two."

John read more than one page. He kept on until he finished the entire seventh chapter of Matthew. It told about judging, about asking, seeking, knocking, and finding. About gates and ways, false prophets, trees good and bad, building houses on sand and rock.

"We'll have to read that again to get it all," John said.

"I believe Elizabeth is going to be all right," announced Anna's mother as she opened the door the next morning. "She's sleeping yet and I don't feel like waking her up. How's our little baby John?"

"Better."

"Good. Then it won't hurt him to take him out, will it?"

"Out where?"

"Where? Well, Anna, where do we take our babies about this time of their life?"

Anna was sitting on the edge of her bed pulling Joseph's stockings onto his plump legs. She stopped. For a long moment she did not look up. Frantically she searched for the right thing to say. "I suppose you mean we ought to be thinking of his baptism."

"Not just thinking about it—making plans."

An awkward silence followed. Slowly Anna pulled up the stocking. "Well, Mother," she stated, "I guess I might as well tell you. John and I talked this all over and we may not have him baptized."

"You mean—?"

"That's what I mean, Mother."

Her mother's face turned pallid. Anna heard her whimper as though she had been wounded.

"What is this gloom hanging over this house?" muttered Anna's mother. "What is it?" she repeated with a look of distress.

"Is what?" Anna's self-defensive words seemed to come out of a large empty room and echo in her aching head and pounding heart.

"Listen to me, Anna." Her mother waved her hand.

"I am listening, Mother." Anna's voice was expressionless. She picked up Joseph's other stocking.

"You can't actually mean what you said." She stepped closer to the bed, raising her arms with her voice. "You *are* going to have your baby baptized."

Anna started to shake her head, then caught herself. She scarcely glanced up.

"And tell me," her mother pointed an accusing finger, "what has brought about this strange notion?"

Anna's arms dropped limp. "I—I just can't explain now. I didn't get home until nearly morning and John got me up early."

"Why?"

"I had to feed him."

"Oh. I thought you meant big John."

"How's Elizabeth?" asked Anna.

"Sleeping. I didn't wake her up to go to school. Tell me, what do you think was the matter with the child last night?"

Anna drew a long deep breath before she spoke. "Something upset her, I guess."

"I know that. But what? I never saw her act quite like that before. I couldn't understand why she kept begging for you. I thought maybe she was going to die. Why did she ask you to stay?"

Anna didn't answer. She acted as if she was dreadfully scared or worried over something.

"Did she tell you what it was?"

Anna was silent. Her mother stood waiting for the words which her daughter seemed to be weighing or determining

235

not to speak. Finally in consternation, her eyes bleary and her feet dragging, she made her way to the door.

"Must you go?" asked Anna.

"Elizabeth might get awake and wonder where I am," she faltered. "You meant what you said about the baby? You're actually thinking of such a thing?"

"Yes, Mother. It's decided. We are not going to have him baptized."

"Decided!"

"Yes, Mother."

"Oh, that poor little John," she sobbed, covering her face with both hands. "He's *got* to be baptized. I'm going to talk to John."

Anna watched her mother go. She knew what was coming next—a dozen questions from the wide-eyed, astonished little girls who had heard the entire conversation.

"After breakfast," she told them, "I will have a little talk with both of you. You are old enough now to understand a few things that must be told."

John agreed that it was the only thing to do now. In spite of her determination to remain calm, Anna's voice did quiver a trifle at first, but she started out forthrightly, a little daughter with uplifted face snuggled close on either side.

"Now," she began, "this is our home and this is our family. There are seven of us now and we belong to each other. We have been a happy family and we are going to keep on being happy living and working together, are we not?"

Both agreed.

"We are not rich. But your papa is a hard worker and good and kind to us all. He loves each one of his children alike. So do I. Now when your papa and I were little babies like tiny John, our parents took us to the priest to have him baptize us."

"What's that?" asked Mary.

"He sprinkled a little holy water on us."

"Why?"

Anna hesitated. "Well, I never did know exactly why," she said. "But that is what the father tells all the people to do."

"Was I?" asked Mary.

"Was I?" echoed Kathrine.

"Yes. You were both baptized when you were tiny. Anna and Joe too. But now we have decided something different for our new baby."

"Why?" they asked in unison.

"It cannot mean that we do not love him as much as we did you. Never. Grandmother cannot understand. That is why she was upset this morning. She thinks we must always do things as they did. But we want you girls to know that no matter what Grandmother or Grandfather or anyone else in the whole village thinks or says, remember we will do our very best for your new baby brother. If you ever want to ask any more questions about this, come to me or your papa. Don't ask anyone else."

They agreed.

"Was Elizabeth scared last night?" asked Mary.

"She was worrying." Anna coughed nervously. "But I talked to her and she—she feels better now. If you get your knitting now, Mary, I will show you how to make a heel."

"Well, Mother," persisted Mary, "was she scared like Grandma was? I mean about our baby not—"

"Our baby will be all right, Mary. God understands all about it, I am sure." She hesitated. "Yes, Mary, I'm sure He does. Want to knit now?"

"Where is God?" asked Kathrine.

"Up beyond the sky somewhere, in Heaven."

"But how can He understand when He is way up there and we are down here?"

"I cannot answer that, Kathrine dear. I do not know how He does it, but I am sure He does. Get your knitting, Mary."

Several times that afternoon Anna noticed Mary and

Kathrine hovering over Baby John in his little bed and whispering something to each other.

"When did things begin to go so wrong over there?" was the question Anna's mother asked over and over, each time with more emotion. And Anna's father usually gave the same answer in conclusion. "I still think John's going to America was not good for him or the family. When you stop and think back, he's puzzled us off and on ever since that time."

Then one afternoon, as Anna was darning John's socks, she lifted her eyes and met the puzzled stare of her father standing in the doorway. His gaze was so solemn and intent that she flushed.

"Father, have you been standing there long?"

"Not long."

"Come. Take a chair. All I heard was the children playing outside."

He was twisting his cap nervously with his large muscular hands. He looked almost haggard.

"Aren't you feeling well today?" she asked.

He sat down without relaxing. He cleared his throat. He bent forward, fumbling with the peak of his cap. He did not look up when he spoke. His voice was husky. "I'm about worn out trying to."

"Trying to what?"

"Trying to feel all right. And trying to pacify your mother. I told her this morning I can't put it off any longer. I'm coming over to find out about it."

"About what?" Anna wove her needle in and out several times, then slowly drew the yarn through.

"Don't ignore me, Anna," he said. "I haven't been able to get any satisfaction out of John. Why all this suspense? You know what's on my mind. What I've got to know." He made a peculiar sound in his throat and transferred his gaze to the tiny blanketed bundle in the homemade wooden bed beside Anna's chair. "I thought," he faltered breaking the silence, "that when you and John got married you were going to be the solid, the firm, the dependable type. I know we brought you up right."

Anna's needle in her hand trembled. She wanted to throw her arms around her father's neck and tell him she knew they had done their best. Her heart ached for him.

"I can't believe," he went on dejectedly, "that you are going to be the first ones in our village to make such a terrible mistake."

Anna scrambled frantically in her mind for the right thing to say. She could not pick it up. She pressed her one hand against her chest. She felt her father's eyes searching her flushed face.

Suddenly he got to his feet. "Tell me," he said impatiently, "tell me one thing, please. That you've changed your mind."

"About what, Father?" she asked feebly.

"Why, about having that baby baptized." He pointed to the bed. "Don't you realize what this is going to mean?" His words did not seem to move her. She sat looking at nothing.

He plunged on. "Shame and disgrace. That's what it will mean. Not only on you, but your whole family and us. What will Father Markum think of us as parents? Looks like we didn't bring you up right."

"Oh, Father, please."

His tall frame sagged. "Hasn't the way you lived before been good enough?"

"I'm—I'm not sure, Father," came her subdued answer.

"Not sure?" Her father's face reddened. "Something—" he stood speechless, shaking his head and gazing with an unfamiliar earnestness at the wall beyond Anna's shoulder— "something or somebody is responsible for this," he said. "If it's America, I wish John had never seen America."

Anna looked up sharply. "America?"

"Then if it's not that," he declared, "it must be that thief Lutz in Daruvar." His breath came faster. "He has no regard.

No honor about him. Going around trying to deceive happy, contented people and break up home ties. It's outrageous. He ought to be put into prison."

Sudden unbidden tears welled up in Anna's eyes. "Oh, no, Father," she cried.

"You mean you're actually defending that man?"

"I didn't mean it that way, Father. Honestly, Father. I mean—," she wiped her eyes with the corner of her apron. "The children are coming in now. I—I don't like to talk about this in front of them."

Immediately his voice became quiet, almost calm. "I hope not."

That day of questioning, warning, criticism, and misunderstanding became a general pattern for many that followed. Some days were better, but more were worse until Anna dreaded to see anyone coming near the house. Sometimes she was dismayed, unsure, even frightened, but like John, tried desperately to appear undisturbed by remarks from anyone.

The thing which hurt most of all was that Elizabeth was not allowed to come over more than once a week, and she was carefully instructed at home not to discuss any phase of religion with either John or Anna, nor to report to them anything she had heard.

Anna was preparing supper one evening when she heard a smothered sound of sobbing in the next room. Looking in, she discovered Mary bending over her bed with her head buried in her pillow, her body shaking. She went to her and gathered her daughter in her arms.

"What's wrong, Mary?"

Mary threw her arms around her mother's neck and laid her head on her shoulder. Her sobs increased.

"Tell me, child."

"Our baby is going to be snatched away," she cried.

"Our baby? Who told you that?"

"Margaret did."

"When?"

"A while ago. Out there when we were playing. She came over and said so."

"But who'll come and snatch him away?"

"A bad devil," she sobbed. "She said he's hovering over our house all the time now waiting his chance. Oh, Mother, will he? Will he?"

Anna held her brokenhearted child close to her and patted her tenderly.

"Why would a devil be hovering over our house, Mary?"

" 'Cause Father Markum is mad at you and Papa and he told him to come get him. Margaret said so. Oh, Mother!"

"It's not so, Mary. Don't cry."

"Margaret made a face at our house too."

"Dear child. That wasn't a nice thing to do. Margaret and you always were such good friends."

"I know. But it's different now. She said her mother might not let her play with me any more."

"Well, you have Kathrine to play with, and Joseph and Anna. If her mother feels that way, we can't help it."

"Why is Father Markum mad at you and Papa?"

Anna never knew it could be so difficult to explain a thing she felt so keenly. What should she say? How could she avert the panic in her little daughter's heart? It wouldn't help to impress her with the fact that they were poor and getting poorer every day; that it was becoming harder for her father to exchange work for food or oil because of the growing barrier between him and the villagers. It wouldn't do to tell her the priest wanted money, the very thing they didn't have; that their house needed a cleansing for years.

"Why is he?" she repeated.

Anna felt a tear trickle down her own cheek. She brushed it away quickly. "I haven't seen Father Markum for a long time, Mary," she said. "He didn't tell me he was mad at us. I don't want anybody to be mad at us. And even if he would be, Mary, he wouldn't have any right to tell a bad spirit to

241

come get our baby. He belongs to us, and remember what I said about God. He understands."

"John!" cried Anna that evening, "I feel as though I can't go on much longer without some kind of help. I've got to find out." She made a deep sigh and wiped away a tear. "It's getting to be one dark day after another until I feel so uncertain, so helpless and sad. I can hardly hide it from the children."

He knew what she meant. They had been reading portions in the Testament every morning. They had marked a number of verses in John that had given rise to questions. "He that believeth on the Son hath everlasting life: and he that believeth not the Son shall not see life; but the wrath of God abideth on him." "Ask, and ye shall receive, that your joy may be full." "I am the bread of life: he that cometh to me shall never hunger; and he that believeth on me shall never thirst." "I am the light of the world: he that followeth me shall not walk in darkness, but shall have the light of life." "Let not your heart be troubled, neither let it be afraid."

"How can we, John?"

"I've been trying to figure out a way for us to get to Daruvar together."

Her eyes widened. "Have you?"

John frowned. "But there are too many obstacles. We have not the money to ride the train and it's too far for you to walk."

"I think I could. I know I could."

John shook his head. "But what about the children?"

"Elizabeth would stay with them. And tomorrow is Saturday. She'd love to."

"Don't get excited, Anna. Your mother wouldn't let her do it."

"I'm going over right now and ask her. Pray hard while I'm gone."

"But what will you tell her?"

"I'll figure that out on the way over." At the door she

called back: "Watch Joseph so he doesn't get into anything. I won't be gone long. Oh, John, if there is a God who hears our prayers, ask Him now."

Chapter 28

It was not a light impulse which sent Anna dashing out of the house leaving John standing there shocked. For days she had been struggling with a constant series of baffling fears and hopes and heartbreaking ideas until she felt torn inside. Had they made a wild, idiotic decision about the baby? A nightmare of noes and yeses had been quarreling within her all that day.

Then when she found Mary sobbing, it cut too deeply. Her nerves were ready to snap. If their innocent children had to suffer because of their indecision, it was time to act. How could she or John attempt to explain to them or offer real comfort when they themselves did not know the answer?

The three, Mother, Father, and Elizabeth, were seated at the table ready to eat. In the dusk, their faces were not clearly outlined, but they looked up, startled, when Anna stepped inside. She made no salutation, but leaned against the casing to steady herself. Her knees shook.

"John and I must both go to Daruvar tomorrow," she announced abruptly. "It's important. Will you let Elizabeth come over after supper so she'll be there when we leave early in the morning?"

She stood erect and without moving. A dreadful silence followed. Anna could hear her father breathing heavier, faster, deeper, as his lower jaw dropped. His eyes were riveted on Anna's with an uneasy frightened gaze. When at last he spoke, his words punctured the bubble of silence with cutting significance.

"She can come," he said with a phlegmish sound in his throat, "if you give us a full report when you return."

Anna chilled. Direct painful thoughts tormented her and made her weak and sick at her stomach. Horrors!

But what else could she expect? What else could she do now but accept this challenge?

"I'll look for you then, Elizabeth." She opened the door and darted out before another word was spoken.

"Are we doomed?" she asked herself on the way home. "Or crazy? My God, help us! Help us!" she half sobbed.

It was early afternoon when the two stood trembling at the front door of the gray block building across the tracks. They looked at each other in silence, worn nerves frayed. John pressed Anna's arm. Then just as he raised his hand to knock, the door opened. Both stepped back.

Mr. Lutz had his hat on and was saying something over his shoulder to his daughter Lillie who was sweeping the floor in the assembly room. Then he noticed.

"Mr. and Mrs. Olesh!" he exclaimed in surprise. "Come in. Come in."

"But I see you were going someplace," John said. "We're intruding."

"Not at all," came the quick reply. "My plans are always flexible. God's ways are better than mine any time. Every time. Come in at once. I was just going to start out and try to hand out a few tracts on the streets. I can do that later. This is the first time you've come together and it is what we've been praying and waiting for. Lillie, go call Mother. You came by train?" He ushered them to seats.

"We walked," answered John. "All but the last three miles. A man with an oxcart gave us a ride."

"But I well realize it was a long tramp at that and you need to sit down and rest yourselves." He took John's hat. "Now first of all, have you had dinner?"

John and Anna glanced at each other. Neither answered.

"You haven't. Agnes," called Lutz, "look who came. There was some soup left over, wasn't there?"

At the sight of the couple Mrs. Lutz's pleasant face broke

245

into a broad smile. "Happy surprise!" She shook hands. "Come on out to the kitchen with me. Then we can all visit together while I warm up the soup. I told Will after dinner there was enough left for two hungry people. The Lord knew you were coming."

"But, Mrs. Lutz," began Anna in an apologetic tone, "we don't like to cause you all this bother. We—"

"Bother nothing. My dear woman, you must not ever say those words again," protested Mrs. Lutz still smiling. "We're here to serve the Lord. This isn't our house. We live here, but it belongs to God. Everything in it, including the food in the cupboard, belongs to God because it has been provided by Him through His people who help us carry on. So, you see, we are only glad to be able to share with others."

Mrs. Lutz quickly set out a plate of sliced bread, apple jam, and a small dish of tasty-looking cottage cheese.

"William," she said as she stirred the soup on the stove, "reach up there and get out two of those soup bowls. And cups. I'll make coffee."

"I will," agreed Mr. Lutz, "but I can't wait another minute. John," he said, looking him full in the face with earnestness, "have you come back to inquire when we're leaving Daruvar?"

Instead of answering, John looked at Anna. A startled expression crossed his face.

"Oh, John," Anna pinched the words from her tightly closed teeth. Color left her cheeks. "What will we do now?"

"Are you?" John asked.

Lutz shook his head. "Not yet, John. I just said that, remembering your last visit. Opposition has not lessened, that is certain. But as long as God gives us the strength and courage to stay here and testify, we're going to stay. Aren't we, Agnes?"

"Of course."

"He's promised never to leave us nor forsake us. He's

246

promised to be with us even to the end of the world. And again, 'If God be for us, who can be against us?' "

"Mr. Lutz." Slowly the color crept into Anna's cheeks and into her tired brown eyes, a faint glow. "All that," she said quietly, "is in the little Testament you gave me."

"It certainly is," agreed Lutz. "And many more promises just as precious. I know now you've been reading that Testament."

Anna clasped and unclasped her trembling hands. She bit her lip to keep back the tears. "Could those promises possibly be for us too, Mr. Lutz?"

"To be sure, they are for you. God is no respecter of persons. Why, Mrs. Olesh, God couldn't be God and love Agnes or me more than He does you. Surely you don't think He would do more for us than He would for you, do you?"

"I didn't know."

"Every promise in the Word of God is for you once you have accepted Him by faith."

Again John and Anna exchanged glances. Anna opened her mouth, but the words seemed to be stuck in her throat. A tear trickled down each cheek. "Then please tell us how," she said softly.

"Nothing could make me happier, Mrs. Olesh. Nothing in the world."

"We simply can't go on like this any longer. We've been floundering around for years."

"Bless your hearts. Agnes says the soup is ready; so please pull up to the table and I'll offer a prayer of thanks." He did.

"My! this tastes very good, Mrs. Lutz," said John.

"Very kind of you," added Anna. "You see, Mr. Lutz, we never knew anything but what the priest and our parents and grandparents told us, until you came that day."

Lutz nodded.

"We've been so mixed up, confused, and distressed ever since. And now—" her voice broke. She bit her lip. Slowly

247

she took another sip of soup.

"Do believe me. I did not intend to make either of you unhappy."

"I'm sorry," Anna answered sadly. "Perhaps you can explain how we feel, John. I'm not saying what I want to at all. Oh"—her sad eyes were downcast for a moment, then she looked up into Lutz's face—"why is it so hard for us to tell you now what we mean and feel so deeply?" She rested her flushed cheek on one hand. With the other she slowly moved the spoon back and forth in the soup.

"You needn't try, Mrs. Olesh," said Mr. Lutz in a gentle manner. "I know what you're trying to tell me."

"How?"

"I was once in the very place you are now."

"You?"

"I was once a very badly confused, miserable, condemned creature myself. Yes, floundering around as you put it. Comparing religions and finding fault with them all. But all the while seeking for the truth. I knew there must be an answer to my troubled, unhappy soul. I had no rest, no peace of mind day nor night. I wanted a lasting peace, something to satisfy, something which passes all understanding. Something which would cast out that fear of what friends, relatives, families, and above all, the priests, would do to me."

"You, Mr. Lutz?" inquired Anna. "You know about families and—and relatives?"

"Do I? I doubt if you can mention a fear, a superstition, a threat, or an agony of soul I didn't experience before and during and after the time I broke away from the church. You see, I was brought up a Greek Catholic."

"But didn't you tell me your mother—?"

"Yes. Yes, I remember telling you on the train. Ten years after I was saved, I led my own dear mother to saving knowledge of Jesus Christ. But for at least eight years she opposed me as bitterly as anyone. Did I lose friends? Did my family and relatives treat me like an outcast? A traitor? A heretic? To be sure. But listen; today I have more friends in Christ than I ever had by the ties of flesh. The Scriptures promise that we will. Let me get my Bible and read it to you."

He was gone only a minute.

"Here it is in Mark 10:29. 'Jesus answered and said, Verily I say unto you, There is no man that hath left house, or brethren, or sisters, or father, or mother, or wife, or children, or lands, for my sake, and the gospel's, but he shall receive an hundredfold now in this time, houses, and brethren, and sisters, and mothers, and children, and lands, with persecutions; and in the world to come eternal life.' You see, God doesn't promise us all this without persecution, but in the end eternal life. Trials for a time, to be sure, but it's the end we're striving for. I remember well the day I was so sick and tired of making penance, confessing my sins to the priest, trying to earn my way to Heaven, counting beads, kissing the father's hand, and all that, that I said to myself, 'I'll walk around the globe to find the kind of peace I need.'"

"Then what?" asked John.

"Then one day a Protestant missionary handed me a tract right there on the street in Budapest. It was sundown. I was just about to cross the street when a man on the corner held out a folded paper to me. It was entitled 'Twelve Undisputable Things Everyone Should Know.' I began to read at once. It told first how we are all born in sin. Let me read to you from the Word. Romans 3:10 reads like this: 'There is none righteous, no, not one.' Romans 5:12, 'By one man sin entered into the world, and death by sin; and so death passed upon all men, for that all have sinned.' So what can we do about it? Matthew 18:3, 'Except ye be converted, and become as little children, ye shall not enter into the kingdom of heaven.' John 3:3, 'Except a man be born again [that is, from above, of His Spirit], he cannot see the kingdom of God.'

"Nowhere in the Word does it say we must go to a man

249

to confess our sins. God did something about our hopeless, helpless situation. He 'so loved the world, that he gave his only begotten Son [Jesus Christ], that whosoever believeth in him [Jesus Christ] should not perish, but have everlasting life' (John 3:16). Listen to this. II Peter 3:9, 'The Lord is . . . longsuffering to usward, not willing that any should perish, but that all should come to repentance.' Christ did the work for us. He paid the price for our redemption. Isaiah 53:5 reads like this: 'He [that is, Jesus Christ] was wounded for . . . [John and Anna Olesh's] transgressions, he was bruised for . . . [John's and Anna's] iniquities: the chastisement of . . . [John's and Anna's] peace was upon him; and with his stripes . . . [John and Anna Olesh] are healed.' "

Amazed, John and Anna looked at each other. "Does it really say our names, Mr. Lutz?" asked Anna.

"No, it says *our*. But if it means me, it also means you, my friends. Listen again. Christ did not shed His blood on the cross for nothing. Ephesians 1:7 tells us how powerful His blood is: 'In whom we have redemption through his blood.' We are not saved from our sins by paying money. And according to the Scriptures, there is no such place as purgatory. If we are lost when we die, we are lost forever. It is the blood of Christ that makes atonement for our sins. Matthew 11:28 says, 'Come.' This is Christ's invitation to whomsoever. 'Come unto me [to Christ], all ye that labour and are heavy laden, and I will give you rest.' Rest of mind. Rest from floundering around. Rest from that heavy burden of sin. Rest from fear, from superstition. John 6:37 says, 'Him that cometh to me [to Christ] I will in no wise [under no circumstances] cast out.' Isn't this good news?"

John and Anna sat spellbound.

"Was He able to save a confused, mixed-up, man-fearing person like I was? Yes, indeed. Glory to God! Hebrews 7:25 told me, 'He is able . . . to save them to the uttermost that come unto God by him [Jesus Christ].' He is able to do it for you too, for He is able to do exceeding abundantly above all that any of us ask or think. That's found here in Ephesians 3:20. He is not only able to save us but to keep us saved. Able to help us over every temptation. And He keeps and will keep every one of His promises. Never once has He failed anyone. When we fail, it's our fault. Do you understand thus far what I've read?"

After a moment Anna spoke. "I had no idea it was that plain," she said softly, "but, how can we—I mean how can we actually get saved? I mean, really know we are? We—we want to, but how, Mr. Lutz?"

"By believing. 'He that believeth on the Son hath everlasting life.' "

"It can't be that easy."

"Do you believe Jesus was born of the Virgin Mary?"

"I do."

"And you, John?"

"Yes."

"Do you believe He was born to save us all from our sins?" Both nodded.

"Do you think anyone living could be good enough, or do enough good deeds to others, or do enough penance to earn his own salvation?"

John shrugged his shoulders.

"No. No one could. No one is saved by good works, by giving money, by prayers, or by penance. Nor by praying to the Blessed Virgin, who is no mediator between us and God. We are saved the moment we accept His sacrifice by faith. 'Believe on the Lord Jesus Christ, and thou shalt be saved.' I'm reading this right here in Acts 16. Romans 10:9, 'If thou shalt confess with thy mouth the Lord Jesus, and shalt believe in thine heart that God hath raised him from the dead, thou shalt be saved.' "

"Oh, Mr. Lutz," cried Anna in tears, "I want to do that.

251

I want to confess with my mouth the Lord Jesus. Does it mean now?"

"Yes, Mrs. Olesh, it means right now—this very moment —you are saved."

"Oh," Anna's face glowed. "John," she said, reaching over and touching his arm.

He nodded. "I too," he said. "I want to confess with my mouth the Lord Jesus."

"Praise God!" Mr. Lutz pressed John's hand in his own, then Anna's. "Let us kneel in prayer. Heavenly Father, bless these two honest seekers for the truth. Bless them for hearing your holy, inspired words. Bless them for accepting Thy Word by faith. Bless them for believing on God who sent Jesus Christ. We thank Thee for Thy priceless gift of everlasting life. We thank Thee that because we believe we shall not come into condemnation but have already passed from death unto eternal life. Be merciful to those who have not yet believed and use us all to tell the good news of salvation to many. In Jesus' name we pray. Amen.

"And now, John, I'd like you and your wife to each pray and tell God what's on your hearts. Tell Him you believe on Him, that you've accepted Him into your own hearts, that you want to live for Him the rest of your days. Ask him to be your strength to meet every new trial and temptation which will come to you. Tell Him with your own mouths what the sins are you want Him to forgive and forget forever. Then thank Him for doing all this for you."

"Mr. Lutz," began John, "I never prayed aloud. But I'll try my best."

"That's all God ever expects of any of us, John."

It was an honest and simple prayer each offered. And when they got up from their knees, there was no need for Lutz to ask if they had found the answer to their burdened hearts. Their faces and tears of joy told that. Mrs. Lutz put her arm around Anna's neck and kissed her affectionately.

"We must hurry on our way now," John said. "And we can't tell you what this means to us."

"Don't go yet," said Lutz. "There's a train going out at three-thirty. That will give us time to talk over a few things yet."

"We haven't the money."

"I'll pay your way home."

"It's too much, Mr. Lutz," objected John.

"I want to do it. Stay. I want to talk to you about obedience to His Word. For if we love Him, we will keep His commandments. One of them concerns baptism upon your own confession. You were likely baptized as infants."

Both nodded.

"Now wouldn't you like to be baptized again with your own request and understanding? Upon your own acknowledgment of Jesus Christ?"

"If that's the thing to do, we want to do it, don't we, Anna?"

"Why, yes, John. There's no use starting out unless we go all the way."

"It may be a long time before we get back here again," John remarked thoughtfully.

"It may never be," added Anna. "After I give my father a full report of what we've done when we get home. John—" she caught his hand in hers. "Yes. That was the agreement. Don't looked surprised."

"You didn't tell me that."

"I'm telling you now. Otherwise he wouldn't have let Elizabeth come over."

"All right," he said after a period of silence. "I might have guessed that much. The blow will come sooner or later. So let's get some more instruction and have Mr. Lutz baptize us while we're here. Have you waited to tell me anything else?"

"Nothing else," she whispered. "What could be worse than that?"

Chapter 29

When Elizabeth returned home early that evening, her father looked up, startled.

"Home already?"

"They came back on the train."

"The train? I thought John was broke. What did he sell?"

"I didn't ask, Father. You told me not to ask them any questions before they left nor after they returned."

"Elizabeth."

"Yes, Father."

"Elizabeth."

"Yes, Mother."

Four eyes marked with dread were riveted on the child.

"What do you think they went for?" Both Mother and Father pressed the question from anxious minds.

"I don't have any idea. I don't," she repeated.

"Did they bring a package, a sack, or anything along home?" asked her mother.

"Nothing that I could see."

"How did they act?" questioned her father.

"Very happy. Happier than I've seen them for a long, long time. I stayed and ate supper with them. Anna insisted."

"Then go back," ordered Elizabeth's father immediately. "It's not too late. Tell Anna I want her to come over. Go now." He walked back and forth across the room rubbing his calloused hands together. Then he stood at the door waiting. "Now let me do the talking," he reminded his wife.

"Try not to be harsh with her."

"Well, we got back the same day," began Anna in a pleasant voice. "We'll never get done thanking you for letting Elizabeth come over. I'll sit down if you don't mind."

254

"Sit," said her father. He tore his gaze from her glowing face for a moment and his Adam's apple went up and down twice. "Elizabeth tells me you walked in and rode back." He turned halfway around and gave her a sidewise glance.

"We did. Otherwise we wouldn't be halfway home yet."

"What you went for must have been extremely important."

Anna pressed a fold of her skirt between her fingers. "It was."

"We're ready for the report." His voice was low and mechanical. Anna could both see and feel he was trying desperately to control his emotions.

"Very well," came her answer. "You evidently have a suspicion or a fear that we went for something quite out of order, Father."

"I—I wish we didn't have, Anna," he admitted. The words seemed to be blown from him with engine force. "Please set our minds at ease," he added. There was both anxiety and impatience in his husky voice. "Your poor mother has been fretting herself almost sick."

"I'm sorry." Anna looked over at her mother sitting beside the dim oil lamp. Her forlorn face was resting on one hand.

"Well, Father," began Anna with deliberation, "what I have to report will not make you feel any better, I'm afraid."

She saw her father press his one large hand on his chest as if something were hurting inside.

"For that," she continued, "I feel very sad. Because I do hate to hurt your feelings or Mother's or go against your wishes. I love you both very much. But I belong to John now. We must live our own lives and bring up our children the way we see best. For years we have been thinking there must be a better, happier way of living."

Her father's arms dropped. Mother sat tense. Elizabeth, standing behind the stove, never took her eyes off Anna.

"Today John and I had a long talk with Mr. Lutz."

255

"No." Her father's voice sounded not angry but wounded, as though his feelings had been slashed to the bone.

Anna heard her mother utter a low cry and saw her clutch her throat with both hands.

"So it's actually come to that! Then he did cast an evil spell over you and your house that day he was there."

"No, Father."

"What else could this mean? I've always had a terrible fear of that sneak."

"I know, Father. But it was no evil spell. He brought us good news. The best news we've ever heard. The news of salvation and peace of mind. Forgiveness through Jesus Christ."

"It can't be true. Anna, this is impossible. Now I know you're under a spell." Nervously he shifted his glance.

Anna continued. "You might as well be the first in the village to know too that we've had one of his New Testaments in the house for some time and—"

"Never!" His eyes bulged. He grabbed the chair back in front of him for support.

"And today John and I accepted God's Christ for our pardon from sin. We are saved by faith without going to the priest or—"

"Impossible! Outrageous! You're beside yourselves!"

"We never were more sure of doing right, Father."

The sweet clarity of her words frightened the three who heard them. Suddenly, after a deathly quiet, Anna's father lunged forward. As he waved his hand it struck the corner of the stove, cutting a gash in the thick flesh below the last knuckle. His legs shook.

"You!" he cried brokenly, peering at Anna from under his heavy eyebrows, "you, of all persons, the first in our village to allow that rascal to make fools of you. Anna," he repeated half sobbing, "my dear daughter, this is so silly, so unheard of."

She could scarcely speak now for the lump in her throat.

"I hope," she said tenderly, "that John and I will be able to prove to you and everyone in the village that the thing we have done is what everyone must do to be saved."

Her father uttered a deep groan.

"We did not decide to do this suddenly. It seemed to us a lifetime of hunting and groping, of doubting, and I never again want to go through all the things we suffered before we finally had the courage to go for help."

"Suffered!" exclaimed Anna's father. "You poor child. You are only going to begin now to know what suffering is. Everything will be against you now. Everything in this life and in the one to come." He stood appalled as though paralyzed. Her mother covered her face in her apron and sobbed as if her heart were breaking. Elizabeth too was crying.

"I know there will be suffering," admitted Anna—she got to her feet and folded her arms behind her—"but Christ knows all about it. He suffered for us, and He will go with us through our suffering; and if God is for us, who can be against us?"

"Everyone will be against you. Don't be surprised, Anna, if you are driven out of Miletinac."

"If we are, God surely will find a place for us to go. He wouldn't be God and accept us as His children, then desert us."

"Bah, such talk. Who ever heard of the like? Father Markum will be seeing you and getting you out of this nightmare of a thing."

"He won't need to waste his time on us, Father. Mr. Lutz is our pastor now. We were received into his church today by water baptism. Just let Father Markum let us alone."

"Let him! Let him!" shouted her father. "You'll see the day when you and John will both be down on your knees begging him to baptize your baby and forgive your sins. Oh, Anna, Anna!" He shook. Never had Anna seen her father so uncontrolled.

She went to him and threw her arms around his neck. "Don't take it so hard, Father."

He held her out at arms' length. "It's a curse on our village, on our family, and on John's family. Worse than that, on your innocent children. They will grow up to curse you for this, Anna." He dropped his arms as though they were so much lead.

"Good-by, Mother." Anna stooped and kissed her on the head as she walked to the door. "Good-by, Elizabeth. Thanks for taking care of the children. Mary and Kathrine said you all had a grand time."

Elizabeth could not answer for crying.

The Testament was no longer hidden under the mattress but wrapped in a clean white cloth and kept on top of the dresser where the children could see it. Instead of reading portions from it in secret in the morning before the children were awake, John read to the family each evening immediately after supper.

"This is God's Book of stories for us," he explained to the children. "Parts of what I read to you I may not understand clearly myself, but I'll explain to you what I can. It is what is in this Book that makes your mother and me happy even though we're poor and even though the neighbors make fun of us and call us names. We won't let that make us feel bad. We know God loves us. Mr. Lutz said if possible he'd come to see us once a month. He's our real friend and when he comes he will help us to understand this Book better. Now when I'm done reading, we'll all bow our heads and be quiet while I pray to God."

Without those daily periods of devotion the trials John and Anna were soon to encounter would have been unbearable. Criticisms, accusations, shunnings, public sneerings flowed uninterrupted from every angle and every age. Children threw clods at the Olesh house and made hideous faces at the children whenever they stepped outside. Some of the older neighbors tried to reason with John and Anna at first on a quiet, personal, intimate level. Then, when that failed to move them, they tried powerful, frantic words. After each interview John and Anna vowed their vows again with spontaneity and thanked God for another opportunity to testify to their salvation.

Then came the season for the annual house blessing. It was a dazzling bright winter day with just enough nip in the air to make a person feel good. There was that usual early morning stir and bustle in the village, children sweeping yards, mothers wiping windows and scrubbing little faces.

"Papa, who's going to sweep our yard?" asked Mary, watching a little wistfully from the window.

"I will," he answered, picking up the broom. "But it's hardly worthwhile."

"But it's dirty, Papa. Look at all the straw and corncobs on it. And there's an eggshell too."

"I swept it last evening. Someone littered it again during the night."

"When the father comes and sees all that, he will think we are very bad and dirty, Papa."

"He may, Mary. But God knows how it got there. I'll go sweep it once more if it will make you happier."

"I think it would."

While John was sweeping, the schoolteacher passed. When he was less than a rod beyond the house, he turned around, raised his fist threateningly, and muttered an oath. "You traitor," he muttered scornfully. "You high-minded turncoat."

It was noon when the long black-robed father appeared with his pewter water jar. Dozens of faces were watching from windows. Some of the villagers were standing outside. One was John's father. Would the father sprinkle the Olesh house? Would he?

He stood stock still with a diagnostic air.

"Come back from the window, Mary and Kathrine," John said gently. "Joe, come here to me. He'll soon go on to the next place."

But he didn't. He stepped up to the door and knocked with vigor.

John answered the knock.

"If what I'm told is true," he said with unceremonious bluntness, "your house does not deserve a blessing this time."

"That is quite all right with us," answered John calmly.

"You mean you don't even care?" He raised his bushy eyebrows.

"Why should I? God has already blessed it as no man can."

"Man? You call me an ordinary man?"

"There is only one Father. Our Father God."

"Blasphemy!" shouted the father, eyes blazing. "Has it occurred to you that you are headed for a terrible disaster, John Olesh?"

"The terrible disaster we were headed for before our eyes were opened to the truth has occurred to me," replied John.

"Truth?" retorted the father. "Who can know the truth apart from the pope?"

"Whosoever seeks to find it. I mean, whoever seeks with all his heart, will sooner or later find it. I am one of those who sought."

"You're damned, John Olesh. It's a terrible sin to go against the church. Unforgiveable."

"But I have a Testament. It tells me something altogether different. It tells me I'm saved through faith in Jesus Christ."

"You'll go to Hell." His face reddened.

"I hope not."

"You will."

"Not unless I turn down what Christ has already done for me."

"Blasphemy! Blasphemy!" shouted the father. "And remember, John, you're going to be doubly punished for leading your family astray. And that is nothing to wink at. I am going to warn every person in this village about you and this vicious doctrine you've given yourself over to. You're going to suffer hunger and want in this life and torment forever in the next. And your baby. I'll see to it that that matter is taken care of too."

In consternation Father Markum gathered his skirts in one hand, and whirling around, hurried to the next house.

"Oh, Father Markum!" cried Anna's mother bitterly after he had sprinkled their house. "Isn't this the most awful thing that has ever happened in our village! My daughter, my son-in-law!"

"The Olesh family?"

"Yes. Oh, Father, Anna is our own daughter. Father, please don't blame us. We've done our best to teach her the rules of the holy church, Father."

"I sincerely hope so," he said tonelessly.

"We've done and said all we know to show them their wrong," she cried. "Here's our offering, Father." Hot tears streaked her pale face. She kissed his hand before giving the coins to him. "We only wish it could be ten, twenty times more, Father." Worn, tired, and harassed from sleepless nights, she anxiously waited to hear a few tender words of thanks, comfort, or something from him.

He spoke four words. Only four. Cool, hasty, cutting. "Woman, they are hopeless."

Utterly depressed, she staggered inside and dropped on the first chair she could reach.

"And does he blame us?" huskily whispered her husband who had been watching from within.

"I couldn't tell. I couldn't tell," she wailed. "But I don't care to live now."

"Mother!" cried Elizabeth. "Why do you talk like that?"

"Because I hate living. I hate myself. I hate the mountains. I hate the sun in the sky. I hate all my wasted efforts trying to live right. I hate everything, even the fa— Oh, go away, Elizabeth. Go out of the house for a while, yes, you and your father both. Go out and let me alone till I get out of this terrible nightmare." She finished with words incoherent.

261

Elizabeth clung to her father, frantically, shaking like a leaf. "What's gone wrong with Mother?" she sobbed.

"Get your coat," he said with dreadful seriousness. "Your mother is beside herself. Let's take a walk."

He knocked on the Olesh door gently, breathing heavily, painfully. John opened.

"John, I want to talk to Anna."

"Come in, Father. She's feeding the baby."

"I'd rather talk to her out here, alone."

"It's warmer inside, Father."

"I can't come in."

"Why not?"

"Because."

"Not because you're not welcome, Father."

He shifted from one foot to the other. His morbid countenance took on a slightly hopeful look. "Well."

"Come in, Father," called Anna pleasantly.

"Come in, Grandpa," called little Joseph.

Reluctantly he obeyed. Elizabeth followed, cheeks flushed, eyes swollen and red.

"This is killing your mother, Anna." She tasted the bitterness of the words hurled at her. Mary and Kathrine looked panicky.

"No, Father," said Anna firmly. "I'm praying for her. For you and Elizabeth, too. Why didn't she come along?"

"Because she is beside herself. She is at home saying things she doesn't mean. She is terribly disturbed and neither of us can do anything with her."

"Did you want me to go over to her?"

"No. Not unless you go to tell her things are going to be different here."

"What do you mean, Father? Turn back to our fear and superstition and darkness? Go back to beads and images and the hideous old witch doctor and all that, after enjoying this peace, this happiness and light? Never, Father. I would be beside myself if I did that. The more people talk to us, the more we are sure we did the right thing. And since Father Markum was here and talked to John today we're happier yet that we've been delivered from— Why, Father!"

Holding his breath he wheeled around and walked out. He groaned in unspeakable anguish.

"What will we do?" sobbed Elizabeth.

"Nothing," he said smitten. "Nothing."

Chapter 30

Wencel walked close behind Elizabeth whistling softly. Gently he pulled on her one braid.

"Don't, Wencel."

He stepped up beside her. "I didn't hurt you, did I?"

"No. But—"

"But what?" He gave her a glance out of the corner of his eye. "You've got pretty hair. Know it?"

"Now, Wencel."

"I mean it."

She blushed and looked straight ahead.

Wencel picked up a small stone and threw it as far as he could. "You've got the prettiest hair of any girl in school," he ventured timidly. "Did you see me hit that tree yonder?"

"Sure."

"Can you throw a—? I didn't mean that. Girls don't do such things. I'll carry your books if you want me to."

She did not resist when he reached for them.

"Going to Djulovac Sunday?"

"Don't know yet. I might if it doesn't storm. Why?"

"If you do," Wencel adjusted his bill cap, "thought maybe we could leave at the same time."

"Why?" Elizabeth asked vaguely. A glint of light crossed her face like the first rays of sun on the horizon.

"Well, I'd like to walk with you if you don't object. And your parents don't."

They walked on in silence. Elizabeth could feel her heart in her throat. Her cheeks colored.

"Think they would?" he asked, knitting his brow.

"I don't know why they should, Wencel," answered Elizabeth softly. "But would yours?"

"Don't know why they should," came his quick reply. "It's not fair you and your parents should be talked about or misjudged just because John Olesh drug your sister out of the church."

"I'm glad to hear you say that, Wencel."

"I never did think it was nice the way some of them pestered you with questions just because she was your sister. You can't help it. Can you?"

"Oh, Wencel," smiled Elizabeth. Funny little prickles danced around her heart. "I'm glad."

"Maybe it looked like I was helping along in it at first, but I will never help again. Pop said last night anyone can see how hard your mother and father are taking it. And I never did think it was nice the time you had to stay after school and the father talked to you."

"That wasn't all."

"I know. All that writing business." Wencel said a bad word under his breath.

Elizabeth raised her chin. "And I don't care," she exclaimed, "what anyone says about my sister. I still love her even if she did turn out this way. And I always will. People just don't know how nice she really is in spite—"

"Pop says it probably all started when John went off to America and he's to blame."

"Well, I don't know exactly who's to blame, Wencel, but it's awful to have a thing like this happen in your family."

"Well, I know one thing," asserted Wencel. "Much as I'd like to see America, I'll never go off and leave my wife like that." He gave her a glance. "If I can't take her along, I won't go. Anyhow, I wouldn't lead her away from the church."

Elizabeth's heart pounded. She swallowed twice.

There was a peculiar solemnity in John's voice. He was reading from the sixth chapter of Matthew. "For your Father knoweth what things ye have need of, before ye ask

265

him." He looked at Anna sitting at the opposite side of the table, little Anna's sleepy head on her shoulder. "After this manner therefore pray ye: Our Father which art in heaven, Hallowed be thy name. Thy kingdom come. Thy will be done in earth, as it is in heaven. Give us this day our daily bread." He hesitated. His eyes scanned the clean-scraped dishes on the table, then his four fast-growing children. "And forgive us our debts, as we forgive our debtors." Slowly he closed the book, bowed his head, and prayed. "Dear Father in heaven." He paused. "We need You if ever we did. This book says You know what we need before we try to tell You. You know then. Right now. For the sake of these our dear children do something for us. The thing we need. And help us to have forgiveness in our hearts toward all our neighbors who feel hard toward us. Dear God, give me as the father of this family special wisdom to know what to do. Give us the courage we need to face what may come tomorrow. Amen."

The urgency of John's prayer that evening in January sent a score of pulses throbbing through Anna's being. She felt it to the tips of her fingers and toes. She drew little Anna closer and a tear fell on her golden-colored hair.

By no means did John and Anna hear directly or indirectly all the criticism that was daily being heaped at their door. The inhuman judgment against the "mad Lutzites" soon had its appalling and infectious influence throughout the village. John Olesh, the most ambitious, the most aggressive, the most intelligent young man in Miletinac, was regarded with contempt. He was a disgrace to the village, a blot on Christ's church. No one wanted to exchange his services for cabbages, pumpkin-seed oil, or potatoes even though some pitied his wife and children in their dire need.

More than once in the gray hours of night Aunt Tena slipped some food in the door and hurried back hoping no one had seen her. Anna's mother did the same and so did John's parents.

The first visit by Lutz did not tend to lessen the malicious village gossip. The air was charged with piercing statements. "Let's kick him all the way back to Daruvar." "Let's have him buried alive." "Let's put him in a cage and let him starve to death."

Yet no one so much as laid hands on him. Lutz walked head erect and smiling in the middle of the broad open street of Miletinac. He even spoke pleasantly to the children who eyed him in puzzled fearfulness and who forgot themselves for the moment and answered his friendly greetings.

"You are both making progress," he said with gladness after spending an hour with John and Anna in the midst of their family. "This is of utmost importance in the beginning of your new life in Christ. I am not at all surprised to hear of the opposition and criticism. I expected that. But remember this one thing: let us not get discouraged and give up because the way is hard. Christ suffered all this and more for us. And remember, too, that wide is the gate and broad is the way that leadeth to destruction and many there be which go on it. But strait is the gate and narrow is the way which leadeth unto life everlasting and few there are who find it. Aren't you glad you are among those few? Another thing to remember is this. When we seek first the kingdom of God and His righteousness, all the things He sees we need will be added to us. Someday in some way, John and Anna, you will come to realize the truth of this promise. We don't know how or when it will all come about, but let's keep on trusting and believing and obeying one day at a time and He'll take care of the rest. I can speak out of our personal experience. We've tried and tested this promise and it's as true as God Himself. When are you coming to Daruvar again?"

"Together?" asked John.

"Yes."

"I doubt if that will be until Mary is old enough to stay with the children. I doubt if we could find anyone in the village who would be willing to come and stay with them even if I had the money to pay them. I may go to Daruvar next week to see about borrowing some money."

"Wish I could help you out, John, but I've never had any to loan. How much do you need?"

John looked at Anna. She shook her head.

"Be sure to stop in," Lutz said. "I'll have something for you. Now I'm going to leave this Bible here for you. It contains the Old Testament as well as the New. It begins with God's creation of the world and man and how sin came into the world. The Old Testament helps to explain the New. You'll enjoy reading many of these Old Testament stories to the children, such as the story of the first home on earth, the first children, the first great ship and why it was built, and the first rainbow. Then there's the beautiful story of a great man Abraham and his son Isaac, and the story of Joseph with his coat of many colors. Your children will enjoy it and want to hear it over and over. Then there's the beautiful story of Baby Moses who was hidden in a basket in the rushes. Then there's the story of David the shepherd boy who killed the giant Goliath, and Daniel who was cast into the lions' den, and Joshua and his army and what happened to the walls of Jericho, and the story of the boy Samuel."

Mary's and Kathrine's eyes sparkled. They clapped their hands.

"You'll want Mother to begin reading right away, won't you?" Lutz smiled at the beautiful, bright-eyed little girls and took Joseph up on his knee and stroked his hair.

"Will you, Mother?" begged Mary.

Anna nodded.

"Just think," beamed Mary. "Now we'll have a storybook in our house."

"The best storybook in all the world, Mary," answered Lutz. "I'd better hurry back to Vilieki Bastaji to get that next train, but I've enjoyed myself here with you so much I'm reluctant to leave."

"But you will stay long enough to eat a bite, won't you?" suggested Anna.

"Thank you. But I have my lunch right here in my coat pocket and I'll eat after I get on the train. Let's have prayer together before I go."

John walked with Lutz to the edge of the village.

"This may make it harder for you, John. Folks are eying us from every side."

"They might as well know we're friends."

"And in sweet fellowship too," Lutz remarked in a jovial tone. "Your wife really gave a good testimony today, John. A fine attitude toward your whole problem. I was amazed. She's a brave little woman."

"That's what I mean to talk to you about," said John with seriousness. "You noticed she shook her head?"

"Yes."

"She didn't want me to say in front of the children what I want to go to Daruvar for next week."

"I see."

"I want to find out if I can borrow money again from that Jewish man to go to America."

"America?"

"I see no other way out. Brother Lutz, I can't see my family go hungry. I thought perhaps I could go and work until I had enough to move the family close to Daruvar. We'd like to be able to attend church every Sunday and get our children in Sunday school."

"I like your idea, John. But of course I hate to see you leave. What does your wife say?"

"She sees where this is bringing us. She's quite thrilled over my suggestion to move closer to church. We talked about it at length last night and she is willing to have me go. I'm positive I can find work. Perhaps the people in the village won't be so hard on her and the children if I get away."

"Might be."

"If I do go, would you try to come over once a month and see how they're getting along?"

"I'd do my best, John. And you can count on me to help them out with food too."

"I didn't mean that. I don't like begging. Please understand me. I meant, look after them spiritually."

"I knew what you meant, John. But as God provides, I'll take joy in sharing. And if God opens the way for you to go to America for the sole purpose of bettering your family spiritually, He wouldn't be God and fail to supply what they need. Remember, I didn't say want, but need."

"Anna isn't choosy. She appreciates anything."

"If I had only known your circumstances, I could have brought you a sack of cornmeal today. Be sure to stop in when you come over next week."

John hadn't reached LeHavre, France, when Father Markum came to see Anna. She knew before he spoke that his mission was not of a pleasant nature. His lips were drawn tightly over his teeth and his eyes snapped.

"We've never yet tolerated such impudence, Mrs. Olesh," he began abruptly, searching her face.

It angered him that she made no answer. "Did you hear what I said?" He spoke each word with preciseness.

"Yes, sir."

"Do you have any idea what this will amount to, Mrs. Olesh?"

"No, sir. I haven't any idea what you have in mind."

"Do you recall ever hearing me say that those who play with fire are liable to get burned?"

"I remember."

"You think I was joking?" He fumbled with the cross hanging from his neck.

"No, sir."

"Saying so many idle words?"

"No, sir."

"Sir?" he shouted angrily. "Insulting isn't the word. I'm still the father. And you are the only person in this village who has ventured such dishonor. You will pay dearly for all this reproach on the church. You are to appear in court in Daruvar Saturday morning."

"In court?" Anna felt lightheaded. She grabbed the door casing for support.

"Your husband has gone to America again, I understand."

"Yes."

"How long will he be gone this time?"

"I couldn't tell you."

"He'd better have taken you with him. I understand too that that devil-worker Lutz was here to see you recently."

Anna made no answer.

"The church will take care of that too. Unless you bring your baby to have it baptized before Friday, you will answer in court Saturday morning."

He waited.

Again Anna made no answer.

"You will talk yet," he said sternly. And his bold-featured face was set. With lips compressed he walked away.

"What did he mean?" cried Mary frantically.

"I don't know exactly, Mary." Anna sank on the nearest chair and buried her face in her apron.

"Why are you crying, Mother?" sobbed Mary, trying to lift her mother's face.

"Oh, I don't know why I should," she answered in an effort to quell her fears. "God will surely undertake for us somehow."

"Undertake? What does that mean, Mother?"

"Dear child." Anna drew Mary close to her. "It means God understands what I have got to go through and that He will help me. Oh, Mary, dear, He will have to. He will just have to. And you. Mary, what would I ever do without you? You will have to help me pray about this too."

"I will, Mother."

The next day Anna received by mail the official notice to appear in court at eleven o'clock or before on Saturday morning.

She went straight to her mother and showed it to her.

"You'll let Elizabeth come and stay with the children, won't you, Mother? I can't leave them alone."

"Of course you can't, Anna. But what a mess you've gotten yourself into now! And it could have all been avoided."

Anna took one long, long breath. "I know, Mother. But it's the price we had to pay to get peace."

Anna's mother had no tears. They seemed to be frozen deep within her. "A very, very strange sort of peace," she said. "I'll have to see what your father has to say."

"If Mary were only a little older, I wouldn't need to bother anyone. Maybe Aunt Tena would come, but the children all love Elizabeth and her ways best. You won't turn me down, will you, Mother?"

"Oh, Anna!" cried her mother with a sudden outburst of emotion. "I never did turn you down. You're the ones who did the turning. We used to be such a happy family. And now—all this."

"Mother, I must go. I'll look for her. You won't fail me. You can't."

272

Chapter 31

"You're in trouble, Anna," Mrs. Lutz said simply. "Come in and tell us all about it."

Anna welcomed the security and friendly warmth of the house. Briefly without tears she told the story between pauses. She was exhausted and her nerves were tense. "I looked at the clock in the depot," she concluded wearily, "and saw I had a little time. So I stopped to tell you, rest a while, and perhaps beg a cup of coffee." She twisted the corner of her homemade handkerchief.

"You'll have more than a cup of coffee, my dear," declared Agnes Lutz. "You shall have anything in this house you want to eat. And we're going to have prayer with you before you leave. Aren't we, William?"

"Of course. And, Anna," he said comfortingly, "remember this. God will not let you be tempted above what you will be able to endure by His divine help. He is with you, in you, above you, around you, before you, behind you, to help you in this particular trial. He is with you right now. This very instant. So don't worry. Don't let any man or group of people on earth frighten you. If you worry, you do not trust. He'll see you through this trial. I'm going over and slip in if I can. Remember, these words are in God's eternal Word: 'If God be for us, who can be against us?' "

"But, Mr. Lutz—"

"Yes, Anna, I know what you're thinking. Some folks are definitely against us in what we believe and do. But remember, some were against Christ too. But did they succeed in destroying Him or His purpose? No. Neither will anyone who is against the right that you do. We know God is with us and for us. I'll pray for you right now while Agnes prepares your lunch and we'll pray again together just before you leave."

The prayer Brother Lutz offered was simple, yet challenging. Anna felt the strengthening power of God run through her veins. Her nerves calmed and her eyes became clear and trusting.

But an hour later, when she stepped forward in the half-filled courtroom, her entire body trembled in spite of that

"And you mean you are still thinking it over?"

274

divine encouragement. The gruff voice of the large shaggy-headed judge startled her.

He pulled his metal-rimmed glasses down on his long nose and looked at her over their tops with a stern, penetrating gaze. Once more he referred to the paper on his desk.

"So you are our next offender," he stated, placing a brass paper weight on the long yellow sheet. "Mrs. John Olesh of Miletinac." He cleared his throat.

Anna nodded as she answered in a subdued voice.

"You have a small child, I understand, a baby boy to be exact, who should have been baptized months ago. Am I right?" His cold, derisive green eyes numbed her for a moment as she stood perplexed.

"Well," gulped the judge, looking at her again over the top of his glasses. "Can't you answer?"

"Yes. Yes, sir. Just a moment, sir. I—" Anna clenched her hands.

"Then do so when I ask you a question."

"I was thinking," said Anna feebly.

"You should have done your thinking months ago." He rapped his knuckles on the desk top.

"Oh, sir, I—I didn't mean, I didn't. I—"

"Then you have thought a good deal about this?" He frowned deep creases into his forehead.

"A great deal, sir."

"And you mean you're still thinking it over?" He lifted his heavy eyebrows and raised himself on tiptoe.

"No, sir. Not that. We decided—"

"Who's 'we'?" His heavy body came down with suddenness.

"My husband and I."

"Very well. And where is he?"

"In America."

"Why America?"

"I mean he's on his way, sir. He may be there by this time. I'm not sure. He's gone to get work."

"Not enough to do at home?" The judge cleared his throat with a professional tone.

"Not enough to provide for our growing family, sir."

"So he's partly responsible then for this decision about the baby?"

"As much as I am, sir. We decided together that we would not have our baby baptized."

"You did? Well, then, Mrs. Olesh, it's too bad he's not here with you to share in the consequences. But"—and again he referred to the yellow sheet before looking at her over the top of his glasses—"undoubtedly he'll have a chance to do his part now, too, for you must both know that this is a very serious offense against the church. Is it not?"

Anna touched the desk to steady herself. She looked him straight in the eyes. "To your way of thinking, perhaps it is. But," she hesitated only a moment, "before God we feel very certain that we made the right decision."

The judge leaned forward and stretched his thin lips tightly across his uneven teeth. "Then this is what you will do, Mrs. Olesh," he said in plainly spoken words, eyes bulging. "We will have no further argument here. You were born and reared in the church and you are familiar with her practices and doctrines, I'm sure. Are you not?"

"Yes, sir."

"Of course you are. Father Markum has been your spiritual adviser for years and you know his deep concern for all the new children born in his parish. You have deliberately set yourselves against him and the holy church fathers. So listen to me carefully. Unless you repent and take that baby of yours to the father for baptism before next Saturday at this time"—he stopped long enough to glance dramatically at the large box-type clock on the opposite wall—"you will pay a fine of twenty-five dollars."

276

The courtroom became quiet—quiet enough to hear a pin drop.

Anna chilled. She gripped one hand with the other in a painful grasp. She could feel her legs wobble sickeningly under her.

"You may go now," blurted the judge, peering at her from under his mop of shaggy hair. "You don't like what I told you, I know. You don't want to believe what I said. Well, I do. You may go now and think it over at your leisure and make your own decision, this time without your husband. It's all in your hands now. You won't have time to write and ask him what to do."

Anna's feet seemed to be glued stubbornly to the floor. She grabbed the edge of the desk to free herself, then turned and walked slowly down the aisle. Every eye in the courtroom followed her to the door.

The eyes of the judge followed her, too. Suddenly he motioned to the officer at the rear of the room. He came promptly.

"At your service, your honor."

"Who was the man that followed that woman out? Do you know?"

"I think it was that Protestant missionary, your honor."

"I see," said the judge nodding. "Did he come in with her?"

"Not with her, your honor. But soon afterward."

"The rascal," muttered the judge, jerking his glasses off and putting them on again immediately.

Heads in the courtroom went together and many low whispers were heard.

Lutz spoke quietly to Anna on the outside at the foot of the steps. "I'll hurry on. You come."

She needed no coaxing. Blinded now with tears, she dropped on her knees in the chapel room. "Dear God!" she cried. "Where will I ever get twenty-five dollars? My God. My Jesus."

"Don't cry, Anna," pleaded Mr. Lutz. "They can't make you have your baby baptized and they can't make you pay if you haven't got it. Let us band together to trust God for this very situation. He must get glory to Himself somehow because you have done His will in this matter."

"You can imagine what my parents will say now," wailed Anna. "How can I go back and tell them this?"

"But remember, 'If God be for us, who can be against us?' "

"No one," whispered Anna.

"That's right, Anna. No one. You will stay for dinner and rest until train time."

"But, Mr. Lutz," cried Anna. "I have no—"

"Sh! You needn't try to explain. I understand. We're paying for your ticket. And what's more, you couldn't walk home and carry the sack of cornmeal and sugar we have for you."

"Mr. Lutz!"

"Call me 'Brother' from now on, Anna. I'm your brother in Christ. And I'm John's brother in Christ. We are closer by the ties in the Spirit than by any earthly ties of the flesh. So don't hesitate to drop in any hour of the day or night and share with us any problem you have. We are here to help you. Are we not, Agnes?"

"To be sure, Anna."

"I can't begin to tell you what this means to me," answered Anna. "Very likely I will be back next Saturday."

And she was, after a week of intense praying and repeated explaining to her parents.

"But this whole thing is so ridiculous and unnecessary, Anna," complained her father. "Of course Elizabeth is ready to come over and look after your children if we say she can. She's in the height of her glory over here. But what satisfaction do you get out of being called into court like this?"

"Only God gets the glory, Father. I didn't plan it this way."

"Well, He doesn't get glory; I'm mighty certain of that. You're making yourself the scandal of the entire village and

278

Daruvar as well. Everyone is talking about this awful thing."

"I realize it, Father. I'm sorry it bothers so many people. But I've got to go back once more. I don't know what the judge will say this time."

"If we didn't pity your children, we wouldn't give in and let Elizabeth come over. We want you to know that. Why don't you go to Father Markum Saturday and have John baptized like you know you ought and end all this fuss?"

"Oh, Father!" exclaimed Anna almost in tears. "You don't understand. Don't try to make me doubt my own sincerity. I can't deny that Christ has saved me. I mean I don't want to, no matter what people say or do to us. Please let Elizabeth come. I've got to go back, Father."

"Very well, then. But," he added as he walked away, "I don't see why I give in."

Again the judge eyed Anna across the top of his glasses. "And what have you to report today, Mrs. Olesh?"

To Anna's surprise she was not as nervous as she was the week before even though the courtroom was crowded. "I have nothing to report, sir."

"What's that?"

"I have nothing to report, sir."

"You mean you didn't have your baby baptized?"

"No, sir, I didn't."

"Very well, then hand over your fine." He held out one hand. "I was already informed you didn't report to Father Markum."

"I don't have it, sir."

His hand dropped. "Did you think I was playing court with you last Saturday?" inquired the judge in an aggravated tone.

"No, sir."

"Then why don't you take this matter seriously?"

"I do, sir."

"I wasn't fooling when I said your fine would be twenty-five dollars."

"I know, sir. But I just don't have it."

"But you will have it," he said with positiveness. "Does your husband have a job in America?"

"I haven't heard from him yet."

"Well, how many children have you got?"

"Five."

"Five too many for a woman who can't take charge of her children better than you do. Am I right?"

"They were given to us by the Lord, sir."

"Huh. How much property do you own?"

"Twelve acres, sir."

"Paid for?"

"Yes, sir."

"A house?"

"Yes, sir."

"You may be forced to sell all you own, Mrs. Olesh. You go home now and think this over more seriously. Look at me, Mrs. Olesh. Look me right in the eye. I mean exactly what I'm telling you. Unless you have that baby baptized by a week from today, you'll be back and pay a fifty-dollar fine. Remember, one week to think this over."

An appalling sensation swept over Anna. Must she make the trip again? Her parents. They would be horrified, furious!

"But remember what I told you before, Anna," reminded Mr. Lutz with tender sympathy before she left the center. "Agnes and I will be holding you up to God in prayer all week. God can't be God and fail us now. Your problem is our problem, Anna."

It took, as Anna expected, a good deal more pleading this time to get consent from her parents to let Elizabeth stay with the children. Harsh, humiliating words were flung at her.

"You just want an excuse to go over there and see that

heretic Lutz," said her father condemningly, with a hurt look in his eyes.

Anna shook her head. "Never."

"Must be," added her mother. "Why is it you always get a ride back on the train?"

"It's not Brother Lutz any more than it is Sister Lutz."

"Brother Lutz!" shouted her father in disgust. "And Sister Lutz. What crazy things are they going to talk you into doing or saying next? So now it is gone so far that he claims you're his sister."

"In Christ," explained Anna. "We've been born alike into the family of God, don't you see? God is our Father; so naturally we're brothers and sisters in the Spirit. Brother and Sister Lutz act as though they really love me. They do. They understand and pray for me and—"

"You mean to infer we haven't?"

"No, Father. No, Mother. I didn't mean to infer that. You've done many nice things for me all my life. And I'll always thank you. Please believe me that I ask you to let Elizabeth come over for one and only one reason. If I didn't have to appear in court, you may be very sure I wouldn't make another trip so soon to Daruvar."

"And what do you suppose John would say about all this?" asked her father.

"I believe I am doing what he would be doing if he were here. John would go in my place. I hate to leave the children like this, but what else can I do? I will have to take them all with me unless you let Elizabeth come over."

"And mark my word, Anna. This is the last time," declared her father.

"Then you will let her come?"

"Only once more. And if I ever detect that she is taking up with your silly religion, she'll never step another foot inside your house. The neighbors can't understand all this action. And I tell you, Anna, I'm embarrassed and don't know what to say to them any more."

"I know it must be hard, Father. But someday I hope you'll listen long enough to me so I can convince you and Mother both that at last I've found what gives me peace and happiness."

"You call that peace and happiness to walk into Daruvar every week and get shamed and threatened in public court?"

"It's not pleasant. Not that part of it, to be sure," admitted Anna, "but underneath, deep down inside a quiet voice tells me that no one who is against me will succeed."

Elizabeth, Father, and Mother all stared speechless.

"That's right," repeated Anna. "I know God is for me. I don't know how, but He will see me through."

"See, Elizabeth," Kathrine said sweetly, pointing to the Bible on the dresser. "Mother reads us stories out of it every evening before we go to bed."

"She does?"

"Yes. They're really good stories, too. You want me to tell one of them to you?"

"Want to?" asked Elizabeth.

"I can't tell them as good as Mary can. Mary, let's all sit around in a ring and you tell us the story about Abraham and his boy he almost killed and didn't. Oh, Elizabeth, Mary can tell it real good and it's so sad and scary, only at the last it ends happy."

An anxious, half-fearful expression crossed Elizabeth's tender face. But without any further coaxing she gathered baby John in her arms and squatted to the floor with the children. She waited with as much eagerness as Kathrine, Joseph, and Anna for Mary to begin her story.

Mary threw both arms around Elizabeth's neck. "We wouldn't know what to do if you couldn't come over and stay with us."

"I'm glad I can, Mary."

"Why did Mother have to go away again?"

"Didn't she tell you, Mary?"

"Not very much. She said she would someday. Tell me all

about it. It's something about giving our little Johnnie all to God, but I don't see why she had to go to Daruvar to—"

The door opened.

"Oh, Grandpa," exclaimed Joe jumping up. "Come and sit down with us. Mary's going to tell a story."

"A story? Where did she hear it?"

"It's one Mother read."

The color left Elizabeth's cheeks. She scrambled to her feet, and almost bumped Joe over. "Did you want something, Father?" she asked excitedly.

"I just dropped in to see if everything was going all right."

"It is, Father. Everything's going all right. Mary and Kathrine helped with the dishes and I swept the house good and now I'm going to try to put the baby to sleep."

"I'll be going on then."

But Elizabeth wasn't exactly happy about the expression on her father's face when he left the house.

Chapter 32

The children often referred to that last day and night before Papa left. It was stamped indelibly on their minds.

"Look," Mary would say. "The sky glows as if it's on fire, just as it did the night before Papa left. He said it meant he'd have a nice day to start on his trip. Remember?"

"Now, Joe," Kathrine would say with one hand on his shoulder, "remember how Papa told you to play nice with Anna. And, Anna, remember what Papa told you."

But sometimes Kathrine, too, forgot. The children in school said Papa was a coward and that he ran off to America because of what the people were saying about him. Kathrine counted the days until school would be let out, the times she would have to cringe under the insulting remarks and jeers of the other boys and girls.

Then Mary would put her arm around her younger sister and remind her that Papa went away because he was very brave. "Don't you remember, Kathrine, what all he told you that last night? He said not to listen to what anyone else says. Papa loves us and will come back as soon as he can. And remember, he is always praying for us and would not have left if it had not been absolutely necessary. Just two more days of school, Kathrine. I wish I could go in your place."

There had been a peculiar sweetness in Papa John's voice, so solemn and subdued, when he read from the Bible that evening. He held baby John in his left arm, pausing now and then to look at him and swallow something which made his voice falter. Then they all had knelt beside their beds while Papa prayed long and tenderly, mentioning each of the

284

children by name and committing them and dear, dear Mother to God.

Then he took each of the children in turn on his knee and spoke words of affection and instruction for their behavior while he would be away. He finished by kissing each twice, on one cheek good night and on the other good-by, for he would be leaving early in the morning before daylight. How could they forget that evening?

"Now, Mary," he said, drawing her last and lovingly to his knee, "you are my oldest; so I have had you longest to love. Not that I love you more than I do Kathrine or Joseph or baby John, but—well," he cleared his throat and bit his lip, "you have been a good girl, Mary, and I know I can depend on you to be Mother's main stand-by and helper. I don't want you to do more than you're able to, Mary. But do you suppose you can take care of the baby and help with the meals so Mother can do the outside work?"

Mary nodded and her arm around her father's neck tightened. She pressed her lips to his warm temple. "I'll do my best, Papa."

"I know you will. I'll come back as soon as I make enough to help us into a better way of living. I don't believe God expects us to go on like this. And until then, Mary, be a good girl and good to Mother. Love her lots because she'll miss me. And don't worry about anything any of the neighbors or anyone else might say about us. Remember, Mary, Mother and I are trying to live to please God. Not people or relatives."

Mary did her part conscientiously and well. Anna was amazed at the way she took over the responsibilities of baby care and cooking. And she was amazed at the cooperation Mary got out of Kathrine and Joe. With her crippled knee she got around inside very quickly and Joe never refused to run the outside errands, like going to the straw pile to fetch potatoes (he could count them out, one for each except John, making five) and bringing in water.

"There are hardly any potatoes left," Joe reminded Mary.

"You go help Mother," Mary told Kathrine. "She needs you outside more than I do. I'll manage."

So Kathrine at nine helped to plant and hoe the garden and led the borrowed-from-Grandpa ox back and forth across the fields while Mother handled the plow. It would soon be time to plant the turnips and pumpkins.

"I hate to have you work so hard," Anna would say, "but you know, Kathrine, we've got to plant to have something to eat. I'll rub your tired legs when you go to bed."

"But who'll rub your legs, Mother? You're tired too."

Then Anna would look sweet and sad and reply, "Mine aren't still growing, Kathrine. Mine have often been this tired."

Anna endeavored as much as possible to hide her problems from her children. It was not always easy nor even possible now. Mary would soon be twelve and readily detected it when her mother's smiles were forced or when she wore that anxious, far-away look into a world of reverie. Anna's loom of life was forming an ever-growing pattern of sorrowful woof with peaceful warp. Mary watched her with a sort of mysterious half-conception. At times her mother was so extremely tender and kind to her it almost hurt. Little did she understand the mental sufferings, the misunderstandings, the extent of the ridicule from relatives and neighbors her mother endured in silence, nor the cruel demands of the court. All this Anna kept hidden in her heart.

"Mother," exclaimed Mary one morning, looking up suddenly from the dishpan where she was busy working on a scorched pan, "I love you."

"Well, dear, I'm glad you do. What made you say it?"

"I just wanted to tell you once more."

"Thank you, dear. It helps to make everything a bit easier."

"Make what easier, Mother?" All that morning Mary thought her mother looked troubled.

"I don't know, Mary. I mean whatever is to come. I'll need your love. I'm glad I can depend on you."

"Must you go back to Daruvar again?"

"Yes, dear."

"You *have to,* Mother?"

"Yes. But I hope it will be the last time."

"But why must you go back?"

"I don't know why, Mary."

"Are you sad, Mother? Your voice quivers this morning."

Anna looked away. "I hate to ask Elizabeth to come again."

"But she said she doesn't mind."

"Yes. Thank God for Elizabeth. But—"

Anna wanted to unburden everything to Mary. But that would be almost cruel. Soon enough she would learn the hardships of living the Christian life in Miletinac. It was enough that she knew about the stones and the straw hurled at the house, the hideous faces and jeers from neighbors' children. Carefully Anna was trying to prepare Mary for the spiritual awakening she would undoubtedly have before long. She must not be unduly frightened—tender, lovely, beautiful Mary.

"They don't know any better," Anna always explained. "We won't make faces or throw anything in their yards. We must try to think of something nice to do in return."

"Like what?" asked Mary.

"I don't know right now."

One evening an idea struck Mary while her mother was reading aloud the story of Baby Moses.

"I know," she said, her eyes dancing. "Let's invite in the neighbor children to listen to you read these stories. That would be something nice in return."

Anna looked up in surprise. "When do you mean?"

"Maybe on Sunday afternoon."

"Well, we could try it," answered Anna. "If their parents let them come, I'll read."

"No," exclaimed Kathrine. "Not read. Just tell it. Like you do to us afterward, so they can understand it better. I like them best when you tell them without the book."

Saturday morning the low-hanging clouds were heavy with rain. Anna thanked God all the way to Daruvar that Brother and Sister Lutz had insisted she accept the money to come by train. Twice she unfolded the letter and read it. When she got to the Gospel Center, she handed it immediately to Agnes.

"My first letter from John," she said. "You may read it."

"I'll read it aloud, so Will can hear it."

May 5, 1913

MY DEAR ANNA,

I just arrived in New York several hours ago. I've decided to go farther west this time where they tell me wages are better. Pray that I will find a good paying job at once. I pray for you and the children constantly. How thankful I am that at last we are fastened securely to a faith that is real and satisfying! I am positive it is God's will that I came over here and I'll do my level best to save up enough to move us close to Daruvar. Won't that be a wonderful day when we can take the children to Sunday school ? It will be such a long time before I will be able to hear from you. I'll write as soon as I get located. Until then God bless you and keep you safe in His loving care. When trials new and hard come, remember I'm praying for you. I will send you money as soon as possible.

A kiss with love to each of the children.

JOHN

"A nice letter, Anna. And it does your heart good to know he's praying for you, even though he knows nothing about this new trial, doesn't it?"

"Without his prayers and yours I doubt if I could have made it back here today."

"Has it been a hard week?"

"Extra hard. I won't relate all I've gone through since last Saturday. Stones thrown at the house and nasty remarks by neighbors don't bother me as much as some of the things my parents say and think."

"We remember what that is like too, Anna," said Brother Lutz. "So does our Lord. He was tried and tempted in all points like we are and without sinning."

"Pray for me before I go. I feel so shaky."

"We'll kneel at once. God will sustain you, Anna."

"And what do you have to report this morning, Mrs. Olesh?" asked the judge with a dreadful blackness of countenance.

"Nothing."

"Again?" he shouted. "You mean to tell me you're back with that same answer? You dared to come back to this courtroom without your fine?"

"I could not bring it, sir."

"Could not? I didn't say bring it if you could. Doesn't your husband have work in America?"

"I don't know, sir."

"Didn't you tell me he went off to America to get work?"

"Yes, sir."

"Didn't you write and tell him about this?"

"Not yet."

"What? And he tries to make you believe he can't find work? Went off and left you here with a pack of children to take care of? The scoundrel. You will write and tell him and he will pay the fine."

"He may be working by this time. My husband is not lazy, sir. You see, I just heard that he reached New York."

"Listen, Mrs. Olesh," the judge eyed her over the top of his glasses with pronounced indignation. "How dare you defy this court like this?"

Anna stood with eyes downcast and sorrowful. A lump in her throat choked words.

"You don't intend to have your baby baptized?"

Anna shook her head.

"By what authority dare you disobey the church of Christ?"

Anna looked up. Her sad eyes met his blazing ones. "By the authority of the Word of God, sir."

The judge pointed angrily to the rear of the room. "That man back there," he said, "is coaching you in this, isn't he?"

Anna did not look back.

"He's put you up to all this action, hasn't he?"

Anna shook her head.

"You are so conscience-stricken you cannot speak," he said icily. "Well, we will see. A week from today you will be back here with your baby." Anna jumped. She gripped one hand over the other. "That's what I said, Mrs. Olesh. You will be here in this courtroom with your baby. You will pay a hundred-dollar fine or the child's head will be cut off."

"Oh!" Dazed with blinding sorrow Anna's trembling hands covered her sheet-white face.

"You may go now. Think it over at your leisure." His fist struck the desk top.

Before Anna reached the door her face was drenched with tears. She stumbled down the steps and on to the Gospel Center.

Agnes Lutz caught her in her outstretched arms, for she knew before either Anna or Will spoke a word that something dreadful had taken place.

"What will I do?" sobbed Anna. "What will I do?"

"Nothing," advised Lutz. "God is on the throne. He sees. He knows. He cares. Let's wait, and trust while we wait."

"You mean I should not come back?"

"Yes."

"Not show up? You mean—?"

"I mean if I were you, I would stay at home and pray. See what happens."

"But if someone comes and snatches my baby out of my arms—" Anna covered her face and wept bitterly— "right there before the children. Oh, Brother Lutz, they would never, never forget it."

"Neither would any of us. Let's pray. Each of us in faith believing that this whole thing will be handled by God Himself in His own way. There is nothing else to do."

The three spent an hour on their knees in earnest prayer. Nor did they get up until Anna said she was confident that God would protect her and her baby.

"Listen, Sister," said Brother Lutz. "Say over and over all the way home that God, who has promised to sustain you when you cast your burden on Him, will do it. 'If God be for us, who can be against us?' God simply cannot be God and fail you now, Anna. He has seen you through so far and somehow He will take you through the rest of the way. God is yours, Anna. You are God's. So rest in Him."

"Will," suggested Agnes, "maybe you ought to go over to Miletinac next Saturday. Just in case, you know."

Anna shook her head. "If I am going to trust God at all, I am going to trust Him altogether. I'm not going to tell a word of this to the children, and," she added, "another thing, it would be best if you stayed away from Miletinac for a while. You know, with John gone, people would really talk."

"You're right," said Brother Lutz. "I wouldn't want to do anything to make the situation harder for you. The best I can do is pray, and you can depend on that."

The week was unbearably long and yet frighteningly short. Anna prayed with every breath she drew. Friday night came. She held her baby close and cried over his soft little head, kissing him again and again. Midnight came. She walked over to his little crib but could not release him. Gently she placed him on her own bed and lay down beside him, her one hand on his plump arm.

There was no need to fight sleep, for her closed eyes were wide awake with live, penetrating thoughts. Until dawn Anna searched her life to see if there could be a reason why her prayers would not be answered. "He is yours, dear Lord," she prayed and fell asleep.

She woke with a start. Someone opened the door. Instinctively her hand clasped tightly the little arm beside her.

Chapter 33

"Aren't you up yet?"

Anna covered her mouth to stifle her frightened outcry. She sat up half-dazed.

"Father, why, Father." She rubbed her eyes. "What's wrong, Father?"

"Nothing. I came over to see what's going on here."

"What do you mean?" Anna jumped to her feet. She smoothed back her black hair. Her hands shook.

"You're not going to Daruvar today?" He remained in the kitchen, one hand on the table, the other on the doorknob.

"No. Why?"

"Well, I just wondered. You didn't ask Elizabeth to come over. So it's all settled?"

Anna stared at her father for a tortuous moment. A pounding in her chest became almost unbearable. "What time is it?" she asked. "I—I must have overslept."

"I guess you did," returned her father. "Well, I'll be going back. We were just inquisitive. You didn't say anything all week. Your mother had to know; so I came over. Did they convince you to have it done now?"

"You mean—?"

"I mean, are you going to take him and have him baptized after all now?"

"Oh, no. No, Father."

"No?" His hand on the doorknob tightened. "Then you paid your fine?"

Four heads raised up from four pillows and looked around. Anna pressed her forefinger to her lips. She shook her head at her father.

But he ignored her signal. "Then how was it settled?" he asked. He looked perturbed, almost vexed.

"Well, Father," answered Anna softly, "I've turned it all over to the Lord. Every bit of it."

"The Lord? I don't understand that, Anna. How do you—?"

Baby John started to cry. Affectionately Anna took him up in her arms and kissed him. She patted him and kissed him again. "That's all right now," she whispered, her face on his head. "Mother's right here. Time to get up, children," she added, turning to each. "Mother overslept this morning." She glanced again at her father who stood mutely at the door, a troubled, puzzled expression on his unshaved face. His lips were drawn and twitching with apprehension.

"But God does, Father," she exclaimed. "I know nothing more to tell you."

Without another word the door opened and closed. Anna watched from the window. She saw her father's heavy feet dragging and his face cast downward as he moved slowly across the wide village street.

The morning was sunny and warm. A gentle breeze was blowing and a sweet quiet hung over the ancient village.

Her cheeks burned feverishly and her knees felt weak and uncertain, but while Anna prepared breakfast she tried humming a tune she had heard the Lutz children sing. It was a song about the Lord leading His children through the wilderness. She couldn't remember exactly, but it had a soothing effect on her nerves.

Baby John gurgled and jabbered happily in his crib. It was God's morning.

After the usual morning prayer period, Anna outlined the day's work to the children. "Today I must get the turnip seed in the ground. First I'll start the bread. There's enough flour for one more baking. Kathrine, you won't need to help me outside today. You sweep the house real good and make

294

the beds the nicest you ever made beds and watch the baby. You may knit on Joe's socks if you have time."

"May I go out and invite the children to come in tomorrow afternoon?"

"Let's wait, Kathrine, until tomorrow morning. We will see then. Mary, for dinner you may make mush again. The same amount you made yesterday. There's nothing else here to fix but apples. Stew about five."

"Then there will be no more," returned Mary.

"I wish someone would bring us some meat again," put in Joe with a hungry smacking of the lips.

"Someday things may be different," answered Anna with wistfulness. An overwhelming pity surged through her. She grabbed Joe in her arms and squeezed him. When she released him, he looked up into her face eagerly, solemnly.

"I wish I were old enough to go to America and earn some money right now," he declared. "Then we'd have sausages. All we wanted."

"You dear boy," replied Anna, stroking his black hair. A sudden new appreciation and love for her children enveloped her. She'd live, she'd work, she'd die for any one of them.

All forenoon her lips moved over the seeds she fed to the freshly prepared soil: "Blessed are the poor in spirit: for theirs is the kingdom of heaven. Blessed are they that mourn: for they shall be comforted. Blessed are the meek: for they shall inherit the earth. Blessed are they which do hunger and thirst after righteousness: for they shall be filled. Blessed are the merciful: for they shall obtain mercy. Blessed are the pure in heart: for they shall see God. Blessed are the peacemakers: for they shall be called the children of God. Blessed are they which are persecuted for righteousness' sake: for theirs is the kingdom of heaven. Blessed are ye, when men shall revile you, and persecute you, and shall say all manner of evil against you falsely, for my sake. Rejoice."

"Mother! Mother!"

Anna jumped. "What is wrong?"

"Nothing's wrong," cried Joe, slapping both knees. "Guess what?"

"I can't. Tell me quickly."

"Someone came."

Anna's heart skipped a beat. She turned anxious eyes toward the house. "Who, Joe?"

"Aunt Tena."

Anna's pent-up feelings gave way. She burst into sudden tears.

"What's wrong, Mother? She brought us each a piece of chicken already cooked. And a coffee cake."

"Aunt Tena did? How nice of her! You see, Joe, God knows what we need. He won't let us go hungry for long."

"But she thought—Well, she didn't know you were here. She said she heard you had to go back to Daruvar again; so she didn't bring any chicken for you."

"That's all right, Joe."

"But we'll all give you some of ours."

"No, Joe."

"Hurry and come in, Mother. Isn't it time to eat now? Mary does not have the mush made yet, but it's time, isn't it? I am terribly hungry."

"Is Aunt Tena still there?"

"She left. Mary's crying now."

"Crying? What—?"

Anna hurried toward the house. Had Tena heard? Would she in her absence, tell the children? Half blinded by fresh, stabbing fear she stumbled barefooted over the freshly plowed earth.

Mary was stirring the cornmeal into the boiling water. Her eyes were red from crying.

"Joe came out and told me Aunt Tena was here."

"Oh, Mother," cried Mary. "I wish Papa was here."

"Why? Tell me."

"Are you going to have John baptized?"

"No. Why, Mary?"

"Aunt Tena said if Papa was here now she bet he would say to go have it done or something awful might happen to him."

"What else did Aunt Tena say?"

"She asked me where you were, and why you didn't go to Daruvar, and were you going to take the baby to Father Markum tomorrow, and did we hear from Papa yet, and did we have enough to eat. Oh, I don't know any more what all she asked. What did she mean would happen to our baby?"

"Mary, I don't know what Aunt Tena meant. But remember what Papa told us about feeling bad over what people say. It was very kind of her to bring you children good things to eat. Look at this coffee cake, Mary."

"But I don't like people to say bad things are going to happen to us. Why do they, Mother?"

"Nothing has happened yet, Mary," said her mother thoughtfully, scanning the street in both directions. "We are the Lord's. He's watching over us. Come, dear. I will wash my hands and help you get the dinner on."

With the last shadows of evening Anna stood in the open doorway, an expression of wonder and relief in her vivid brown eyes. She held her baby firmly against her tired shoulder. The day's experience of watching for the unseen, waiting for the unbearable (which she had as yet not been called upon to bear) had made heavy demands on her body. She ached all over. Even her fingernails throbbed and pained her. Slowly a tear trickled down each cheek. "The mercy of the Lord," she whispered. "Send mercy again tomorrow. Blessed are the hungry, the meek, the merciful."

One little girl was permitted to accept Kathrine's invitation to the Sunday afternoon storytelling and that was because the child's mother had gone to Djulovac to church

She held her baby firmly against
her tired shoulder.

and the father, wishing to take his Sunday afternoon nap,
was glad to get rid of talkative Susan for a while. "Run
along," he said. "You are too little to be polluted anyhow."

The child sat in rapt attention while Anna vividly retold
the complete story of the great flood, the ark, the first
rainbow.

"Where did you hear that story?" asked Susan, taking
a long deep breath when Anna had finished.

"She got it out of that Bible up there," put in Joe before
anyone else had time to answer.

"Bible?" asked Susan, looking at the black book Joe
had pointed to on the dresser top. "What is that?"

"Come, children," Anna advised tactfully. "If you want
me to, I'll tell you another."

"Yes, do," exclaimed Susan.

"Mother can tell them good. Can't she?"

"I never heard any stories before about God." Susan
answered. "Tell it all over again, Mrs. Olesh."

Anna smiled. "Well, how about a story about a man who thought he could run away from God? And what he saw in the night?"

"Tell us that story you read to us last night," suggested Joe. "About Daniel, you know, who was thrown into the den of lions. That's more exciting. Tell it, Mother."

"Let Mother tell what she wants to," cut in Kathrine. "They are all exciting."

Two hours passed before they realized it. Little Susan still was not satisfied. She sat cross-legged on the floor, her eyes fixed intently on Anna's face. "I could listen to you tell stories all day and all night, Mrs. Olesh," she exclaimed.

The joy in Anna's soul was manifested in her tear-misted eyes. She looked lovingly, lingeringly at innocent, bright-eyed little Susan whose mother had strictly forbidden her to play with the Olesh children. More than that, only the week before Susan had helped several of the other neighborhood children litter the Olesh front yard with eggshells, onion tops, and other bits of refuse.

"Much as I'd love to go on with storytelling," explained Anna, "and much as I'd love to keep you here with us until dark, maybe you'd better go home before your mother comes after you, Susan."

"But Papa said I could."

"Stay until dark?"

"No. I mean come over. He is probably still sleeping. Anyhow, my mother doesn't know how nice it is over here listening to stories. I bet she would like to hear them too—I'll bet; and I hope she goes off to church again so I can come back."

"Well, next Sunday afternoon you come back if you can, Susan," Anna said. "And see if you can bring some other children with you."

"I will. But do I have to go now?"

"You don't have to, dear child, but it might be best."

"Couldn't you tell it just once more? That first one about

that great big boat and how all the bugs and birds and animals and creeping things got inside before the water came up?"

Anna laughed softly. But before she had Noah cutting down the first tree there was a sharp, vigorous rapping at the door. Kathrine, nearest the door, jumped up and answered.

"Is my Susan in there?" It was none other than Susan's mother, the pretty but quick-tempered Mrs. Lazotin. Her dark eyes flashed as she held her arms akimbo.

"Yes, Mother," answered the child, scrambling to her feet. "I'm coming."

"You'd better hurry about it, too." Outside the door the little one got a whack across the shoulder and was ushered home with a series of sharply spoken words.

Anna sat in silent sorrow for dear little Susan. Her children clustered around her full of awe, waiting for some word of explanation. In her overburdened heart Anna hunted for the words to quell their astonishment.

Then suddenly two entered without knocking. Elizabeth, pale-faced, and Wencel. Elizabeth looked frightened.

"Anna," she said in an unsteady voice, "we just got back from Djulovac."

"Yes."

"Father Markum—well, come here, Anna."

Anna obeyed. Elizabeth put her face close to her sister's and spoke in a frightening, defeated tone. "Father Markum is enraged."

Anna made no comment. She asked no question.

"I'm just telling you, Anna. Something awful's going to happen here if you don't watch out. Please do something quick."

"I've turned it all over to the Lord, Elizabeth," answered Anna softly.

"He's not doing anything for you that I can see."

"But *He* sees, Elizabeth." Anna's words were spoken with firm conviction. "I do not need to."

Elizabeth stared. Wencel stood blank-faced, shifting nervously from one foot to the other.

Anna continued, "I know the way seems dark. Awfully dark. And uncertain. But God sees through the blackest darkness. And right now I know He's leading me through it. I feel His hand holding mine. Now."

Elizabeth shook her head. "I don't understand it, Anna. Do you, Wencel?"

Wencel shook his head. "Let's go," he whispered.

There was something unusually beautiful, even reverent, about Anna's face when she gathered her children around her once more that evening.

"I will read something from the Psalms tonight. I guess it's not exactly a story, but—well, we will see what it says. Psalm 91. That is where the Bible opened to. 'He that dwelleth in the secret place of the most High shall abide under the shadow of the Almighty. I will say of the Lord, He is my refuge and my fortress: my God; in him will I trust. Surely he shall deliver thee from the snare of the fowler, and from the noisome pestilence. He shall cover thee with his feathers, and under his wings shalt thou trust: his truth shall be thy shield and buckler. Thou shalt not be afraid for the terror by night; nor for the arrow that flieth by day; nor for the pestilence that walketh in darkness; nor for the destruction that wasteth at noonday. A thousand shall fall at thy side, and ten thousand at thy right hand; but it shall not come nigh thee. Only with thine eyes shalt thou behold and see the reward of the wicked. Because thou hast made the Lord, which is my refuge, even the most High, thy habitation; there shall be no evil befall thee, neither shall any plague come nigh thy dwelling. For he shall give his angels charge over thee, to keep thee in all thy ways. They shall bear thee up in their hands, lest thou dash thy foot against a stone. Thou shalt tread upon the lion and adder: the young lion and the dragon shalt thou trample under feet. Because he hath set his love upon me, therefore will I deliver him: I will set him on high, because he hath known my name. He shall call upon me, and I will answer him: I will be with him in trouble; I will deliver him, and honour him. With long life will I satisfy him, and shew him my salvation.' "

"Look, Mother," whispered Mary. "Anna and Joe and the baby all fell asleep."

"We can all sleep better now," answered Anna. "I am sure I can."

Chapter 34

Four days passed and nothing unusual happened—only more of the same kind of shunnings and jeerings, shamings, and blamings from onetime good neighbors. As Anna read her Bible more diligently, her faith in God grew steadily. He did prove His sufficiency for each day's temptations and trials.

The fifth day brought two letters, one from Sister Lutz containing a stamped envelope. "Please let us know what the Lord has been doing for you. We've heard nothing from Miletinac."

The other was even more welcome.

Lancaster, Pennsylvania
May 12, 1913

MY DEAR ANNA AND CHILDREN,

Now that I am located, I will hardly be able to wait until I hear from you. Send my letters general delivery. It seems months since I left home. How are you getting along? Has our good friend from Daruvar, Brother Lutz, been over to see you? God bless him for coming to our village. God bless him for stopping at our house. God bless both Brother and Sister Lutz for all their kindness to us. I'm lonesome for all of you, but our separation is different this time. Now I know Christ and know that you do too. We trust Him; we know He hears our prayers and is watching over us. This is a great and constant joy to me. Otherwise I never could have left you again. My Testament always goes with me in my shirt pocket. I read a little at lunch hour and commit you to God. I get laughed at, but it speaks to me deep inward joy no one knows. I could not explain it if I tried. Why were we so long in finding its meaning? You all mean so much to me. You seem very near—Mary, Kathrine, Joe, Anna, and baby John. Every

303

breath I take is a prayer for each of you. Mother dear, have the neighbors been tormenting you any more? You are continually in my thoughts.

This is a most beautiful country. I wish you could be here with me. I suppose you are now having evening worship with the children. It is seven o'clock here. Only God knows how I hated to leave you. Tell each of the children Papa loves them dearly.

Oh, yes, I have a job smelting iron. It will do until I find something better. I get forty cents an hour. I'm sending you five dollars this time. My room is in the basement of an old apartment house about ten minutes' walk from the plant. It will do. I am going to get along on as little as possible so I can send more to you each month. I may go west later on. I visited a church Sunday, but it was hard to understand much. God keep you.

JOHN

"Children," said Anna, struggling to control her emotions, "we ought to bow our heads right now and thank God for Papa and that He found him his job. And, Mary, you and Kathrine together could look after things here while I hurry to Vilieki Bastaji, couldn't you?"

"Sure we can. You mean you will bring home something from the store? To eat?"

"It may be a little late before I get back. But we will have something to eat when I do get here. So you children be good and mind your big sister while I am gone. Let us pray."

It was no secret long. The neighbors soon discovered that Anna Olesh went off to the store because she received money from John. The villagers commented freely and frequently on the fact that, much to their astonishment, as yet nothing disastrous had happened at the Olesh house.

"Does beat all, does it not, how those disobedient and condemned folks can keep on going like they do? Like nothing was wrong between them and the church?"

"John's wife get out and works like a horse while that

crippled little Mary tends the baby and does the cooking like nothing ever did ail her. Can't understand where they get their strength. I thought they would fag out before this."

"And how is it she evades the court? Someone ought to tell the judge she is getting money from her husband."

"I don't want to be the one to report the fact. Just wait. Her time is coming yet. She won't always go around with that satisfied, serene look on her face."

September 3, 1913

DEAR JOHN,

Truly the Lord has been very good to us. The children are all well, the pumpkins look fine, and with your monthly help we have not had to go hungry. Thank God. I am daily amazed that no notice has come from the court about the fine. This week I received two unsigned letters mailed at Daruvar saying I was to expect severe punishment for not having the baby baptized and for joining up with that Lutzite gang of outlaws. I would like to go into Daruvar and see Brother and Sister Lutz again, but I'd better stay close at home now. Something is brewing. I don't know what to expect. I'm sure Brother Lutz would come over if I would say the word, but I have told him not to try it until you come home. I wish I could send you their last letter to me. They are always such an encouragement. They report two new converts to the faith. But they are being persecuted and threatened too. But at last—at last, John, it's so wonderful to know we are on the straight and narrow way which leads to Heaven. At last to have the peace we longed for! If we can only keep on and never be turned to the right or to the left. Pray hard these coming days for Kathrine and Joe. They dread starting to school. The shoes you sent them fit perfectly. But that may make things a little harder for them. Other children will likely be jealous. Mary almost eats the cake of perfumed soap you sent her. She carries it around in her pocket most of the time.

Sam Nikabica is very sick. They had the witch doctor twice, but I heard he was worse. But still they believe in her. The poor, blind people. If they only knew Christ!

305

You will be happy when I tell you of something wonderful that took place Sunday afternoon. I don't know yet how it came about, but little Susan came here with three other children and asked me to tell stories. Only the day before these same children tormented Kathrine and Joe every time they stepped outside the house, calling them all kinds of names and throwing things at them. It must have been the grace of God, John. I don't know what else could do it. They behaved perfectly in here and drank in every word as if they were starved. Pray for me that I will be the blessing and light God expects me to be to our neighbors.

But Elizabeth is getting more distant right along with her growing friendship with Wencel. I feel sure he and Father Markum influenced her against us. It hurts. I've shed tears over it. I think, too, Father questioned her about Bible stories Mary told her. Mother and Father seldom show their faces. They act almost scared of me. I haven't seen your parents more than twice since you left and they had little to say. I know we are despised of men, but how wonderful to know God loves us and has His hand over us!

John, why don't you save some of your money over there? Don't send it all to me. Somehow I feel it would be safer with you. I know I am being watched. I am so eager to get moved to Daruvar. I long to go to church and worship God with His true followers. We miss you more than I can tell in words. Don't worry about us. Just pray.

ANNA

Part of John's letter of November 28 read as follows:

I am facing a new problem and I am asking God to show me His answer. I have been asked to work as foreman over a gang of colored men on Sundays. I did it once and asked God to forgive me if I did wrong. I told the boss I always go to church someplace on Sunday, but he laughed at me and said I can do as he says or look for another job. It was difficult for me to explain to him. You know I still cannot express myself in English very well. So I do not know how long I'll be here. I wish I could talk it over with Brother Lutz. I surely don't want to grieve the Lord who has done so much for us. I think I am as alone with God here as you are in Miletinac. I have not met up with any men I would call Christians in this plant yet. I'm a stranger in a strange land but dreaming and working and praying hard for a better day when we will be united. And I hope this time it will be for the rest of our lives. I don't enjoy this separation.

December 30, 1913

DEAR JOHN,

I had to go to Daruvar to have a tooth pulled yesterday. I did a thing I did not want to do. I left the children in the charge of Mary. I prayed much for them and they got along all right. I couldn't stand the toothache any longer. It was keeping we awake at night.

Of course I went over to the Gospel Center and what a reunion we had with tears of joy, rejoicing, and praying! But, John, they are being persecuted more than we are. I wouldn't be surprised if they would be ordered out of town soon. The priests are very angry and the court joins with them. Brother Lutz was called in recently to answer many questions and was shamefully ridiculed.

But the miracle! They have never asked me again for that fine. Maybe they will demand it of you when you come home. I have no idea who sends me these unsigned letters. I got the third one Monday. That is another reason why I dreaded to leave the children alone. But I went in and came back on the train. Brother Lutz is going to write to you. He shakes his head at the idea of working on Sunday. Oh, John, whatever you do, be true to God and His Word! We are both so young in this new life. I hope we will not stumble or sin. John, would we still move closer to Daruvar if Brother and Sister Lutz have to leave? It breaks my heart to think of it.

Your

ANNA

Then came a letter mailed at Gary, Indiana.

DEAR ANNA,

Don't write to me again until I let you know where I am. I lost my job today because I refused to work on Sunday. At first I got a transfer to work in another department with less pay. But next it was work on Sunday again. I said "no." I cannot. I have nothing now. No job. I will do my best. I pray our dear friends will not have to leave Daruvar. That would change things for us completely. What would we do? Where would we go? I hope you are not worrying about it. God will surely work out something for our good. Good-by now. I am going west to hunt for work.

Love,

JOHN

Anna had mailed John a letter January 29. It was a short one, but Mary had enclosed a beautifully printed page which she had spent much time preparing.

DEAR, DEAR PAPA,

Our new baby is the sweetest that ever was born. She does not look like anybody but herself. Kathrine stayed home from school one day to help me with the work. She wants to stay home all week, but Mother is afraid it will make the teacher very angry. He is cross at Kathrine and Joe most of the time because they would not kiss the priest's hand. He visited school last week. He made Kathrine and Joe stand outside while he talked to the other children a long time. All the way home the children called John "Baby Bimbo." Kathrine and Joe came home crying. Mother always knows what to say to make us feel better when we are sad. We all love you, Papa. We pray for you the best we can. In the spring I will be old enough to take care of things so Mother can go to church on Sundays. Don't you think so? I wish Elizabeth would come over like she used to. We are lonesome for her. Hurry home. Don't you think Lydia is a pretty name for our baby? I do. I still have the soap you sent me.

Very many loves from

MARY

But John never received that letter.

Anxiously Anna waited and prayed over the almost-empty flour sack. Weeks passed but no word came from John. She measured the cornmeal, the oil, the matches, the sugar. She counted the turnips, the potatoes, the dried beans, and the coins hidden in the top dresser drawer.

"Today, today," prayed the children, "send Mother a letter from Papa. With money, dear Jesus. Please."

"Here," cried Kathrine, holding her highly prized shoes out to her mother after the day had brought no letter, "maybe someone will buy these. I can wear my old scuffs."

"Who would buy them?" asked Anna sadly.

"Doesn't the storekeeper in Vilieki Bastaji have a little girl about my size?" Kathrine's eyes were shimmering in tears.

"I believe he does. But, Kathrine, Papa would be grieved if he knew we sold them. I know he will send money as soon as he can. We can make out a few more days if we have to."

"If only Aunt Tena or Grandma or someone would bring us some chicken or something," cried Joe.

The end of the week came, but no letter.

Father Markum came to perform his annual house-sprinkling ceremony. Jeers, hootings, and bold-spoken shamings from the most faithful church members who were following the father in the village street penetrated Anna's tightly closed door as he neared the house. At least a dozen men and boys were in the group.

The father stopped abruptly. There was a sudden quiet. He lifted his black skirts and shook both feet in front of the house. Horrified, Anna watched from the window.

"They've got a new baby in there," one of the men shouted. Anna held her breath.

"It will go to Hell with the other one," answered the father.

Anna drew her frightened children away from the window. "Come," she said tenderly. "Jesus tells me no such thing. Oh, how awful!" she whispered. "Oh, I never supposed. Never.

Our neighbors. Children, stay by me. Close. Now sit down. Each of you. Be quiet. He's coming to the door."

Anna paled. Her knees knocked together. She did not wait for him to knock. She stood trembling before the open doorway.

"I'm told you have a Bible in this house." There was no touch of warmth in the father's voice. "Is it true?" He eyed her sharply. The group of scoffers stood within hearing distance.

"Yes," answered Anna. "It is true."

He lifted his eyebrows. "That's all right," he said with a cynical grin. "No one said you couldn't. But you've been reading in it, haven't you?" he frowned.

"Yes."

"And that's all right," he said cuttingly. "No one said you shouldn't. No one said you couldn't. We don't care if every home in Miletinac has a Bible in it. We don't care who reads it. You thought the church fathers did. Didn't you?"

"Yes." Anna's voice was scarcely audible.

"There you are altogether mistaken. You did not need to sneak it in and hide to read it. The sin you are going to be punished for is that you have interpreted it yourself. Not according to the consent of the holy fathers but according to your own weak mind and conscience. No one has enough intelligence to do such a thing. No one. It is a very grievous sin for you to even attempt to interpret one single word of that Bible." He shook his finger at her. "That act alone will send your soul to eternal burning Hell. The Holy Bible is an awful book. It is a most dangerous book. You have been tampering with sacred things. With fire, Mrs. Olesh. You and your husband both. And as I said before, there is a terrible burning awaiting you. It would be far kinder to take the lives of your little ones now. I understand there are two now."

He waited. She made no reply. She was frozen.

"I say it would be an act of mercy to take their lives now

310

rather than to let them grow up to maturity to follow in your ungodly footsteps."

Again he paused for her comment. Her lips did not move. Her face was white.

"You are not afraid of Hell?" he shouted demandingly.

"I—I am very much afraid of Hell," answered Anna. "That is where I was bound for." She took a breath. "That is why we made the change. I'm not going there now."

"You're not? How do you know that?"

"My Bible," came her answer. "It tells me I'm saved by grace through faith in the Lord Jesus Christ. I didn't work for it. I didn't pay for it. I didn't have to beg Mary for it. It's a gift I accepted by faith. It's real. I know it. I believe it. I feel it. And no one can take it from me." Anna was trembling. She could hear the children in the other room crying with fear.

Father Markum stood for a moment as though puzzled and ashamed of it. He shifted. His face reddened. "You poor woman," he said at length. "You are badly deceived and going to pay a very dear price. You are banking on fables. Christ is too busy to take time for anyone like you. You can't reach Him except through Mary."

Uncontrolled tears oozed and hung trembling on Anna's thick black lashes. "But I have," she answered. "He took time to come down and reach me. Why can't you see it, Father Markum?" she cried. "He paid that dear price for me and for you and for all our dear neighbors who scoff us."

Like whipped dogs the group of scoffers behind the father turned and walked away. Father Markum cleared his throat and with head bent moved on his way.

Milwaukee, Wisconsin
April 3, 1914

DEAR ANNA,

At last I have a job at the International Harvester Company. I make fifty cents an hour and I like the work fine. Write to me at once general delivery. I got the cheapest

311

room I could find. I had quite a time getting out here. Had to walk part of the way. The country is beautiful and it makes me terribly homesick for you all. I wish you were here with me. Sometimes I wonder, Anna, if I shouldn't look around out here for a small farm and bring you all to America. I am praying about it. You pray too. Are Brother and Sister Lutz still in Daruvar? Write at once. God be with you tonight.

My love as never before,
JOHN

Chapter 35

But Anna could not mail an immediate answer to John's letter. She had been out of postage, paper, envelopes, and money for weeks.

Work! How she had worked to get the ground ready for spring seeding!

Skimp. Stretch. Save. Patch. Anna Olesh experienced the deeper, more painful meaning of those four words, especially since the baby had come. Every night she prayed herself to sleep.

The children. Their anxious eyes, their hungry faces, their endless flood of questions, "When will Papa come home?" "When will he send money again?" nearly overwhelmed her. Sometimes alone in the field she would give way to her feelings and cry aloud to God while the tears streamed down her cheeks.

But besides her loneliness for John and their startling scarcity of food, she learned from personal, daily experience about the roughness of curiosity, the injustice of contempt, and the sting of sneerings fresh and to-the-face. Would there be no end to this ridicule from the villagers who once loved her?

One evening Anna came in from the field early. A thunderstorm was blowing up from the distant Blue Mountains, moving in toward the village.

"It's going to storm, children," she said. "I didn't want you to be here alone."

Anna had no more than closed the door when there was a loud, rapid knocking. She opened. There was no one in sight. On the low wooden step outside the door was a cardboard box about a foot long and half that wide. She stepped

313

out. Carefully, hesitatingly she opened it. What? Her eyes were surely deceiving her. It couldn't be. But it was. On the sack of cornmeal FOR ANNA OLESH was printed in bold letters.

She carried the box into the house. "Look, children."

"Something to eat!" cried Joe, clapping his hands.

"Something to eat!" chimed all four.

There was not only cornmeal in the box, but sugar, a small sack of white flour, some dried beans, and prunes.

"Who brought it, Mother?" they all asked.

"That's what I don't know. I wonder. It must have come from a friend." Anna was half-laughing, half-crying. "There must be someone in our village who cares a little bit for us. Is the water in the kettle hot, Mary?"

"No, but it soon will be."

"Then we'll have mush for supper. Think of it. With sugar on it. And tomorrow I will bake bread. Come. Let us stand around the box and hold hands and bow our heads to thank the good Lord for sending us this wonderful gift."

"I wonder," said Anna after the prayer—"I wonder if Brother Lutz brought this to our door."

"Listen," Mary grabbed her mother's hand. "I think I'd be old enough now to stay with the children if you want to go to church on Sunday. You want to go. You want to ask him, don't you, Mother?"

"I'd love to go to church, dear. But I don't know. I don't know, Mary, if I should. And the children may come again for stories, strange as it seems. I can't understand why their parents let them come."

"I could tell them stories, Mother. Not as good as you do, but I could try."

Anna drew Mary to her and planted an affectionate kiss on her forehead. "What would I do without you? Mary, you are such a little woman already."

And while it thundered and lightninged and the rain poured down, Anna and her family enjoyed a delicious supper.

314

Mary did persuade her mother to go to Daruvar on Sunday. Anna started on foot before daylight. It was noon by the time she reached the Gospel Center. Morning services would be over, she feared.

She tiptoed inside. Sister Lutz and her children and a few adults were standing in the corner of the assembly room talking in undertones. Two of the children were crying.

"Anna!" Sister Lutz ran to her with outstretched arms. "You've heard already?"

"Heard what?"

"William's in jail."

"In jail?"

"They came and got him early this morning. Before we were up. Anna, you know about this, don't you?"

"About what?"

"How it all came about?"

"No."

"Did you get the box we sent you?"

"The box? With the cornmeal and sugar and—"

"Yes."

"Yes. Last night. But I—"

"Last night?"

"Yes. Just about dark."

"What did he tell you?"

"Who?"

"Who brought it to you?"

"I never saw anyone. Someone knocked. That's all I know. When I answered, no one was in sight. The box was outside the door. My name was on the cornmeal sack."

"Yes. I put it on."

"You?"

"Yes, Anna. I kept telling William all week that I had such a strong feeling that you were in need."

"We were, Sister Lutz. God sent that box in answer to our prayers."

"Well, I told William, let's have a box ready so if you do

315

come to Daruvar we could give it to you. We've been watched very closely. Every move we make. When you didn't come, we watched for a chance to send it to you. 'Somehow,' I told William, 'I can't get it out of my mind that Anna is in need.' So Tuesday William came in here in a hurry and said he met your father in the depot waiting for the train."

"My father?"

"Yes. That's who he said it was. He asked him if he wouldn't deliver that box to you."

"And he said he would?"

"He said he would, but William said he looked at him awful queer. But why didn't he deliver it before last night?

"Early this morning two officers came here and got William out of bed and said, 'So you're the man who claims to be doing true Christian service in Daruvar. Well, we've got the goods on you now. You're smuggling things to women. Yes, all the way over to Miletinac.' "

"Smuggling?"

"They accused William of hiding Testaments and money in sacks of cornmeal. You know he has been warned."

"But he didn't, did he?"

"He never did that. No. But I did tie some money in a cloth and put it in the sugar for you."

"You did?"

"You didn't open the sugar yet?"

"Yes. We used some last night. But I never noticed anything in it."

"I thought perhaps you needed stamps. We hadn't heard from you for so long."

"I do need stamps. Oh, Agnes, surely my father—Oh, I can't think of it. Maybe it's still in there."

"But why did he wait so long to give it to you?"

"And why did he bring it over, then run away? You think he reported this? Oh, Sister Lutz! My own father!"

"I don't know who, but whoever it was has certainly put the wrong construction on William's motives. Anyhow, I was

316

the one who suggested sending you the food and the money. I thought of your children, Anna. And perhaps John was out of work. God knows our hearts, Anna."

"Of course. And how we all did appreciate it! I wish you could have seen the children. But poor Brother Lutz."

"And you didn't come because you knew about this?"

"I came because I wanted to worship with you. Mary offered to stay with the children. She begged to, to let me come. I knew nothing of this. What will my father think now if he finds out I came over? What is going to happen next?"

"I do not know, Anna. But this is one thing I do know, we are not going to stop trusting God now."

"How long will he be held?"

"I've no idea. The church leaders are furious at us. Come, join us in prayer for William. He is depending on us. He will need a double portion of the wisdom of God to know how to answer his accusers."

They all knelt in the corner of the chapel. Anna shook with sobs.

"Don't cry," said Sister Lutz.

"But it looks as if I'm to blame for this."

"To blame? No. Don't say that. William has always been kind to people. He's helped others. Widows and children."

"But why does God allow such a good man to be falsely accused? I can't understand it."

"Listen, my dear." Sister Lutz put her arm across Anna's shoulder. "If we had no trials, no troubles, how would God test our strength and genuineness? God is allowing this for a purpose and He must get the glory to Himself because of it. Why were good men like Abraham and Noah and Paul tested and persecuted? Why wasn't life always easy for them? Their glorious characters stood out by the way they met their troubles and trials. In I Peter we read a verse like this, Anna: 'For what glory is it, if, when ye be buffeted [that means struck at, or accused, or made fun of, or persecuted] for your faults, ye shall take it patiently? [We ought to do that.] but if, when ye do well [the best we know by God's help and live according to His Word], and suffer for it, ye take it patiently, this is acceptable with God.' That pleases the Lord. Oh, Anna, I can hear William saying that verse over and over right now."

Anna looked up and smiled through her tears. "Then you don't think he is discouraged?"

"William discouraged? No, Anna. This will not shake his faith in God. He lives every moment by faith. I've seen William burdened many times but never discouraged. No matter what's been tossed in his face these past months, underneath he has a calmness, a peace, a joy that all the priests in Serbia put together couldn't equal."

"And you're sure he'll never be sorry he sent the box over with my father?"

"Sorry? Sorry he did a kind deed? Anna dear, you know better. Has he ever been sorry he went over to Miletinac? Has he regretted he helped you and John find peace with God even though you were called in to the Daruvar court three times, and the head of your baby was threatened? Yes, he suffered with you. He was deeply concerned and prayed night and day for you, but he was not sorry he testified to you."

"I hope not."

"And those threats. What has come of them?"

"Nothing yet."

"Nothing."

"But the suspense at times—"

"Has been almost unbearable. Yes, Anna, I believe that. But somehow the grace and peace and the unspeakable love of God reach down and lead you through those times of dreadful suspense. God never felt nearer or dearer to me than He does right now. He's wonderful. He's my Saviour. He's everything to me."

Agnes Lutz jumped. A warm hand gripped her shoulder.

"William!" she cried. "William! When did you come in?"

"Right now." He dropped on his knees and a prayer of thanksgiving poured from his soul. Then he prayed for the officers who took him to jail, for the priests, for the lost of Daruvar, and finally for the little group of Christians in the circle. "And, dear Lord, bless Sister Anna and her husband, Brother John, in America. Bless him with health and strength and work, that the needs of his family may be supplied. But, above all, keep him true to Thee under all circumstances, and guide him and Anna day by day, that the peace and joy of this glorious salvation which is theirs and which has put a glow into their lives will always be theirs in an ever-growing abundance and be handed down and received by their children and children's children. Amen and amen."

Together the little group sang praises to their Creator. Anna could feel the goose pimples come out over her entire body. She had never felt so stirred to pledge her allegiance to God. Something like a soft-whispered prayer spoke sweet words of peace to her heart.

And little did Anna imagine the strength and encouragement she would draw in the days and months to follow from that morning's experience at the Gospel Center. She was the first to tell of her trials and how God had protected her. The words came sparkling and fresh from her newly thrilled, happy soul; sentences she had never thought before, nor tried to put into words.

One of the first things Anna did when she got home was to empty the sugar sack. Yes, the money was in the bottom, in a tightly tied piece of cloth. But there was something more than two coins in the cloth. A small strip of paper contained two sentences: "Be careful if you accept this. Beware if you spend it."

"Did anyone come today, Mary?"

"Just two. Sarah and Edith. That's all. I told them three stories. The one about Moses, and Baby Jesus born, and

319

the flood. They said they didn't think they could come any more."

For days John had been catching startling bits of the talk among the men during the noon lunch hour. That and what Anna had written in her last letter startled him. What was it all about? If he could only understand everything the men were discussing. He wouldn't edge up. He wouldn't show his ignorance by asking questions. Some of the men poked fun at him as it was because he didn't smoke or drink. And again because he carried his Testament in his shirt pocket and read it after he was through eating until the bell rang. "The Jesus man" they called him. John let on he didn't hear. But he turned his head to listen when one man said unmistakably, "Now Russia joins Serbia against Austria. And you men watch what France and Germany will do next. I'm glad I'm in America."

"America," said John under his breath. "My wife! My children! O God! If I only had them here with me. Keep your hand over them while we are separated from each other."

It was very difficult for John to keep his mind on his work that afternoon. If he could only read a newspaper. He must find out if what he thought he heard was true. He prayed. He listened. He watched. He waited for word from Anna.

Then one evening when he arrived at his rooming place the daily paper was lying on the floor inside the door of the dingy hallway. He picked it up. Two of the top words he readily recognized. He held the paper in his trembling hands and waited. In a few minutes the landlady came in, her arms full of groceries.

"Why, good evening, Mr. Olesh."

"Good evening, ma'am," answered John, removing his cap. "Vot is?" He pointed to the bold-typed headline.

"BALKANS BECOME BOILING POT OF EUROPE. That's what

320

it says, Mr. Olesh. Sounds like there's plenty of trouble across the water, doesn't it?"

John looked perplexed.

"What's on your mind, Mr. Olesh?"

John rubbed one hand over the other. "Mine vife," he said. "Good vife. Mine Mary. Mine Kathrine. Mine Anna. Mine leetle John un mine baby vot so schmall."

"You mean you've got a family like that over there where they're fighting?"

John nodded.

"Oh, Mr. Olesh! No wonder you're anxious. War is a terrible thing. I sure hope we stay out of anything like that. We will. President Wilson has a head on him. But men are funny creatures. They can start fighting over almost nothing sometimes."

John didn't understand half of what the woman was saying.

At once he wrote Anna a long letter and took it to the nearest mailbox.

Anna dreaded leaving the children in the house alone, but she must go to the field and hoe weeds if she was to have oil to burn and food for her growing children. Every time she prayed with them first before she went out. The terrible reality of war was upon them. No more wondering or speculating. The low, thundering rumble of cannon was coming closer day by day.

One morning a young man brought Anna a government notice ordering her to haul a wagonload of food to the soldiers at the edge of the mountains.

"But I have six children," pleaded Anna.

"This is an order issued by the government, Mrs. Olesh. Other women are going to help. It's this or go to prison. Are you going to obey?"

"I will."

"Katie," she announced in tears. "I'm sorry, dear. But it's

321

got to be. There's no other way. You'll have to go to the field and do the hoeing. I've got to haul food to the soldiers. Mary, be brave and pray hard. God will see us through somehow."

Chapter 36

Anna had already made a dozen day-long trips by horse and wagon hauling food to the soldiers. Part of the road wound through a thickly wooded area. To steady her nerves Anna always sang and prayed aloud while going through the forest.

After dark one evening two Austrian officers burst into the house without knocking.

"Hand over your pistol," one of them demanded. His rough voice and fierce eyes frightened the children. They buried their faces in the bedcovers.

"I have no pistol," answered Anna.

"Don't tell us that," shouted the other officer. "We know better. Out with it."

"I'm telling you the truth," insisted Anna. "There is no pistol or gun of any sort in this house."

The first officer flashed the point of his pistol in Anna's face. "You expect us to believe that? Get it at once or I will kill you on the spot. Yes, right here in front of your children." She could hear smothered sobs.

Anna whitened. "God knows I'm telling the truth, sir. Please believe me. If I had one, I'd give it to you without any argument."

The officer lowered his aim. "Did you ever have one in your house?"

"Yes, sir."

"All right, then." He pressed the pistol tight against her chest. "Where is it? And say it quickly."

"My husband put it in the repair shop over a year ago."

"Where?"

"In Daruvar. It's still there."

"Your husband," snarled the officer. "And where is the rat?"

"In America."

Anna felt his saliva spray her face. "You expect us to believe that too? The rat. In America!"

"Ask anyone in the village," Anna said.

With volcanic eruption vile cursings poured from the two enraged officers. "If the rat was only here," swore the one with the pistol as he flashed it back and forth, "we'd love to beat his measly brains out." The two went out and slammed the door. The whole house shook.

Anna stood for a moment as though trying to grasp what had just happened.

Then a sudden power seemed to possess her. When she spoke, there was something deep, primitive, yet new and fresh in her simple statement. "Children," she said, "look up. Look at me. Come. You see, God did not hide His face from us in this hour. Let us thank him." And while they clustered around her, she prayed.

In no time Austrian soldiers simply poured into Miletinac and raided every other home in the village.

"My God! My God!" John held his breath. The letter from Anna was but two sentences: "Don't try to come home now. Not safe to walk in the streets any more."

Anna clasped John's letter to her breast while hot tears rolled down her cheeks.

"Why, Mother!" cried Mary. "I can't keep from crying when you cry. What's wrong? Mother!"

"It's from Papa. I can't keep the tears back, Mary. He wants to know all about us. But I can't write now. My last letter came back. And it has been opened. Oh, God in Heaven," she sobbed, "do be good to John."

In a few days Anna received another order from the government.

"You're to be a watchwoman from dark until dawn beginning tonight. And this order stands until you are officially released. You're to walk an eightmile beat around the village. An officer will tell you tonight what to watch out for, what to expect and what to do under any circumstances."

"Yes, sir." Anna asked no questions. She made no excuses. It would almost tear her heart to leave her children alone at night she knew, but it was that or go to prison.

All color left her cheeks.

"You heard what he told me, children," she said, wrestling to be calm. Their sad uplifted faces and startled eyes smote her. She nearly staggered across the room. She picked up the Bible and held it, looking at it. Her heart throbbed. Her hands shook.

War. How crushing! How fearsome! What started it? Some said a lad of Serbian ancestry had shot and killed the Grand Duke and his wife, heir to the Austrian throne. But who knew?

The children's anxious silence, their frightened upward gazing into her face was crushing. She wanted to cry out with all her powers, "O God, why? John! Come home. Please come home!"

But something held her. Her throbbing heart steadied. The Book she held in her hard-worked hands told of One who had gone the inhuman limits of pain, loneliness, suffering, and death for her. And because He was near, and would give strength, she could go on.

She reached out and pressed each child to her. She kissed each one, then sat on the edge of the bed.

"I'll read to you before I go," she said quietly. "Without this Book and what it means to me I never, never could leave you. As I watch for the enemy, I'll be doing it to protect you. I'll be praying for you. Remember, God is watching over you. Your papa in America is praying for you too. God helping me, I'll be back before you're awake in the morning. Joe, you and John sleep together. Kathrine,

325

you and Anna sleep with Mary. God bless little Lydia. I'm glad she's not old enough to know anything is wrong. I hope she sleeps soundly all night."

"I wish Elizabeth would come over and stay with us," whispered Kathrine half-crying.

"I'd rather not ask her," Anna answered, opening the Bible. "What shall I read to you? I must hurry. It will soon be growing dark. I'll read the Twenty-third Psalm. 'The Lord is my shepherd.' "

She could not tell whether the children understood much of what she was reading or not. Even though they seemed to be listening with unbroken attention, she wasn't sure.

Suddenly she realized that she herself was the Bible they were reading. She closed the book.

Her serious face became soft and radiant. Her sad eyes glowed over them with the warmth of tenderest mother love.

"Children," she said scarcely above a whisper, "my God is your God. And He loves and watches over each of us. I must leave you for a few hours now, but He will be right here with you. Now I am going to pray for you. Try not to be afraid. Just go to bed and sleep."

And on those quiet, lone watch-walks in the dark Anna talked continually with God. In the still coolness of the nights she learned more and more about His limitless love for the sinful world. Her faith grew steadily and her soul strangely calmed.

As she watched the shifting clouds, she begged them to carry her love across the ocean to John. Foolish. She knew it was. Yet from her soul's need she did it night after night. She had to express her feelings in some way. For as her love for God grew, so did her love for John. Anna was not old. She was mother of six, but she was still young, vigorous, ambitious, full of life and fervor. And John was the man she loved.

Brave. If he could see her now, would he tell her again

that she was brave? He had called her brave the evening he told her for the first time he wanted to go to America. Mary and Kathrine were the brave ones now. In the fair, tender bud of their lives they had to experience this stab of war—work, loneliness, fear, hunger, plus reproach because their parents were Christians.

One chill, rainy morning when Anna came home, she knew at once something was wrong. Mary was bending over the baby's crib.

"She's not acting right, Mother. She whined and fretted all night. I held her and did everything I could think of. See how she jerks and flutters her eyelids."

Anna touched the tiny flushed cheek.

"She has a high fever, Mary." Anna picked the little one up in her arms and carried her to the kitchen. She sank on a chair, exhausted, weak from hunger and now from fright. She knew without a shadow of doubt that her baby was desperately ill.

"You go back to bed and rest a while, Mary. I'll take care of her."

The dark, dripping day wore on. Anna sat by the baby's crib in silent vigil. Her soul reached out to God for mercy. What could she do but pray? There was no medicine in the house, and if there were, how would she know it was what the child needed?

"Joe, you go out to the garden with Kathrine and help her dig a few potatoes. See if the turnips are big enough to eat."

Little Lydia. Sweet-faced, fair, delicate, pretty as a picture. The one John had never seen. The purest, the most helpless, the most dependent.

Was this sudden sickness because of—? Anna shuddered. The villagers—now what would they conclude? "Ah! an evil spirit. Something terrible is going to happen." She could hear all their sneers and jeers and dark forebodings now as she sat and watched her baby suffer. She knew her baby was innocent. She knew, too, that somehow God was still loving and caring for them.

If only John knew, and could join her in prayer! If only Brother and Sister Lutz knew!

Brother and Sister Lutz. How was it with them? Were they still in Daruvar? It was wearing to wonder about so many things.

Death. Anna was certain it was hovering lower, closer each hour. Lydia refused water. She did not respond to a mother's touch. Not even her loving words.

Anna dropped on her knees beside the crib and shook with sobs. "But, after all," she prayed, "you know what's best, dear Lord. Lydia is yours. I will not ask to keep her if you want her. In this trying hour, O God, when I think my heart is going to break, show me your love. So I can show it to my neighbors, my children, my children, my children, O God. Show me, teach me, take me, make of me what you want me to be. I want to prove to these people your glory."

Kathrine and Joe brought in the potatoes and turnips, and Mary peeled and cooked them. But no one was really hungry. Anna ate a few bites so the children would eat.

Brave? John's voice, his hand, his footstep, his very being seemed present. But more real the voice, the hand, the presence of God. She watched. She waited.

Over the lifeless little face very, very gently she placed her best homemade handkerchief.

"Kathrine," she said softly, "will you go and tell Grandma to come over? Right away. Joe, go along with Kathrine. You won't need to run."

"I did the best I knew, Mother," sobbed Mary on her mother's shoulder.

"I know you did, dear. No one will ever think you didn't. This would have happened if I had been here. The Lord wanted her, Mary."

"Is that where she will go?"

"Absolutely. Our baby has gone straight to Heaven. Don't ever let anyone make you think anything else. People will talk, but we can't help it, or keep them from it. I know God loves us. And He has love in all He does. I trust Him."

Mary stared at her mother. Then she kissed her.

Anna's parents could not comprehend her reaction. They and all the other villagers were completely baffled. She wouldn't give in now and have John baptized? She wouldn't try to call the witch doctor? Would Anna Olesh ever learn? What they called punishment Anna called suffering for God's glory. What they called reproach she called her strengthening in Christ. Strange. How very strange!

Four little girls (those who had come to Anna's house to hear stories) consented to carry the tiny casket to the cemetery.

Little by little John learned to understand what the men were discussing at the plant. Every evening he asked his landlady what the paper had to say about the conflict in Europe. Every evening he shook his head and groaned.

"It's getting to be a grand mess, Mr. Olesh."

"Vot?"

"A grand mess. Listen to this. The present war which really began with the Austrian ultimatum to Serbia, with Germany's support and under Germany's direction, has now grown to involve every first-class power and most of the lesser nations in Europe. It will by all appearances become the most extensive war in history, involving greater economic loss, casualties, and civilian suffering than ever known."

John groaned.

"You didn't get all that, did you?"

John shook his head.

"Sounds bad, Mr. Olesh."

"Yeh. Bad. I pray Got."

"There's nothing much more you can do about it, Mr.

329

Olesh. Just so they stay over there with their guns and airplanes. Listen. Here is a list of nations involved. I don't think anybody knows who is fighting whom any more or for what. It says right here many simply found themselves being attacked without any formal declaration of war. Now here's a list: Austria, Serbia, Germany, Russia, France, Belgium, Britain, Japan, Turkey, Portugal, Italy, Bulgaria, Rumania—"

"Stop!" cried John, putting his fingers over his ears. "I no see. I go pray."

Every Sunday John attended some Protestant church in Milwaukee. There were many. Most of the songs were new and strange to him, but he found the page and followed along as best he could. Without fail he got at least one helpful nugget of truth from the Sunday school lesson discussion. Some teachers he could understand better than others.

The preachers in the pulpits always seemed to be trying to remind God about the awful condition in Europe, and wouldn't He do something about it before it involved all the rest of the world—including their own glorious, peace-loving United States?

Unless it was raining John took a long walk every Sunday after church. He would find a quiet spot in some public park where he could read his Testament undisturbed and talk to God. No one could understand his need, his anguish of heart. No one in happy, prosperous, pleasure-mad America cared. No one but God.

Passers-by glanced at him and grinned stupidly. Some laughed out loud.

Slow, torturous weeks were those for John with no word from Anna. He was afraid to send any more money. Did she receive what he had sent? Did they have enough to eat? John lost his appetite.

"You're getting thin," remarked the landlady one evening. "Are you sick?"

330

"I no hear mine vife is. Mine Mary. Mine Kathrine. Mine Joe un Anna un mine new leetle one. Mine," he pressed his shaking hand over his heart, "so feel," then his gray eyes filled with sudden, uncontrolled tears. He turned and walked away abruptly.

"I wish I could help you out, Mr. Olesh," called the landlady.

John shook his head sadly. "I more pray. I vait. I votch. I say to Got, help."

It happened. The inevitable. It was the first week in April when newsboys all over town called out, "Extra! Extra! Read all about it. Extra! United States declares war on Germany!" The papers were soon gone. John bought one himself although he didn't know exactly why. Everybody on the streets was grabbing for them.

Immediately posters were pinned up throughout the plant requesting all employees to buy liberty bonds. "Be patriotic. Buy United States bonds today."

John studied. He debated.

"Olesh," exclaimed the foreman at the end of the week, "I see you're the only fellow in this plant who hasn't bought a bond. Some have already bought more than one. How about it?"

"I no get."

"I know you haven't yet. But you will."

"I no get. No." He shook his head.

"You mean you want to live here and enjoy the liberties of our country and not help Uncle Sam?"

"I no make mad. I no fight."

"No one is asking you to get mad or fight. But we're to help the government keep our young men who have to go fight. You aren't ready to help?"

"I no like war."

"Who does? That's why we must hurry up and have this mess over with. You mean you aren't interested in helping?"

John shook his head. "Christian no fight. No kill."

331

"You're the only man in International Harvester who has tried such an argument. Olesh, I'd be ashamed. I'd feel mighty cheap if I were in your shoes. International won't hire any slackers. We're going to go 100 percent in here."

The next day John was handed his final pay check.

He went to his room, gathered together his few belongings, and tried to explain to the landlady why he was leaving.

"I don't exactly understand your religion, Mr. Olesh, but maybe God does."

John nodded.

"And I hope God, who knows your heart, will overlook it and pardon you if you've done wrong. I think as long as we live in this country it's our Christian duty to be loyal to it in every way. And right now this is one way we can all help. I do not have any sons to give Uncle Sam, but I will give in this way." John knew it was useless to try to explain in his crude way his convictions; so he left the woman with a bow and a smile.

"Come back sometime, Mr. Olesh," she called. "You've been a nice, quiet roomer. Don't you have any relatives here in America?"

"Uncle Jose in America. I not see. No. I go mit me un Got."

The months for Anna were far more torturous and uncertain than for John. Sometimes she got only a few hours' sleep in a week's time. Daily she warned the children not to leave the house night or day without her permission. Army planes were roaring overhead continually. Great billows of dust, smoke, and fire could be seen at frighteningly close range.

The tiring night watching continued. To be sure, God's very presence was with her, but sometimes Anna thought her legs would break before dawn. And when she reached home, there was not time to rest. To the garden, to the field she must go for the sustenance of her family. Their very breath of life depended solely on her and the patch of ground they owned. As long as she had feet to carry her she'd keep going for them. As long as she had hands they would dig and scratch for them. She prayed over every living, growing thing on the farm and for energy for one more day.

Three strange men broke rudely into the house one evening while Anna was reading her Bible to the children. With curses they ordered bread and cottage cheese.

"I have no cheese in the house," Anna told them.

"Then bread and syrup."

"But I have no syrup."

"Sausage."

"I have no sausage."

They filled the house with curses and vile talk.

"Be careful, men," she said. "Remember, God is in this house. He hears every word you're saying."

"That's not so," one retorted. "God is a prisoner over in France. He can't hear 'way over here."

"Don't be surprised," answered Anna. "God will not be mocked. He *is* in this house."

The three men left immediately. Anna waited until she was certain they were gone. "God really is in this house, children," she said softly. "Never doubt it for a second."

They stared at their mother in silent wonder. She was not aware of the strange heavenly light on her face.

Chapter 37

"Where did you last work? Why were you fired? Why didn't you stay home and help your Serbs and Slavs in this bloody mess?" That and similar humiliating and confusing retorts John had to encounter daily in his search for a job. Seemingly no one wanted to hire a foreigner who could scarcely speak English. And definitely not one who refused to buy liberty bonds.

All the way across the state of Minnesota John tramped. Footsore, heartsick, and disturbed, he sat down on the dusty grass along the country railroad. He buried his face in both hands. "Is this what I get for trying to help my family?"

"Dear Lord. You know my condition. I don't want to give up, but help me soon."

He pulled a blade of grass and rolled it slowly between the palms of his hands.

A man inspecting the tracks walked by. He hesitated. He looked back and tossed John a friendly greeting—just a simple "good day" with an open, easy smile. John looked up in surprise.

"What's on your mind, stranger?" inquired the man pleasantly. "Looks like you're trying to carry the whole world and all its problems." The man chuckled. "That's too much of a load for any one person."

John nodded in partial comprehension. "I no vork," he said.

"Why not?" asked the man. "Maybe that's what's ailing you. If you'd work, you'd get rid of most of your troubles. Take a job like mine. I walk mine off."

John got to his feet. "I vork I kin. I do goot vork. I no lazy. No."

The man laughed softly. "I see. Well, pardon me, sir. You mean, then, you really do want work?"

"I vork anyzing. Anyzing," repeated John. "I no make money. I—"

"But," interrupted the man, "you have worked?"

"Yeh." John took a step closer to the man. "I vork goot."

"Where?"

"In rock quarry. Un mid horse un wagel. In schmelter. I do so hard vork anyzings I kin. Got no machines. Vork wid han'."

"Can't even drive a tractor?"

"Tractor? I learn, I kin."

"How about farm work? Ever done any of that?"

John's face brightened. "I have farm. Yeh. I like a farm."

"Where do you come from?"

"Europe. Serbia. No kin go home now."

"I suppose not. War's tough on that point now. Mind working for a German?"

John blinked. "I vork anyzings. Any farm."

The man pushed back his straw hat and scratched his head. "Well, I tell you. First what's your name?"

"Olesh. John Olesh."

"I tell you. I've got an uncle living over near Aberdeen, South Dakota—about five miles out from town, west on the highway. He's got a big farm. Needs help right now. Just had a letter from him yesterday asking me if I knew of anyone."

John wanted to leap. Instead, he stepped closer to the man. "Vot? His name vot? I vonce go see."

"His name is Al Weissinger. If you look him up, tell him I sent you. Hank, the track walker. He'll know. I've worked for Uncle Al and he's all right. Good, honest, and straight. But a hard worker."

The Lord heard his prayer! John whispered words of praise and started on with renewed energy.

He had little difficulty in locating the Weissinger farm.

Al, short, stocky, and muscular, gave John a hearing. Then he invited him into the house to a delicious supper. Potato soup, sliced onions, Dutch apple pie, and fresh just-out-of-the-oven homemade bread. Food never tasted better.

But it wasn't until after the meal that Al gave John any satisfaction about hiring him.

"What wages do you want?"

"I work. You pay."

"What do you mean? I'm to pay you what you think you're worth or what I think you're worth?" Al ran his hands into his hip pockets and backed away from John, studying him.

"Vot you dink," answered John. "I no smoke. I no drink. I no lazy. I vork you goot."

"All right, John. Start in tomorrow morning. We get up at 4:30 every morning except on Sunday it's 5:30. We have an hour off at noon and quit at 6:00 except during harvest. Harvest here will begin the latter part of next week. Can you take that?"

John nodded. "I take."

"All right, then. We keep a room for hired help upstairs. It's the northwest corner room."

John smiled.

"My father," remarked Al, "was a newcomer to this country when I was a lad. That's one reason why I'm ready to help men like you. I remember those days well. My dad was a hard-working man and he taught us boys to work. Most of these Americans like the easy life. Little work but big wages. Never could see it come to me that way."

Many were the methods of successful farming John learned from Al Weissinger in the months to come. He learned other things as well. Words and their meanings, important matters about business, the government, taxes, laws, and American culture.

Al was a smart man without acting smart about it. Gradually John confided in him about his problems, his

336

longings, and his fears about his family back home. Al and his wife learned to understand and respect John. They could tell at times that his heart was nearly bleeding. Every evening John asked Al to give him the newspaper developments about the war.

Eight months and no word from Anna.

"There's nothing to do but wait until this comes to an end," Al told John.

But one evening Al looked up from the paper and said, "Say, I have an idea, John. The next time I go to town I'm going to stop at the Red Cross office, and ask if they'd know of some way you could find out about your family."

"How?" John had been especially quiet and serious that day. "Mine Anna be dead I know nozings. She live I know nozings. I pray. I cry. I more pray." John buried his face in both hands, then went immediately to his room.

Before the week ended Al brought home the report. "There's one thing they can try, John. They said you could send your wife a French telegram through their office. It's your only chance."

John looked up confused. "French? Vot I say? Anna no read French."

"Leave that to the Red Cross. It's the only chance. I'll take you in and they'll help you word it. Remember, a telegram can't say much. You can't tell her how much you love her and all that."

"Anna know I love," answered John.

The next day the telegram was sent. "Is family living? Shall I come home?"

"That's enough, Mr. Olesh," said the Red Cross woman. "We'll see what happens. If an answer comes back, I'll call Mr. Weissinger."

Their meager supper was over. Anna was sitting in the dark talking to her children who were snuggled close around her.

"God sees us in the dark," she was saying. "He knows what we need. He knows where your papa is and I believe he's all right. I'll tell you the story about the little girl who told a sick man about the good—"

Someone knocked. Before Anna got to the door it opened. It was Susan's father.

"It is a fact, Mrs. Olesh," he announced bluntly. "I just came from Daruvar." He laughed. "Out of oil?"

"We've been out for some time."

"Like sitting in the dark?" He laughed again.

"We learn to do many things we don't like," answered Anna.

"Well, that preacher Lutz and two of his followers are in prison and his church was raided. It is a fact, Mrs. Olesh. Did you know it?"

"No." Anna didn't gasp. She asked no questions. "The Lord will work it out."

"He will? Would you say He has been working things out for you too?" This time his laugh was louder.

"He does," answered Anna. "He has never let us down yet."

"You would say He is working things out when you don't know what's become of that man of yours?"

"God is with John wherever he is. He knows all about our need and will work it out in His own time and way."

"You say God will?" Almost hideous was his laugh.

"I believe Him. I trust Him. I know He will."

"You're not worried John has gone off with some gay woman over there in America?"

Such experiences were harder on Anna than going out to haul food to the soldiers, or walking all night alone in the dark. It was far more tormenting than the hunger pangs she had become so familiar with.

How many more reproachful, scandalous, insinuating remarks would her children have to hear about God and their father? Anna shivered. Weren't the horrors and grimness of war going to soften the attitudes of her once kind-hearted, friendly neighbors?

"These children have a good father. He loves every one of them as much as you do your little Susan."

"Oh, no," came the mocking reply.

"Yes, he does," answered Anna. "Right this minute I believe he is praying for them. That is more than you are doing for your little Susan."

The man grunted and walked away.

The following afternoon a lad from Vilieki Bastaji came running.

"There's a telegram at the store for you," he announced.

"For me? Are you sure?"

"Aren't you Mrs. John Olesh?"

"Yes."

"You are to come and get it yourself."

Although it had been gravely dangerous many times to be out on the street or on the road, not a structure in Miletinac or Vilieki Bastaji had been damaged. The actual fighting was miles to the north. The past two weeks, however, there had been a decided lull in tension throughout Serbia. But that did not mean the war was over. There still was dread and uncertainty.

It was a chill December day. A thin blue-gray haze hung drearily over the mountains. Anna pulled on an extra pair of stockings and her leather-soled homemade scuffs. She tied a woolen scarf on her head and buttoned her jacket at the throat.

"I'll not be gone a minute longer than absolutely necessary, children. Mary, don't wait till I get back to feed the children. Yes, it will have to be potato soup again. I'm sorry, dear."

Anna noticed Mary's pensive look. It was almost forlorn. "Someday things will be different, I hope. Let's be thankful we have one thing to eat."

"I am, Mother," said Mary. "But I hope it's not bad news about Papa. Oh, Mother, do you think it is?"

A puzzled expression crossed Anna's face. "I can't make this out," she cried in utter disappointment, holding the telegram in her hands.

"Let me see it," said the storekeeper. "Huh. That's French if I know anything."

"But it's from John."

"Your husband?"

"I'm sure it is."

"You'll have to find someone who can read it for you. You'll have to take it in to Daruvar, I suppose."

Anna's heart sank. She looked with agony at the mysterious words. "I will have to try to go tomorrow. It is too late now."

"Say," said the storekeeper, "take it over to the depot. That is where it came in. Why it was brought over here I don't know. Maybe the ticket agent can read it to you."

He did. Trembling with excitement Anna repeated the words. She pressed the paper against her thumping heart. The joy for the moment was almost more than she could contain. A message from John! He would come home if she said the word. Anna wanted to shout it at the top of her voice so everyone in Miletinac could hear it.

But no. He wouldn't dare. The uncertainty, the nervously shifting armies, the new unexpected turn of things, and the declaration on Germany and Austria made his home-coming unthinkable now.

"Could I send a telegram back right away?"

"Do you have the money?"

Anna stood speechless. Of course she had no money.

"Why don't you send an answer back through the Red Cross?" suggested the ticket agent.

"Could I?" cried Anna. "Could I really, sir?"

"Why not? That's how this came through. What do you want to tell him? I'll send it in. They can reject it, you know."

340

"You will? You will send it for me? Why will you do it for me, sir? I—"

For a moment the ticket agent looked at Anna thoughtfully. He picked up his pencil. "I don't know why," he answered dryly. "I wouldn't have to. What is it you want to tell him?"

"Tell him, 'Living. Not safe to come.'"

She watched him write the words.

There was a new request in Anna's prayer that night, a new tone of thanksgiving, and a new conflict in her anxious heart.

She worked as never before—as if driven by the impulse of an irresistible urge to help the days pass more quickly. When would it be safe for John to come home? What was John doing in South Dakota? Where was that? Her arms longed to encircle the earth to find him.

Her five-word telegram brought John's second message: "Sell everything. Come to me."

The air was suddenly full of dancing needles in the stuffy little store. Anna stood with muscles quivering. Was this of God? Sell everything. Go to America.

She fairly flew home to tell the children. They jumped. They laughed. They danced. They cried. They all wanted to sit on her lap at once and hug her. Go to Papa! To America!

"But the place isn't sold yet, children. Perhaps no one will care to buy." She caught herself. It wasn't necessary to remind the children it hadn't been blessed by the priest for many months. "If it is God's will, someone surely will," she added.

"Oh, Mother," exclaimed Kathrine, "if you pray real much, someone will buy it right away."

"But even so, we can't cross the ocean until this war is over, Kathrine."

"Let's ask God to make it stop tonight," said Joe, pounding his fist on the table.

"Bless your heart, Joe," said Anna, patting his head.

341

"We've been praying that every day for over three years now. But God will work it all out somehow. I know He will. We must keep on trusting Him," and while she was talking she reached for the Bible.

Like wildfire the news of Anna Olesh's telegrams spread over the village. Her parents called immediately to get first-hand information.

"But, Anna," began her mother in an utterly horrified tone, "you wouldn't actually consider doing such a thing!"

"Why not? God will go with us. I wouldn't undertake it without Him."

"But you don't know the first thing about traveling. And with five children. You don't realize how far it is to America."

"But John told me to sell and I am going to. He said to come and we are going. By God's help we will get there."

"Well," said her father with an uneasy and unhappy countenance. "You can't change your mind once you get halfway there. Remember that. But I guess it is with this like it was about your strange new religion and that Lutz. There is no use trying to change your mind. At least if you go," he concluded, "everyone in our village will be true to the church."

Anna bit her lip. "Yes, Father. I understand what you mean."

"Nor will that Lutz be doing any more of his evil work. His church has gone to nothing." He waited for her comment. "Hasn't it now?"

"No, indeed," answered Anna. She held her head erect. "Not as long as John and I are living, for we're part of his church."

Aunt Tena called and expressed herself on the matter of Anna's leaving. "It's ridiculous. You don't realize what you're getting yourself and these poor children into. John ought to wait until this war closes and come home and get you if he wants you over there. I wouldn't listen to him."

Not one person in the village said Anna was doing the

342

right thing. Not one person spoke one word of encouragement to her. Her action was unheard of.

Nevertheless Wencel's father came and looked over the place several times during the next month. "Looks like Wencel and Elizabeth will be getting married when the war ends."

"I sincerely hope it will be soon," answered Anna.

"Well, I'm going to do all I can to keep Wencel on this side of the ocean if it takes all I've got and more. This is the only place around Miletinac I know of that's for sale or going to be."

Anna made no reply, but kept praying silently.

"Tell you what I will do, Mrs. Olesh. If this war ends and Wencel and Elizabeth decide to get married, I will be back to talk business."

"You mean I am to go ahead and see about getting passports?"

"You can do as you like about that, Mrs. Olesh."

But Anna soon found that getting passports for her family would be no small matter. She made a trip to Daruvar, but would have to come back with Mary, Kathrine, and Joe, have their pictures taken, and first of all secure clearance with the Serbian, American, Austrian, French, and Swiss consuls. That would mean going to the courthouse in several cities.

Anna was almost overwhelmed. There was but one thing to do—go home and sell the very things they needed— potatoes, oil, and turnips—so she could pay their train fare.

Chapter 38

Never had Anna been grilled with so many questions. More than once fear gnawed at her spirits like a sudden fierce storm threatening a village. Would the application go through? After all their efforts? She prayed unceasingly. Each time that comforting voice within spoke assuringly. "Fear thou not; for I am with thee." "With God all things are possible." "If God be for us—"

"Your permit will be mailed to you," she was told. "But please don't ask me when, for I cannot tell you that."

Seven weeks passed. No permit. But the glad news everyone was waiting for came. Germany had taken definite steps to obtain an armistice.

"Now can we go?" asked the children again and again.

"When God makes it possible, we will," answered Anna.

Wencel and his father came together to look over the farm.

"You are still planning on going?"

"Yes indeed. Even though no one around here seems to think I'm doing the right thing. We will go as soon as the Lord opens the way."

"Understand, Mrs. Olesh, I am not saying I think you should. But your parents said you had your mind made up."

"I am only waiting now for the permit for our passports."

"Send me word if they come."

If? The word was like a slap of cold water in her face. She prayed the more. Eagerly, expectantly, daily Anna walked to the mail depot. Her parents as well as others in the village speculated, ridiculed, and even made bets.

She knew her own children were wondering if after all their mother's God was hearing her prayers. More than a few times they saw her brush away a tear of disappointment. "Not yet, children," she told them, "but I will keep on praying."

Then came a letter from John. Anna couldn't wait until she got home to read it.

MY DEAR ANNA,

I pray God will help you get this. Have you sold the place? I am buying a small farm near Lebanon, Pennsylvania. I saved all I made in the west. I had a good chance to ride this way. I will be closer now when you come. I hope to have the house furnished and ready for you. God bless you and the children and keep you well and safe is my every moment's prayer. Come, Anna. God help you. Anxiously waiting.

Always with a heart of love,

JOHN

The next day the permits came! "Look, children. They are here!"

Everything suddenly became brighter, even the hard beaten path under her feet. Anna worked with renewed vigor. But she didn't know whether to plow the ground for spring seeding, or leave that for Wencel. She prayed; she waited; she watched.

It was two months before she received the passports, and the sailing notice. The *Leopodena,* the first ship to cross the Atlantic since the war, was scheduled to leave Le Havre, France, on April 25. Tickets would need to be picked up at Basel, Switzerland.

"Thank God!" cried Anna. "Listen, children, we must never, never doubt God. Again He has heard and answered our prayers. This means we must be ready to leave Miletinac not later than April 11. We're going to have to work and plan together and pray together. Are you all ready to help?"

In unison they pledged their allegiance.

345

With the flour and cornmeal left, Anna baked five sizeable loaves of bread. She wrapped them carefully in a freshly washed blanket. That's what Kathrine would carry. Joe would carry another blanket with some of their clothing wound inside. Mary, of course, wouldn't be expected to look after anything but herself.

"But I surely can carry a little something, Mother," suggested Mary with a tinge of disappointment.

"Perhaps the Bible. We will wrap that in one of the winter scarves."

"I can carry something," insisted little Anna.

"To be sure, I'll fix each of you a bundle. One you can sit on or use for a pillow."

Inside her dress Anna tucked the 80,000 dinars, the price she received for all their possessions—the farm, the house, and the furniture. The bills she tied securely in a cloth bag, fastened it with a cord, and hung it around her neck.

Anticipation. Those months of dreaming, of reaching out to an unexpected bliss. At last the *now* had come. Could it be true? None of them, not even little John, slept much that last night at home. They had said good-by to their neighbors and loved ones. That part was not easy, especially when Elizabeth wept aloud on her shoulder.

"I will write to you, Elizabeth," whispered Anna. "You and Wencel will be happy here working together. But happier," she added, "if you knew Jesus Christ as I do. It's wonderful what He means to me. I never knew true happiness before."

Elizabeth made no answer. She only squeezed Anna's hand and cried the more.

They were scarcely off the train at Daruvar when a red-faced Ukrainian with a shaggy mustache stepped up to Anna and said in a low, frightening voice, "You've got money on you. Haven't you?"

Anna walked on, calling her children to stay close by her. The man persisted. "Wait. Where's your money?"

"Come, children!" cried Anna. "Joe and John, stand right here for a minute. Anna, hold on to Joe." Quickly Anna took Mary and Kathrine with her into the women's washroom. She got out her bag of money. "I'm going to hide part of this on you," she whispered. "We're being watched." Her hands shook. "Keep an eye on that door."

She tore her handkerchief in two pieces and folded a bunch of the paper bills in each. She pinned one securely to each of the girls' underwear.

"Talk to no stranger," she warned them. "Watch. Stay close to me. Never mention a word about money to each other. Someone might hear you. Our next stop will be Zagreb. And then on to Basel where we'll get this exchanged. God help us. God help us."

The depot was swarming with people buying tickets for Zagreb. Others were waiting for the train to arrive. And when it did, most of the people jammed and pushed like cattle. It took several police to hold the mob back until the train was emptied. Soldiers—some who had been war prisoners—were coming home. People shrieked; some cried; some cheered; a few fainted.

It wasn't an easy task to keep her flock together. "Throw your packs on your backs. You all go first; I'll follow. Stay together."

Anna was carrying the largest bedding bundle on her own back. It was the only thing that saved her from getting hurt, for several grown boys jumped up on the seats behind her and stepped on her back bending her halfway to the floor. They leaped like monkeys over the children in front of her.

The train was dark. And cold. Every windowpane had been broken out. Men cursed. Women shivered. Children cried and clung to their parents.

The conductor elbowed his way through the crowd, holding a lantern above his head. "Now let's have a little order in here," he said in a stern voice. "Show your tickets."

After he had gone his round, a man came up to Anna and leaned over John beside her. She could feel his breath on her face. "You can't take that money out of this country."

Anna shivered. She knew at once it was the man who had confronted her at the depot. "There may be a police on this train," she said.

"You're trying to get smart now, aren't you? I am the police."

Anna looked straight ahead. "God knows the truth."

Muttering ugly words under his breath the man backed away.

Not once did Anna close her eyes that night. She opened the bread blanket and broke off a piece for each of the children. They sat in silence and ate it.

The depot in Zagreb was also dark. And colder. A few people were moving about carrying flickering candles.

"Hold on to each other," whispered Anna. "Kathrine, you and Joe and Anna stay together. Mary, hold on to my one arm. John, the other."

They sat in cold silence for four hours waiting for the train.

At Basel, Anna's 80,000 dinars were exchanged for 1,000 American dollars. The boat fare for the six was $475.00.

But at Le Havre they were put on a battleship! Not the *Leopodena*. The boat was crowded. Rough-looking characters of many nationalities got on.

The first ordeal was a complete stripping of each child on board before the ship doctor. In the process little Anna's passport dropped out of her dress pocket and a man beside her immediately grabbed it and stuck it in his own pocket.

Joe saw it happen. "That's my sister's passport," he said. "Sh!"

"Give it to me," cried Joe.

The man scowled.

"She's got to have it. We're going to America. She's my sister. It's hers."

348

The man swore at Joe and drew back.

Joe raised both arms, waving them frantically. People were pressing in from every angle. Parents were busy stripping their children, and everyone was talking louder than the other.

"I'll jump the ocean if you don't give it to me," cried Joe at the top of his voice. "Mother, Mother!"

"What's wrong here?" inquired a large man making his way close to Joe.

"That man grabbed my sister's passport. I saw. I know." Tears were streaming down Joe's face.

"Here"—the large man's hands were on the culprit—"hand it over."

The man drew it out of his pocket, but before he handed it to Joe he whacked him on the head with it.

"Thank's, mister. Thanks," cried Joe, quite out of breath.

The children slept in hammocks. Anna could have had a cot bed, but she did not trust to lie down once on the eleven-day voyage. She hardly trusted to close her eyes. Constantly, as her lips moved in prayer, she kept close vigil on her children.

A gentle rain was falling that balmy midmorning, May 5, 1919, when the boat stopped at Ellis Island. "It won't be long now," Anna reminded her children. "Soon we will be in America with Papa. The Lord has been very good to us and brought us safely so far. And you children have all been obedient. I'm glad I can tell your papa that. Kathrine, you and Joe go ahead."

"Oh, won't we be happy!" Mary beamed, grabbing her mother's arm. "Let's hurry."

They were halfway down the gangplank. Mary was the first to notice it. "Oh, look, Mother," she cried. "Isn't it the prettiest rainbow we've ever seen? Look at the rainbow, Kathrine, Joe, all of you, quick before it goes away."

"It's the prettiest and biggest I've ever seen," remarked Anna.

"Look," said Mary; "the end of it is clear over there in America, isn't it?"

"Could be, perhaps."

"Maybe right where Papa is this very minute."

Anna's tired eyes danced at the thought of it.

"Do rainbows always mean there's happiness at the end, Mother?"

"It means the sun is shining through the rain, and it's God's way of painting the sky with His promise. Move right along, children. Follow the man and do as he tells you."

They had been on the island for three days. Torturous days. Especially for the children. They were put through all kinds of examinations both physical and mental. They were tired, nervous, and frightened. And now fresh terror struck their mother.

"Oh! No!" Anna turned white when she finally comprehended what the immigration officer had said. Tears streamed down her cheeks. Mary threw her arms around her mother's neck.

"What did the man tell you, Mother?"

"Oh. Mary! My darling!"

"What is it, Mother? Something about me?"

"Oh, my child! My dear Mary!" sobbed Anna. "He said because you are a cripple you will not be allowed to enter the United States. Oh, Mary! He said they will send you back to Yugoslavia!" Anna turned her tear-stained face to the officer and shook her head in inexpressible grief.

"Oh, no! Why, Mother? No! No!" Mary clung to her mother and cried as though her heart would break.

"Oh, Mary, my child! If you have to go back, we all go back. I will never, never go on on without you."

"Pray!" cried Kathrine. "Oh, Mother, God always hears your prayers. Pray quick, Mother. Ask God to change the man." Kathrine threw her arms around Mary and shook with sobs.

All the children were crying now. While hot tears streamed from her bloodshot eyes, Anna lifted her face toward heaven and cried out to God for pity. The officer stood dumbfounded.

Presently he called for an interpreter.

"Tell that woman to stop her crying and we will try to talk sense with her. Bring them into my private office."

"The officer wants to know how your daughter came to be crippled. Was she born that way?"

"Oh, no! She fell. My husband even came over to America to see if he couldn't find a doctor who could operate on it."

351

"Is that why he is there now?"

"Not this time. The doctor thought it was no use. We had waited too long, I guess. He is there preparing a home for us now. Oh, can't we take her with us, sir?"

"Are you going to see what can be done for her?"

"As the good Lord leads, we will."

"The officer wants to know if you will be able to be financially responsible for this child."

"Yes, of course."

"Will you see to it that she receives a proper education?"

"Yes, sir. She can read and write now."

"She can?"

"If she had her books here, she could show you."

The man handed Mary a pencil and piece of paper and asked her to write something.

"What shall I write?" asked Mary.

"Anything," said the man. "Show me what you can do."

Carefully Mary moved her pencil across the paper. "Dear Papa, We all hope to see you soon. Mother loves you. We all love you. We pray every day God will help us find you. Our baby was so dear and sweet, but you never got to see her. God took her to—"

"That will do," said the interpreter. And he handed the paper over to the officer. "She's not stupid," said the interpreter.

"What did she write here?" demanded the officer.

The interpreter read the simple but well-written sentences.

"Take her along," said the officer. "We ordinarily don't do it, but—well—"

"You may take her along," repeated the interpreter.

"Oh, Mother! Oh, Mary!" cried Kathrine. "He changed, didn't he? God heard Mother's prayer."

Mary was clinging to her mother, crying now for joy.

"Yes," added little Anna. "God hears Mother's prayers always. I'm glad."

"Thank you. Oh, thank you, sir!" cried Anna while tears

of unspeakable gratitude streamed down both cheeks. "You can't possibly know what this means to all of us."

John looked at the letter once more: "Leaving home April 11 to sail April 25 on the *Leopodena*. That's all I can tell you now. God keep us until we meet. Oh, John! Happy days surely are ahead for us. We are all so excited. Anna."

He had made arrangements with the neighbor to meet his family if and when they would arrive at the Lebanon train depot. He had no car of his own and no telephone. The neighbor had inquired as to when the *Leopodena* was due to arrive in New York. John had made three trips with the neighbor to the depot only to be disappointed.

The *Leopodena* had arrived, but where was his family? John felt weak.

The four-room house was ready. John swept and scrubbed until the bare floors were immaculate. He had purchased from a secondhand store three good beds, a cookstove, a kitchen table, six chairs, a Coleman light, one small glass oil lamp, some dishes, and a few cooking utensils. In the cupboard was a week's supply of groceries, a sack of flour, sugar, and lard. Out in the pasture was a handsome milk cow and a hog big enough to be butchered whenever Anna was ready. The garden was up. The onions, lettuce, and radishes were ready to eat.

John opened his Bible and read Psalm 111, closed the Book, and sat thinking, thinking, thinking. He opened it again and read Psalm 112, closed the Book, and sat again in deep thought. Where was his family? Dropping on his knees beside the bed he poured his troubles out to God in prayer.

"Papa! John! Papa! Papa!"

The voice echoed throughout the house.

John sat up. Was he dreaming?

"John!" cried Anna. "Are you here?"

John jumped to his feet. "Anna! Anna! When did you come?" He crossed the room and folded her in his arms.

"Right now, John. Haven't you any oil either?"

"Yes. Yes."

"Hurry, Papa," cried Mary. "We want to see how you look."

"Just a minute. I want to see how you all look too." Trembling with happy excitement John lit the Coleman lamp. The children gasped in wonder. What a wonderful bright light! The house! How lovely!

John stood speechless for a moment. Then he took each of the children in his arms and kissed them. "I can't believe it," he exclaimed. "You're all so big. So big already. Why, Mary, you're a young lady. And Kathrine is as big as you are. And Joe! Anna! John! Where is—well, isn't there another?"

"Lydia," said Anna. "She didn't stay with us long. God knew best. It was hard, John, but God knew best."

"Oh! . . . And what more has happened of which I know nothing?"

"We will have many things to tell you, Papa."

"I suppose, but tell me first how you got here. I intended to meet you."

"Some kind-looking man and woman met us at the depot. They acted as if they were expecting us. They kept motioning to their machine and said Olesh, John Olesh, over and over. So we finally got in. And here we are. We couldn't understand anything else they said. The man got out and led us up to the house, then drove away."

"Couldn't have been anybody but our neighbors around the bend. No one else knew you were coming. Oh, Anna, Anna!" cried John. He held her out at arm's length. "You are beautiful, but tired."

"Do I look as if I am?"

"Yes. I can tell you have had some strenuous experiences."

"I have, John. But not alone. The good Lord was with us."

354

"And that's what makes the glow on your face, even though you're tired. Come." He led her to a chair. "Sit here, Mother dear." He placed his arm gently about her shoulder. "All you children sit down too. I have milk for you. And sugar cookies the neighbor woman baked."

"Oh, Papa!" cried Joe. "We are almost starved."

"The Lord, children," said John, trying to control his emotions—"we must thank Him for all this."

Chapter 39

Anna's heart vibrated a new uncomposed song each time she heard John's quick, firm step on the porch.

"Breakfast about ready, Mother?" He and Joe entered the kitchen and Joe set the pail of milk on the floor beside the stove.

Anna glanced up from the kettle of steaming breakfast cereal she was stirring. Her face was radiant. "Just about, Papa John. I will fry the eggs now. Eggs," she repeated. "Think of it, eggs for all of us."

John patted her on the shoulder and she answered with a smile. "It's taking me a while to get used to this American stove, but I really like it."

"Mother, I milked the cow myself this morning," proudly announced Joe.

Kathrine skipped barefooted across the kitchen. "And I want to try it tomorrow morning."

"I do, too," chimed little Anna.

"Me, too," added little John, buttoning his shirt.

"As tired as you children were from playing so hard last night," laughed John, "I thought you'd want to sleep in those good beds until noon." He glanced at Anna and winked.

"We're going to all work together," concluded Mother. "Papa and I are planning what each one will do to help. Right now, Joe, you may put the chairs to the table. Kathrine, you put on a pitcher of milk. Mary, you get out the sugar. I'll dish up the cereal."

After the blessing John looked at Mother across the table, "Are you really pleased?"

"Pleased?" Those expressive brown eyes were no longer

tired and bloodshot. They were rested and sparkling. "Why, Papa John," she exclaimed, "I'm more pleased every hour of each new day. And this is our fourth morning in America. I love this place. The house is cozy and bright inside. These wooden floors, John. I love every board in them. The doors have windows in them. I think I love every shingle too, John. And sometimes I can hardly work for looking at the fields and hills, the woods, the sky, the garden you made. I love the big yard, the cherry tree, the apple tree, the grape vine, the bridge across the creek, the well with good fresh water. What could it be I wouldn't love here, John? It's home. Best of all, you won't ever have to leave us again. It's almost too good to be true. Today I just must take time to write and tell the folks and Elizabeth all about how wonderful God has been to us."

The May morning was a dazzling one. There was a compelling grandeur in the bursting, green-growing world. The clear, cloudless sky throbbed with the radiant brightness of the sun. Through the open door came a tender musical bird chorus. The atmosphere had never smelled purer, more stimulating; a breakfast had never tasted better.

"Where will we go to school?" asked Anna a little wistfully.

"We will all take a walk one of these evenings," answered Papa. "There is a red brick schoolhouse down around the bend where you will be going."

"And where will we go to church?" asked Anna.

"That I don't know," John admitted. "I have gone along into town a few times with the neighbors, but I can't say I feel at home in their church. It is a little too fine for us, I fear. I must get the children shoes. And you too, Mother. I'm glad you asked about the church. This is one of my great concerns for our family. We must all pray about it."

"Until the Lord shows us where to go we will have to have church right here with our family," remarked Anna.

"We are part of Brother Lutz's church and we can't let it go to nothing."

John smiled and nodded. "That is right, Mother."

The year unfolded one memorable experience after the other. There was the excitement of exploring and learning, the satisfaction of working and planning, the joy of planting, of reaping, and eating together.

"This is what I call real living," remarked John, not once, not twice, but many times. And each time he knew Anna and each of the children would smile a big *Amen*.

The children were overjoyed when the twins came. But that particular occasion for joy was of short duration. Tiny Eve lived but one day and Adam only a few more.

"God knows best," Anna explained to the children. "He has answered many prayers for us; we won't allow this to discourage us. God must want them in Heaven."

John pressed Anna's hand. "You are a constant inspiration to me," he whispered.

John was in the field one forenoon plowing, when he noticed a group of about thirty men in the pasture less than a quarter of a mile distant. He stopped. The men seemed to be discussing something. It wasn't a funeral, was it? There was no hearse in sight. No women. The men formed a circle. John walked over to the lower fence corner. The men all removed their hats and bowed their heads. John held his hand to his one ear. More than one seemed to be praying. He listened. Over the field floated rich blendings of harmony. Sacred music. Touching, meaningful, powerful music.

As if drawn by some irresistible, undefinable force John started walking closer, closer until he could comprehend some of the words they were singing. He hesitated. He stood spellbound. "Lead Us, O Father." He repeated the words as if his thirsty soul had sent out feelers in longing pursuit of fellowship with men who knew and loved God. Then came the firm, rich melody of another verse. John repeated

358

the words he understood. Some power of the immortal seemed to penetrate the very pores of his flesh and touch a pleasant chord in his starved soul. A fresh reverence and love for God and men of God welled up within him like a fountain.

Slowly he moved toward the group. No one noticed him until he was almost upon them. One turned. He smiled and extended a friendly hand. With a friendly firmness he held John's calloused earth-soiled hand.

"Neighbor? Friend? How do you do? Fine morning."

Others, every one of the thirty, shook John's hand.

"Mr. Olesh. Glad to meet you."

It was an unforgettable morning. The men had given John an expression of something. Of what? He couldn't understand it. Something pleasing. Something precious. Something lowly yet powerful.

"Vot mean dis?" ventured John.

"We have gathered here," answered one, perhaps the leader of the group, "to find the will of God."

"Vill of Got?"

"Yes. For the right spot on which to erect a church."

"Church? Oh," John's eyes widened. His heart jumped.

"We're certain now," continued the man. "This is the place God would have us build. We are here, all brethren in the Lord who believe in prayer."

John nodded.

"We have prayed much individually, in our own homes, and this morning we met together to pray unitedly. We are all agreed now that this is the spot. There's nothing like knowing you are being led of the Spirit of God for such an undertaking. A church must answer the spiritual needs of the people. It must be a home where all the people can worship together like one big family and where every member will feel they are wanted and needed."

John listened intently. He understood a good bit of what the man had said.

"You live in this neighborhood, Mr. Olesh?"

"Yeh." John pointed to his humble dwelling up the road.

"And do you know the Lord?" The man's face had a spontaneous sincerity about it.

John smiled. "Yes," he said and placed one hand on his heart. "Jesus mine. Mine own."

"I'm glad to know that. What church do you attend?"

"Church?" John shook his head.

"Do you go to church anywhere?"

John shook his head. "Mine church in Europe. Brother Lutz. I no find mine church in America. I look. I votch. I pray. Mine vife Anna pray. Mine five children need church."

"When this church is built, Mr. Olesh, we sincerely hope that you and your family will come. One thing I am certain of, you will be welcome. Isn't that so, brethren?"

"Yes. Yes, indeed. To be sure." A chorus of invitations followed.

John's feet felt feather-light when he walked back to the house. "They are going to build a church down there, Anna."

That delicious yeasty smell of rising bread about ready to be baked greeted him when he entered the kitchen.

"What kind of people were they?" Anna was peeling potatoes. "I saw you go down."

"People of God. That is all I can tell you. I could see it on their faces. I could feel it in their handclasps. I don't know what else to tell you, Anna. But I somehow have a feeling that is going to be where we will belong." He came close to her. "Haven't we been praying for God to show us? And those men have been praying for God to show them."

"And, John," said Anna, dropping the potato and looking full into his face, "I have a sure feeling in my heart that wherever Brother and Sister Lutz are, or whatever has become of them, they're praying, too, we'll be led to the right church here in America. Could it be? Oh, John! So close. No walking miles and miles and miles? All walk along

360

together? And we'll get to watch them build it? God gives us more than we ask for. Even more than we dream or hope for. Remember the day when Brother Lutz reminded us that if we seek God and His righteousness first, all the other things we need will be added to us. We now have a home, a cow, our children, a school, and can it be, the best of all, a church? What will they call it?"

"What do you mean?"

"Will it be a Gospel Center? You know what I mean, John."

"They said it will be a Mennonite Church."

"Mennonite? Mennonite?" repeated Anna. "Do you suppose the women will be as friendly as you say the men were to you?"

John stood at the window, his hands behind him, gazing down toward the spot where the men had been standing. Kathrine and Joe were in the garden busy at their assigned tasks. Mary was singing while gathering wild flowers down close to the road. Little Anna was clipping tall grass along the garden fence and John was squealing while playing with a barrel hoop and stick. The chickens were cackling proudly over their morning's egg laying.

Anna watched John.

He seemed lost in his thoughts.

"Well, I tell you," he said presently, turning and walking over to the table where she was peeling potatoes, "I would suppose so. Wasn't Sister Lutz as friendly as he? Back of every good man I dare say is a good woman—a wife, a mother, or a grandmother." John sat opposite her and looked into her delicately flushed face. Her brown eyes were shining. Her black hair, parted in the middle, was gently lifted from her temples. Nothing but her own purity of soul deep within could have put the heavenly glow he saw on her face at that moment. "Anna," he reached across the table and took her one hand in his, "whatever good comes from me, or those children playing outside, will be because of you."

361

Anna's gentle eyes were modestly downcast for a moment.

"Why, John." Her eyes met his. They were shimmering in tears. She could not speak.

"Where would we be today if it hadn't been for you?" he asked. "You've never thought about that?"

She shook her head.

"I have. Often. You couldn't forget the man Lutz. It was you, Anna."

"Neither could you, John."

"You took the Testament."

"But you got it out of its hiding place, John."

"You were the one who made arrangements for Elizabeth to come over and stay with the children so we could go to Daruvar. Remember? You were the first to accept Christ."

"But, John, you were ready, too."

"But, Anna dear, let me talk. Let me tell you now what I've been wanting to tell you for years. If it hadn't been for you, and your desire to know the truth, and your devotion to God since that day we were baptized, we wouldn't be here together like this today."

A tear fell on Anna's dress. "We would have all gone back with Mary, John."

"You have been brave, Anna. This morning, when I was out there plowing, I got to thinking back again step by step over my experiences during these lonely years here without you. Two things stood out before me day and night. Always."

"What?"

"You couldn't guess?"

Anna shook her head.

"The second time I left for America, before I got on the train at Daruvar, I looked across the tracks and saw a light in the window at the Gospel Center."

"A light? What kind of light?"

"Just a soft glow. That was all."

362

"What about it?"

"I couldn't forget it. Inside that window where the light glowed, lived that man Lutz that you couldn't forget."

"It wasn't the man, John. It was what he believed, how it showed in his life."

"Yes, Anna. I'm telling you."

"Yes. Go on, John."

"That was the one thing. The light in the window. The other was your face."

"My face?"

"The way you looked the moment you accepted Christ that day in his home. Your face—you didn't know it— but all at once it glowed."

"Because I was happy, John. I will never forget how I felt all over, what joy came over me, what peace when I realized I was accepted and my sins were all forgiven."

"Those two melted together like one."

"What do you mean?"

"Your face seemed to glow from that window. It came before me in every trying place I went through. It was like a rainbow shining through a storm. It followed me everywhere and gave me hope and courage and a desire to be true to you and God."

"John," whispered Anna. Her face was radiant. Her lips quivered. "It's sweet of you to tell me this. Oh, John, you've made me so happy. I have so much to live for. So much I must do now. So many to pray for. So many to love. My task overwhelms me. Our dear children, John. I must help them know Christ, too. They will. I have faith. But I feel so small, so weak. I ask God every day to just use me as a lamp to help light their way and to supply the oil it takes to keep me burning. Here comes Mary with a bunch of flowers. John, look! Isn't she sweet?"

"Like her mother," whispered John.

Miss Evans was exceptionally patient and understanding

with her four new pupils from Yugoslavia who struggled bravely and persistently with the strange new language. She very readily discovered they were far from stupid, although their lips often could not frame the correct answer to her questions. She kindly chided the children who laughed at the amusing mistakes the newcomers made.

Kathrine helped Joe whenever she mastered a new word first. Anna helped John. In turn John more than a few times helped the others, and at home each took pride in teaching Mary. With book assistance, encouragement, and occasional home visits by Miss Evans, Mary was able to move along steadily with her elementary education.

Long before the church was completed, the minister and his comely, sweet-faced wife called one evening at the Olesh home to tell John and Anna how glad they were to have them in the valley. "We want to be of assistance to you, not only physically, as good neighbors should be, but spiritually as well."

John and Anna listened intently.

"When the church is finished," said the minister, "it will be dedicated. We invite you to come. All of you. Yes," he added, noticing John and Anna glancing at the children, "the whole family is invited. Children are always welcome in our church, where parents take their children. We hope you will feel our invitation is sincere and from the heart, Mr. and Mrs. Olesh, and that after you have once come, you will find our people humble and friendly and above all, true fol lowers of Christ."

John smiled and nodded. So did Anna.

Chapter 40

Anna got the children ready Sunday morning and together the family walked down the road. It was a lovely church, beautiful in its simplicity and immaculate newness. Everything was new—the faces, the songs, the papers they distributed—all but the One they came to worship. That was the "in-common" thing that made the Oleshes feel at home from the beginning. That, more than the warm handshakes and smiles.

"I liked it," confessed Anna on their way home. "We will go again."

And they did. But to become members, lifelong members, to pledge undying allegiance to a "body-of-Christ" group was a thing that required careful and prayerful consideration. So it was two years later when John and Anna Olesh made their decision.

"Ve now feel ve know vot step ve take," John told the minister.

Anna's eyes, brown and trusting, shone with peace and confidence. Her face was calm and serene. Her lips parted as if to speak, but she didn't. She only nodded. John had voiced her sentiments. He could say it best.

"We are glad you have carefully thought through this step, Brother John," remarked the minister. "We have tried to explain to you both what we believe and why, according to the Scriptures. And if at any time, as we live and go on and work together in the church, you see anything or hear anything you don't understand, please be free to ask one of us. None of us is perfect—our little church isn't perfect, and we all need each other's help. Sister Anna, this is for you too. If at any time you have a certain conviction about anything, be free to express it."

Anna's warm cheeks pinked. "Me?" she said in a sweet subdued tone. "Me," she reached for John's hand and touched it gently. "Mine John says vords. I so feel." She pressed one hand over her heart. "I more pray mit mine Jesus."

The next Sunday John and Anna were received into church fellowship.

It was a warm October afternoon when the bright sun was shining through the kitchen window where Anna sat knitting. So rapidly were her fingers moving one could scarcely be outlined from another. The soft navy yarn cap she was about to finish for Joseph matched the small neck scarf hanging over the back of her chair.

Close by sat Mary, knitting a similar cap for John. On the short-legged stool beside her lay an open spelling book. Occasionally she glanced at the book and her lips moved.

Anna's fingers stopped for a moment, then suddenly both hands dropped into her aproned lap. She looked out the window, down across the leaf-carpeted yard, and beyond to the church in the distance.

"You didn't make a mistake, did you, Mother?"

Immediately Mary knew she had asked the question only for want of a better one. Mother make a mistake when she could knit almost any pattern in the dark? "What are you looking at?" added Mary quickly.

Anna gathered the fringe of her thoughts together. "I was just thinking," she answered with a long breath.

"What about?"

"The letter, Mary. It's about all I can think of today. Almost makes me homesick."

"Not to go back to live in Miletinac?"

"Oh, no. Not to live. But I would love to walk in on

366

Elizabeth right now. And Mother and Father. Get the letter, Mary, and read it to me again."

"Again?"

"It's good practice for you, dear."

"But I never will learn to read English well," said Mary getting up.

"Yes, you will, Mary. If the other children can learn it, you can too. But I want you to keep brushed up on Slavian too." Mary cleared her throat before she began to read.

Miletinac
September 10, 1922

MY DEAR ANNA,

I'm always so glad for a letter from you. It seems that's what I live for any more. Wencel, too. He says nothing new or different happens here and that is about true. Your letters are always so full of news about the children, the school, the church, your life in America, and everything you do over there.

But, Anna, I do have something new to tell you this time. Something that will likely be a great surprise to you. Mother and Father went to Daruvar Saturday afternoon and stayed at Preacher Lutz's house overnight and attended his church on Sunday. Think of it. Wencel and I had to promise not to tell anyone in the village. They said they had been thinking about going sometime just to see what Lutz was like and why he had had such an influence on you. I wouldn't even be surprised if they had one of those New Testaments in the house. They act so different of late — I mean so strange or something. After all they said to criticize and accuse you, Anna, it's almost unbelievable. What have you been writing to them? Mother doesn't give me your letters to read, but she always tells me when they hear from you and acts greatly pleased. I must admit you write very convincingly about what you believe, but that is not why Wencel likes to read your letters. At least I hope not. We have promised each other we are not going to be impressed or misled by anything you write or by what the folks do. You are happy in your way of believing and I am glad you are; so stick to it.

367

Wencel is good to me and his parents take lots of interest in our place. But the pumpkin crop isn't going to be any good, and for some reason the potatoes have a new sort of blight. We are so disappointed, for we had figured strong on trading potatoes for chickens, and, well, you know what all. Anna, I just simply don't see how you ever made ends meet for your family.

Wencel is considering doing the very thing he said many times he would never do. Can you guess? Yes, leave me to go to America to find work. I don't see how you ever lived through letting John go off like that three times. Of course, you are together now, but it is so hard to even think of. Do you think he could actually get work? Ask John. He told me to. When would be the best time of year to leave? And where would be the best place to go to look for work? You know Wencel can't say a dozen words of English. Have you ever seen Uncle Jose? Aunt Tena thinks he's gone farther west, for she hasn't heard from him for seven weeks now.

Mother was here for almost an hour. She just left. So now I will finish this letter. She said that Mr. Lutz said he will never go back to Budapest unless another missionary who believes and teaches as he does comes and carries on the church. Anna, I can't understand Mother. What has come over her? Wencel says he thinks she misses you and the children so much that she's losing her senses. I can just hear you say something quite the opposite. Well, whatever it is, I for one am not going to cause a fuss about it. But I can just see Father Markum coming around to sprinkle our houses before many months and I dread what might happen now. Mother just wasn't herself today. I about know what you will do, Anna. Yes, pray. Well, when you do pray, pray for me, too. I mean about whether or not Wencel should leave me and go to America. From your last letter I see everything isn't sugar and cream and easy going for you either. There, too, you have to skimp and save.

My, I wish it would rain. The ground is very thirsty.

Love to John and all the children,
ELIZABETH

"Thirsty," whispered Anna.

"What did you say?" asked Mary.

"The ground in Miletinac is very thirsty, Mary," said her mother thoughtfully. "And so is Elizabeth's heart."

"How do you know, Mother?"

A tear fell. She looked up into her teen-aged daughter's questioning face. "How do I know, dear?" she asked with unusual tenderness. "Could I ever, ever forget how dry and parched and hungry my own heart was one day? Before I realized what was wrong? Thank you for reading it once more, Mary."

"What are you going to write and tell her about Uncle Wencel coming to America?"

"Papa and I must talk it over some more first."

"Just think," said Mary, "how lonesome Grandma and Grandpa would get if Elizabeth came over here."

"That's what would happen if Wencel found work. I thought about all that."

"Maybe Grandpa and Grandma would come, too, then."

"That's very doubtful, Mary. Grandpa would be too old to get out and try to find a job over here. No, Mary, if Grandma and Grandpa accept Christ, I'd sooner believe they would sell their place and move into Daruvar. Oh, Mary." Anna drew a long, deep breath.

"What, Mother?"

"Only yesterday I read that verse in Hebrews again that says, 'No chastening for the present seemeth to be joyous, but grievous: nevertheless afterward it yieldeth the peaceable fruit of righteousness.' "

"What does that mean?"

"I can't explain exactly what all it does mean, but when Papa and I decided to follow Christ, which meant for us breaking from the Catholic Church, we had to go through some unpleasant experiences. You remember some things, Mary. God allowed us to be tested, I guess, to see if our love was sincere. Now I am more glad than ever we didn't

369

give up because we were persecuted. To think that Grandpa and Grandma went to Brother Lutz's house! And slept there overnight! And listened to him preach!"

Anna picked up her knitting. "Put the letter on the dresser. I will read it again before I go to bed."

"Again?" Mary looked back as she walked toward the bedroom. She noticed an extraordinary beauty about her mother's face. For a second it held her motionless.

Chapter 41

John came running. "From your mother," he announced, tearing open the letter. "Read it out loud."

Miletinac
Christmas Day

DEAR ANNA AND FAMILY,

How we wished all day we could have eaten Christmas dinner together with you! Elizabeth and Wencel were here and we roasted a goose. We miss all of you more than you have any idea. How are you all? Have you ever found a doctor who could help Mary's knee? We are beginning to understand what you meant when you said you learned to cast your burdens on the Lord and He was ready and able to sustain you. We want you to forgive us for asking the witch doctor to come over that time.

Anna's arms dropped. She stared at John, mute, stunned. Then he saw two delicate tears creep to the edge of her lower lashes. Then a smile brushed her face.

"It was them? John!"

"Read on, dear."

It is remarkable how Jesus Christ can change a person's whole life and attitudes. It makes me very happy to tell you that Papa and I plan to be baptized next Sunday.

Anna hesitated. She handed John the letter. "Here," she choked. "You read it." Uncontrolled tears of joy flowed down her cheeks.

John cleared his throat. He, too, shed a tear or two before he read,

We never knew any two persons could be like Brother and Sister Lutz. So humble, yet so knowing and ready to help a person grasp the things about God and His Word. We feel now we understand partly what all you two went through. We beg you to forgive us. Of course, we know you said you would long ago, and that's one of the reasons why we were convinced there was something real and right about what you believed. I could write pages about our new experiences in Christ. What sweet peace inside! No one knows who hasn't experienced it. We have found some wonderful new friends in the church in Daruvar. To be sure, the villagers are shocked and resentful. Father Markum is bitter with anger. Pray for us. We surely don't want to get fainthearted or scared now. If things work out, we want to sell our place and move to Daruvar so we can be close to our new friends.

"Just what I expected," whispered Anna with emotion. John continued reading:

If such a thing would happen that Wencel goes to America and Elizabeth would also go someday, there would be nothing to hold us in Miletinac. Papa would be more likely to find work in Daruvar, perhaps a part-time janitor job or something like that. Just enough to support us two is all he would want. He is ready to assist Brother Lutz in any way he can. That man and his sweet wife surely have endeared themselves to us.

I never supposed two years ago Wencel would ever think of going to America. Elizabeth is trying her best to be brave. Remembering how you went through those times when John was gone, of course, helps her. I might as well tell you this, too, that Wencel has emphatically declared he is not going to mingle much with you folks if he comes. And if he does get ahead enough to take Elizabeth to America, they are not going to live near Meckville. He is dead set on sticking to his faith. Father Markum and his parents have already gotten him to sign a written oath to that effect. So I wouldn't be too insistent. You know what I mean, don't you? This is a matter you can't rush or force. I, yes, even I who was once blind, now see the way, the truth, the light. Papa and I are very happy. Everything looks different now. Even the raindrops make

372

music when they dash against our windowpane. The things I once hated I love now, and the things that once seemed vain and useless now have meaning. We knew you had something, but were afraid of it. Love casts out fear. Yes, perfect love casts out the most terrible fears. We've learned much of the Word since the first day we let Brother Lutz talk to us, and since he gave us a Bible. But we have much more to learn. We hope you are having a happy Christmas in Pennsylvania. Snow, I suppose, is on your lawn and garden. What do the children think of it all? If you ever have a picture taken, please send us one. I'm anxious to hear that your new baby arrives safely. God bless and keep you all. Kiss each of the children for us.

Love from
MOTHER AND FATHER

"Oh, John!" cried Anna, and she dropped to her knees beside the table. John knelt beside her. "We've got to thank God right now. This is wonderful, wonderful!"

It was eleven months before Elizabeth joined Wencel in Norristown.

Four years later Wencel died unexpectedly. Anna went to the funeral, which was held in the Most Blessed Mother Mary's Catholic Church.

"You'd better go home with me, Elizabeth," Anna pleaded.

Elizabeth shook her head. "Thanks, Anna. But you have your family to care for. One more would be too many. I'll stay here and find work."

"Work?"

"I might clean in a hotel or do something like that where I wouldn't have to talk much to the people."

"But you will be so alone here, Elizabeth."

"I must learn to be alone. I would be alone if I went home with you."

"What do you mean?"

"You know what I mean, Anna," she sobbed. "I wouldn't fit in. There's a sea between what you and I believe."

373

"Yes, dear. But there's a bridge that can span that sea." She pressed her sister's trembling hand.

Elizabeth sobbed the harder. "I can't think of it now. I must stay here and fight it through."

"Not fight," corrected Anna tenderly. "That is the human way. But God's way is to submit to His will. Can't you see what I mean, Elizabeth?"

"It's not fair!" cried Elizabeth bitterly. "Wencel was working so hard to make us a comfortable home, and now this."

"God is kind, Elizabeth."

"Kind? I can't see any kindness in this. No, it's not kind."

"It often takes time to see that part of His plan, Elizabeth. It is there but you just can't see it."

Elizabeth shook her head. "Thanks for coming to me in this sad hour. It was all I wanted. Just to have you here with me." She pressed Anna's hand.

"I was only glad I could come, Elizabeth. Remember the night Papa called me over when you were sick?"

Elizabeth nodded.

"You are still my little sister," said Anna softly. "Even though you are bigger than I am now. I'll always be ready to help you, comfort you, share with you all that I can. Remember, the latchstring to our door always hangs on the outside for you. When you are tired fighting this alone, come to me. Will you, dear?"

Elizabeth could not speak for crying.

Several years passed. Elizabeth never came. But one day a letter did. Anna answered it at once and wrote a second.

June 16, 1929

DEAR MOTHER AND FATHER,

Today I received a letter from Elizabeth announcing her marriage to a Mike Farina. It came as a complete surprise. Did she write it to you? She says he is a good, hard-working man and thrifty and is anxious to meet us. They plan to come to see us before long. I'm confident you are still praying for her as we are. We will do our best to show them a happy time when they come. I am very anxious for them to come.

I wish you could see our family and they could see you both. Henry is doing well in school. You should hear how he can read from the English reader. Steve can hardly wait for the day when he can go to school, too. Mary and Kathrine both have steady boy friends, and Joseph is looking toward the girls with a serious eye. We have tried to bring our children up in the love and fear of the Lord, and now if they establish Christian homes of their own, we will know our prayers have not been in vain. No, we never found a doctor who thought he could correct Mary's knee. Her lover loves her deeply and accepts her as she is. She has become very efficient and is an attractive young woman. She will probably be married soon. I was deeply touched to hear of Aunt Tena's passing. But even more so when you wrote of Sister Lutz's death. She was a great soul with a heart of love and I look forward to meeting her in Heaven someday.

The valley here and the Blue Mountains in the distance were never more beautiful. They always remind me of the Blue Mountains back home. Sometimes I really get homesick to see both of you, and beautiful Yugoslavia once more. But that will hardly come to pass. It has taken every cent to provide for the needs of our growing family. But my spirit, my thoughts, my prayers, my never-dying love are with you now, today, tomorrow, and always until the end of time. God bless and keep you both. To know we will meet someday in Heaven gives me joy unspeakable.

Lovingly and sincerely, your daughter,

ANNA

Not many months later Mike and Elizabeth bought a small farm near Meckville. Although Mike seldom attended church, he was deeply impressed with John's and Anna's sincerity. It was his dying request a few years later that their pastor conduct his funeral. "And instruct my wife," he whispered, "in the better way of living, that she might have that faith by which to safely die."

375

After that it did not take Elizabeth long to grasp whole-heartedly that better way.

"This must be what I've always wanted and longed for," she cried. "Oh, Anna, why have I been so stubborn and blind?"

Thirty budding springs, thirty blossoming Mays came and went. Thirty times John and Anna and their children rehearsed and recounted, and relived the events which preceded that memorable evening when they were reunited as a family in the humble little home Papa John had purchased and furnished for them.

"Surely," Kathrine would say, "it was God who sent that kindhearted neighbor past the depot at the right moment."

Then Joe: "And remember how funny we all must have looked standing there on that platform in those quaint home-made clothes and with those odd-shaped blanket packs on our backs." Then everyone would laugh.

John spoke next. "And we thought we would starve before we got here."

"And Mother seemed tireless during those eleven days," said Mary.

The grandchildren, big and little, listened alike, wide-eyed and with emotion. "Tell it all again," they would beg. "Tell more this time."

There was something unusually fascinating about the people who gathered for Sunday morning worship in the church. Was it the earnestness of their four-part singing, or their attentiveness to the reading of the Scripture by Brother Doutrich? Or their response to the well-delivered sermon by Brother Shank? Was it the fatherly remarks by the bishop, Brother Bucher, or the volunteer prayers from the lips of a number of laymen? All were impressive.

On the front pew sat Steve, John's and Anna's youngest, chosen by the congregation to be ordained as their deacon. Not far behind Steve sat his father. To the right, Anna; to

376

the left, Joe and Henry. The others were also present.

There they sat, men of God and their fruitful wives. The young, the fair, the vigorous, the sturdy, the onetime strong, now feeble, bent, and white. Mothers, fathers, grandparents, grandchildren, the well-to-do, the all-but-poor, the middle class, the really poor, the babes in Christ, the deep-rooted saints; like one big family they sat together in worship.

After the closing hymn and the benediction, no one seemed in a hurry to leave. They lingered to shake hands with one another, but especially with Steve, then with Steve's parents, who had become such a living, loving, vital, illuminating part of the church.

"This must make you very proud," one woman said to Anna.

"Not proud," answered Anna. "Mine all for God."

On a gentle slope in the beautiful valley far below the scenic Blue Mountains and not far from the church, John built Anna a handsome new house. The dining table by the big picture window was opened to its full length and spread with Anna's most delicious dishes: baked smoked pork, mashed turnips, wilted green beans in savory sauce, hot strawberry gravy, glazed potato halves, raised Yugoslavian coffee cake, fried salted nuts, cream pie, and apple tarts with stuffed prunes.

Mary, mother of seven beautiful children, had come with her husband and family from Milwaukee. Henry, Joe, John, Kathrine, Steve, and Anna were all married and nestled close by in their own homes. They did not have far to come to get there in time for the family gathering. Elizabeth, too, was there.

The house rang and vibrated with laughter. After dinner Anna suggested they gather in the living room and sing for a while. Mary's second daughter played the organ. It wasn't the most perfect harmony, nor the rarest combination of musical quality, but they made music nevertheless. Words in song about spiritual blessings and the joys of God's free grace in Christ Jesus. John and Anna helped as best they could. Every now and then Anna lifted her eyes to John and his eyes smiled a response.

"Now mine little ones sing," she said.

"Yeh," added John, "Please."

"Vonderful, vonderful," beamed Anna when they were finished.

"And now," suggested Kathrine, "why don't all you children go out on the porch steps and play school or church while we clear the table?" The children ran for the door. "There's a nice big lawn to play on too," she added.

In a comparatively short time one of the children burst into the kitchen. "Grandma!" he shouted, quite out of breath. "Come quick! Hurry!"

Dropping everything, everyone obeyed.

"Someone hurt?" gasped Anna.

"See! See!" shouted the children, pointing toward the mountains.

"A rainbow," whispered Anna in relief. "How beautiful, beautiful! Raining yonder?"

Mary moved over and put one arm across her mother's shoulder. "It reminds me of the rainbow we saw when we got off the boat at Ellis Island."

Her mother smiled. "I believe this one is even bigger." Her gaze was fixed intently on the shimmering, dazzling splendor of color. "Remember, Mary," she remarked, "how you thought the one end surely reached 'way over here where Papa was waiting for us?"

Mary laughed softly. "And maybe it did. Who knows? Looks like this one goes over the mountain. Perhaps clear over to Yugoslavia."

At that everyone laughed.

"Children," said Anna, and a tender, sober, yet radiant expression crossed her face. Her trusting brown eyes shone. She pushed back the corner of her black head kerchief and the gentle breeze blew across her creamy white cheek. As

378

she raised her hand toward the farther end of the rainbow, it disappeared. Her arm dropped.

"What were you going to say, Mother?" asked Steve.

"I was going to say—" She seemed to grope a moment for the right words. They clustered close around her. "I say," she began again, "my rainbow, and your rainbow too, starts 'way over there in little old Miletinac, under the mattress. The other end that we cannot see yet reaches to Heaven. Yes. That's it. But if I had always kept the Testament hidden— I mean if I had never taken it out and opened it—" She stopped short. A sweet, sweet something no one could have named was poured out from her beautiful love-burning soul, and passed around from heart to heart in the group. Like a treasured polished chalice they all sipped from it in silence. They knew. They felt. They understood what it was she was trying to express.

It was young Anna's husband Nick (who shortly before had been won from darkness to light) who finally broke the silence. "Let's all go inside now," he said. "Let's have Grandma Anna tell us the whole story about her hidden rainbow. When she told it to me, that's when I first got a glimpse of mine."

Anna glanced upward at Nick and smiled happily. There was a beauty on her face, a simple purity born alone of the Christ of her treasured Book. Not only Nick but each of her children and their companions, and her grandchildren returned that glance with one of tender devotion.

"Come," she said. But she did not know that just as she was going through the door another rainbow appeared in the heavens for a few seconds. John saw, and knew, as never before, that her story had a meaning, an eternal purpose their children could never ignore.